Otter
St. Onge
and the **Bootleggers**
A Tale of Adventure

Otter St. Onge and the Bootleggers

A Tale of Adventure

Alec Hastings

The
Public
Press

First Edition

The Public Press
100 Gilead Brook Road
Randolph VT 05060

ThePublicPress.com • info@ThePublicPress.com

ISBN-13:978-1484826003

Cover art and book design: Carrie Cook

For additional information about this book contact:
alecwhastings@hotmail.com

Printed in the USA

DEDICATED TO DEBORAH GOVE, LOVING WIFE AND MOTHER

ALWAYS MISSED AND ALWAYS LOVED.

SEPTEMBER 25, 1950 – JANUARY 7, 2003

Your granddaughter, Charlotte Lucy Niles,
has arrived!

And there's a hand, my trusty fiere,
And gie's a hand o' thine,
And we'll tak a right gude-willie waught
For auld lang syne!

ROBERT BURNS

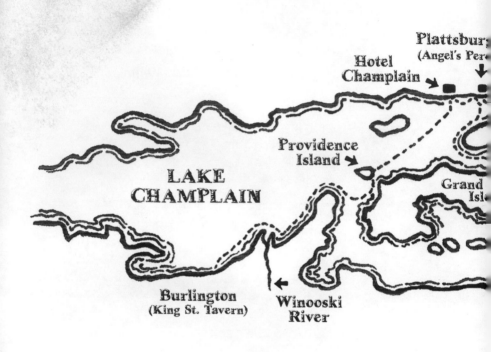

Plattsburg
(Angel's Perc

Hotel
Champlain ➤

Providence
Island ➤

LAKE
CHAMPLAIN

Grand
Isl

Burlington
(King St. Tavern)

Winooski
River ➤

- - - - - - - - - Otter's Journey by Boat - - - - - - - -

Otter's Route on
Lake Champlain during
the Flood of 1927

Contents

Introduction

Alec Hastings

*O**tter St. Onge and the Bootleggers* is a rollicking tale of adventure. I have loved such stories since I was a young scamp eavesdropping on my elders when I was supposed to be in bed. My mother often found me hiding at the foot of the stairs, listening to my relatives visiting in the farmhouse kitchen. From my perch on the last step I could hear the clink of whiskey glasses and every word being spoken around the old clawfoot table.

When Mom found me and sent me upstairs with a spank, I didn't mind. I had just heard some exciting stories I wasn't supposed to hear, and a stinging bottom was a small price to pay. Which of my friends would not have done the same to hear my grandfather tell about setting off some dynamite in Newbury on the Fourth and breaking all the storefront windows on Main Street? He hadn't meant to break the windows, of course, but I suspect the price he paid for that little caper was more than a stinging bottom!

With a dad who not only told stories but brought an

armload of books home from the library every week, it wasn't long before I discovered the magic of the *printed word*. What fun it was to fall under the spell of fiction! I will never forget my storybook heroes from those days. Jim Hawkins, the Hardy boys, Robin Hood, Huck Finn— they were all crowded in the back of my mind when I decided to write *this* book, the very one you have in hand. It's a rollicking tale, as I said. Rollicking, according to Webster, means "exuberant and lively." I can think of no better description for the hero of this story, that likable rascal, Otter St. Onge. Some corners of his tale are darker than those of the books I read as a boy, but Otter will take you safely through the shadows. Whether you be man or woman, boy or girl, seat yourself in his canoe and lean back against the middle thwart with Jake, the wolf dog, curled up at your feet. As the waves lap against the hull and a loon calls mournfully from the open water, listen to Otter tell his tale. St. Peter on a pogo stick— it's a whopper!

April 24ᵗʰ, 2013

INTRODUCTION

CHAPTER 1

Mississquoi Moonbeam

OUT ACROSS LAKE CHAMPLAIN, past Hog Island and the Alburgh dunes, the sun drifted down the sky. Under the trees, I could only see it in my mind's eye, dropping into those big old Adirondack Mountains like a hot-air balloon, fiery red, God leaning out from the basket, agog at his kingdom. *He's headed west,* I thought, *across the Great Plains to cowboy country. He'll stop to rest on Pike's Peak. Maybe he'll drink a little ambrosia and puff on his pipe before he heads for California. But back up, Otter St. Onge,* I said to myself. *Don't let your daydream run three hundred leagues across the prairie to the great beyond. You've got some ambrosia of your own to worry about tonight.*

So I took my imagination in hand, and for the umpteenth time that afternoon I thought about the night ahead. I had just turned eighteen, and I felt the beauty of sunsets and pretty girls keenly, but I had business to tend to, and the business at hand called for a sharp eye and an ear tuned to meddlers.

I dipped my paddle in the water and kept the bow of the

Melodie pointed down the Mississquoi River. The sun was sinking below the treetops, and shadows were spreading. If I timed it right, no one would see me when I reached the opening hidden beneath the overhanging branches of the riverbank. The only light would come from a half moon waking up in the Cold Hollow Mountains, and I would be a ghost disappearing in the dark. Nobody would see me leave the river, and nobody would follow me along the tiny creek that led to Granddad's still in the heart of the swamp. I was counting on that. Granddad had invited me on a bootleg run for the first time. Tonight was the night, and I didn't want an infernal revenue man or anyone else following me to where Amos Waters made his famous Mississquoi Moonbeam.

I had left Granddad with the last batch of whiskey that morning and returned to the farm to help Petrice with the chores. I cleaned the gutters and wheeled barrows of manure up a sloping plank to the top of a pile outside the barn door. While Petrice finished milking Granddad's Jerseys, I bedded them with fresh sawdust and fed out some hay. For the rest of the morning I fixed fence where the heifers had been getting out of the Mooney lot and then split and stacked chunks of maple and beech in the woodshed.

At noon I went to the kitchen for lunch. After eating a heaping plate of brown bread and beans and ham, *and* a sizeable bowl of Indian pudding, I sat back and sighed with contentment. Then Petrice sprung her surprise. She came out of the pantry holding a brown-paper parcel tied with string.

"This is a big day for you, yes?" she asked, handing me the parcel. "You're eighteen today? Happy birthday, Otter!" I put the string in my pocket, pulled the paper apart, and lifted out a brown flat cap. I turned it over in my hands and marveled at the tailoring.

"It's a beaut!" I said with a grin. "I'm going to look like a movie star. Thanks, Petrice." I got up from the table and hugged her.

"Go on with you," she said and pretended to push me away, but when I gave her a bear hug and lifted her off her feet, she laughed and laughed.

"It's Johnson Company wool," she said, smiling. "I sewed it when you and Amos were out fishing." Petrice thought it bad luck to ever mention Granddad's still in the swamp, so she always said he was fishing instead of making Moonbeam.

"Well, I'm going to wear it this afternoon when I go after some catfish."

"Good," she said. "Now you better skedaddle if you want to meet your grandsire by dark. Give him this letter. It came day before yesterday." She handed me an envelope, and I stuffed it in a leather pouch I carried on my belt. "And take your wool jacket. Feels like rain to me."

That had been a few hours ago. Petrice had packed a hamper of leftovers for Granddad, and I had stowed it under the rear thwart. Now, I was about to enter Dead Creek, a branch of the Mississquoi that emptied into Goose Bay. The river was pretty full for the first week in November, not up in the weeds, but well up on the banks.

It had rained a lot in October, and that was good because on those rainy days, it was hard to see the smoke from Granddad's cooker, and sometimes we could even fire the whiskey boiler in daylight.

So I was thinking about all and sundry, about the new cap Petrice gave me, about smuggling whiskey on Lake Champlain, and even about Annie Perkins back in Burlington where I'd attended high school, when I saw a wiggling of stalks in the cattails to my right. *What kind of creature is it?* I asked myself. Then a motor roared to life, and bold as brass, Warden Asa Finch and his brother Orvin burst from cover and swept alongside my canoe. Some of the swashbuckling effect was lost when Orvin grounded the keel on a stump, but Asa grabbed the gunwale of my canoe and nevertheless assumed a heroic pose. Orvin sat in the stern, in charge of the outboard, and the portly, steel-eyed Asa crouched in the bow pointing a side arm. When he recognized me, he pushed his campaign hat back disgustedly and lowered his gun. He looked foolish, but I didn't say so.

"What are you doing out here, Otter," he asked sternly. "Did you skip school this afternoon?" Without giving me a chance to say *boo,* he pointed at the oiled, brown tarp at my feet. "What's under that? Some of your grandpa's moonshine?"

"Afternoon, Warden Finch. I graduated last June, sir, and I'm working on Granddad's farm nowadays. He gave me the afternoon off, so I thought I'd catch some catfish for supper. I love pan-fried catfish, don't you? Mmm," I said, licking my lips and grinning. "They sure are delicious. Have you ever cooked them with a little bacon in the skillet? Now, what you do is...."

Palm outward, Asa signaled me to stop and then pointed again at the tarp. I had purposely ignored the question about the tarp just to get him worked up, but now I lifted a corner so he could see the basket Petrice had packed. Then I opened the lid of the basket so he could see Petrice's cold chicken and the rest of Granddad's supper. He looked wistfully at the Indian pudding and the jar of cream. Petrice was known for her desserts.

"Just in case I get hungry while I'm out here fishing," I explained. I emphasized the word "hungry." It was Granddad's supper, of course, but I couldn't resist having a little fun with Asa. Truth was, I couldn't have eaten another bite if you'd paid me. Well, that's not quite true. I can always eat, but I was pretty full.

He stared at the basket and then at me. He was suspicious, I could tell, but then he always was. "I got my eye on you, boy!" he said fiercely. "Remember that. And you tell your grandpa his goose is cooked if I find his still." He let go of my canoe and waved Orvin upriver, forgetting that they were hung up on the stump.

As I headed downriver, I looked over my shoulder and tipped my new hat in his direction. "Yes sir, Mr. Finch. I don't know what this still is you're talking about, but I'll tell him. And try your catfish with some bacon if you get a chance. You can get a bunch of 'em down at the rivermouth. I found where they had their holes in the mud last Saturday when I was swimming."

"Never mind, young fella. Just get about your business, and don't let me find you with any contraband."

"Yes sir. I mean, no sir. You won't find me. I mean, well, you know what I mean. What kind of band, sir? I don't actually dance that well...." And by then, I had paddled too far to make conversation practical, so with a friendly wave of my hand, I dug my blade in the water again and widened the gap even more. I looked over my shoulder, and Asa was crouched down, gripping both sides of the skiff as he wiggled his ample rear end toward Orvin to take some weight off the bow. Sure enough, the bow lifted and came clear of the stump. Asa let go of the gunwales and stood up to catch his breath. The boat pinwheeled in the current, and Asa—off balance and eyes widening—tumbled overboard with a great splash. Orvin held out an oar, but the boat had already drifted out of reach. Asa flailed and shouted. When I looked one last time from the next bend in the river, he was still in the water, sputtering and blowing, and Orvin was trying desperately to start the motor and come to his rescue.

Holy human bobber, I thought, *you couldn't sink the warden if you tied him to a cannonball.* I'd never taken Asa too seriously—he did that himself—and this meeting only shored up my opinion. But still, I remembered what Granddad had said. He said if the wind was blowing in favor of the law and against the miscreant—meaning me—

even a fool and a bungler like Asa could be dangerous. Usually, I saw Asa long before he saw me, but he had surprised me this time. Tonight we would be carrying more than catfish, and if the feds caught us, Granddad might lose the farm. *Keep your eyes open, Otter St. Onge,* I said to myself for the umpteenth time, and now, as I neared the hidden route to the still, I paddled the way my dad taught me, never making a splash.

Twenty feet ahead of me, two soft-shelled turtles slid from a downed tree into the water, and then, just as I reached that spot, I saw a strange sight. A bunch of ferns shivered on the riverbank, and a big coyote walked out onto the trunk of the old tree. At least, I thought it was a coyote. Then I realized it couldn't be because it was too big. No, big isn't the word. That doesn't tell anywhere near the size of it. The darned thing was humongous. You prob'ly won't believe it because I barely could, but there in front of me stood a wolf.

Now before you jump the gun, I know I've mentioned Mississquoi Moonbeam several times, but I want to make it clear that I hadn't been sampling any of Granddad's latest batch when I saw this animal. I was still on my way to pick up that batch. So here was this wolf, come to the river for a drink, and just as curious about me as I was about him, and we watched each other, eye to eye, as I floated on past. I studied him close, from about fifteen feet away, so I know he wasn't a coyote.

But I could still scarce believe my eyes. I had never heard

of anybody who had seen a wolf. Vermonters had trapped
and shot them all—at least, that's what Granddad told me.
Now I was looking at one close enough to see his whiskers.
He was enormous, one mean son of a gun if he wanted to
be, I suspected, enough to make me reach for my rifle, but
I didn't pick it up. I lay one hand on the gunstock, but his
eyes held me in a spell, and I stopped. He stood quiet and
kingly and as magical as the sunset still glowing in the red-
tipped crowns of the trees, and I whispered, "Hey there, big
fella. Where'd you come from?" He didn't answer but only
followed me with his eyes, and I couldn't strictly tell whether
he was hungry or just curious, but darned if I didn't think
it was the second of the two. I looked back over my shoulder
through the shadows trying to fix the sight of him in my
mind, and then, as he faded in the dusk, I turned away. I
needed to spot the stream that would take me to Granddad,
and it was hard to see even in daylight.

ABOUT HALF AN HOUR LATER, I found what I was looking
for. I nosed the bow of the canoe toward the right bank and
under some alder branches that brushed the water. Hidden
behind the alders, a tiny creek meandered out of the
woods. It was November, as I said, and the air had cooled
since sunset. I could see my breath now, and I pulled on
a wool sweater before I picked up my paddle again and
vanished into the gloom under the trees. After countless
forks in the swamp, I made the croaking call of a great blue
heron. In the heart of this maze, where the creek could no

longer float my canoe, my grandsire had built a still at the beginning of Prohibition. It wasn't likely that the revenuers would ever find it—they hadn't in seven years—but it was just as well to signal Granddad I was coming. I didn't want to get shot at if he mistook me for one of them fellas. As I stepped onto a hummock of grass, Granddad slipped out from behind a cottonwood, his Savage 99 cradled in one arm. His eyes gleamed in the moonlight, and his long, grey beard hid his expression. When he spoke, his voice rasped, but I knew he was glad to see me.

"Right on time, young fella," he said. Granddad was a man of powerful presence, even if he wasn't a big man physically, and I loved and admired him. He was kind but as tough as hickory and as smart as a down-country lawyer even if he was born and bred in the backwoods. He'd read the *King James Bible* from cover to cover and the *Complete Works of Shakespeare,* and he said whatever he didn't know about the human animal from experience, he knew from those two books. He wore a broad-brimmed crusher and logging boots winter and summer. The union suit and Johnson Company wool pants and shirt went on in late October and didn't come off until April. Suspenders held up his heavy trousers and a wide leather belt carried his hunting knife.

"Let's load up so we'll be ready to go," he said. "Then, I want to see what Petrice sent in that basket." Once the canoe was pointed back toward the river, he started handing me the burlap bags he had piled behind the tree.

I swung them carefully into the bottom of the canoe and
filled most of the space between the thwarts. Other than a
muffled clink from jostled whiskey jugs, we worked quietly.
After the bags were loaded, Granddad covered them with
the square of canvas and strode off through the woods
toward his camp. I followed with the basket of food.

His lean-to blended into a knoll shaded by locust trees
and safe from high water. Granddad had cleared the odd
bush and branch from the sides of the knoll so he could
see anybody coming, and his rifle was never out of reach.
The still was cold now. Granddad had been stilling shine
for a week. We had run the latest batch the night before,
and he had bottled it that morning. A coffeepot was
simmering over a bed of coals. He leaned his rifle against
a tree and poured a cup for me and one for himself. He
added a tot of Moonbeam to each cup from a Mason jar
and then motioned me to sit down with him at the narrow
table he had hewn from a couple cottonwood logs. I gave
him the letter from my bag. He glanced at the address,
looked more closely as if curious, and then stuffed it in
his jacket pocket.

"What's for supper, Grandson?" he asked. "I'm famished."

"Petrice's home cooking," I said and handed him the
basket. "This should taste pretty good after all the fish and
frog legs you've been eating."

"Oooh, yes," said Granddad, as he lifted the lid of a pot.
"I do love baked beans, and," he added, looking through
the rest of the basket, "I do love smoked ham and cheddar

cheese and Petrice's bread, and—what's this?" he asked, pointing at the dessert.

"Indian pudding, Granddad."

"Indian pudding, eh? I wonder why Petrice went to all that trouble." I thought I detected a sly tone in his voice, but maybe not. We didn't talk for a bit because he tucked right into the beans and ham. Then he lit a pipe, and I saw him smiling in the soft glow of the fire.

"Indian pudding and ambrosia," he said, pointing to the Mason jar, "the drink of the gods. Or," he continued, "the drink of the Devil if you have too much of it." He fell silent and puffed on his pipe. I waited. "How was your trip out here?" he asked finally.

"I saw Warden Finch"—Granddad raised his eyebrows—"but I told him I was going fishing, and he believed me." Granddad lowered his eyebrows. Then, a little worried that I might sound like a kid, I told him the exciting news. "I saw a wolf, too." Granddad grinned, and right away I wished I'd kept quiet. I could see I was in for some ribbing.

"A wolf. Is that so?" he chuckled.

"I didn't expect you'd believe me," I said.

"I thought you might be a little old to be crying wolf. How old are you, anyway?" he asked.

"Eighteen."

"You don't say. I could have sworn you were seventeen. When did you turn eighteen?" he asked. He was grinning like the cat with the cream now, and I could definitely feel my leg being tugged.

"Today."

"You mean to say today is your birthday, and I didn't even know it?" I didn't reply. Granddad wasn't a great one for remembering birthdays, so I didn't find this as surprising as he apparently did. "Well, I'm a poor excuse for a granddad," he said. I looked at him curiously, but he changed the subject. "Let's finish our coffee and get going. We'll sit tight at the mouth of the Mississquoi and look around. If it seems safe, we'll strike off for the shanty."

"I stopped at Pardo LaFontaine's Feed Store this morning before I went to the farm," I said, "and he claims the feds have only been looking for bootleggers coming down by Rouses Point, so we probably don't have to worry much about them bothering us on Goose Bay."

"The feds aren't the only ones we have to worry about," replied Granddad.

Who else should we be worrying about? I wondered. *Asa?* Well, it didn't matter. I was just glad to be going on this trip. He swigged the rest of his coffee. I was surprised to see that he was leaving a good helping of the ham and beans behind. Before he doused the fire, he whistled low and peered into the dark. A moment later, I started up from my seat.

A man stepped out of the shadows with a very large dog at his side, and then the two of them came into the firelight. The man was Indian, maybe French too, but Indian for sure. He wore his black hair long like some of the Abenaki around Swanton, and his face was dark-complected. He looked at me with pretty much the same grin Granddad had sported a short time before. I stared at the dog, fascinated, and realized we had already met. He was the animal I'd seen on the riverbank, the one I'd thought was a wolf.

"Grandson, say hello to Bill Three Rivers," Granddad said, nodding toward the Indian.

"Howdy, Bill," I said and continued to stare at the dog.

"Bill's an old friend of mine from Quebec. He's headed south to Whitehall to visit a cousin, and he's in need of some cash. Since a few bottles of whiskey are the next best thing, I've traded for his canine friend here. This, ahh, dog, Bill calls him—he *does* look more like a wolf now that I think on it—he's yours if you want him. Happy birthday."

I was still tongue-tied and wide-eyed, which is not my usual condition. Then—I smiled. And kept on smiling. The dog, if he was a dog, was magnificent. He sure as hell did look like a wolf though. "Thank you, Granddad!" I whispered excitedly. "He's a great, huge beast isn't he?"

Granddad laughed. "Yes," he said, "he's all of that. 'Bout big enough to pull a hay wagon." I knelt down beside the dog and reached my hand slowly toward his muzzle. He watched me impassively and then stretched forward and licked my fingers. "What's his name, Bill?" I asked.

"His secret Indian name is Dog Who Rolls in Dead Fish, but his everyday name is Jake."

"Oh," I said, not quite sure if my leg was being pulled again. "Well, Jake is all right, I guess."

"Yut," replied Bill still grinning. "That's what 'jake' means."

"Huh?"

"Jake means 'all right' or 'everything's okay.' You comprenez?"

"He's been to school," interrupted Granddad. "He understands just fine. Not to be rude, Bill, but we've got to shove off. We've got a considerable piece of work ahead of us. You can camp here tonight if you want. It smells like rain to me, but suit yourself. There's still coffee in the pot, and I've left you some ham and beans. The whiskey's in your canoe already."

"Merci, Amos. I don't care what anybody says—you're a prince among men," said Bill. Then he followed us down to the water. I stepped into the bow, and at Bill's command, Jake jumped into the middle of the canoe and curled up next to the Moonbeam. Granddad laid his rifle next to Jake and knelt in the stern. I waved goodbye to Bill, and with a few, quick paddle strokes we were gliding toward Dead Creek.

IT WAS SOME TIME BEFORE GRANDDAD finally decided it was safe to venture out onto Goose Bay. A few rags of cloud scudded across the sky, hiding what was left of the Hunter's Moon and leaving us in shadow. We had been drifting near the mouth of the river for an hour, scanning the shores of the bay. For a while, a couple loons, fishing or just swimming around out there, called back and forth to each other in the moonlight. *Such a lonely, weird sound,* I thought. *How strange for the Great Giver of Voices to put that one down the gullet of this beautiful bird that swims like a fish.* And then I thought, *No, it's just the right voice, a voice first heard when the earth was newly born.*

Chance thoughts like these were passing through my mind, and I was being lulled to sleep by small waves lapping against the sandbar where our canoe had come to rest. Then Granddad spoke, and what he said set my heart to pounding.

"Otter," he whispered, "we might as well go, but I've got to tell you something first. Don't get too excited because I'm not sure if it's true. If it is, it'll be the best birthday present you've ever had."

"What is it, Granddad?" I asked.

"I just read that letter. Don't raise a ruckus when you hear this," he warned, "but—your dad—he might be alive." The news hit like a lightning bolt. My father, Sergeant Royal St. Onge, went missing at the Battle of Vimy Ridge. That was ten years ago during the Great War, and I had long since decided he was dead.

"I don't believe it, Granddad. Why wouldn't he have come home?" I demanded.

"I don't know. All I know is that he'll be at the fish camp on Goose Bay tonight."

"Can I see the letter?" He pulled a paper from his jacket and passed it forward. I dropped it in the bottom of the canoe and crouched over it, shielding a match. In the wavering light I could just make out the words.

No doubt you figured me for dead, Amos, and now you prob'ly think I'm some kind of Houdini (or maybe you've got

*a worse name) the way I up and disappeared. When you
hear what happened, I think you'll understand. Anyway,
I'm back on this side of the pond, but it's not safe for me
to come to the farm. I'll be at the fish camp the night of the
boy's birthday. Bring him if you judge it the right thing
to do. I've got a boat, a fast one called the* Thorpedo, *and
I'll be bringing some custom to taverns in Burlington and
Plattsburgh that night. Want to come along? Please tell
Sweet I love her.*

"Do you think it's really him?" I asked.

"Looks like his hand, Otter."

"I still can't believe it. He's alive, Granddad!" Then, more
slowly, I said, "He doesn't know about Mom." Granddad
didn't reply. It was still hard.

The waves kept lapping, but now they only made me
restless. I wanted to go. A minute passed. Then, pushing his
paddle into the silt, Granddad finally slid us off the sandbar,
and we left the shadows of the swamp and entered Goose
Bay. Taking long strokes, we cut through the water quickly.
We stroked and stroked, and excitement welled up in me
like a bubbling spring. My breath came quick, and blood
pumped through me like sap climbing to a treetop in the
spring. This was my first time carrying a load of shine, but
that wasn't the only reason I was excited. The other reason
had me wound up tighter than a watch spring.

Calm down, mister, I said to myself. *Nothing's ever
gained by getting all bent out of shape.* I turned back to
the job at hand and scanned the lake for trouble. Well, of

course it came. In the moonlight we were close enough now to see the silhouette of the family fishing shanty perched on stilts out in the shallow bay. We heard the thunder of an engine, and a dark shape separated from the shadows of the opposite shore and sped toward us. There wasn't any escape, and Granddad cursed.

Damn, I thought, *it must be the feds. Them or Asa.* The boat bore down on us at full speed, and suddenly we were blinded by a spotlight turned on in the bow. At the last moment, the launch turned broadside, and the wave it raised nearly swamped the canoe. Then, as the helmsman cut to an idle, a man's voice boomed above the noise of the engine.

"Raise your hands, you," he said, and as I looked down the barrel of the shotgun pointed in our direction, I thought I'd follow his orders with fair alacrity. As I did, Granddad whispered, "Be ready to go over the side," and I felt a twisting in my gut because I saw what he saw—these men were not wearing uniforms. The boat we were looking at did not belong to the United States government, and the men in it were not feds. Who they were, I didn't know, but I was sure of one thing—the man behind the gun barrel didn't wish us well. Jake growled menacingly, and Granddad and I raised our hands.

CHAPTER 2

Too Tall

AKE GROWLED AND BARED HIS TEETH as the
boat came near. I kept my hands up and blinked in
the glare of that confounded spotlight. Then, after squinting,
I could see that the motor launch drifting broadside toward
us was good-sized, maybe thirty feet long. *Le Bûcheron*
was the name on its bow, and I thought, *Well yes, that big,
strapping fella staring down the shotgun barrel does look like
a lumberjack.*

He was wearing green wool trousers and a black wool
tuque, and he wouldn't have needed a pair of oxen to twitch
logs because he was about as tall as a tree himself. His black
hair bushed out from under his cap in all directions, and his
beard, just as black and bushy, would have been the pride
and joy of one of those biblical prophets Grandma Melodie
was always trying to get me to read up on. But what I noticed
most of all on that giant was his eyes which were screwed
right down tight on me and Granddad. I know he must have
blinked, but I sure don't remember seeing him do it. Those
eyes of his just bored in on us, and I remember thinking that

we were prob'ly bound for the bottom of the lake.

When I marked the other men in the boat, I saw a small, shifty-eyed character at the wheel who reminded me of nothing so much as a weasel. His face was pitted with scars from pimples or pox. His greasy, gray hair hung limp and sparse on his scalp, and his features all crowded forward with his long nose. The two in the stern made the Weasel look smaller, maybe, than he really was. They were young men but big—not as big as the giant, whose shotgun looked like a pistol in his hand—but they were big enough, and as I looked from one to the other, I realized they were twins. I also had a hunch they were part Indian. They had the same high cheek bones and whiskerless chins of the Abenaki, and they had glossy, black hair that reached to their shoulders. Funny thing was, they reminded me of somebody, but I didn't have time to think who. The twins held their rifles loosely, like they didn't really plan on using them, but I suspected the safeties were off, and I wasn't fooled for a second into thinking they were a couple of friendly fellas. They might have *looked* easy in mind, but they were watching me and Granddad real careful.

The Weasel cut the engine, and as the motorboat drifted within reach, the giant with the shotgun muttered something to the twins, and they laid their rifles down. One of them reached in his pocket and flipped Jake a piece of dried meat. Jake stopped growling and gobbled it up. *Hah!* I thought. *Great loyal companion and protector you are!* Then the twins grabbed the gunwales of the canoe fore and aft. The giant still had the shotgun aimed in our general direction, and now he spoke gruffly to Granddad.

"What you carrying under that?" he asked and pointed the gun barrel at the tarpaulin. "Show me. Real slow. My trigger finger twitches when I get much nervous."

"Yes sir. You can look all you want since you're holding that Browning," said Granddad, and he lifted a corner of the canvas and produced a bottle from one of the burlap bags."

"Whiskey?" said the big man.

"You won't find any better north of New York City," said Granddad.

"Is that so? That's a strong claim, you."

"It's a strong liquor. I call it Mississquoi Moonbeam. My own recipe. Care for a taste?"

"Pass it over here!" the man growled.

Granddad reached across the gunwale, but instead of giving the giant the bottle, he gave him his hand, and the two shook like they were old friends.

"Granddad—What?" I began.

"Nephew, you look surprised, you" laughed the lumberjack. I guess he said this because my mouth had dropped open. I closed it, but now I was more than just surprised. I was dumbfounded.

"Nephew?" I asked.

"Oui!" he said. "I'm your father's brother. This broken-down farmer at the wheel is my long-time friend, Luc"—here, he pointed to the Weasel—"and these are my sons, your cousins, by the way, Louis and Little Roy." I stared, wide-eyed and amazed. The twins nodded, and the corners of Little Roy's mouth turned up with the trace of a smile.

"That's right, Otter. Meet your Uncle Hercule St. Onge that they call Too Tall. He's a bull-and-jam logger from that bug-ridden swamp they call Quebec."

"Don't listen to your pepere when he talks about Quebec," said Too Tall. "He's never been any farther north than St. Jean."

I was listening, with one ear at least, but now questions unspooled in my head like thread flying off a bobbin. *This Too Tall is my uncle? Louis and Little Roy are my cousins? That's why they looked familiar! Spin me around and knock me down,* I thought, *they do look like my father.* On my bureau back at the farm was a picture of my dad in uniform just before he shipped out with the 4th Canadian Division in 1916. His face was as familiar to me as my own, and as I stared at this new uncle of mine, it spooked me to see my father's eyes staring back. *What kind of man is this Too Tall?* I wondered. *Were he and my dad close?*

They sure looked a lot alike. Too Tall was bigger and of course, taller, but he had the same brown eyes as my father. Under his bushy beard, I thought Too Tall might also have a handsome face like my dad. I hadn't seen Dad since I was seven. I had never even met any of my father's family, and here I was, meeting my dad's brother and his sons, and about to be reunited with my dad all in the same night. *Jumpin' Geronimo,* I thought, *they say crazy things can happen on a full moon, and I guess they're right.* I turned my attention back to Granddad in time to hear his reply.

"And St. Jean was far enough. Anybody with two coins to rub together was up to their boot tops in cow manure, and the rest were so poor they made their pants out of grain sacks."

"Amos," laughed Too Tall, "I swear. You're hard on us poor Canucks."

"Well, be that as it may, meet your brother's son, Otter St. Onge."

"Otter!" said Too Tall laughing again. "What kind of name is that for a young man? Can you swim like an otter? Can you fish like one? Or are you just full of mischief, you?" He turned back to Granddad. "I'll bet you gave him that name, Amos. And you call us Frenchmen cracked. Who would name a boy this way? You Anglaise are the crazy ones. Good thing his mother is watching out for him from heaven." He looked skyward and grinned. "He needs an angel looking after him if you're his grandsire."

I didn't know what to think when this Too Tall uncle of mine joked about my mother. I like a good laugh, but my mother was dead, and that was no laughing matter. My grandparents and I hardly ever talked about her. If we did, it was—well, not like Too Tall joking about my mother being an angel. But then, on thinking about it, I decided he didn't mean any harm. I figured maybe it was just his way, and I soon learned how true this was. Too Tall laughed easily and often but never from any meanness.

Anyway, Granddad handed Too Tall the bottle, and my uncle glugged a substantial amount. Then he grimaced. "Amos," he sputtered, "you got to filter out the pond scum when you make your mash. This stuff is worse than the lemon extract we used to drink in the logging camp up on the Nulhegan Stream."

"I notice you didn't spit it out," said Granddad dryly.

"I don't waste whiskey, even as bad as this. Luc, you try. Tell this doodle dandy he has to stop using swamp water for his mash." He handed the bottle to Luc who gulped from it, wiped his sleeve across his mouth, and beamed with satisfaction.

"Is damn good, Too Tall."

"Luc, you fool. I was going to buy the whole load. Now, he'll hold out for a big price down on King Street in Burlington. All those railroad men like to drink, eh?"

"Too Tall, I wish we could all sit here under the moon and flap our gums," said Granddad, "but it's starting to rain, and we were just about to meet your brother."

"Royal!" cried Too Tall. "You're out here to see Royal, him? I thought he was dead!"

"We got a letter from him. It was his handwriting. I'm sure of it. Said he'd meet us tonight at the fish camp."

"Well, I'll be blessed and bedeviled all to once. Gone eleven years, him, and now the prodigal returns."

Granddad nodded. "Yut. His letter said he'd be here tonight with a load of whiskey. We're bringing a batch of

Moonbeam, and I figured we'd make a run to Burlington and Plattsburgh. Why don't you come on over to the shanty. He should be there waiting for us."

Too Tall's expression was blank, and then I saw a flicker of worry. "Amos," he said, "we just came from the shanty. He's not there."

Granddad didn't answer. He stared at Too Tall, waiting.

"Somebody *was* there, and not so long ago maybe. We found a half-drunk cup of coffee on the table and a dinner plate with some dried egg on it. There was a cigarette stubbed out on that same plate. A Gauloise," said Too Tall. "Odd. That's a French cigarette. Hard to find over here."

"That *is* odd," said Granddad. "I never knew Royal to smoke. Still, he might have taken it up over there in France." He paused and stared at Too Tall grimly. "Here's an even stranger thing. Royal's been gone eleven years. Eleven years. All of a sudden, he writes and says meet him at the fish camp, and we can run a load of bootleg. No visit to the farm, no "glad-to-be-home," just all business. Well, here we are, but where is he? If Royal was at the shack earlier, why did he leave? If somebody else was there, what were they up to?"

"I haven't told you all of it, Amos." Granddad stared at Too Tall, and when he finally spoke, his voice had an edge.

"Let's hear the rest then."

"The shack was all shot up, splinters and bullet holes. If I didn't know better, I'd say somebody let loose with a Tommy gun."

I couldn't be quiet any longer. "Holy Toledo, Ohio!" I said. "What do you think happened? Did you see any blood?"

"No. No blood. I don't know what happened, Otter."

"Well—I'll swear an oath right now," said Granddad solemnly, "I'm going to find out."

"Sign me up for that job," I said, and Too Tall nodded. My mind was spinning. *Is my father alive?* I wondered. *Yes. He has to be.*

"Let's go," said Too Tall. "If we're going to look for Royal, the best place to start is Burlington or maybe over in Plattsburgh. We can take your Moonbeam with us.

IT BEGAN TO RAIN ON THE WAY TO BURLINGTON. It wasn't a bucketing downpour but just a light, steady rain. Granddad and I had set my canoe on the port side of Too Tall's boat. In it were our rifles, the Moonbeam, and a couple bedrolls we grabbed from the shanty. Now, we were settling in for a couple hours of wet boat ride. Granddad spread his wool blanket on a bench under the roofed-over section of the stern. He stretched out for a nap but looked at Luc with sudden surprise when he heard soft, clucking sounds coming from under the plank where he was about to lay his head.

"Strange traveling companions," he said.

"Too Tall's Uncle Henri owns a chicken farm," said Luc. "We brought a couple in case we run out of food. You know Too Tall. He eats a lot."

"You're not telling me anything new. The man visited my

farm for three days, and that's all he did. He's a walking biblical pestilence. He could cause a famine all on his own." Luc grinned and agreed.

I saw that Jake was curled up in the bottom of the boat next to Granddad, or to be more accurate, next to the chickens. I put on a slicker and went up front to sit with Too Tall who was hunched over the wheel.

"Do you think Dad's okay?" I asked.

"Certainment, nephew. If your papa has come back from the Great War, he has more lives than a cat. Who knows what happened at the shack? Maybe the feds came, and he had to leave in a hurry, eh? They'd prob'ly have a hard time catching him. If your father has a new boat, as Amos tell me, you can bet it's a fast one. He was always one for speed." I should have been comforted by my uncle, but I wasn't.

"Too Tall," I said, "tell me the truth. I saw the way you looked at Granddad when you mentioned the cigarette. You're worried about something, aren't you? What? Tell me."

He didn't answer right away. Then he must have decided I was old enough to hear the bad news because he didn't candy coat it. "Simple fact is, Otter, smuggling is a wicked dangerous business. It's not so much the law. It's the other bootleggers. There's a lot of money in smuggling, and some fellas want more than their wedge of pie. They want the whole pie, 'specially the fellas coming up from New York and down from Montreal. I'd bet an American Ben Franklin that it was other bootleggers made those bullet holes at the shanty. If they did, your dad may already be dead."

"But you said there was no blood? That's a good sign, isn't it?"

"Bien sûr. Yes. Maybe they took him along, but—I'm sorry, Otter—maybe don't get your hopes up too much, you."

We stopped talking then, and I sat there in the rain, thinking. Too Tall turned on the spotlight again. In the rain and mist, I could see my hand in front of my face but just barely. Uncle Hercule didn't want to attract the law, but it was too dangerous to run down the lake in total darkness. We had left Woods Island behind and were headed south toward Burton Island when we got a shock. A spotlight shone on us from behind, and a smooth voice hailed us through a megaphone.

"This is the Lake Champlain Boat Patrol. Cut your engine. We are coming alongside to inspect your craft."

"It's Jack Kendrick from St. Albans," said Granddad hurrying forward. "Let him come. Pull your hat brims down low, boys. Don't let 'em see your faces. Hercule, when I give the word, hit the throttle—hard!"

Too Tall dropped the engine to an idle. The patrol boat pulled alongside *Le Bûcheron* with Kendrick at the wheel. His sidekick, Eddie Halstead, held a service revolver. "Put your hands in the air, fellas," he said genially. Both boats rocked on the waves, and Eddie grabbed the rail of our boat to steady himself. Just when he was stepping across

the gap to plant a foot on our deck, Granddad shouted.
Too Tall slammed the throttle forward. When *Le Bûcheron*
leaped ahead, Eddie lost his grip on the rail, waved his
arms wildly, and fell into the lake.

With the engine roaring and the bow of *Le Bûcheron*
cutting through the waves like an arrow, we looked back
and saw Eddie thrashing about in the bright circle of the
spotlight, and Jack leaning over the side, reaching for
Eddie's hand to pull him back into the boat.

"I'll bet Eddie is sputtering," said Too Tall.

"I don't imagine he'd want his mother to hear him right
now," replied Granddad.

"They'll be after us," said Too Tall, "and I don't know if
we can outrun them with six of us in the boat."

"Can any of you young fellas swim?" Granddad asked.

"Louis and Little Roy can," said Too Tall.

"Good. Otter can swim too—like an otter," he said with a
grin. "Head south 35 degrees west."

"The Gut?" asked Too Tall.

"Yut. If we can't shake Jack by then, I and the boys will
jump overboard and strike out for Grand Isle. Jack will
follow you, but without our weight, you and Luc will have a
better chance of giving him the slip. We'll hike to the ferry
and meet you in Plattsburgh tomorrow night at the Angel's
Perch."

"Not Burlington?" I asked.

"No. I've been thinking. Your dad said it wasn't safe
for him to go the farm. If that's true, he won't go to your

grandmother's place, not if he has a choice. Plattsburgh's a better bet."

By this time, we had put some distance between us and Jack, but now we heard another engine roaring like an echo of our own, and I turned and saw the patrol boat in pursuit, its spotlight a pale, yellow blur in what was now becoming a heavy rain. Too Tall had shut off our lights, and with the lead we had gained, Jack could no longer see us, but he could still follow traces of our wake. Unfortunately, he was already gaining on us.

"Damn that Jack, him!" yelled Too Tall above the thundering engine. "He's got a new boat. Prob'ly belonged to a bootlegger! It's faster than a greyhound." I pulled my flat cap down low on my forehead and looked back. The patrol boat's headlight shone in the dark, maybe three hundred yards back, and Jack was gaining. We were taking a wicked chance, running without lights. Somewhere in the gloom ahead of us was the railroad bridge to North Hero. Our only hope was to see its lights and zip under it. If we missed, we'd crash into the causeway between North Hero and Grand Isle. It seemed like a pretty flimsy hope, but Too Tall kept the throttle wide open, and that new Chrysler engine screamed so loud I thought it would shuck its mounts.

The minutes passed and Jack's light crept closer. I wondered if some of us were going to swim, but then I saw Granddad pull his deer rifle from under a canvas where he had hidden it earlier.

"We must be right on top of that railroad bridge, Too Tall," he said.

"We get much closer, and we'll be wearing it," Too Tall replied.

"Turn your spot back on."

"He'll see us, him."

"That's the idea. He's close anyway. Let him get a little closer. When you're lined up with the bridge, hold your course and turn off your light."

I wasn't sure what Granddad had in mind, but I was pretty sure it wasn't a good time to ask questions, so I just watched. He stretched out on a bench in the stern and used a coil of rope for a rifle rest. Once settled, Granddad flicked off the safety and waited. He didn't have to wait long. Jack zoomed toward us, and now I could see his slim, military figure standing behind the wheel. I could also see Eddie standing in the bow, taking aim with a rifle himself.

"He's going to shoot at us!" I cried.

"Get down!" hollered Louis.

I dove for the deck along with the twins and Luc. Too Tall called out that he could see the bridge and was headed for the channel. Granddad sighted down the barrel of his gun. *What's he going to do*, I wondered? I knew my grandsire was not a man to trifle with, but was he really going to shoot a federal agent? Jack was close now, in shooting range, and in seconds his spotlight would reach us. Just then Eddie fired. I heard the bullet slap against the boat, and then I heard a grunt.

Too Tall turned off our spotlight just as Eddie fired again, and then Granddad squeezed the trigger of his deer rifle, and Jack's spotlight winked out. I whooped like an Indian. What a shot! I could still see the dim shape of the patrol boat through the rain but just barely. If Too Tall could bring us safely through the causeway, we had a darned good chance of getting away because without his spotlight, Jack would have to slow down and search for the channel Too Tall had already sighted.

But Too Tall had to get us through the channel first, and he had not backed off the throttle at all. The engine still thundered and the bow slapped against the waves as we sped into the darkness. If Too Tall veered off course even a little bit, we might come to a sudden stop. I looked up just in time to see the huge, iron bridge trusses looming faintly overhead. Our luck held, and we passed through the causeway without piling *Le Bûcheron* onto any rocks, and that was all right with me because I had no desire to make the acquaintance of Jack and his pal Eddie—not, at least, in the present circumstances.

"Looks like we might give old Jack the slip," roared Little Roy with a grin.

"Yut," called Granddad, "we might at that."

"I hope so," said Louis, "because Luc has been hit."

Before Granddad could ask how bad he was, the bow jumped. I heard a sharp bang like another gunshot and then the sickening sound of the hull grating on a rock—a big rock. Our momentum carried us over it, but it wasn't a good sound. Moments later, Little Roy called from the stern.

"My feet are getting wet," he said.

"Stop the boat!" called Granddad. "Quick! Could be we'll *all* have to swim. Let's look." Under the canopy Louis struck a couple matches in unison and held them low. Water was rising between the floorboards in the stern and beginning to lap at Little Roy's boots.

"Jumpin' Jesus and a band of angels," he cried. "What the hell is this?"

"Trouble," said Granddad. "Trouble with a capital T."

OTTER ST. ONGE AND THE BOOTLEGGERS

CHAPTER 3

Trouble

ET'S TAKE A LOOK AT YOU, LUC," said Granddad. Luc pulled up his hunting jacket, and in the lantern light Granddad cut away a piece of bloody union suit and peered at the gunshot wound. The Weasel had been hit in the back, and blood welled from the bullet hole. Luc grimaced with the pain, but he was still standing.

"I think that slug ricocheted off something before it hit me, so it ain't buried in my gut. Least, I don't think so. Feels like the Devil's got his hooks in me though!"

"That he has," said Granddad. "You hang on, Luc. Otter, cut a piece of your shirt for a bandage. Make it thick enough to soak up the blood and tie it on tight. Luc, when he finishes, you lie down. Let the blood clot." Granddad hung the lantern from the roof of the canopy so I could see to Luc, and so he could check the boat at the same time. Louis and Little Roy had moved a couple bags of liquor and pulled up the floorboards. I glanced down, and in the dim light I saw that the rock had opened a seam and water was flooding the bottom of the boat.

The lake's comin' in faster than we can bail," Granddad said. *"Le Bûcheron* is headed for the bottom. No doubt about it."

"Jack's right behind us," said Too Tall. "What are we going to do?" He paused, and we could hear the engine of Jack's boat thumping rhythmically a couple hundred yards away. He was coming, slow but steady. We only had a minute or two before he and Eddie would be on top of us.

"Grab your rifles," Too Tall said, "and swim for shore. You'll fetch up on the causeway. I'll stay here with Luc."

"Wait," said Granddad. "I've got an idea. Stuff some sacking in that hole. It'll buy us a little time. Luc, how are you at playing possum?" Luc tried to grin, but what his mouth did couldn't have been called anything happy looking. Still, to the Weasel's credit, he said he was game.

"All right, here's what we need to do," said Granddad, and I thought to myself, not for the first time, that my grandsire was always as ready as Caesar at the Rubicon.

A COUPLE MINUTES LATER I WAS TREADING water in my union suit and clutching the bow line of *Le Bûcheron. Hells bells, the smuggling business is nothing close to dull,* I thought. I had stripped off my clothes and boots and stowed them under a tarp. Then I had cut a swatch of cloth from a liquor sack, sliced two eyeholes, and tied on a makeshift mask. The others had done the same, all but Luc. He had pulled his felt crusher down low on his forehead and tied a bandana over the lower half of his face. Now, he and Jake were the only ones left in the boat, Luc lying face down in the bow. Too Tall was hidden on the other side of the bow from me, holding another dangling rope to stay afloat. With just our eyes and noses showing, we must have looked like a couple frogs in the swamp. My worry wasn't being seen by Jack; it was turning into an icicle and dropping to the bottom before he finally showed up. Christ with a Christmas tree, it was November, and that lake was some cold! Little Roy, Louis, and Granddad, were treading water out in the dark. The *put-put-put* of Jack's boat grew louder, and Eddie's ring of lantern light finally penetrated the gloom. We waited.

"Jack!" cried Eddie, "I can see their boat. It's just ahead. Hurry up! It's sinking."

"Keep your eyes open," said Jack. "Don't let those hooligans surprise you again."

"Oh, my poor mother," whispered Eddie.

"What is it?" asked Jack.

"I-I thought I aimed high. I think I hit one of them. Oh, Mother Mary, Jesus, and Joseph. I didn't want to kill him."

As they eased alongside the smugglers' boat, Jack saw what had caused the quaver in Eddie's voice. An old man was sprawled lifeless in the bow, one arm stretched above his head as if he had grabbed air while pitching forward. The other arm was trapped beneath him. As they drew closer, Jack saw that the man's jacket was stained with blood.

"Come take the wheel," said Jack. "I'll tend to that fella." Jack left the engine idling and came forward. "Go on back," said Jack. Eddie felt for the railing and shuffled backward, still staring at poor Luc who lay there as quiet as a dead man. Never taking his eyes off the body, Jack tied the patrol boat to a stanchion on *Le Bûcheron*. Then he jumped aboard. As he turned toward the bow, he heard a growl. He stared into the shadows and was amazed to see a wolf baring its fangs and snarling.

"You calm down, boy. You calm down and stay right there." He pulled his revolver from its holster and released the safety. Keeping an eye on the wolf, he addressed himself to the body again, "All right, bub, you'd better speak up." Luc the Weasel didn't say a word. "Answer me now!" cried Jack, "or I'll put another round in you."

Lord love a duck, I thought, *is he really going to shoot Luc again?'* Jack cocked the pistol, and he was so close, Luc must have heard the click, but the Weasel didn't make a sound. Jack sloshed through water that was now above his boots. When he reached for the gunwale to steady himself, Jake leaped and sunk his teeth into

Jack's britches. At the same time, Too Tall's hand shot up out of the water, grabbed Jack's wrist, and tumbled the lawman and the dog into the lake. Then, Luc rolled over with a groan and aimed a pistol at Eddie, but Eddie was quicker this time. He was already sighting down a rifle barrel at Luc.

"You better give up, mister," he said. "I'll shoot you again if I have to."

"Yes sir," said Luc, "I'm puttin' my gun down right now," and gingerly he placed his pistol on the seat where it would stay dry.

Eddie smiled, pleased in spite of himself, and Luc smiled in turn because of Little Roy. Under cover of Jack's splashing and indignant, shouted threats to Jake and the rest of us, Little Roy had slipped quietly into the patrol boat and was now standing behind Eddie with a blackjack in his hand. He flicked it against the smaller man's skull, and then Eddie swayed and crumpled to the bottom of the boat.

This seemed like a good time to call off Jake. He was swimming in circles around Jack, and between curses, Jack was huffing and puffing and sounding tired. Too Tall and I clambered back into *Le Bûcheron,* and when I whistled, Jake left off his persecution of the poor lawman and swam over to the boat where he allowed Too Tall to hoist him back aboard. Granddad, now in the patrol boat, told Little Roy to throw Jack a rope before he drowned.

"Too Tall," he called, "help Luc get over here, and then pass us the liquor and the rest of our gear." I patted Jake on the head for his recent service and then helped Too Tall pass the Moonbeam to Granddad and Louis. As the water rose to our knees, Jake and I abandoned ship and jumped aboard the patrol boat. Meanwhile, Jack had caught hold of a rope, and Little Roy was reeling him in like a big-mouthed bass. With a sigh, Too Tall bent over the foredeck of his boat, wrenched the spotlight from its fastenings, and then stepped aboard our new prize. Seconds later, *Le Bûcheron* disappeared beneath the black water with a sucking sound.

Soon after that, the sky opened, and the rain poured down so hard I didn't know if I was on the lake or in it. I guess it didn't matter much because all of us but Luc were pretty waterlogged. I'd never before been so wet and cold and miserable as I was that night after *Le Bûcheron* sprung a leak and we jumped in the lake to ambush Jack. Still, they say misery loves company, and we were all laughing about it before long. I can't say the same for Jack. He was downright cranky, especially after Granddad put a hood over his head so we could turn on the spotlight and take our masks off without being recognized. I will say in Granddad's defense that he let Jack change into a dry pair of wool trousers and a dry wool shirt from the patrol boat's storage locker. That says a lot about the kind of outlaw Granddad was because Jack only had the one extra set of clothes,

and he and Granddad were about the same size, and
Granddad every bit as wet as he was.

To warm himself up, Granddad uncorked a bottle
of Mississquoi Moonbeam, swallowed mightily, and
passed it to Too Tall. Too Tall, naked as the day he was
born and wringing out his union suit, raised the bottle
and drank a toast to our new boat which he promptly
christened *Jack's Comeuppance.* Then the rest of us,
shrugging back into our clothes, had a good shot of
Moonbeam ourselves to ward off the chill. Granddad
offered Jack a drink, but Jack was a teetotaler, I guess,
and didn't even have a sip. He was awful mad, partly
because he had just been fished out of the lake half
drowned but mostly, I imagine, because Granddad
had outfoxed him, and he was threatening Granddad
and the rest of us with prison once the tables were
turned which, he assured us, would happen soon
because we had assaulted an agent of the United States
government, and that was no laughing matter, even
though Little Roy and Louis were chuckling quietly to
themselves while they rigged *Le Bucheron's* old spotlight
in place of the one Granddad had shot to pieces.

Granddad was ignoring Jack and motoring slowly
toward the west side of the Gut where we would pass
out to the open waters of Champlain again. Little Roy
and Louis finished screwing down the spotlight, and
soon its beam searched the murk ahead. Too Tall had
bound Jack and Eddie hand and foot, and then tied

them to the rail aft of the cabin. Eddie had revived, but he wasn't too perky. I think he might have taken a nip of our moonshine but for his headache and the fact that Jack was there. Louis was watching over them from the cabin to make sure they didn't get into any mischief. He was looking after Luc too, who vented his spleen toward Eddie in a colorful streak of insults aimed at past generations of Halsteads. He had worked his way back to the cowardly, bootlicking son of a monkey that passed for Eddie's grandsire when shock and fatigue set in, and he slowly unwound like the mainspring of a watch. Louis eased him down on a bench in the cabin, and his ranting turned to muttering and then ceased altogether.

In the bow, Little Roy and I peered into the night in search of shoals. The spotlight penetrated maybe forty feet ahead of us, but with the rain sheeting down, it was still as dark as a coffin. Little Roy stretched out at full length on the foredeck and slowly swiveled the light back and forth in search of hazards. Granddad gave Too Tall the wheel and rummaged through Jack's storage locker again. Out came a stub of pencil and a chart of the upper lake. He unrolled the chart, and I held a lantern so he could see. He tugged his pocket watch from a waterproof pouch on his belt and noted the time. Then he drew a line on the chart and ciphered.

"This Jack," he said with grudging admiration. "The

man has *all* the aids to navigation. I think I'll take this compass and chart with us when we leave. Keep us pointed south 80 degrees west, Too Tall. We'll pass out of the Gut in a few minutes, and then we'll head for the Cumberland Light. We can go south from there to the ferry landing and get Luc to a friend of mine who can take that bullet out and patch him up."

"Who's your friend, him?" asked Too Tall.

"His name is Doc Eastman. If we can borrow a car, we can be at his house ten minutes after we tie up. His place is just a mile up Moffitt Road." Too Tall nodded, and I saw a look of relief on his face. I figured he and the Weasel must have been friends for a long time. We sped through the darkness without talking, and my thoughts turned to my father again. *Where is he now?* I said to myself. *What happened at the fish camp?* Most of all, I wondered if he was alive. The minutes passed, and the rain fell without let-up. Jake sat up and laid his chin on my knee, and I stroked his shaggy head. Finally, Too Tall broke the silence.

"This Doc Eastman—he won't call the cops, peut-être?"

"No," answered Granddad. When Too Tall looked at him with eyebrows raised, he continued.

"I saved his grandson's life. It's a story quickly told." Knowing better, I settled back in my seat and got comfortable—or as comfortable as I could be without being a frog or a duck. Then I listened.

"I met him twelve years ago," said Granddad,
"in 1915. I was taking the ferry from Grand Isle to
Cumberland Head, just where we're going now. It was
September, the time of year when we can get the tail
of a hurricane coming up from the West Indies. A few
folks drove Model T Fords onto the ferry, but most of
us were foot passengers. I had a few bottles of tax free
Moonbeam in my knapsack to help with expenses along
the way, but of course that teetotaling Volstead hadn't
got those ninnyheads down in Washington to vote for
Prohibition yet, so I wasn't smuggling on any grand
scale.

I told Petrice I was going to a farm auction across the
lake over in Beekmantown to bid on some Jersey heifers
a drummer had told me about. Leastways, I was going
to bid if they looked like good milkers and promised to
sell reasonable. Truth be told, though, I was on a lark.
Every time I turned around the week before that, I kept
thinking *winter's comin', winter's comin'*—Jack Frost on
the windows and a vee of honking geese headed south
almost every day—so I just wanted to be out and about
before settling in.

Anyway, this Doc Eastman drove onto the ferry
with a brand new Model T Touring Car. I was at the
rail taking in the view and thinking that the wind was
picking up, and he and I struck up a conversation. He
introduced me to his daughter Evelyn, and Evelyn's two
kids, Scotty, a boy eight years old and Marian, a girl of

six. The kids explored the boat before we left Grand Isle.
They were excited about that ferry ride. They dashed up
the stairs to the wheelhouse deck, and a gust of wind
hit them so hard, it almost blew them off their feet. They
loved it. They grabbed the rail and held tight, grinning
with pure joy. I'll never forget their faces. They were
amazed by Mother Nature's wildness. I wish to God
Mother Nature had stayed tame that day.

I remember thinking that Marian was going to be
a knockout. Had her mother's looks, and her mother
was a beautiful woman. The little darling was wearing
a bright, red beret, and she was as proud as could be
of that little hat because Doc had just given it to her.
I watched those children while I talked with Doc and
Evelyn, and I noticed that Evelyn kept her eye on them
every second. She loved those kids more than anything
else in the world. Any fool could see that."

"Hold on, Amos," said Too Tall. "Little Roy, what's
that?" Little Roy peered through the curtains of rain
ahead. I could see nothing, but Too Tall said Little Roy
had the eyes of an owl.

"I think it's the channel on the west side of the Gut,"
said Little Roy. "Hold her steady. You be headed right
up the middle." Too Tall pulled the throttle back, and
we slowed down, chugging along slowly so Little Roy
could warn us about rocks. Sure enough, as we passed
through to open water, we could see the Cumberland
Light across the lake. In clear weather, it was a bright

beacon that could be seen more than ten miles away. Tonight, it glimmered watery and faint in the distance. Too Tall pushed the throttle forward. The pitch of the engine rose again to a roar, and we surged forward into the wall of rain and the chop of the open lake. I thought of Luc, wondering if he was okay. Then I figured we had done what we could, and I settled back again for Granddad's story.

"Okay, Amos," said Too Tall. "You were telling us about Doc?"

"So I was. He and I talked, and soon we were half shouting against the wind. It had been blowing all day, and now it was blowing harder than ever. We commented to Captain Beecher, who was climbing the stairs to the wheelhouse, that the crossing might be rough, but he claimed he'd made the trip many times in weather just as bad, and that's what he said later in the *Burlington Free Press*. It was the last trip of the day, and a lot of New Yorkers wanted to get home come hell or high water, so off we went. The storm gathered all the while, and by the time we'd made it half way across the lake, we were facing waves that looked like they'd rolled in from the mighty Atlantic. It's a long reach from the Narrows at the south end of the lake to Cumberland Head, and when the wind blows, the waves build. The sky filled up with oily, black clouds, the rain pelted down stinging and cold, and the wind began blowing the white caps right off the waves. It was up to a gale before long, and those waves were fearsome, fifteen feet or more from trough to crest.

It didn't get bad all at once, of course, but when the rain came, it got miserable on deck. Doc Eastman had seen it coming, so he had already put up the top on the car. He and I buttoned up the side curtains, and then Evelyn and the kids took cover inside when the rain started. They were snug and safe for the time being. Doc put on a slicker, and I was already wearing a wool hunting jacket and a felt hat. The two of us stayed out in the weather to see what the storm was going to do.

Well, it came on, and it came on, and the waves kept building, and it seemed like each new one was a little bigger than the last. By this time we could see the Cumberland Light, but just barely. With all the rain and overcast, it was almost dark even though the sun hadn't dropped into the Adirondacks yet. We were still a good distance from the ferry landing, maybe a mile or more, and now the waves were getting nigh onto biblical.

By the time we decided to get Evelyn and the kids into the passenger cabin, it was too late. We didn't dare take the little ones across the heaving deck. Before we knew it, Doc and I were gripping the rail and bracing our legs as the ferry banged down into the trough of one wave and swooped up to the crest of another. Up and down we went, juddering and banging, banging and juddering until it seemed the ferry must come apart. This went on for maybe half an hour. It didn't seem possible that it could get worse, but it did. As the waves built bigger and bigger, and the boat was tossed to and fro, the cars began to slide around on the deck. Then, a monster wave came. I saw it rear up like the hand of the Almighty and then come crashing down. Doc's Model T skittered sideways and hit a truck. The door to the back seat popped open, and Evelyn screamed as Scotty was thrown out across the deck and over the side into the water.

'Doc,' I shouted above the howling wind, 'Get a life preserver!' I threw off my jacket and hat. I pulled my knife from its sheath, cut my laces, and shucked my boots. Then, as the deck tilted steeply once again, I climbed the rail and jumped in. I swam furiously for the spot where I'd just seen Scotty sink beneath a wave, and I dove. I swept my hands blindly through the water, snagged his coat—a crazy piece of luck—and kicked hard for the world above. Just when we broke the surface, I looked for the boat and saw Doc with a ring buoy in his hand. Scissoring the rail with his legs just as the ferry rose upward again, he heaved the buoy for all he was worth, and his aim was true. With a couple kicks, I was able to grab it with one hand while holding Scotty with the other.

Doc started hauling us in, but then the terrible thing happened. Evelyn had jumped out of the car with Marian in her arms as the ferry had begun this same roll upward. She was running as best she could for the ship's cabin, and she was almost there when the ferry crashed down again, harder than ever. One of the crew had braced himself in the cabin doorway and was stretching out a hand to grab her, but she couldn't reach him. She lost her footing and careened down the wet deck out of control. She struck one of the railing posts. Doc told me later she hit her head. She was badly stunned. The boat plunged, the rail dipped down to the level of the lake, and that section of the deck went under water. Suddenly, Evelyn was afloat with Marian still in her arms, and in seconds she was ten yards from the ferry.

Doc and I watched in horror. I couldn't help them without leaving Scotty to drown, and neither could Doc. The deckhand who had tried to help Evelyn gain the cabin saw what had happened and came running with another ring buoy. He flung it, and by some miracle it landed right beside her. In a last, brave effort, she managed to drop the ring over Marian's head and get it under her armpits. I was sure they would be saved. The deckhand had just taken up the slack in the rope when the ferry lurched again. And again, the cars slid on the deck, and one of them skidded all the way to the rail and hit the deckhand in the back. He got clipped hard and almost tumbled into the lake himself, but somehow he gritted his teeth and clung to the rail. What he *couldn't* do was hang onto the rope. It slithered into the water like a snake, and Doc and I watched Evelyn and Marian disappear as the crest of a wave rose between us and them. Marian was screaming with terror, but I didn't hear Evelyn call back to her. When she rose to the crest of another wave, I saw Marian one more time, the red beret still visible, but there was no sign of Evelyn. Then Marian dropped out of sight again, and that was the last we saw of her."

"Damn," said Too Tall softly. "Damn. Tragique, Amos. Mama and l'enfant? Both drown?"

"They must have," said Amos. "Doc said Evelyn cracked her head hard against that post. He saw blood. She prob'ly blacked out right after she got her daughter into that life preserver. I can't imagine Marian survived. She was only six."

"That's a sad story, Amos. Très désolé. The doc, he must have been very tore up."

"Broke his heart. His only child? *And* his granddaughter? As you said—tragic. His son-in-law, John Prince, fared even worse. He and everyone else had come to Burlington that day to celebrate Marian's birthday with his parents. John stayed the night—he had some business in town—and was going back to Plattsburgh the next day. The telephone rang that evening when he and his father were sitting in the parlor after dinner, talking about how much Marian had enjoyed her party. It was the ferry company calling about his wife and daughter.

After the double funeral, John asked Doc if he and Beverly would raise Scotty. Doc said they would, so John Prince joined the Lafayette Escadrille, those American boys who flew with the French air corps before we entered the war. He was shot down over a place called Vimy Ridge in 1917. Officially, he was missing in action, but the flyboys said he must have died in the crash. That left Doc and Beverly to raise Scotty on their own. He was all they had left, the spitting image of his father, they said." Amos paused and looked away. "So. That's the story. Doc and Beverly wanted me to be Scotty's godfather," he continued, "because, well, because of that day, you know. I used to stop and see them once in a while when Scott was younger, but I haven't been by in a few years. Scotty would be twenty now. Anyway, you overgrown Canuck, that's how I come to save Doc Eastman's grandson, and that's why Doc won't call the cops."

"Bon, Amos. Très bon. I am sorry for this poor man's trouble, him, but I am glad he will help us with Luc."

Yes. He'll help us. After what Granddad risked to help him, he will surely help us, I thought. I sat there in the rain, picturing that little girl drifting away, lost in those terrible waves, and the sadness of it pierced my heart, and tears welled up in my eyes, but it didn't matter because with the rain streaming down my face, neither Granddad nor Too Tall could tell. Then I realized Granddad was talking again.

"We're south of the Cumberland Light," he was saying, "so we must be close to the ferry landing. Stay close to shore. The water's deep, so we shouldn't hit a rock. It's as dark as the soul of Satan, so look hard for the landing. We don't want to miss it." Just then, Louis called from the stern, and I could tell from his voice that something was wrong.

"Amos," he called.

"What is it?" Granddad asked.

"You'd better look at Luc."

"What's wrong?" asked Granddad.

"He's lost a lot of blood," said Louis. "He's not doing so well." Louis lit the lantern and held it while Granddad rested a finger on Luc's throat. He took it away and cursed.

"Too Tall!" he yelled to make himself heard above the engine and the downpour. "Turn this thing loose. Luc's bad. Hardly has a pulse. We've got to get him to Doc."

"Damn and damnation!" said Too Tall. "Hang on Luc! Don't you die!"

Too Tall shoved the throttle forward, and the boat rocketed into the night. Jake leaned his sodden flank against my leg seeking a little reassurance. I stroked him, closed my eyes and said a silent prayer. *We're flying across the waters like an arrow from your bowstring, oh Lord, and if you would, Sir, please deliver us to the shore in one piece. And while you're at it, Lord, please keep Luc in the palm of your hand until Doc Eastman can get that bullet out. Thank you, Lord. Amen.* Then I opened my eyes as wide as I could and stared into the dark hoping to see whatever we were going to hit in time to jump clear.

OTTER ST. ONGE AND THE BOOTLEGGERS

CHAPTER 4

The Angel's Perch

A T THE UNHOLY RATE WE WERE TRAVELING toward the ferry landing, I thought we would ride the boat right up the beach and into the woods before we came to a stop, but Granddad knew what he was about. He had that giant uncle of mine cut the engine at just the right time, and we coasted to the pier. Drifting in quiet-like, Granddad hoped to escape notice, which was advisable since he was intending to "borrow" a car. It wasn't late yet, but the last ferry had made its run, and with any luck no one would be hanging around the landing in the pouring rain when they could be toasting their toes in front of a crackling fire.

Too Tall almost did a jig when Little Roy spied a Model T parked at the ferry captain's house. My uncle laid Luc down gently in the back seat and covered him with a blanket because the poor fellow was shaking. Then the bunch of us pushed the car out of the yard and around the first curve on Moffitt Road where we thought we could start it without being heard. Granddad spoke quietly to Louis.

"We'll take care of Luc and be along as soon as we can. You take care of my grandson."

"I will," promised Louis solemnly.

"All right. We'll meet you at the Angel's Perch."

Granddad and Too Tall got in the front seat, and Little Roy cranked the motor. It sputtered a couple times, but praise the patron saint of spark plugs, it finally caught, and they drove off into the murky night looking for Doc Eastman's place.

We got back aboard *Jack's Comeuppance* and set off once again for Plattsburgh. When we rounded the point and entered Cumberland Bay, we could see the lights of town twinkling faintly on the darkened shore ahead. Little Roy had already gagged Eddie and Jack before landing at the ferry dock, and now the plan was for him to stay on board with them while Louis and I went to find the Angel's Perch. Louis carried a lantern to signal his brother when we returned. Little Roy was to wait a hundred yards out in the harbor on the unlikely chance that any of the local constabulary should wander down the rain-driven street to the docks.

The rain still poured down, and I could hear water gushing from a storm drain nearby. As black as the Devil's coattails it was, and just as we expected, not a soul stirred on the waterfront. We pulled our caps low and slogged up Bridge Street. Five minutes later we passed the Delaware and Hudson Railroad Station and knew to keep our eyes peeled for the Angel's Perch. We found

it just before the bridge over the Saranac River. It was a
two-story brick building that looked like it had once been
a working mill but was now beset with cracked windows
and crumbling mortar. It had no sign, only a crudely
carved angel above a door below street level, and believe
me, the place didn't look anything like the way I pictured
Heaven. The Perch was a blind pig that catered to hard-
drinking railroad men on the west side of the lake,
and it was only open to customers who were less than
upstanding. We huddled in the doorway of A. C. Waldo's
Pawn Shop across the street. It must have been something
fancier at one time because it had a small portico with a
roof that stuck out just enough to keep us dry. Beneath
it, we waited for Granddad and Too Tall as the rain hissed
on the paving stones.

By the time they arrived in the clattering Model T two
hours later, my teeth were chattering, but we were glad
to hear that Doc Eastman had removed the bullet from
Luc's back and that the old boy was resting peacefully.
Granddad said he had learned some interesting news
from old Doc, but he'd tell us about it later because, for
the moment, we had more important fish to fry. With that,
he rapped on the stout, nail-studded door of the Angel's
Perch. A narrow panel slid sideways and uncovered a
peephole. He spoke softly to the man inside, and the door
opened. Granddad nodded to the burly fellow standing on
the threshold. Although not tall, the fellow was a strong,
barrel-chested man who looked like he could discourage

most any customer from disturbing the peace of his establishment.

"Good evening, Parson," said Granddad cordially.

"Evenin', Amos!" answered Parson excitedly. "Come on in outta the rain! It ain't a fit night for man nor beast lest you're a fish or a frog. Cozy up to a table by the fire. You must be froze to the bone. I'll throw on another log so you can drive off the damp, and I'll send one of the girls right over to tell you what they got hot in the kitchen. By the pagan gods, Amos, you and your boys look like you swum here. Deacon's in his office if you're here to do business as well as pleasure, and I hope you are, because I'm partial to that—what do you call it—Missus Whiskey's Moon Cream?"

"Parson," laughed Granddad, "your hospitality is only exceeded by your exuberance and your erudition. Moon Cream is much the better name. I license you to change my Mississquoi Moonbeam to Missus Whiskey's Moon Cream and to sell it as such henceforth. I'm sure the custom will crowd the bar for the name alone, and, yes, I *have* brought some of this elixir for the Angel's Perch, but let's tend to pleasure first and business later. Dinner and a warm hearth would be most welcome. I don't know about the other fellas, but a mug of Irish coffee would go down smoothly too."

"By all the saints, Amos, you'll have the best the house can offer. Right this way fellas. What's that animal you've got there, boy? He looks like a darn wolf. Is he friendly? Ah well, bring him in. His bite can't be any worse than that of some of these boys working for the Delaware and Hudson. Come in, come in! Sit down and warm yourselves!"

In no time we were all seated at a scarred, round table. Jake curled up and rested his chin on my feet. A cheerful fire blazed in the stone hearth, and the heat of it soon sent steam rising from our clothes. The strains of fiddle music came from a far corner of the room, and the railroad men were singing "Paddy Works on the Railway." Granddad drew a corncob pipe and a tobacco pouch from a jacket pocket, and blew smoke rings toward the ceiling. I glanced around the room and noticed the tavern's namesake, a three-foot, hand-carved angel sitting on a shelf behind the bar. The statue's face *was* angelic, but in one hand the angel held a whiskey glass and in the other an unwound scroll which read, "Spirits Sprouteth Wings."

"Parson?" I said, once Granddad was settled. "And people say my name is odd. Were his parents religious?" I asked.

"His mother was," answered Granddad, "but his father, old Nick Gates, was about as irreligious and as mischievous a rascal as I ever saw. When he proposed marriage to a Temperance woman, a woman named Angelina, she said yes, but only if he promised to give up the drink. He said he would be temperate, but he would never give up spirits entirely for he was a spiritual man. Also, he pointed out, his living came from his tavern, and it was incumbent on him to sample all his liquors to ensure their quality for his customers. He said that to demonstrate his good faith in temperance as a principle, however, he would, with her consent, christen their children with names that would signify to the world that they were a devout and reverent family. Hence, the names of the children: Parson, Deacon, Reverend, Cherub, Angel, and Pearly.

"Pearly?!"

"Yut, as in Pearly Gates," he said with a broad grin. "She's the youngest. Angel, the oldest daughter, is behind the bar right now. You may think her a trifle large for an angel, but then, who's ever really seen one?" I glanced over at the bar and noticed a woman whose features resembled Parson's, but whose girth was even greater.

"Parson is the eldest, and he makes sure no one comes in the Angel's Perch who's not supposed to. He's got a sixth sense when it comes to recognizing a lawman. His brother Deacon keeps the books and does the buying and selling, and that reminds me of why we're here. You boys order some good, hot food for us. Too Tall and I will go dicker with Deacon. And don't forget that Irish coffee." He said that last over his shoulder, and then he and Too Tall disappeared into the milling crowd. I saw a door open behind the fiddler, and they entered Deacon's office.

Louis leaned back in his chair, impassive and silent as usual, and soaked up the warmth of the fire. He tipped his hat brim down, but I could see that he wasn't napping. His eyelids had lowered, but they hadn't closed.

I looked around, still curious about the Angel's Perch
and its clientele. It was a rougher version of Grandma
Melodie's place, the King Street Tavern. It was crowded,
a working man's bar, and the men were wearing what
they'd worn all day. Some of their coats and coveralls
were ripped and tattered, some were neatly patched, but
all were more or less grimy. Looking around, I figured
every man jack in there had spent his day repairing
track, unloading a boxcar, or cleaning a Delaware &
Hudson locomotive. It was time to unwind. It might have
been Prohibition, but you couldn't prove it by the Angel's
Perch. The men were all drinking beer and whiskey, and
at several tables they were playing cards. They listened to
the rousing tunes of the white-haired fiddler and forgot
the long work day.

As Parson promised, a barmaid soon came to tell us
what the kitchen was offering. She was lovely, but I confess
from the start that "lovely" is a weak and uninspired word
for what she truly was. There are times when I think I
should be like my grandfather, a man, for the most part,
of few words, a strong, silent woodsman, but if I don't do
justice to Mary and the first time I saw her, it's not because
I'm like Granddad in that way. It's because I don't have the
poetry in me to describe how comely and sweet she was.
Some women have beauty in the face, some in the figure,
and some in the soul, but I was to find out soon that dark-
haired Mary had beauty in all three, and these beyond any
woman I had ever known. I will never forget her coming

toward me through the jostling crowd, her skirt swinging gracefully with every step, and her blues eyes shining. Her smile lit me up, I swear. She balanced a tray of drinks with her right hand, and fended off a patron's groping fingers with the left. She was a vision. If the truth were told, that little imp with the bow and arrow shot me right in the heart the moment I saw Mary.

I wasn't the only one who noticed her. Eyes turned as she passed, and a self-appointed ladies' man, who was swaggering back to the table next to ours, gave her a pat on the behind as she walked by. Maybe I was quick to take offense over a girl I didn't even know, but that was the way of it. I didn't take to that fella from the first, and I didn't take to him any better at the last. He treated her like she was his, and the crazy thing was, she didn't seem to take offense. For the life of me, that didn't cipher. He was a loudmouth and a braggart with the manners of a pig. She was graceful and lovely, the only woman in the Angel's Perch that looked anything like one. *What can she see in him,* I wondered? *Maybe she sees something I can't see. I'd need the eyes of an eagle to see it, but maybe it's there for all of that. Maybe his brass and bluster cover up a heart of gold.* Heck, I didn't believe it for a second, which just goes to show you how lunatic a fella can get when he comes under the spell of an angel.

As all this passed through my mind, she unloaded the drinks and made her way to our table. When she spoke, much to Louis' amusement, I was struck dumb. I know this makes me sound like a lovesick mooncalf. Maybe I was, but I wasn't in all ways ignorant of females. Some of the pretty girls at Burlington High School found me easy enough to look at, or so they said. I had thick, black hair and high cheek bones from my father's Indian blood. I was broad shouldered, an inch or two over six feet, and the good Lord had given me the gift of a keen eye coupled with quickness and strength. I played basketball all four years of high school, and I helped put some banners in the gym.

That led to spooning with the cheerleaders, and then to Annie Perkins who was not only pretty but smart. She was two years older than me, but we courted anyway—for a short time. Her father was a professor at the University of Vermont. He was friendly enough until he found out my last name was St. Onge and my father was part Abenaki. He had a theory that Indians and Canucks would throw off the bloodline of the regular Yankee Vermonters, so that shut the door on me and Annie. Then I met Bridget Murphy. She was the closest I ever came to having a steady. She worked at the Queen City Cotton Mill, and she was a firecracker—pretty, bright, and full of fun. From her, I learned all I needed to know about girls, and I was lucky enough to get the lessons without becoming a father.

So, I'd come to love girls by this time, but I'd also learned to rein myself in because I wasn't yet ready for the most holy bonds of matrimony. At least, the idea hadn't appealed to me so far. Then, this girl in front of me turned my notions topsy turvy. She spoke to Louis and me so sweet and lovely, she scrambled my wits like eggs in a pan, and I couldn't hear the words, just her voice like a songbird's. If you've ever heard a hermit thrush, you'll know what I mean. The first time I did was on a hillside above Granddad's farm in high summer. Slipping quietly through the hardwoods, I stopped dead in my tracks to listen. The notes were like water falling— clear—liquid—like music from the otherworld. Laugh if you want, but her voice was that beautiful to me, and I couldn't even speak when she wished us both a good evening. Louis, trying to keep a straight face, told her I had "spells" now and then, and I'd be right as rain in a minute.

She laughed. "I'm Mary," she said. "If you're hungry, we've got a pot roast coming out of the oven with carrots, onions, potatoes, and brown gravy. We've got a fish platter with fresh lake trout, and we've got beans baked in maple syrup and salt pork with turnip greens and brown bread on the side." I'd been too busy to think about food for hours, but now I was famished. I smiled like a simpleton and let Louis order.

"We'll need five dinners. Why don't you pull from all three dishes. D'accord, Mademoiselle?"

"Sure. Anything else?" she asked with a friendly smile. Louis grinned widely—too widely—and before he could reply, I jumped in.

"Yes, a mug of Irish coffee for my grandsire."

She nodded without looking at me directly. Before she left, she reached for the full ashtray on our table, and as I handed it to her, I stared at one of the cigarette butts. It had dark tobacco, and on the stained paper I could read the letters *G-a-u*.... She saw my interest and looked at me, wondering, but when I said nothing, she left. She passed lover boy's table, sidestepped his busy hand, and pushed on toward the swinging doors of the kitchen.

Louis peered at me, and I thought, *Uh-oh, he's onto me.* Louis was quiet. If either of the twins was at all like their garrulous father, it was Little Roy; it definitely was *not* Louis. Louis wasn't exactly shy. He was just—as I said already—quiet. He was also a hawk, and I had already sensed why Granddad had put him in charge when he and Too Tall had driven off with Luc back at the ferry landing. When other people talked, Louis listened. And he watched. As I was thinking all this, Louis grinned again which is another thing he doesn't do that often.

"What?" I said.

"You like her?" he asked.

"I think I'm in love with her," I said. I told the truth because Louis knew anyway.

"Trés bon!" he replied. "Maybe she can help us." I frowned and looked at him questioningly.

"It was a Gauloise, oui?" he asked. I hesitated, wondering what he had in mind.

"The cigarette?" he said.

"Yes, it was."

Louis grunted. A few minutes later, the waitress named Mary reappeared from the kitchen, and I tried to watch her without being too obvious. She passed by lover boy's table, sidestepped what was, I'm sure, some wicked clever remark as easily as she had sidestepped his roving hand earlier, and reached our table without spilling a drop from the various cups and bowls on the enormous tray she carried. She set steaming cups of coffee in front of the two of us, laid the table with plates and silverware, and then emptied the tray of serving dishes containing the pot roast, beans, fish, and so on.

"You gentlemen look a bit damp," she said, "so I made sure the coffee was hot. I'll bring coffee for your friends when they finish with Deacon."

I murmured my thanks and Louis said, "Merci." I gazed at her angel face until I was just shy of ogling, and then I looked away and realized I was heating up from the inside. She left, and Louis and I tucked into the meal with the whole-hog appetite of two fellas who have spent a long, cold day out of doors. Every so often, I snuck a piece of pot roast or fish under the table for Jake, who took these offerings from my hand with surprising care, which was just as well considering the size of his teeth. Before long, we had gulped down our coffee and wiped our plates clean with crusts of bread. We tilted back in our chairs expecting Granddad and Too Tall to return from Deacon's inner sanctum at any minute.

Mary came back, not only to refill our coffee mugs but to offer us apple pie. She cut big, steaming wedges from an oven dish and set them before us. She bent down a little closer than necessary to set the pie in front of me, and I whispered gently, "Careful, this might get you in trouble with your boyfriend."

She looked disconcerted and then whispered back. "He's not my boyfriend, but if he was, would you be afraid?"

I shook my head slowly. I was hoping to look like a handsome young blade, the kind of fellow this girl would like to know better, and I was also hoping I could think of another witty remark, one that would make lover boy's clever talk appear the work of a mental midget, but I wasn't quick enough. She took the rest of the pie and went back to the kitchen. Once again, I admired her as she left the room. I didn't know yet if she had any poetry in her heart, but she sure had it in the way she walked. Louis chewed thoughtfully, obviously liking the pie.

"You know what would go good with this pie?" he asked.

"What?"

"Some cheese. Why don't you go find that girl and see if she's got some good, sharp cheddar."

"Can't it wait until she comes back from the kitchen?" ·

"No. It can't. I want some cheese before I finish. Besides—I want you to ask this young lady you are so quickly falling in love with if she remembers the man who sat at this table and smoked some rank-smelling cigarettes before we got here. Best to do that away from other folk. Comprends?"

"Sure," I said. "I understand."

I passed by the swinging doors as if I were on my way down the hall to the indoor privy. Once out of sight of the taproom, I stopped and leaned against the wall. I didn't have to wait long. The doors swung open again, and Mary came through, all business, carrying a tray of clean mugs for the bar. Seeing me, she paused.

"You look lost," she said.

"Not exactly."

"Can I help?" she asked.

"I hope so," I replied.

"What do you mean? What do you want?" She wasn't smiling now.

"Please—I'm not—," I stammered and stopped. All of a sudden, I was tongue-tied. What was I supposed to tell her? My grandsire and I are smuggling whiskey, and, by the way, we're also looking for my father who has been kidnapped? Sure. That would cinch my spot on her dance card. *Oh fiddledy toot,* I thought, *what do I say?* She stepped closer and stared at me, waiting for an answer. I couldn't tell if she was suspicious or curious. Maybe she was both. One thing I saw as clear as a saint's conscience—she was achingly beautiful.

"Yes?" she said more softly, encouraging me.

"Can you tell me about the men who sat at our table earlier this evening?"

"What men?"

"That's what I'm asking. There were some, weren't there?"

"Why do you want to know?"

"Because I think they kidnapped my father. Maybe they did even worse." I thought she might tell me what a liar I was and laugh in my face, but she didn't. She told me to wait. She brought the mugs to the bar, and then she came back and tugged my sleeve to pull me after her. We slipped into a storage locker where a butchered pig and some plucked chickens were hanging from hooks in the ceiling. A tin-lined box packed with layers of sawdust and blocks of ice stood over a drain in the middle of the floor and kept the room cold. One little voice in my head was telling me to concentrate on my father and what I could do to rescue him, but another, much to my surprise, was regretting the not-very-romantic surroundings for my first real conversation with the girl of my dreams.

"What's your name?" she asked.

'Otter," I said before I could think.

"What!" she laughed. "You're kidding."

"No. I'm not." I turned red, but then I said to myself, *Otter, you've never been flustered by your name before. Don't start now.* I stood up straight and held her gaze. "Can you help me or not?" I asked. It was her turn to be flustered.

"There were three of them," she said. "Are you telling me the truth? Do you really think they kidnapped your father?"

"Yut."

She twisted a curl of her wavy, brown hair between her thumb and forefinger and considered before she went on. "Well, it doesn't surprise me. They were tough customers. The one that smoked those cigarettes? One of the others called him Chance. They all spoke Canuck French. This Chance wore a hat even at the table and a coat with a high collar turned up. He might have been handsome once, but not anymore. He had a strong chin and long, dark hair that spilled out from under his hat. He kept back in the shadows, and I only saw his face clearly when he got up to leave."

"What did he look like?"

He had a black patch over his left eye and a jagged scar that went from his missing eye to his chin."

"Was there anything else about him you think I should know?"

"I think he was the top dog of that bunch."

"Why do you think that?"

"On the face of it, he and the other men were equals, but I could see they looked to him, and they listened if he spoke." She frowned and thought. "Working in this place I see a lot of rough men. They're rude, even mean some of them, but they don't make the hair stand up on my neck. He did. Whoever and whatever he is, he's a dangerous man." She paused and looked at me. "You need to be careful."

"I will be," I said. "Do you know where they went when they left?"

"I heard one of them mention the name Ruth and the Hotel Champlain. Then the one they called Chance gave him a dirty look, and the man clammed up."

"The Hotel Champlain? Well, that's pretty interesting. I can guess his business there. I'll bet a lot of the hotel guests like the whiskey that comes down from Canada. From the way you describe this Chance, I'm not the only one who should be careful. You should too. Don't mention any of this to anyone else."

"I won't. He gave me the creeps."

"By the way, what's your last name?" I asked. She hesitated, and I had to ask her again before she would say.

"Mack," she replied. "My name is Mary Mack."

"Mary Mack?" I asked, "as in Miss Mary Mack, Mack, Mack, all dressed in black, black, black...." She scowled and moved toward the door.

"Okay," she said, "I've got to go back to work."

"No. Wait. I'm sorry. Mary, what you've told me may help me find my dad, and I haven't seen him in eleven years. I appreciate it," I said, and I smiled because I truly did.

"Don't mention it. Before you leave, tell me—are you going to the hotel?"

"I think so. I've got to talk to my grandsire and see what

he says. I'm with him and my Uncle Too Tall. That's my cousin Louis out there at the table."

"Too Tall?" she asked.

"You'll see," I said.

"Listen," she continued, "I could go with you. I could help. I know a girl at the hotel named Annie-Marie. She's a chambermaid, and sometimes she works in the dining room or the bar at night. She has a passkey to the rooms. Maybe I can help you get inside. It's pretty swank. They have a detective there full time, and, no offense, but you and your friends don't exactly look like the swells that stay at the hotel. I'll be done my shift in about ten minutes."

"Let's go to talk to Granddad," I said with a grin.

"Okay. But first I have to tell you something."

"What?"

"That guy at the table next to you? The one you called my boyfriend. His name is Roddy Bragg. *He* thinks he's my boyfriend. I don't. He might get riled if he sees us come out together."

"You said he's not your boyfriend. Why does he think he is?"

"It's a long story. We went dancing a couple times. He took me to the moving pictures. I guess he thinks that gives him some claim on me."

"And you think maybe I can help you get rid of him?" I knew I shouldn't have said it, but I couldn't help it. I had the feeling there was something she wasn't telling me.

She was annoyed. "I'm just telling you that if he sees us together, he'll try to beat the living daylights out of you. Look, I'm sure you don't need my help. Like I said, I've got to get back to work."

"Okay," I said. "Sorry. I seem to be putting my foot in my mouth tonight. Thanks for the warning."

"I'm serious," she said. "He'll try to kill you."

"Don't worry," I replied.

She looked at me doubtfully, but I opened the door, and she passed into the hall. When I followed her, there stood Roddy Bragg, hands on his hips and a cigarette dangling from his mouth. From the look on his face, I figured he must have eaten a lemon.

"I guess you didn't know Mary's my girl did you, hick?" He reached for his cigarette and blew a puff smoke in my face."

"You know, I didn't, and I can't believe it even now that you're telling me. Call me daft, but I just can't imagine it, Romeo." Roddy, as I suspected, didn't know his Shakespeare, so he wasn't completely sure *how* he was being insulted, but he knew he was. That made him feel stupid, and feeling stupid turned up the flame under old Roddy. Suddenly, his temper was on the boil. I guess in his little circle, he was King Tut and used to getting what he wanted, but Granddad taught me never to take any guff from a bully, and I wasn't about to start now. Another thing Granddad taught me was how to box, and it was a good thing because Roddy was about to blow a gasket.

"Okay, chump," he snarled. "You're gonna wish you hadn't opened your big mouth."

"No doubt," I said. "I just can't help it. When I see a bully, some devil in me makes me poke him with a stick."

"Roddy, leave him alone!" cried Mary. "He just delivered some chickens, and I was showing him where to put them in the cold locker." *Bless her heart,* I thought. *She's a quick thinker, but it's too late now.*

"I saw you looking at him," said Roddy, "and we'll talk about *that* as soon as I ring his bell." Then he rushed me, throwing a punch as he came.

CHAPTER 5

The Hotel Champlain

RODDY BRAGG'S PUNCH ALMOST LANDED, but at the last second, I sidestepped. His fist sailed by my cheek, and his rush carried him into the coats hanging on the wall. He got tangled for a second, and then he whirled, furious.

"You just made a big mistake, slick," he said. His face was as red as a ripe tomato, and I guess he wasn't too happy that Mary was watching us. If he had hit me, he prob'ly *would* have killed me. Luckily, Roddy wasn't overly bright nor overly quick. I knew if I got him fired up, he'd come at me again like a charging bull, and that was just what I wanted.

"Gosh, Roddy," I said. "What a swing! I could feel the breeze from that one. For a second I thought you were Jack Dempsey the way you sailed into those coats. Let's see some more of that fancy footwork, champ."

Then I danced around a little and threw a couple jabs at the coats just to get him riled. I confess—I enjoyed mocking Roddy. Normally, I'd consider such a thing meanspirited, but in Roddy's case, I was willing to lower myself. As I said already, I didn't take to him from the first. Of course, that had to do with Mary Mack, but that wasn't all of it. I just don't like a bully, and Roddy?—you could've put his picture in Mr. Webster's dictionary beside the definition. I could see that he liked to throw his weight around, and he had plenty to throw. He was a good bit bigger and stronger than me, so I was playing with fire by needling him, but I couldn't help myself. Besides, I had a hunch that if I got Roddy mad, he'd be his own worst enemy.

And wasn't he fired up now! He sucked in great lungfuls of air and blew them out like he was a steam engine building up pressure, and then he roared and came at me again with fists flailing. I heard a snarl and another roar, and saw Jake bullet toward us from the taproom. Ducking under Roddy's punch, I drove my own fist into his stomach like I was going to park it in his backbone. The air *whooshed* out of him like out of a punctured balloon. Somehow though, wheezing and caving in on himself, he managed to stay on his feet even though Jake had him by the seat of the pants. I stepped behind Roddy and crooked my elbow around his throat to choke his windpipe. He flopped like a fish on land, and then I eased him to the floor where he passed out. Jake, deciding that Roddy was no longer a threat to his newly adopted master, wagged his tail, and I gave him a piece of pork I had absent-mindedly peeled from the carcass in the storage room and put in my pocket.

"I thought an Otter was playful," said Mary with a surprised smile.

"It is," I grinned, "but it's also a wild animal."

"You'd better get out of here. His friends are coming," she said and nodded toward the bar. "Go through there," she said, pointing, "and you'll find a door to the alley. Hurry!"

"All right. No sense in creating a ruckus. Tell my grandsire about Chance, and tell him you want to go with us. His name is Amos Waters. I'll wait across the street. Come as soon as you can, and we'll take a boat ride to the Hotel Champlain." I smiled, and when she smiled back, the good feeling spread through me like sunshine. Then I ducked down the hall and disappeared.

Later, Mary said she explained to Roddy's cronies that he had gotten the worst of a fight, and by the time they had carried him back to the taproom and begun to revive him with fumes from a bottle of whiskey, Granddad and Too Tall had completed their business with Deacon. Mary brought them coffee and introduced herself. Quickly and quietly she told them of the man named Chance, the Hotel Champlain, and my dustup with Roddy Bragg.

"Where's my grandson now, miss?" asked Granddad.

"He's waiting across the street, Mr. Waters," she said. "Could I come with you? I-I need to leave the Angel's Perch."

"And why's that, miss?"

"I've got my reasons. Please, Mr. Waters, I might even be able to help. I know a girl who works at the hotel."

Granddad stared at her. Then he stared at her some more. Finally, he made up his mind.

"All right," he said, wiping his mouth with a napkin. "Let us finish our dinner, and we'll go find my grandson."

"Thank you, Mr. Waters. You don't know what this means to me. I'll be right back," said Mary. "I have to pack a bag."

"Ten minutes, young lady. Then we'll be gone."

ONCE SHE LEFT, GRANDDAD TOLD LOUIS that a couple of Deacon's men would follow him to the waterfront with wheelbarrows and replenish the tavern's stock of Moonbeam or "Mooncream" as Parson was wont to call it. Granddad had also come up with a scheme to rid us of Jack and Eddie, and he gave instructions to Louis on that account as well. Then he and Too Tall finished their pie and rose from the table. When another waitress appeared, Granddad gave her a wad of bills and drained the last of his Irish coffee with a happy grin. Roddy Bragg was just coming around as Granddad and Too Tall turned to leave, and Too Tall caught the waitress's sleeve.

"Tell that young fella, him, to be careful with strong drink will you, ma chérie?" He winked, and then he followed Granddad out the door, and the two of them once again stood on Bridge Street in the pouring rain. They found me back in the doorway of Waldo's Pawn Shop. We talked about Chance and the Hotel Champlain, and I could see that Granddad was busy cogitating a plan.

Ten minutes later, just as I was regretting that I had
left Mary in the Angel's Perch with Roddy Bragg, she
slipped out of the same dark alley I had just left and
hurried across the street to join us. Her wool cape and
her cloche hat were lady-like enough, but the men's wool
pants and the brogans she had lifted from some poor sot
caused Granddad and Louis to stare. Me, I remember
being surprised that she was just as beautiful in a pair of
pants as she was in a dress. I was a goner! *Pants or not,* I
thought, *she's a girl altogether sensible. Those pants and
boots will serve her well on a night like this.*

We all hurried down Bridge Street to the lake, but
after we passed the train station, Granddad kept looking
at a line of boxcars hitched to an idling locomotive. Sure
enough, as I followed his gaze, I spied Louis midway down
the line. When we reached him, he was peering into the
gloom of a boxcar at Jack and Eddie. Jack, growling in
protest, was practically choking on his gag, irate once
again over his ongoing persecution. Jack was not the type
to accept fate quietly and was wearing himself to a nubbin.
Still, he settled down to listen when Granddad spoke.
I could see from the twinkle in Granddad's eye that he
wanted to laugh, but he did his best to sound sympathetic.

"Jack," he said, "I hate to leave you boys in such a fix,
but time and tide, as they say, wait for no man, and we've
got some important business to prosecute tonight. I'm
afraid you'd slow us down in our endeavors, and besides
that, if we were to meet more of such as yourselves, we'd

be hard-pressed to explain how you and Eddie came to be trussed up this way. So, I hope you'll understand the need of sending you on a little trip to our neighbors in Canada." This got Jack all agitated again, but the gag held, and he could only make strangled noises that made Granddad grin even wider.

"This freight," he continued, "is headed to Montreal, but Louis loosened your ropes, and I'm sure you'll work your way free before you get that far. You can get off the train somewhere an hour or so up the line. I've left you and Eddie a pint of spirits, which I know, strictly speaking, is against regulations for government men, but maybe on such a godforsaken, miserable night, a snort or two to warm your insides won't go amiss. There's a half a loaf of bread, too, and some cheese. Sorry it ain't more, but we're travelin' pretty light ourselves.

Oh, and one last word. If you feel a mite embarrassed by this whole misadventure"—and here Granddad's voice revealed a mix of sympathy and amusement—"maybe it'll comfort you to know that we take no pleasure in your misery, and we don't intend to broadcast this chapter in your careers to the newspapers and cause a detriment to your reputation. We'll leave your boat at a public landing here on the upper lake, don't know where just yet. We may be smugglers, but we're not thieves. Fare thee well, fellas."

As if to signal the end of this uncharacteristically long-winded speech by Granddad, the locomotive blew its whistle, and the rumbling of the engine grew louder. The train chugged slowly down the tracks, and the five of us turned toward the lake again.

HALF AN HOUR LATER TOO TALL CUT THE engines of *Jack's Comeuppance,* and we slipped alongside the dock at the Hotel Champlain a few miles south of Plattsburgh. A floodlight lit the shore, and in its pale glow we inspected the other two boats berthed at the pier. The fancy script on the stern of the bigger vessel proclaimed it to be the *Simon Weed.* Since Weed was the tycoon who built the Hotel Champlain, it didn't take a genius to figure out that this sixty-foot, steam-powered double-decker was the hotel launch. The other boat was half as long and as much like the launch as a hawk is like a chicken. When the floodlight finally revealed the name on that boat, I almost forgot myself and shouted it out loud. It was the *Thorpedo,* my dad's boat! No one was aboard, and after a quick search, Granddad discovered that Royal's whiskey wasn't either.

High above us on Bluff Point loomed the Hotel Champlain, shadowy and huge. Even tonight, with the rain pouring down like we were Noah and his boys waiting for the waters to float the ark, we could still see the lights of the hotel shining like watery haloes. On clear summer nights I had sometimes seen those same lights from all the way across the lake, and during the day the hotel was such a colossus it was a handy landmark from almost anywhere on the upper lake. Once I had seen it on a summer morning from only a mile or so to the east. Mist was rising from the lake, and with its huge, red-roofed gables and its hundreds of windows reflecting the sun, it had seemed a mirage, a magical fortress in a shimmering cloud, and I had always wanted to see it up close.

Now that I had arrived under its very walls, I wasn't quite as thrilled as I had thought to be. The Hotel Champlain wasn't for the likes of us. It served the rich and their ilk. Teddy Roosevelt had stayed at the hotel, and three years ago Hollywood had even shot a picture there called *Janice Meredith*. I saw the movie with Bridget in Burlington. Marion Davies played a pretty heroine who helped Paul Revere in the Revolutionary War, and wasn't she a peach! *So anyway,* I thought, *how are we going to get into this place?* Like Mary said, we weren't exactly fancy folk. With his long beard, Granddad looked like a biblical prophet, and Too Tall—well, he was about the most conspicuous person I'd ever met, which was not exactly an advantage in our present situation. Even if Mary managed to sneak us in, what then? Any one of my family would blend in about as well as a fly in the buttermilk. Then I thought, *Hells bells, my father might be in there, and if he is, I'm not leaving without him.*

Mary came to my side while we waited for Granddad to finish fiddling with the engine of the *Thorpedo*. "You might be getting in a serious scrape if you get mixed up with us," I said. "Those two men my grandfather put on the train were feds."

"I'll take the risk. I need to leave the Angel's Perch."

"You don't like working there?"

"Oh, it's not that. And it's not just because of Roddy Bragg."

I raised my eyebrows in question, but she didn't answer. Instead, she asked if she could go with us after she helped us find Royal. Something in her tone made me turn and study her face, which was about as good an idea as that Greek guy Odysseus taking out his ear plugs when he sailed by the sirens. She was so beautiful I'd have promised her my first-born son, which—when I came to think of it—I might have wanted to give her anyway. Ringlets of hair that billowed from beneath her hood and framed her face were flecked with drops of rain. It struck me that the Angel's Perch was well named—at least, it was while Mary was still there. I thought I heard fear in her voice when she said she wanted to leave the bar, and I saw that fear for a second in her face, but then she smiled, and it was gone.

"Yut," I said, "I'll help you as best I can, but you *don't* really know what you're getting into. I've got ten dollars in my pocket, and that's *all* I've got. I guess you've prob'ly gathered that my family is in the whiskey-running business. Granddad has a farm, but he's not exactly catching up with the Rockefellers, so he does a little smuggling on the side. What you don't know is that the danger you're in is more than just getting arrested. Some of these fellas in the bootlegging line—they don't carry guns for show. If we catch up with Chance, somebody might get hurt, and that might happen before we get out of the Hotel Champlain with my father. You still want to go with us?"

Before she could answer, Granddad beckoned, and we all gathered round him. "Little Roy and Louis, I want you to stay with the boat," he said. "I don't want to leave this whiskey for any Tom, Dick, and Charley to walk off with, but more to the point, you might have to discourage this Chance bandit from leaving if we miss him up at the hotel, and he comes back here."

"But Amos," said Little Roy, "we don't even know what he looks like. How will we recognize him?"

"He'll be the one headed for the *Thorpedo*," said Granddad patiently. "Don't show your cards unless he starts to leave the waterfront. He prob'ly won't be doing that by boat. I just undid the coil wires from Jack's boat and Royal's, so if he turns the key to either one, the engine will turn over, but it won't start. Here, Little Roy, put the wires in your pocket. Louis, glue yourself to the wall of the ticket office over there. You can stay dry under the eaves, and you can get a clear shot at anybody near the boats. Roy, why don't you hunker down on the upper deck of the hotel launch. Play it safe, both of you. This Chance is a dangerous man if he got the drop on Royal. When Too Tall and I go up to the hotel, I'll be ready to shoot that sorry son of a dog if I have to. I advise you to be ready as well. If that doesn't set right with you, say so now."

"Don't worry, Amos," said Louis quickly. "We'll be ready."

"Good," said Granddad, "because your uncle's life and

your own might depend on it. From what Mary says, there shouldn't be more than three of them, but maybe there were others she didn't see. I don't expect them to get by us up at the hotel, but stay sharp boys."

For the second time that day I was seeing a side of my grandfather I'd never seen before. I watched him stride toward the hotel with the loose-limbed gait of a deer hunter and disappear into the shadows. His advice to Louis and Little Roy echoed in my mind, and I realized Chance wasn't the only dangerous man out and about that night. I knew then that someone might die before we rescued my father. With that thought to sober me, I glanced at Mary. From the look on her face, her thoughts had taken the same turn. I smiled grimly, and we followed Granddad on up the path with Jake trotting ahead. We soon found ourselves outside the hotel kitchen where Granddad turned to Mary.

"This Chance must know someone who works for the hotel, someone who helped him get inside to sell his liquor without tipping off the hotel detective. Be careful who you trust, Mary, when you start asking about Chance, and that includes your friend. Now—you said you could get us inside. How?"

"I know Mrs. Brettell. She's the head cook, and she'll still be working in the kitchen. I'll tell her I've come to see my friend Annie-Marie, and then I'll go up to Annie's room, put on one of her uniforms, and go to the boiler room next to the big brick smokestack. If nobody's on duty, I'll let you in through the service door."

"And if someone *is* on duty?" asked Granddad.

"I'll tell him the manager, Mr. Richards, wants him to make sure none of the culverts are plugged on the hill so the hotel drive won't get washed away in all this rain. I'll let you in when he leaves."

"You'll do, Mary," said Granddad with a grin. "We'll wait by the smokestack."

THE MINUTES PASSED, BUT NONE TOO QUICKLY, and I was getting as restless as a two-year-old racehorse at the Saratoga track. Then, hinges creaked, and I saw the silhouette of a girl framed in the doorway by the chimney. Mary beckoned for us to hurry.

"Jake," I whispered. "Stay here, boy." He trotted alongside me as we strode toward Mary, but when I told him a second time to stay, he sat down and watched us enter the hotel. Once inside, we followed Mary and slipped into a storeroom on the ground floor. Too Tall stood guard at the door. Granddad asked in a whisper if Mary was ready to search for Chance.

"Mr. Waters, I already looked in the lobby, the dining room, and the bar. I was careful, sir," she said as she saw his eyebrows raise, "but I didn't see Chance. He must be in a private room." Then she took a red bellboy's uniform off a rack and continued, "If Otter wears this, maybe he can get a peek at the hotel register."

"How is he going to do that with the desk clerk on duty?" asked Granddad.

"Maybe," she hesitated, "maybe I can distract the clerk."

"Mary," said Granddad, "I like your style, girl. Otter, she's right. Put on that monkey suit and go check the register for the name Ruth."

I grumbled about working for an organ grinder, but then I swallowed my pride and ducked behind a stack of boxes to change. Minutes later, Mary and I were climbing a short flight of stairs to the lobby. Fortunately, the hotel detective was somewhere else when we arrived. I stayed out of sight around a corner and watched Mary walk confidently across the lobby with just enough girlish beauty to make any man notice. The clerk brightened at her approach. He was a fairly good looking fella in his twenties, good looking if you fancy a fella whose hair is slicked back with pomade and whose smile is about as oily as his hair. He was dressed to the nines in a pin-stripe suit, and I imagine he thought well of himself. He was reading a newspaper, head in his hands, elbows propped on the counter, but he shifted his gaze on hearing her footsteps, and when he saw her, he stood right up.

"May I help you?" he asked, and he looked her over in a way I didn't much like.

"You might at that," she replied coyly. "I'm new here and just started working in the dining room tonight. It's slow, and the maître'd' said I could take a break. I thought I'd step out on the porch and get some air—it's very hot in the kitchen—but ...," and here she paused and looked down shyly.

"What?" asked the clerk. "What is it?"

"Well...," she paused again and then lifted her face to gaze into his eyes. "Well, I know this will sound silly, but one of the guests pestered me earlier in the dining room, and I don't want him to bother me again if he should chance to come out on the porch and find me alone. Do you suppose...?" and again her voice trailed off, and she looked down. "Oh never mind. What am I thinking? You can't leave your desk. I'm sorry to have bothered you." She turned and was already walking away when he replied.

"No, no, that's okay. You're right, I shouldn't leave the desk, but a few minutes won't do any harm, and we'll be right there on the porch."

"Oh, you're so kind. I thought you would be when I saw your face. Thank you so much. Perhaps you can tell me about the hotel and your job here. You must meet a lot of important people."

"I do, but I'm not supposed to talk about our guests. We have to safeguard their privacy you know."

"Oh, of course," she said. "I'm sure Plattsburgh has its share of disreputable characters. These are frightful times aren't they? I'll bet all the rich people at the hotel are a temptation for bootleggers and pickpockets and God knows what else. Of course, you need to protect our guests." She put her hand on his arm, and the two of them strolled out to the porch. I slipped behind the desk as soon as they left and opened the register. I ran my finger down the list of names searching for Ruth. I heard footsteps coming from the main entrance, and I scanned the list frantically. There it was! Ruth! George Herman, room 204. I stepped out from behind the counter just as a short, middle-aged man and his short wife entered the lobby. The man had a skinny little mustache and wavy, black hair streaked with gray. He wore a navy blue blazer, carried a rolled umbrella, and stalked toward me with his head bobbing forward like a rooster. She was well dressed too, clucking about the rude porter at the train station and hanging on her hubby's arm like he was the cream of the aristocrats.

"You, young man!" he cried when he spied me. "Our luggage is with the driver out front. Fetch it now, so we can register and go to our suite."

"Yes sir, your excellency," I replied with the faintest hint of a smile.

"Are you being smart with me, young man?" he demanded.

"Oh, no sir. I heard there was a count or a duke coming to the hotel tonight, and I thought it must be you. A thousand pardons, sir!"

"Humph! A likely story, young man. I've a mind to report you. Now, are you going to stand there gawking or are you going to get our bags?"

"I'll just put my slicker on, sir, as it's raining."

"You don't need a raincoat," he said scornfully. "The car is parked under the portico. It is completely dry." He stared at me, annoyed and suspicious.

"Yes sir. Of course." I smiled brightly and bowed deeply.

"My humble apologies, your lordship."

"I am not a lord, you insolent pup. I'm J. T. Parrts, president of Nagrom's Investment Banking, Inc. in New York City, and you...."

I interrupted before he could bawl me out anymore. "I knew it, sir. I could tell you was important, sir, that good suit, you know, and your language being so educated and all. I'll fetch your luggage this instant, but first let me find that confounded clerk so he can register you."

"Well hurry up!" shouted Mr. Parrts indignantly. "I don't suffer fools gladly!"

I popped around the corner just before Mary and the desk clerk walked in from the porch. The clerk had heard the commotion and panicked about his absence from the desk. As I disappeared down the stairs, I heard Mary thanking him for a pleasant stroll, and the clerk apologizing backward and forward to his unhappy guests. I waited until Mary caught up with me at the landing, and the two of us hurried back to the storage room.

"GEORGE HERMAN RUTH?" ASKED GRANDDAD when we returned. "You're sure that was the name?"

"Yut," I said, and suddenly I understood the look in Granddad's eyes. "The Babe?!" I asked, my voice rising. "You honest-to-God think it's Babe Ruth?"

"Hey," Granddad cautioned, "Let's not tell the world just yet. Maybe it's the Babe, and maybe it isn't, but I don't imagine there are too many George Herman Ruths who can afford to stay at the Hotel Champlain."

"No," I agreed, "I don't imagine so. What are we going to do now?"

"You," he said, "are going to knock on the door of room 204, and when someone asks what you want, you are going to say you have a telegram for Mr. Ruth."

"And—?" I said.

"And when someone opens the door, Too Tall will knock him down. I'll be right behind Too Tall pointing my pistol at anyone who needs to be persuaded that we mean business."

"Where will I be?"

"You'll be in the hall, to one side of the door. Then, if this Chance is with Mr. Ruth, we'll ask him about your dad. Here, take my trapper's pistol. It's not much more than a pea shooter, but it's better than nothing. Mary, you wait here. We'll come back for you. If you hear a shot, go down to the boat and wait there. We'll be right behind you."

"Yes sir," she replied.

MOMENTS LATER WE WERE STANDING OUTSIDE 204. I knocked and announced the telegram.

"Slip it under the door," someone said gruffly. I looked at Granddad. He pressed his thumb and first two fingers together as if holding a pen, and he moved his right hand in small circles.

"The hotel requires me to have you sign for it, sir."

I heard the scraping of a chair, and I stepped to one

side. The door opened just enough for me to see a man with a baseball bat in his hand and a round, familiar face peer out suspiciously. Then things happened fast. Too Tall threw himself against the door, the man backpedaled toward a woman seated on a couch, and Too Tall and Granddad burst into the room. The man landed with a resounding thump, the woman shrieked, and Granddad spoke.

"Mister Ruth, if you could put down that bat, I'd like to ask you a few questions and be on my way." And then I heard another voice, and it sent a shiver down my spine.

"And you, old timer, better put that gun down if you want to live."

When Too Tall had burst into the room, I had flattened myself against the wall right next to the doorway. I turned my head and leaned toward the opening as slowly as a turtle poking his head out of his shell. Barely three feet away stood the man who had just spoken. He had been standing to one side of the door when Too Tall and Granddad had rushed in. Now his gun was jammed into Granddad's back.

CHAPTER 6

Meeting Babe Ruth

I PULLED THE TRAPPER'S PISTOL from my belt and then I froze. Someone had just clutched my sleeve. I turned my head. Mary stood right behind me. She had a sock in her outstretched hand that bulged in the toe like Santa had already put some coal in it. *Holy Mahoney, I* thought, *where did she come from?* Since I couldn't ask her, I took the sock which, as I suspected, was a homemade sap weighted with birdshot. It *did* seem like a better idea. At least it wouldn't make much noise. I handed her the pistol. Granddad was saying calmly and clearly that he *would* put down his pistol, and I whispered to Mary, "Be ready if this doesn't work."

Then I stepped through the doorway, and before the guy with the gun had a chance to say lollapalozza, I swung the sock at the back of his head. His knees buckled, and he toppled like a tree under a Canuck's crosscut saw. His fedora rolled across the floor toward the middle of the room. I watched it come to rest at the feet of the big, round-faced man sitting on the fancy couch. The big man's dark brown, pin-striped suit looked like it was right out of the box. His elbows were placed on his knees, and his mournful, hound dog face was resting in his hands like he was deep in thought. Leaning against the couch on his left was the baseball bat. On his right, her feet tucked up under her, sat a buxom blonde in a sequined dress. She looked like she might be pretty used to men, but I bet men never got used to her. I didn't actually see flames, but she was smoldering. The man I had "socked" was now out cold at my feet. Too Tall took the man's revolver and checked his pockets, but the gun was all the weapon he had. Mary stepped into the room beside me, returned the trapper's pistol, and quietly closed the door. The man on the couch looked at me with interest.

"Wow, slugger! I think you hit a home run there. I hope Bump is okay." I studied the man on the couch with even more interest than he had for me, and sure enough, his face was the one I'd seen in the *Burlington Free Press* all summer, often as not on the front page. Babe Ruth! Sixty home runs in one season! The mighty Bambino of Murderer's Row! Knock me over with a downy feather, there he was, the Sultan of Swat, the Colossus of Clout, a legend come to life, and I admit, I was in awe. But then, I remembered myself. As Granddad always said, whenever somebody blathered on about a big shot, "he still puts his pants on one leg at a time." With that in mind, I composed myself.

"I'm sorry, Mr. Ruth," I said, a tad sheepishly. "I think

I just knocked him out is all. He should come to in a few minutes."

"Say, you're kind of young for this business aren't you?" he asked. Before I could answer, Granddad interrupted.

"Excuse us for barging in, Mr. Ruth. I recognize you from your picture in the newspapers, and I'm embarrassed to meet you in this way, but we had no choice. We're looking for a man named Chance who may have kidnapped my son-in-law, and we heard he was meeting a Mr. Ruth at this hotel. I know busting in on you like this isn't likely to favor us, but we sure could use your help." To my surprise, Granddad fished a photo from his wallet and showed the Babe a worn picture of my dad in uniform just before he left for France in 1916. "This is a picture of my son-in-law," he said. "His name is Royal St. Onge, and he's this boy's father." Then he nodded toward me.

Babe Ruth peered at the picture, looked at me, and then turned his mournful gaze on Too Tall. "I can see the family resemblance," he said, "especially with the human skyscraper here. What's your name, mister?" he asked.

"They call me Too Tall," grinned my uncle. "Royal is my brother."

"Too Tall," mused the Babe. "That fits well enough." He looked down at Too Tall's pant cuffs which ended above his boot tops and then at his shirt sleeves which stopped midway between elbow and wrist. "Can't say the same about your clothes. Well, sir," he continued, addressing Granddad, "I'll tell you what. You're right. Pulling a gun on me and May here, and sapping Bump, doesn't exactly get us off on the right foot. How do I know you're on the level? I see the picture of the boy's father, and if that's legit and what you say about this Chance is true, I'd like to help, but how do I know I can trust you?"

"You don't. We broke into your room thinking to find him here, but if this isn't him on the floor" and glancing at Mary, he saw that it wasn't—"then we'll look elsewhere. My apologies for intruding, Mr. Ruth." Putting a finger to the brim of his crusher and nodding to the woman the Babe had called May, he said, "A pleasure to make your acquaintance, Ma'am."

May smiled. "Yours too," she said.

Then Granddad turned to go, but when he put his hand on the doorknob, Mr. Ruth called him back.

"Hold on," he said, and Granddad paused. "Do you know anything about baseball, mister?" he asked.

"Mr. Ruth," said Granddad, "I'm a farmer and a woodsman, and sometimes I smuggle a little whiskey to make ends meet. You could write what I know about baseball on a postage stamp, and you wouldn't fill up the space."

"Is that so? But you say you smuggle liquor? What do you think of this stuff?" He pulled a bottle labeled MacAskill's Skye Whiskey from a cardboard box at his feet and poured Granddad a couple fingers of the hard stuff.

Granddad took the proffered glass. "I know more about this than I do about baseball," he said. "A toast to you and

yours, Mr. Ruth." Granddad grinned—a little crookedly as
is the way of the Waters' folk—put the drink to his lips, and
swigged it down. Then he set the glass on a shiny table in
front of the couch, a table just the right height to rest your
boots on, but which, I'm sure, was just intended for tea
cups and such. Granddad was no longer grinning when he
passed judgment. "Mr. Ruth, there are horses, and there
are racehorses. Here, try some of this," he said, and he
handed over his hip flask.

Before long, he and Babe Ruth were happily tootling
Moonbeam, and the Babe was telling Granddad about
Chance. When they first met, Mr. Ruth had bought a few
bottles of whiskey at a rather high price and half-joked that
he was being robbed. Chance had pulled out a revolver,
casually spun the cylinder, and told him if he'd wanted
to rob him, he wouldn't have bothered with the whiskey.
He would simply have stuck the pistol barrel against the
Babe's stomach and lifted his wallet. With a ghastly grin,
Chance had slipped the revolver back into a shoulder
holster under his jacket, and he and his pal had left. Then
Granddad told Babe Ruth about our rendezvous with
Royal, Royal's disappearance, and our visit to the Angel's
Perch where we had picked up Chance's trail.

"The more I hear about this Chance, the more I think he
sounds like a snake," said the Babe.

"And a skunk," said Granddad.

"Well, friend," said Babe, sipping once more from the
flask, "this Moonbeam may be steamed off in the cold,

pale dead of night, but it's got some fire in it just the same, and in honor of that and the fact that we suspect Chance of snakish and skunkish behavior, I'll tell you more about him. Last weekend I bought a ticket at Grand Central Station, left the Lady of Liberty right after lunch, and stepped off that old, clickety-clack steam train in time for dinner Friday night. Originally, I came up here to play golf, but now I come even when it's too cold to play. I've met some good people up here"—at this he nodded toward the woman beside him—"like my very dear friend, May."

"Thank you, Babe," she said, and listening to her throaty voice, I didn't wonder at the Babe's long trip from New York City. *My,* I thought as I gazed at her again, *she does fill out all the nooks and crannies of that gown.* I only point this out with an eye to your entertainment, not because I was particularly interested myself. You'll remember that Mary was standing beside me, and I was already beginning to think that she was all the woman I could ever want, and all the woman I could ever handle. So May wasn't in my sights, as you might say, but I'm guessing that she'd been in many another man's, and now she was in Mr. Ruth's. She was, no doubt, as luscious and sweet as a ripe Georgia peach. But back to Babe Ruth. When I began listening again, the Babe was still talking about his trips upstate.

"As I say, I've made some friends here, and I come up to relax now that the season's over. Anyhow, last Saturday night, May and I had supper downstairs, and we saw

some fellas pass by the dining room with instrument
cases. Then the waitress says, 'Oh, that's Mr. Jack
Teagarden, sir. He plays the trombone. He and the rest
of his jazz band just arrived on the train from New York
City.' Needless to say"—and here, the Babe winked at his
companion—"May wanted to be in the middle of all the
excitement, and after dinner we took ourselves into the
ballroom.

That was when I met Chance. Some randy lookin' fella
with white hair whisked May away for a dance—now that
I think on it, I bet it was one of Chance's boys—and this
Chance sidled up to me and said I looked like a fella that
wanted a nip of something stronger than mineral water. I
took one look at him and decided maybe I *did* need a drink.
With a black patch over his left eye and a scar that zig
zagged from his cheek to his chin, his wasn't exactly a face
to put people at ease. Anyway, we soon found ourselves
down by the lake sampling a pint of some pretty smooth
Canadian whiskey. I bought a few bottles from him then
and there, and that was when he agreed to come back
tonight and sell me a case.

The point of this little story is that, if you're looking for
Chance, he might be in the ballroom right now picking
up new customers. There's a crowd in there again tonight
making a fuss over some guy named Bix Biederbock or
Beederbeck or I don't know what. Everybody says he's a
wizard on the cornet. I like that. I like to watch somebody
with genius, don't you? Doesn't matter whether it's a genius

for making moonshine or playing a jazz horn or swinging a baseball bat. You know what I mean?"

I was raised in a time when the children-should-be-seen-but-not-heard school was in session, but Grandma Melodie didn't hold with that school, and neither did Granddad, so I couldn't help but chime in.

"Mr. Ruth," I said, "I bet that's what people felt watching you hit home runs this summer. Sixty of 'em! I've never seen a major league baseball game, but I read about you and Mr. Gehrig in the newspapers. They called you the Homerun Twins! I guess when you grab a baseball bat, you've got some genius of your own."

"Well, I hope so, slugger. I *do* like hitting a baseball. Anyhow, I guess this Chance figures most of the people here at the hotel come and go, so if he doesn't visit too often or stay too long, he can probably peddle some booze without getting caught. Who knows, maybe he's been slippin' the hotel dick some of the good stuff, and the crumb is turning a blind eye."

"Mary," said Granddad, "you said this Chance wasn't in the ballroom earlier?"

"He wasn't, Mr. Waters, but maybe he's there now. I could look," she replied.

"That's what I hoped you'd say, young lady. You can bet I won't forget it. But listen. You be careful. Chance won't expect to see you, but he'll be as skittish as a fox in a chicken coop, and if he recognizes you, he's going to wonder why you're here at the hotel. Don't walk right into the middle of the crowd down there. Keep your distance and see if you can spot him before he spots you."

"I'll be careful, Mr. Waters. And speaking of that, I think I'd better go back to Annie's room and borrow one of her dresses. This uniform might get me in trouble if her boss sees me, and he's likely to be in the ballroom."

"Granddad," I said, "I'm going with her."

"Why?"

I gave him my best imitation of a piercing look before I answered, and hoped that he would remember his speech about me being a man now and realize I had a say in this.

"I might learn something that could help us. Maybe he'll let something slip about Dad. Besides, I've never heard jazz before." I grinned crookedly, hoping to win him over that way if not with my piercing stare. What I'd said was true, but it wasn't the whole truth about why I wanted to go with Mary. I just wasn't easy in my mind about her being near this Chance. If what the Babe and Granddad had said about him being a snake and a skunk was true, then I wanted to look after her. Granddad hesitated just long enough for Mr. Ruth to come to my rescue.

"Why don't I go down with them? Maybe I can help. I've met the fella after all."

"That's generous of you, Mr. Ruth," said Granddad, "but you may be getting into something risky here. Are you sure you want to do that?"

"Not exactly *sure*. It's probably that damn Moonbeam of yours talking right now, but I'll give it a try. I guess if I survived getting struck out by that woman Jackie Mitchell, I can try my luck against this hellion Chance."

"Well then, I'll take you up on that offer, Mr. Ruth, and I thank you kindly for it. Mary, you're right. Go get the dress. Yes, Otter, you go too. You'd better change back into your other duds. And keep your eyes open and your wits sharp."

"Yes sir," I said. I was outwardly calm but already wondering if Mary liked to dance, wondering if I should ask her to dance, and basically wondering about one thing after another that had to do with Mary and whether or not she might be interested in a guy like me.

TEN MINUTES LATER BABE AND MAY ENTERED the ballroom arm in arm, and while a lot of folks were noticing them, Mary and I scouted the room for Chance from behind some potted plants as tall as my Uncle Hercule. The ballroom was huge, longer than Granddad's cow barn with a ceiling as high as the hayloft. Crowds of people were dancing something Mary called the Black Bottom. She knew about it from Annie-Marie, and speak of the Devil, who should appear right then but the girl herself carrying an empty tray and startling both of us when she whispered in Mary's ear.

"Mary, what are you doing here, and what are you doing in my blue dress?"

"Lord, Annie-Marie! Don't sneak up on me like that!" Mary whispered back. "Believe me, I wouldn't be doing

this if there was another way. I'm sorry about taking your
dress. I'll put it back before I leave the hotel. There's a man
here named Chance. I don't want him to recognize me, so I
have to wear something that will blend in. I can't afford to
be noticed."

"Mary, you'd be noticed no matter what you wore."

"You're right about that, Annie," I said, and I was
completely sincere, but Annie scowled.

"And who are you?" she asked skeptically.

"He's a friend," replied Mary. When Annie-Marie didn't
look convinced, Mary continued. "He bested Roddy Bragg
in a fight back at the Angel's Perch, and he's helping me get
away from Plattsburgh."

"Oh. Well, if you got the better of Roddy Bragg, I'm
pleased to meet you. Any enemy of his is a friend of mine.
What's your name, hero boy?"

"Just call me Otter," I said and tipped my hat. "I
apologize if we're causing you any trouble. Mary is helping
me find my father. He might be in danger."

"Are you kidding me, buster?"

"Not a bit, sister." I grinned, crookedly of course, in
that Waters' way that is mischievous, fun-loving, and
just a little bold all at the same time. She made a face,
but I could tell she was starting to warm up to me. Bix
Biederbocker's band switched to a new number, and when
I asked her what kind of dance people were doing this
time, Annie said it was the Lindy Hop. Then she said she
had to get back to work, and she sailed off to the kitchen

for another tray of those fancy finger foods. I don't know what the great Slim Lindbergh would have thought about having a dance named after him—from the newspapers, I got an inkling that he was a sober type, prob'ly not a fella that leaned at all toward the Moonbeam—but who knows what he would have thought at the ballroom that night? Maybe he would have admired how one of those fellas out on the dance floor threw a girl right over his own head so she landed on her feet behind him, how the two of them twirled around the room again like a runaway merry-go-round, holding tight to each other's hands so they wouldn't fly off into space and then letting go so they would. Maybe he would have admired those folks, and maybe he wouldn't have, but if he had been there that night and tied a little tight, I like to think Lucky Lindy would have unwound once he heard old Bix toot that horn. It sure got the rest of the crowd jumping I can tell you.

After the band finished that number, a fella they called Tram stepped to the microphone and said they were going to play "Singin' the Blues." Folks clapped and cheered, and then, when that Tram took up his saxophone, they hushed. In that room, big as a barn, the notes of that tune rose all around us, and my right foot began tapping all on its own, and Tram's saxophone got inside me, sweet and swinging and fine, and my body began to sway from side to side. *Is there anything so beautiful as music, I wondered?*

I remembered my mother singing me lullabies when
I was a tadpole, before she was taken by the influenza.
I remembered Grandma Melodie playing the piano and
singing for the railroad men and the Queen City Mill
workers in the King Street Tavern on winter nights.
I remembered the Canuck fiddlers at barn dances in
Swanton during summers past, their bows sliding and
hopping on the fiddle strings, the excited young men and
their girls rounding the dance floor, glancing in each
other's eyes, and the shoes of the French farmers and their
wives clattering on the barn floor, echoing the snappy
fiddle notes.

And now, here was this jazz, this Bix and Tram, the
trombone man, the bass fiddler, the clarinet player, and
the banjo player, all of them "singin' the blues," making
this music I'd never heard before, that came in through
my toes and started strings vibrating up and down my
spine.

Mary and I stood behind those potted plants, on the
edge of it all, feeling the swing of the song, watching the
dancers hold each other close and pinwheel across the
floor like apple blossoms floating down the Mississquoi. I
was struck by how beautiful it was, and I began to feel the
pull. I'd never heard any music like that before, and I guess
Mary hadn't either. We kept eyeing the room, but neither
of us saw any sign of Chance. *Here we go, mister man,* I
thought, and then I found her hand with mine.

"I've only *seen* this done," I said, "but it doesn't look too hard. What do you say?" She laughed and said, "Sure, I'd love to," and then she put her other hand on my shoulder and rested her cheek against my neck. We slipped into the sea of dancers, and soon we too were floating across the room, and I felt like a cloud, light and drifting, but I couldn't let myself go completely. I couldn't forget Chance, and just as I was about to ask Mary, she said, "I see him. Turn slowly and look over my shoulder. He's in that parlor just off the ballroom. He's with Mr. Ruth and May."

Sure enough, I saw Babe Ruth lounging on a love seat with his arm around May. I don't know what May was saying, but the two men seated opposite were very much taken with her. All I could see was the backs of their heads. One of them had dark hair. Was that Chance? He seemed completely intent on May, but if he happened to look our way, I knew he might see Mary.

"How do you know it's him?" I asked.

"His hair," she replied, "and that narrow, black band circling the back of his head. It's the strap for his eye patch."

"Let's go," I said. "No sense in taking risks." Just as Bix Bieder-something finished his cornet solo and Tram started in again with the saxophone, we left the ballroom and climbed the central staircase to the second floor. Back in 204, we told Granddad and Too Tall what we had seen, and then we all settled down to wait for the Babe and whatever he could tell us about Chance's next move. Well, they did, anyway. I was impatient. I moved restlessly around the suite. I studied the large painting that hung above the fireplace—an old-fashioned Champlain canal schooner loaded with lumber—and then I pressed my nose against a window facing east and tried to see into the night. I started thinking about my dad again, whether he was nearby, whether Chance was hustling him down to the waterfront at that very moment. Then I opened the window a few inches. I could only tell that it was pitch-black and still raining. *Will the rain ever stop?* I wondered. *What if it keeps raining and raining until the rivers rise and flood the towns?* Suddenly, the pattering of the rain seemed more than dreary. It seemed unnatural, and it made me feel uneasy.

Then Bump came to, and I thought about him instead. I guess his head was like to split because he groaned a lot. Granddad explained why we were there and told him where the Babe was. When Bump finally shook off the cobwebs and saw Too Tall, he decided to sit back again and rest his throbbing head. Not long after Bump woke up, we heard a rap on the door, and Too Tall let in May and Babe Ruth. I had left the window to pick up the Babe's bat and was swinging it slowly and deliberately over an imaginary home plate, pretending to be tied with the Detroit Tigers and down two strikes in the bottom of the ninth.

"Sorry, Mr. Ruth," I said. "Just thought I'd get my mind off waiting."

"That's all right, slugger. Why don't you take that bat

with you? It'll be a keepsake of an unusual night."

"St. Peter on a pogo stick, Mr. Ruth," I said. "I don't need your bat to remember tonight. No sir, that's prob'ly your lucky bat. You should keep it, sir."

"It *is* a lucky bat, young fella. I've hit more than one home run with it, but I'm giving it to you. Maybe it'll bring *you* some good luck. You could use it. And call me Babe. Everybody else does."

"Thank you, sir," I said. "Thank you very much."

"I wish I could give you something better, like some information about your dad. We tried to find out what Chance is up to, but he was about as open with his secrets as a banker with his wallet."

May smiled and pushed a wayward curl back from her cheek. Then she looked at Granddad. "He did say one thing."

"What was that, Miss May?"

"He said, 'I've got some unfinished business from the war that's going to be settled soon.' When Babe asked him what kind of business, he pulled his coat back and showed that pistol he carries in the shoulder holster. 'This kind,' he said, 'the kind that closes somebody's account. Permanently.' "

Granddad paused before answering, and in that second of silence, we heard a bang through the open window. It was muffled by the driving rain, but it was the unmistakable sound of a gunshot.

"Granddad!" I cried. "That came from the waterfront!"

Still holding the Babe's bat, I bolted through the door and shouted over my shoulder, "Goodbye, Mr. Ruth! Goodbye, May!"

Too Tall's voice boomed from down the hall behind me, "Run, Otter! I'm right behind you," but I didn't need any encouragement. *What if they're shooting at Dad?* I thought. *What if he's caught in a crossfire?* I ran, you can be sure. I ran like a deer with the dogs right behind.

CHAPTER 7

Muff's Wild Ride

OO TALL WAS AT MY HEELS, and maybe Mary and Granddad were close behind, but I never looked back. I didn't bother to sneak out one of the service entrances either. I raced down the hall, and when I reached the central staircase, I jumped on the banister and slid down to the lobby like my namesake on the banks of the Mississquoi. Too Tall bounded down after me. A portly man in a dark suit with a black trilby pushed back on his forehead was sitting on a sofa reading a newspaper. His mouth dropped open in amazement as we streaked by. He started up, stuttering and indignant, but we were already gone by the time he asked what we thought we were doing.

"Detective?" I said to Too Tall. He nodded. We took the porch steps three at a time and raced down the walk toward the lake. A gray shape flashed past me, and Jake took the lead. Then we heard more shots.

"C'mon!" I said. "Run!" Then, scared for Dad, I sprinted ahead. Too Tall warned me to be careful, but I was too out of breath to reply. I left him behind, and I ran until my lungs were exploding. When I got to the landing, I heard a sharp crack and saw a muzzle flash from where Louis had hidden, and then answering gunfire from the *Thorpedo*. I called to Jake and then dropped into a slide and landed behind some wooden barrels like Babe Ruth stealing third base. We hid there until the men on Dad's boat started shooting at Louis again, and then I ran full tilt to the *Simon Weed*. I dove from the dock and somersaulted onto the boat as a bullet whistled over my head. Jake leaped aboard right beside me as more shots were fired, and I heard a rumble I didn't recognize at first. It was the engine of the *Thorpedo*. *Jumpin' John Henry*, I thought, *somebody bottled a hurricane when they built that engine*. But how had Chance started the *Thorpedo*? Somebody must have put the coil wire back.

One of Chance's men, a stocky fella but wicked short, suddenly appeared near the bow and untied the *Thorpedo's* painter from a cleat. Then he scuttered along the dock to untie the stern line which was right across from my hiding place. I still had the Babe's bat in my hand, and when he reached the other rope, I flung it. I hit the poor little duffer spang on the noggin. He looked at me, stunned, and I ducked as he dropped in a heap. Someone fired from the *Thorpedo* as it drew away from the pier, and bullets splintered the woodwork where my head had been a second before.

"Stay down!" yelled Louis. "They've got an automatic rifle!" *Lord love a duck*, I thought, *this is getting serious*.

Maybe we've bit off more than we can chew. Maybe Chance works for Al Capone. I crawled on my belly farther along the deck of the *Simon Weed* and popped up over the rail with the trapper's pistol in hand. The *Thorpedo* was clear of the dock now, and the rumble of the engine exploded into thunder. I swear on a bundle of King Jimmy's Bibles, Dad's boat was rocking as gentle as a baby's cradle one minute, and the next it shot like a rocket into the darkness of the midnight lake. When the roar of the *Thorpedo* faded, I heard the man I'd walloped with the bat. He was moaning and groaning, but soon he got his gumption back and began swearing like a sailor. I thought once again how even a string of curses sounds pretty in French. He was trying to sneak away, but Jake, true to form, had leaped back onto the dock and was tugging at the man's pant leg.

Then Too Tall appeared and bound the fellow tight as a Christmas goose, stuffed his mouth with a bandana, and tucked the wriggling desperado under one arm. Granddad and Mary came out of the shadows with Louis. Then my heart sank to my shoes. *Where is Little Roy?* I wondered. Granddad, coming aboard the *Simon Weed*, was wondering the same thing.

"Where's your brother, Louis?" he asked.

"I don't know," said Louis, and I could hear the worry in his voice. "Roy never fired a shot. When you left, he hid on the steamer, and I slid around the corner of the building like you said. We stayed quiet and out of sight, and then about ten minutes ago, I heard three people coming down the path, but before I could see faces, somebody from over by the boats shot out the streetlight and shouted for them to run. I didn't know if they had Royal or not, so I fired into the air and hollered for them to stop, but they didn't. They fired back, and one of those hellions had an automatic rifle! Well, I wasn't about to trade bullets with that fella, so I ducked around the corner again. As soon as the shooting stopped, I heard somebody else tearing down the hill, and I figured it had to be one of you boys. I took another shot to distract the bootleggers, and they returned the fire, which gave Piston Legs Paddock here, the fastest human on earth, and White Fang," pointing to me and Jake, "a chance to run into the middle of it all and jump aboard the *Simon Weed*."

"So Chance must have left a man on the steamer," said Granddad. "He must have seen Little Roy come aboard and then he clobbered him. He must have taken the coil wires, too. C'mon. Maybe Little Roy is still here."

I grabbed my bat and helped searched the *Simon Weed*. Sure enough, Louis heard a thumping as he passed by a broom closet, and when he opened it, Little Roy tumbled out, tied, gagged and none too happy. While Louis tended to his brother, Granddad quickly returned to the problem of rescuing Royal from this lunatic, Chance. Only a few minutes had been lost since Chance's gang had left the pier, but we'd all seen the *Thorpedo* in action—everybody, that is, but Little Roy.

"Amos," said Too Tall, "how are we going to catch

that hound? Did you see the *Thorpedo?* Left here like a lightning bolt." Granddad only stared at the squirming character Too Tall still had tucked under one arm. Then his eyes met Too Tall's, and they both smiled.

"This tub," said Granddad, "is as slow as Geehaw"—that was one of his old workhorses—"but it'll have to do for now. I'd rather get caught with the *Simon Weed* than Jack's boat, and anyway, we're missing a coil wire. Too Tall, set your new friend down and go fire up the boiler on this contraption. Louis and Little Roy, get our gear from Jack's boat. Don't forget the canoe and don't forget the chickens. We'll head east for now," said Granddad, "and maybe this fella can help point us more directly. What do you say, friend? Where are we going?" The little man just shook his head and made angry, gargling noises through the gag.

"Just as I thought. Not going to talk, eh?" grinned Granddad. The man made more strangled noises, and I felt sorry for him, so I reached over and pulled Too Tall's bandana out of his mouth.

"I ain't talking," said the man, "and you and whose army can't make me."

"I can see you're a tough customer," said Granddad. "What's your name? Maybe I've heard of you?"

"I ain't sayin' nothin'. My name's Muff Morrisette if it's none of your business, and that boy dere conked me in the head. Now what call did he do that for?"

"Well," I said mildly, "you were shooting at us."

"Not me," replied Muff. "Not me. I don't never handle

no guns. I don't like guns. I shoot myself in the foot once. Hurt bad! Then Boyce say stay away from guns, Muff. I just cook. Do odd jobs."

"You shot yourself in the foot, Muff?" asked Granddad, incredulous.

"Muff did. Boyce took gun away." Here, Muff flushed and shifted from one foot to the other. "Boyce just shake his head. Take Muff to doctor. Muff don't shoot no gun now."

"Who's Boyce, Muff?" asked Granddad.

"He a farmer I hired out to up in Quebec if you so much wanna know, and boy will you be singing a different tune out of the other side of your face when he catches you."

"Well, Muff, he was traveling pretty fast in the opposite direction a few minutes ago. I don't know if he's real worried about you right now, but I am. I'd like to get you back to Boyce, and I'd like to get Too Tall's brother back to him. Too Tall's the guy that was carrying you under his arm."

At this, Muff glanced in Too Tall's direction and gave him a venomous look. Too Tall winked.

"We think your boss Chance is holding him prisoner, so if you tell us where your boss is going, we can bring you back to Boyce."

"Nope. Can't do that. Can't do that. Chance said don't tell nobody 'bout our hideout on the island. Nope. Can't tell nobody. He'd be mad. Don't make Chance mad says Boyce."

"On the island, you say? Which one would that be, Muff?"

Muff put his hands up to cover his mouth and stared goggle-eyed at Granddad. "Oh boy, oh boy! Now Muff's had the radish. Now Muff's a goner. Chance be mad. Goin' to squish Muff like a potato bug. Oh boy, oh boy! Muff's not talkin' now. Not talkin' no more. Mum's the word, Muff. Deef and dumb, deef and dumb."

"Your boss sounds like quite a charmer, Muff. But aren't you worried about what *I* might do?" Muff shook his head again.

"You don't scare me," he said. "Not like Chance. That Chance give Muff the wollygobbles. Besides, don't remember island name. Just a island. Look like any island. Maybe don't even have no name."

"Wollygobbles?" asked Granddad looking amused.

"Wollygobbles! You know—when shakin' in your boots you is."

"I see," said Granddad. "You're right, Muff, I'm not a bad man. Well, I guess that's that."

"Granddad," I said. "We've got to find out! What about Dad? He might be killed!"

"I know, Otter, I know, but what do you want me to do? We can't cut Muff's throat can we?"

"No, but there must be some way we can make him talk."

"That's easy to say, Grandson, but what way? I can't think of one. Unless…." He paused and scratched his chin as if studying the matter from all angles, but I think he was only pretending and had already hatched another of his shrewd plans. "Yes," he said slowly, "there might be a way. Louis, how much rope do we have left?" Louis was standing on the dock, sliding my canoe over the rail of the *Simon Weed.*

"About fifty feet, Amos."

"Yes," continued Granddad thoughtfully, "that should do," and he pulled out his hip flask and offered Muff some Moonbeam. "Have a good snort, Muff. You'll need it, lad. You're going fishing." Muff suddenly looked uneasy, and Mary looked at me. She whispered in my ear.

"What's he going to do?"

"I'm not sure," I replied, "but I think I have a pretty good idea. Let's wait and see."

Minutes later the deck lights came on, steam pipes clanked, and thick, black smoke poured out of the stack. Mary and I were helping Little Roy and Louis load the last of our supplies when the hotel detective came huffing and puffing down the path from the hotel.

"Better late than never," muttered Granddad. "Too Tall, douse those lights."

"You there," cried the detective. "What do you think you're doing?" Too Tall had taken the helm moments earlier, and now the *Simon Weed* was chugging away from the wharf. "Stop! Desist! Halt! Reverse engines, or I'll shoot." He raised a pistol and took aim, but Little Roy had passed Granddad his deer rifle, and now Granddad brought the stock to his shoulder and fired in one motion. *Blam!* Mary jumped, splinters flew at the detective's feet, and the aspiring but now terrified sleuth promptly dove behind a piling.

"Well, he's not entirely thick," said Little Roy.

"Not entirely," said Granddad, "but he's no Thomas Edison."

The *Simon Weed* picked up speed, and Too Tall put more distance between us and the detective. Granddad sent one more bullet in the detective's general direction to discourage more heroics, and then we chugged off into the darkness and out of pistol range.

"All right, Muff," called Granddad. "Are you sure you can't tell us where Chance is hiding?"

"Nope. Can't do it, mister. I forget. You can hang Muff from the highest giblet, draw and cauterize him, or boil him in a oil tank, but Muff ain't gonna squeal, no sir, no sir. Muff ain't no school pigeon."

"I was afraid you'd say that, Muff," said Granddad. "I guess there's no help for it, then. You're a hard nut to crack, I can see, but maybe if you soak for a while, you'll soften up." He untied and then retied Muff's ropes. When he was done, Muff stood with his hands clasped and tied in front of him like he was about to dive into the lake. The fifty-foot rope was knotted around the lashings like Muff was a piece of bait at the end of a fish line. Which he was.

"Cut her down to about six knots," Granddad said to Too Tall, and then he motioned Muff toward the stern. Little Roy and Mary and I followed. Louis was up in the bow with the spotlight looking for whatever we might run into.

Jake was at my side, curious about the small, strange man named Muff. I don't mind telling you, I was curious too, but not so much about Muff. I was wondering if Granddad was really going to toss poor Muff over the side.

"Have you heard about the monster that lives down on the bottom of Champlain, Muff?" asked Granddad.

"What you talkin' about?" asked Muff. "Ain't no monster in dis lake. Fish is all dere is in Champlain. Don't try put that one over Muff's head."

"No doubt but what you're right, Muff, but the Indians say he's as old as time. They call him Tatoskok, and the white folks where I come from call him Champ after the lake, you know. A lot of New Yorkers say they've spied him over on this side of the water. It's deep over here, you know, more than three hundred feet I've heard tell. They say this monster, if such there is, looks like a giant snake, like some kind of legless lizard from the ancient times, some prehistoric creature. Comes right up out of the Devil's hidey hole and stretches out thirty feet or more swimming along on the surface. It has humps come up out of the water, and it wriggles along as fast as an adder after a bullfrog. Folks talk about a farmer over here said he lost a cow that was pastured next to the lake. He found drag marks right to the water's edge. Folks say it was the monster that came right up on land and took that poor beast away."

" 'Folks say, folks say,' hah! Folks say lot of things, and lot of folks crazy as bug beds. You ain't scare me, mister!

You tell folks mind they own business and Muff mind his."
Muff spoke bravely, but I noticed him looking left and right
like a hunted animal.

"Yes, you're right, Muff. I'm sure there's no such
creature. I can't think what I'm saying—a sea serpent in
this day and age? But then, I've always wondered, and
since we're here—well, Muff, we've got to know where
Chance has my son-in-law, and if a monster doesn't scare
you, maybe a cold bath will clear your head and jog your
memory about just which island he headed to." With a nod
from Granddad, Little Roy grabbed Muff's hands, I grabbed
his feet, and Little Roy sang Muff a song.

"One for the monster, two for the ride,
Three for your luck, now over the side!"

We let him go on "side," and Muff hit the water with a
splash and went under. The rope paid out, and we waited
for him to surface. Granddad turned on the spotlight at the
stern, and then the rope pulled taut, and we saw Muff's
springy, black hair break free of the waves. He sputtered
and hollered, mad as could be, but we couldn't hear
what he said over the noise of the *Weed's* engine. Soon
he stopped his bellowing and concentrated on keeping
his head above water. Muff was having a wild ride, but I
thought he was holding his own, so I was surprised when
Mary spoke up and scolded Granddad.

"This is cruel!" she cried. "How can you do this? He'll
drown!"

"He won't drown, Mary. He might get a little waterlogged,

but I don't think he'll drown," said Granddad. He had taken out his pipe now and was striking a match. He put the flame to the bowl, sucked on the pipestem, and blew out a cloud of smoke.

"How can you stand there smoking a pipe and act like it's nothing? He may well drown. There must be some other way to find Royal."

"What way, young lady? If you've got an idea, I'll listen. I hate to do this to the poor little fella, but I can't see another way. We've got to find Royal, and time may be running short."

"Granddad," I said.

"Hold on, Otter. I want Mary to have her say on this."

"Granddad," I said again. "Look!" This time he caught my tone. Everyone looked where I was pointing, and there, just reaching the cast of the spotlight, was the fantastic monster Granddad had described, the one he didn't believe in, the one none of us believed in. It was a many-humped, writhing creature of gigantic size, and as we watched, its head rose from the lake and its cold, reptilian eyes turned on poor Muff.

"Haul him in!" cried Granddad. "Haul him in!" Little Roy and I had already leaped to the rope with Granddad and were pulling, hand over hand, trying to save Muff from the jaws of the serpent. "Put the wood to this tub, Too Tall, and get us out of here!" hollered Granddad. "Mary, go grab one of those chickens we brought."

We tugged hard and brought Muff toward us in fits

and starts. He was submerged in a wave one second and catapulting out of it the next. The monster swam after him in all its terrifying splendor, its humped body slithering through the water, its terrible head plunging into the waves and out again, its great maw opening now to swallow Muff whole.

"Throw him a chicken, Mary, and for pity's sake, land it beyond poor Muff or he's a goner!" yelled Granddad. I glanced at Mary and saw that she gripped a flopping hen by the legs. Without hesitating she wound up, swung the chicken in a high arc overhead, and hurled the bird underhand like she was firing a softball across home plate. That little feathered beauty soared into the air like the stone from David's sling, and I worried that it would keep going, but its wings were clipped, and—God bless the Rhode Island Red—it was too surprised to fly anyway. It sailed through the air and plopped right down in the monster's path. The monster was surprised too, I think, and when he stopped to gobble it up, we put more distance between him and Muff. Then on came the serpent again, and for the first time he made a serpent sound. Above the splattering rain, the rushing wind, and even the thumping steam engine came an angry, eerie hissing, and we hauled all the harder to bring poor Muff over the side before he went the way of the chicken.

Little Roy grabbed Muff's belt just as the monster's head burst from the water again, right at the stern. He reared up, and for all I could tell, he was coming right into the boat with us, but Granddad had grabbed his rifle, and he put a round into the creature's mouth. At the same time, Little Roy heaved Muff into the boat and out of the monster's reach. The monster let out a bellow that, for sheer volume, would have shamed the Cyclops when crafty Odysseus put his eye out with a stick. Then, lashing his tail and almost capsizing the *Simon Weed*, the serpent dove into the lake and vanished from sight.

Muff, meanwhile, was spewing lake water onto the deck, gasping, talking in tongues, and rolling about like a fish out of water. Little Roy, with the kindness he exhibited to all dumb creatures, cut Muff's lashings, propped him against the rail, and talked to him softly like he was settling a spooked horse. As Little Roy comforted Muff, the rest of us talked about the monster. After agreeing that we had, indeed, seen this behemoth, and that it was the strangest, most terrifying sight any of us had ever seen, we agreed that we would not blab about it since we would just be called liars and crackpots. We were all a little shaken, even Granddad, but Muff, of course, was especially excited.

"Him almost got me!" he cried. "One bite, that be the end of Muff! Monster's mouth full of ax blades and smell like a outhouse. Give Muff the wollygobbles! Still shakin'!"

Granddad, never one to miss a chance, figured this was a good time to question the mouse when he'd just escaped the cat. "What a terror, eh Muff?" he said. "He swam right up from the bottom of the lake. I'm sorry he threw you a scare, young fella. To tell the truth, I didn't expect ever to see such a beast. But that's Mother Nature in all her glory. She has a strange brood living in the deeps, doesn't she? Folks say this one is as old as old can be. Must be a hole down there, some kind of underwater tunnel that leads to the beginning of time."

" 'Folks say, folks say.' There you go again, with what folks say. Mean somepin' bad for Muff. Don't never want to hear what folks say ever again. Why don't you, mister, put Muff back on land where he get his sea legs under him and hit the road back for Canada?"

"Well, Muff, my lad, I wish I could, but we've still got to find your boss, so your best chance of getting back on land is to tell us where he's gone. Once we catch up with him and get Royal back, we can talk about Canada."

"And what if Muff still don't talk?" As he looked around defiantly, I started humming and Little Roy began softly singing, "One for the monster, two for the ride...." Granddad only tilted his eyebrows.

"All right. Muff beat down. Mean old skunk almost drown Muff, almost feed him to giant snake could eat a cow in one bite. What choice, Muff have? None, that's what. Now Chance goin' to shoot Muff fulla holes and leave him dead for crows. Muff in tight corner. Him caught like a rat trap. Muff gonna squeal. Him gonna double back on Chance and tell mean old skunk where Chance go. Otherwise, him don't, old skunk worse than Chance and feed Muff overboard."

Granddad sighed. He had resigned himself to Muff's

long-winded, circular, and eccentric mode of conversation, but he needed an answer. He stared at Muff and put on his sternest expression, but I could see a twitch at the corner of his mouth, and I knew it was all he could do not to bust out laughing.

"Where has he gone, Muff?" asked Granddad gruffly.

"Him gone to Proverbs Island."

"You sure you don't mean Providence Island?"

"Proverbs! Proverbs! Just like in a Bible. You hard a hearin'? Proverbs Island! Big rich man house, but he gone now. Too nasty cold this time year. Go back to Montreal up dere. House got big room widda fancy chairs anna big stone fireplace. Gotta kitchen, special room just to eat on a fancy big table, four room widda beds, even two outhouses inside. Very fancy, rich person home. Chance stop dere at night sometime, tie up at big concrete dock. Need any porthole in a storm if it get windy, wavy on Champlain."

Granddad nodded as Muff rambled on, but he was already drawing another line on the chart he had lifted from Jack. "Too Tall!" he yelled. "Bring us onto south 60 degrees east. We're heading for Providence Island. Muff, do we need to tie you up again, or can you stay out of trouble?"

"Don't tie Muff no more. Had enough trouble. Got any food? Muff's stomach cavin' in. Feel mighty peckish. Maybe faint dead away, keel over and fall down. Got any meat maybe or bake potato?"

"How about some cold beans and salt pork?"

"With mable syrup?"

"Don't push your luck." Mumbling something about
not having any luck to push, Muff followed Granddad
forward to our larder. I heard him talking long after he and
Granddad were out of sight. Little Roy went forward to the
engine room to stoke the fire with coal and keep steam up.
Mary and I and Jake moved into the passengers' dining
room, out of the wind and rain. I lit a kerosene lantern and
then opened the valve on a steam radiator. Pretty soon it
clanked and clinked, and I knew steam was coming from
the boiler. Mary found a couple wool blankets in a locker
and handed me one. She wrapped a blanket around herself
and collapsed in a booth.

"Will you sit down with me, Otter? Or do you have to
help Granddad?" Her teeth chattered as she spoke, so I
draped the other blanket over her shoulders, and then I sat
down across the table from her. She smiled tiredly, and I
smiled back. Her hair still glistened with stray rain drops,
and I couldn't help thinking again that she was beautiful
and that I wanted to know everything about her.

"So Mary," I said. "How did you come to be waiting
tables at the Angel's Perch, and why did you want to
leave?"

CHAPTER 8

The Orphan Train

MARY DIDN'T ANSWER ALL TO ONCE. She looked out the window where we could see the rain pouring down again in the dim glow of the deck lights. Then she looked at the table. Then she looked across the dining room at a photograph of the Hotel Champlain. What I mean to say is—she looked everywhere but at me. She reached down and stroked Jake between the ears, and I waited like I do when I'm hunting, and I have to stay very still. Finally, Mary looked at me.

"It's a long story," she said.

"You don't know, Granddad," I replied. "I'm used to those."

"That's not really it," she said. "It *is* a long story, but that's not why I'm afraid to tell you. If I tell you, you might not—you might think differently about me. You—you're...."

"I'm what?"

"Well, don't get mad, but you're so innocent. No, I don't mean that either." She paused, trying to find the right words. "You seem like such a good person, so happy, so fun-loving. I'm just afraid that when I tell you about what's happened to me, you'll be sorry you met me." I turned on the bench seat, so I could look into her eyes.

"Mary, my mother died nine years ago. Two years before that, my father kissed my mother and me goodbye and traipsed off to the Great War, and until last week I thought he was missing in action and most likely dead. Tonight, I beat up Roddy Bragg, knocked out Bump with a sap, and hit poor Muff on the head with a baseball bat. If I seem good to you, I'm glad, but no doubt Muff would beg to differ. If I seem happy and fun-loving to you, I'm glad, but I've seen my share of ups and downs. Whatever you tell me, I'm not going to be sitting up high and mighty on my throne, passing judgment. You don't have to tell me anything, if you don't want to.

As far as what you first said—about me being innocent—I am if you mean that I haven't seen much of the world. I haven't. Only this little corner up here in the North Country. After tonight, I'm not sure how much more of the "world" I want to see. I'm not sure I like knowing that Granddad can be ruthless, that *I* can be ruthless. What I do like, is you. I know that prob'ly makes me sound even more innocent. I don't know if it's love—we've just barely met, and I'm not even sure what love is—but I look at you, and I'm filled with joy. You're beautiful, but I don't just mean your face and your hair and your voice and the way you walk. I mean *all* that, but

I mean something else, too. I think it's your heart that pulls me toward you. I think you've got a true heart, a heart brave and kind, and that's what's most beautiful about you. I want to know you better, but fast or slow or not at all—it's your say-so. If I know more about why you had to leave the Angel's Perch, maybe I'll know better how to help, but it's up to you."

She didn't answer at first. She was so quiet and drawn into herself, I thought the tears might come, but not for Mary. Maybe they'd come one too many times in the past, or maybe she was never the crying kind. In any case, she decided to tell me her story. Once she started, that story was like a train leaving the station. It rocked along slowly at first and then gathered in the miles. I listened in wonderment.

"I WAS RAISED BY COBY AND HELEN ROTMENSEN. Coby said he found me abandoned by my parents, a ragamuffin wandering the streets of Plattsburgh. They took me in out of Christian charity, so they said, and for months they thought I was a mute, for I didn't speak a word. I couldn't remember what had happened to my parents or how I had ended up in Plattsburgh, so I had little choice but to live with the Rotmensens. I soon found out they were no Christians. They only wanted me for a drudge. Coby had a farm in Whitehall, New York. He milked twenty-five Holsteins, but he wasn't much of a farmer. And his wife, Helen? She was the worst kind of witch you can imagine." Mary grinned at this, but it wasn't a happy grin.

"We lived just east of the village on County Road 18, next to Our Lady of Angels Cemetery. Helen told the neighbors that she and Coby had adopted me, but I don't think they ever did. Leastways, they never showed me any papers to prove it. About the age of ten, I got so I wanted to know more about where I came from, and I kept asking questions. Helen cured me of that notion. She had hold of a hot skillet she'd just taken off the cookstove with a potholder. She swung around and banged my bare arm with the edge of it. Then she told me I'd keep my mouth shut if I knew what was good for me." Mary rolled up her sleeve to show me an ugly burn scar above her left elbow. I decided I would remember the name Rotmensen. "From then on," she continued, "I didn't have a whole lot to say.

I went to school long enough to learn to read and write and cipher, but only because the Rotters, as I secretly called them, didn't want to pay a fine. It was hard to keep up with the other kids because Helen sent me to school just enough to keep the truant officer off her back. The rest of the time, she put me to work. That's all the Rotters wanted from me. I was their bound girl, and I never got a nickel nor a word of thanks. Helen fed me, but she was stingy. The prime cuts and the cream went to her and Coby, and the gristle and the skim went to me and the pigs, so I didn't exactly pop the buttons off my dresses. In Helen's cast-offs,

I looked like a poor excuse for a scarecrow. I had a room in the attic where I froze in the winter and died of heat in the summer. I didn't mind the work so much—not when I got used to it—but Helen and Coby? The Devil designed them just to make my life a hell on earth. I'd have been glad to pitch either one of them to the monster instead of the chicken.

When I was a child, Coby didn't bother me much because he was always out in the barn or the fields, but that changed when I began to fill out Helen's old clothes and look more like a girl than a kid. I was probably twelve when he first started looking at me. He would slide along real quiet on the carpet runner in the hall upstairs, open the door to my bedroom, and catch me undressing. Then he took to touching me when Helen wasn't looking. At dinner he might walk behind me if she was in the pantry and rest his hand on my neck for a moment before he went out on the porch to smoke his pipe, or he might touch my hair and smile and say how pretty I looked. I told him to leave me alone, told him I'd tell Helen, but he just grinned and said that wouldn't be smart.

'If you do that,' he said, 'I'll say that you've been making eyes at me, that you've been trying to tempt me. Then I'll tell her we need to turn you over to the Poor Farm. She'll agree. She doesn't want you here. You'll go live with the idiots and the cripples.' I knew he was right. She didn't want me around, and I was scared to death of the Poor Farm, so I didn't say a word.

One day, Helen was in the backyard hanging the laundry, and I was washing the breakfast dishes. It was a glorious morning in April. It had rained off and on all night, but then the sun came out, and the grass and the daffodils and the budding trees were sparkling. Looking out the kitchen window, I saw a flock of robins on the lawn tugging worms out of the ground. A Model T clattered down the county road from Whitehall, so I didn't hear Coby Rotmensen sneak up behind me. He put his arms around me, Otter, and then he pressed against me."

I growled at this. I couldn't help it. Jake sat up, wondering what was going on. Mary stroked his head between his ears, and he settled down again. I wanted to hold her hand, but it didn't seem like the right thing just then. "What did you do?" I asked.

"I didn't know what to do. He began to grope me, and then I remembered the knife in the dishwater. When I got my fingers around the handle, I gripped it tight. 'Coby,' I said, trying to stop the quaver in my voice, 'Let me turn around and face you.' I wasn't supposed to call him by his first name, but I think he liked it right then, so he let go of me. When he did, I whirled with the blade in my hand. He jumped back, but not before I put the knife in his stomach. His eyes went wide, he stumbled back, and then he grabbed a dishtowel from the table to staunch the blood already streaming from the wound.

'You slut,' he said hoarsely. 'You'll pay for that.' Without another word he ran out to the driveway, cranked up the

Model T, and drove to town to get stitched up. That was when I ran away.

I stole all ten dollars of Helen's "ready money." She kept it out of my reach—or so she thought—on top of the kitchen cupboard in one of Coby's old tobacco tins. I saw her climb up on a stool one day and squirrel away some bills in her hiding place when she thought I was still out feeding the chickens. I emptied the money into my apron and replaced the tin. I grabbed a loaf of bread from the breadbox and a wedge of cheese from the icebox, and then I ran upstairs and stuffed my few clothes in a pillowcase. As I ran out the front door, I heard the back door slam, and I knew Helen was entering the kitchen. She called me, but when I didn't answer, she must have thought I was in the outhouse. By the time she came looking for me, I had raced into the woods behind Our Lady of Angels Cemetery and disappeared. I circled back to the road where it joined the highway from Fair Haven, and then I kept on running.

I headed for the Delaware & Hudson railroad station at the north end of Whitehall. I knew where it was because I rode there once with Coby to pick up his sister Ethel who sometimes took the train from Plattsburgh when she came to visit. I got winded after running for a while and slowed to a walk. I was scared that Doc Collins had stitched Coby's wound already, and that he would see me on his way home, so I turned up Williams Street, which was a less traveled road into town. I crossed the Champlain Canal at noon. I remember it was noon because the fire whistle blew. I was worried that Helen might have gone to the Speer's farm up the road and used their phone to call the town cop. Sure enough, I saw him heading up Skenesborough Drive in the direction of the railroad station as I was crossing the canal.

Maybe he was headed there, and maybe he wasn't, but I didn't want to take a chance. I crawled down under the canal bridge and stayed out of sight for the rest of the afternoon. My plan had been to get aboard a freight train headed for New York City. I didn't think the Rotters would ever find me there. As I lay in the shade, scared to death of what was going to happen, I thought up a better plan. I would stow away on a boat headed down the Hudson River. Just after the last glimmer of light left the sky that evening, I heard the sound of one entering the canal from South Bay. The engine boomed low and deep, and I wondered what it was. Finally, it turned the corner north of me, and I made out the dim outline of a tugboat pulling a barge. I waited for the tug to go by, and then I crept carefully to the edge of the canal. The barge was piled high with cargo, but it was covered with an enormous tarp. What was it carrying? Something soft I hoped. It was my best chance to escape the Rotters, so I said a quick prayer, jumped, and—happily—landed in a pile of hay.

I crawled under a corner of the tarp and slept, and by morning we were in Albany. The barge was tied up to a riverside pier when I awoke, so I decided New York could wait. I snuck off the barge at dawn, only to be challenged as soon as I set foot on the dock.

'Whatcha doin', girlie—hitchin' a ride?' a voice asked. I looked for the speaker and saw a tough-looking boy leaning against one of the pilings. He took a pipe out of his mouth and smiled, but I didn't smile back.

'Don't be scared,' he said. 'I don't mean you no harm. I'm just a wharf rat, and it's such a fine day I'm takin' my ease here in de sun and havin' a smoke. Ellery Addens, is me name. Now you're off de barge, nobody will be the wiser, and I won't tell. Are ya hungry? Here.' I looked at him suspiciously, but before I could reply, he tossed me an apple he pulled from a pocket in his ragged coat. I gave him a crust of bread and some cheese, and that was how our friendship started. He was a few years my elder and could easily have conned me, but he didn't. Like me, he didn't know exactly how old he was, but I'd guess he was fifteen or sixteen. When his parents died, he had taken to the streets. I only knew him for a week, but I will never forget him. He was like a big brother to me, and he never once tried any funny business. He showed me where I could eat for cheap, and he showed me a safe place to sleep up in Washington Park.

'C'mon, girlie,' he said after we finished eating. 'Let's go uptown and take a look around. Whadda ya say?' With Ellery as my guide, I saw a city for the first time. I had seen pictures of city buildings in one of my school books, but now I was seeing real ones lining the avenues, towering above me, huge and grand. We walked up Quay Street to Maiden Lane, down Pearl and then up State. I saw the Delaware & Hudson Building, the Million Dollar Staircase at the Capitol, City Hall, St. Johns Church, and Union Station. I was, as you would say, Otter, all agog. I spent so much time looking up, I got a crick in my neck. The city was new and strange, full of marvels and wonders, but terrifying too, with so many people and so many accents, and so much hustle and commotion. When we went to Union Station I saw a group of boys and girls boarding a train, and I thought they must have been school children on a trip, but I was wrong.

'That's the Orphan Train,' said Ellery. 'This preacher, Mr. Brace, sends dose kids up here from New York City. Dey ain't all orphans. Some a dem, de parents is just no good, you know, boozers or crooks. Some a dem beat der kids. Dey leave der kids on the streets to make der own way. And some a dem only got one parent, maybe, who's sick or crippled and can't take care of der kids. Mr. Brace, he puts dem on de New York Central and sends dem out West where some people don't have no kids, but dey want some. De kids don't have no parents, so dese people take dem in, and de kids is happy den.'

'So why don't you go?' I asked.

'Cuz maybe some kids ain't so happy if dey get a bad parent who fools de church people inta tinking de're good.'

I mulled this over for a couple days, and in spite of

Ellery's doubts, I wanted to get on that train. I thought
I had found a way to escape from the Rotters for good
and maybe even find a home. I would go west to Kansas
or Nebraska, one of those frontier states I learned about
in school, where cowboys ride horses and the sky is big
and full of sunshine. Sometimes, dimly, I remembered
my father and mother, and I missed them terribly. I
remembered being loved. What if I could find new parents,
people I could love and who could love me? That was how I
ended up on the Orphan Train.

Not right away though. I was too busy looking for food.
Ellery showed me where I could find leftovers in the alleys
behind some of the better establishments, places like the
Boulevard Restaurant and the Kenmore Hotel. Once, when
we were lifting lids off garbage cans behind the Kenmore, a
boy came out with food to dump and gave it to us instead.
We sat down to wine-soaked beef, potatoes and cheese,
and green beans. I'd never had such food! But then,
some nights we sat down to nothing and gnawed on our
knuckles.

I was also too busy staying away from the wrong
people. Ellery told me Uncle Dan O'Connell ran a tight
city, but he warned me off Nighttown. This was a year
after the government said nobody could drink, but
you could sure get a drink in Nighttown. A bootlegger
named Legs Diamond brought the booze in. He sold it
in whorehouses, speakeasies, and gambling joints, and
he'd shoot people as quick as he'd shoot a rat if they

got in his way. The cops in that part of the city were on the take, so he could get away with it. We kept clear of Nighttown.

And we stayed away from the kids in Nighttown and the toughs in the other bad neighborhoods. We steered clear of Scruffy Joe Jackson's gang down near Madison and Van Zandt, and we stayed well away from Mick "Pigsticker" Murphy who always carried a blade and sometimes came uptown from the Pastures. Most days we panhandled near the Capitol, up in Washington Park, and over near State Street. We didn't spend much time on the waterfront, and we didn't venture south of Madison— that was dangerous. Even uptown, pickpockets and smalltime hoods mingled with the crowds, and the cops were always after kids like me who were supposed to be in school.

Without Ellery, I wouldn't have lasted a day, and I still thank him and the angel who sent me to him when I stepped off that barge. If not for him, I'd be a pile of bones in one of those dark ravines in Nighttown. Ellery was my first true friend, and he taught me how to stay alive, but I didn't want to roam the streets forever, always looking over my shoulder, always wondering where I was going to eat and sleep. I started visiting Union Station hoping that I might one day figure out a way to board the Orphan Train. Maybe it would have been better if I hadn't.

My chance came near the end of May. I learned the schedule for the trains headed west on the New York

Central Railroad and wandered about in the station at those times day after day to watch and listen. It wasn't hard to spot the orphans. New groups of thirty to forty kids arrived almost daily, always tended by a couple placement agents. The day I left, I cleaned up as best I could in the station washroom, and then I waited on the platform with Ellery. When it came time for the orphans to board the train, I loitered nearby, as I often did, to see if a moment would come when I could slip aboard unnoticed. That day, it did.

One of the agents, a young woman with spectacles and a round, cheery face, had already climbed on the train with half of the children when a Negro porter appeared from the station calling for a Miss Laura Templeton. Miss Templeton, the other placement agent, was also young, but unlike her companion, she was as beautiful as a Gibson girl, and suddenly I wished with all my heart that I could be like her. She had pinned up her honey-colored hair on top of her head, but curling tendrils framed either side of her face. Her bright, blue eyes and constant smile were full of sweetness and good humor. I found out later that all the orphan boys had a crush on her. As the porter handed her some missing luggage, Ellery said, 'Here's your chance.'

'Goodbye,' I said.

'Goodbye, girlie. Keep yer wits about you,' he replied. I was already walking toward the passenger coach, and I glanced over my shoulder and saw that he was grinning. I

knew I was going to miss Ellery's bold grin. He was happy
for me but sad too. Neither of us expected to see each other
again. I looked at him wistfully. Then I climbed the stairs
to the coach behind a red-haired girl my age.

Hearing sudden footsteps, she turned and stared down
at me. 'Please don't tell,' I whispered. She studied me,
said nothing, and then marched quickly up the steps. At
the far end of the coach, a blonde girl of six or seven was
crying, and the round-cheeked agent hurried forward
to comfort her. The redhead stopped in the aisle and,
still facing forward, put one hand behind her back and
pointed to the window seat. As soon as I sat down, she
slid in beside me and pulled a navy blue cape from a
carpet bag.

'Put this on,' she whispered. 'Put the hood up. Lean your
head 'gainst my shoulder and pretend to be asleep. My
name's Cara. What's yours?'

'Mary,' I replied. 'Thanks.'

'Just don't get me into no trouble. Why'd you sneak on?'

'People I lived with—the husband—he was after me.'
Cara nodded. She didn't seem surprised. I did as she said
and rested my head against her shoulder. I heard shuffling
feet and a few whispers as the rest of the orphans boarded,
but they made scant noise. They had ridden the Delaware
& Hudson line from New York City that morning, and
they were tired and scared and awed by the prospect of a
journey to the West. They didn't know what was going to
happen. I knew even less. I heard Miss Templeton's skirts

rustling as she walked past, talking to the conductor over her shoulder. I heard the conductor call, 'All aboard!' Then the engineer blew the whistle, the coach rocked, and we lurched forward in a tumult of hissing steam and goodbyes shouted to other passengers by loved ones still standing on the platform.

THE TRAIN RIDE WAS WRETCHED. It took days, hours and endless hours cooped up in that coach, victims of tainted food and a rocking motion that made many of us queasy. Miss Templeton discovered me before we had even reached Rochester, but she took pity on me. As long as I was truly an orphan—and she would find out, she said, if I wasn't—I could travel with the others and, the good lord willing, find a home and parents. I was just wise enough now to be wary, but I hoped she was right with all my heart.

When we reached Kansas City, Missouri, we pulled into Union Station, which not only had the same name as the station in Albany, but looked the same too, with three huge arches in a gigantic building. Members of the Grand Avenue Methodist Church were waiting with cars, and they drove us uptown. When we arrived at the church, the Methodist minister, Reverend Addyman, put us up for adoption. We sat on wooden folding chairs on a raised platform at the front of the church. The people who came to see us sat in the church pews while the minister explained about placement.

I felt funny when the church members stepped up,
one by one, to look us over. A tall, handsome man with
a thick mustache and black hair, glossy with pomade,
politely asked each of us to open our mouths, and then
he inspected our teeth. Dressed in his pin-striped suit, he
was very distinguished looking, and the orphans stared at
the diamond stick-pin in his tie rather than meet his eyes.
Would it be good to have a rich man for a father? Maybe.
And then again, maybe not. The minister followed him,
chattering like a magpie, hoping for a crumb from the
hand of his social better.

He stopped for a long time in front of me, so long I
flushed with discomfort. He gazed at me, looking from
head to toe, and then he held my chin in his hand
while he stooped to look in my mouth. With his face
inches from mine, he said, 'Would you like to come
home with me, missy?' I felt a quiver of alarm, but I
didn't know why. Wasn't this what I had come for? To
find new parents and a home? The preacher scolded
me and told me I must answer when I was spoken to,
but Miss Templeton said I was exhausted after the
long train trip. When Mr. DePrae—that was the man's
name—signed the placement papers, I followed him
out through the towering doors of the church and sat
in his car. It wasn't a Model T either. It was a Peerless
Model 56 Touring Car he told me proudly. Like him, it
was polished and smooth. The seats were shiny, black
leather. The fenders and running boards were shiny

black. The body was a bright, shiny red. It was all strange to me, and as we drove to Quality Hill, I was both excited and uneasy.

I soon learned why the preacher kowtowed to this man. Coby the Rotter had just been a farmer and not a very successful one. In the weeks and months that followed, I was to learn that Mr. Todd DePrae was an important man in Kansas City. He was president of a bank on Walnut Street, and he was as rich as Croesus. That was all I knew about him for a long time. By the time I escaped from Kansas City five years later in May of last year, I had learned a lot more. I had learned that my so-called "father" was also a close friend of Boss Tom Pendergast, the most powerful man in Kansas City and also the biggest crook. Nothing happened without Boss Tom's say-so, and he had a stake in every deal in town, good or bad. The more I found out about Kansas City, the more I forgot my dreams of cowboys and sunshine and a better place to live.

The crimes and secrets of Kansas City were like those of Albany. Every well-lit street had a shady back alley. Even though Tom Pendergast had finally moved up on the bluff with the other swells, he had started out working his brother's saloon in West Bottoms down by the Missouri River, and the saying that you can't make a silk purse out of a sow's ear was surely true of him. No matter how well dressed he was on the outside, no matter how much money he spent to make himself look respectable, he was still a crook. And Boss Tom was one of my father's closest friends.

But when I reached Todd DePrae's home that night, I didn't know any of this. For all I knew, Todd DePrae, President of the Kansas City Savings and Loan, was a pillar of the community, a prince among men. When we drove through the wrought-iron gates and up the paved drive to 73 Janssen Park, I could easily imagine that he *was* a prince. The DePrae home wasn't quite a palace, but it was a stately mansion. The towering chimneys, the two-story walls of golden limestone, the floor-to-ceiling windows on the first floor, the massive front door with its heavy brass knocker—all these impressed me. It was a rich man's home, Otter, and for a short time, it became my home. Over the next four years it also became my prison.

Leah DePrae had no children, and that's why I was there—to be the daughter she wanted but couldn't have. She hugged me on the doorstep and welcomed me with a great show of happiness, but even on that first day I sensed she was broken. She hid this so well at the time, I thought I'd imagined it. After all, what did I know about mothers? I could barely remember mine. But now, when I look back, I know I didn't imagine a thing. I remember a marble goddess that sat on a table in the front hallway, and one day, as I looked at its face more closely, I realized the sculptor's model was Mrs. DePrae. I don't know if this will make sense, Otter, but he had caught her soul exactly—beautiful, but under that beautiful surface what sadness!

I never saw Mrs. DePrae smile. Eventually, I learned why. Mr. DePrae was a monster. I only learned this slowly over the next four years. The knowledge came like grains of arsenic in my morning cup of tea, a slow poison that almost paralyzed me.

In the first months, my fears were lulled to sleep. I attended school, and life was tolerable. I addressed Mr. and Mrs. DePrae as "father" and "mother" and acted the part of an affectionate daughter. They, in turn, acted the loving parents. It was all a sham. Mrs. DePrae did her best to be a mother to me, but she needed more help than I did. Only her daily dose of laudanum could draw the curtain on the horrors she wanted to escape. And Mr. DePrae? Before the first year was out, I was given a clue to his true nature. One day my adoptive mother pulled her sleeve back to avoid getting it wet as she reached into our backyard pond to pluck a water lily. She suddenly remembered the ugly burn on her forearm and covered it up it again, but not before I saw it. It was the size of a nickel—or maybe the size of one of Mr. DePrae's cigars. I was pretty sure I knew then the cause of her sadness, and soon I began to worry for my own sake.

Nothing happened until the end of my fourth year in Kansas City. I was probably seventeen and looking more and more like a grown woman. One evening last spring, after the maid and the cook had gone home, he came to my room. He chatted about school, about how I was getting on with my friends, about whether or not I liked the new

prom dress he and Mrs. DePrae had bought for me. Then
the conversation took a strange turn. 'Mary,' he said. 'You
know what I want now, don't you?'

I didn't answer, not at first. I was shocked, but I
shouldn't have been. I should have seen it coming. He came
closer, and I retreated a step.

'I'll scream,' I said.

'No one will hear you. Mother has gone to bed.
Occasionally, when she is fitful or restless at night, I give
her a potion concocted from jimson weed which helps her
sleep. She won't hear you, my dear. She wouldn't hear
cannon fire, I'm afraid. And if you make too much fuss, I'll
simply gag you. Kissing is not necessary to my enjoyment.'
He stepped toward me then, and light glinted on the
straight razor in his hand. 'This, of course, is persuasive,'
he said, holding up the razor. 'Be a good girl and do as I
ask.'

I saw no escape. Mr. DePrae was no Coby Rotmensen.
He was smart, and he had worked out every detail of
his plan. I didn't have a chance." Mary looked at me
now, trying to gauge my reaction. "It went on for weeks.
He told the principal at the Quality Hill Public High
School that I was being privately tutored and would be
attending a preparatory school the following year. He hired
"bodyguards" to take turns watching over me, saying
that it was for my own protection, that the children of the
wealthy were sometimes kidnapped. They were really my
jailers.

By now, Otter, I had come to hate Todd DePrae. I was desperate to escape and willing to take any risk. One night, when the door finally creaked, and he appeared on the threshold, it was two o'clock, but I was awake. I had his own straight razor under my pillow, and when the chance came, I snatched it up and cut him with the quickness of a snake. He reeled out of bed, blood gushing from his throat, and called for Leah, but he had already drugged her, and she was floating down an underground river out of his reach.

For a second time in my life, I hurriedly packed for an escape. I stole the two hundred dollars that was in his wallet. I had already stuffed two dresses, some underclothes, and some bread and dry sausage in a carpet bag earlier that afternoon. Before DePrae had entered my room, I heard him send the bodyguard downstairs to get some sleep, so I left without being discovered. I walked to Union Station in the dark and slept on a bench until I woke up groggy and stiff as the sun was coming up. I bought a ticket on the first train to St. Louis and reached the station on Market Street in the early afternoon.

I stepped off the train and walked along the platform to stretch my legs, and then I decided to explore the headhouse and find some lunch. Inside, a great crowd of people hurried along a concourse. In ones and twos and threes they veered off and entered various shops, the station restaurant, or the hotel. They bought tickets to go east or west, north or south. They searched for bathrooms, greeted relatives who had just arrived from Chicago or New Orleans, waited for trains going out or trains coming in, or they hurried off to taxis waiting on Market Street. It was a busy place. I paused, trying to decide which way to go when a boy hawking newspapers caught my attention.

'Extra! Extra! Read all about it!' he said. 'Well known Kansas City banker gets throat cut in Quality Hill mansion. Daughter goes missing.' He was holding up a copy of the *St. Louis Post-Dispatch,* and I caught a glimpse of the photo on the front page. It was me! I gave the newsie two cents for a copy and sat down on a bench to read it. I was suspected of having a part in DePrae's death, and the police wanted me for questioning. Boss Tom had offered a reward for information about my whereabouts and was hiring Pinkerton detectives to find me. I was scared, and when I looked up from the paper and glanced around the station wondering what to do, I got even more scared because the first thing I saw was the Western Union office. I had forgotten the telegraph! Of course—the police would have sent word to the railroad.

No sooner did I realize this than I looked out a tall window and saw two policemen stepping off my train headed for the station. *They're looking for me,* I thought. *They have to be.* I saw a knot of people clustered next to the entrance, and I acted almost without thinking. Walking briskly toward that same entrance, I reached it just in time to stand behind that group of people as the cops entered the station. They walked right by me, not more than ten feet away, to the edge of the crowd still swarming along the concourse, and then one went one way, and the other went the other. I hurried out the great, arched doorway and got back on the train. I figured if they had already checked it, it might be the safest place I could find.

That was the only time I came close to getting caught. In the next city, I had my hair bobbed in a beauty salon. I bought lipstick, a cloche hat, and a new dress with Mr. DePrae's money. I disguised myself as best I could, arrived in Albany a couple days later, and disappeared. Nobody knew I had come from Whitehall originally because I had borrowed Ellery's story and told Miss Templeton that I had lived on the streets of Albany after my parents died in the great flu epidemic of 1918. When I arrived in Albany, I took a train to Plattsburgh because I thought the Pinkertons might eventually question Miss Templeton.

I started waitressing at the Angel's Perch in June, and the owners treated me well and gave me a room above the tavern, but then Parson came to me the night before you showed up. He said a shamus had come snooping around the Perch on my day off. He showed Parson a picture of me. And that's why I had to leave, why I asked if I could come with you."

"I'm sorry," I said. "About all of it. I'm sorry about what DePrae did to you, and what you *had* to do to him. I saw the look on your face when you talked about using the razor, but Mary, if ever a man deserved to die, he did. I wish I could turn back the clock and take away the hurt. I can't do that, but I'll do what I can, Mary, and I'll sure help you get away from those detectives." I held her face gently in my hands and kissed her on the forehead. Then I held her tight. A minute passed before we let go of each other. Then—I don't know why—I asked her one last question.

"Mary, do you remember anything about your life before the Rotmensens?"

CHAPTER 9

The Way to Providence

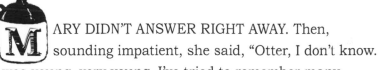 ARY DIDN'T ANSWER RIGHT AWAY. Then, sounding impatient, she said, "Otter, I don't know. I was young, very young. I've tried to remember many times, but I can't."

"Nothing?"

"Oh, for the love of Pete, this will sound crazy, but I remember a hat, a little red beret."

"A hat?"

"Yes. A hat."

"A hat," I said again thoughtfully.

"Yes! I loved that hat. Helen used to make fun of me when I wore it, and she threatened to throw it away, but I told her if she did, I would break her favorite china. She put welts on the backs of my legs with a buggy whip when I said that, but she didn't take the hat."

"She *was* a witch, wasn't she," I said gently. "Sorry to bring up more unpleasant memories. After all you've said, I just wonder what happened, how you came to live in Whitehall. Your parents couldn't have lived there, or someone would have told you."

Mary didn't answer. The rain drummed on the deck outside, and she was lost in thought. She stared out the window with a strange expression on her face and reminded me of Pearl Giddings who ran the Village Store in Swanton. When I was eleven, I went to see the Bardosi Brothers' Circus, and I saw Pearl hypnotized by the Great and Wonderful Fontana Bardosi. The Great Bardosi asked for a volunteer from the audience, and Pearl got right up there on stage. We couldn't hear what the Great Bardosi said, but his voice was as smooth as butter from the churn. It rose and fell like waves lapping the shore of Champlain.

I hardly noticed when he did it, but he pulled a shiny, gold pocket watch out of his vest and swung it back and forth on a little chain. The only light on the stage came from a candle, and when the watch swung back and forth, it flashed with the reflected light. Outside the tent I heard the cooing of a mourning dove. I'd been pounding in fence posts all day, and between the dove and the voice of the Great Bardosi, and the flashing watch, darned if *I* didn't end up half in a trance. Pearl was in one all the way. Her eyes were wide open, but she wasn't seeing the Bardosi or any of us. She was looking off to some faraway place.

Wherever it was, Mary had just gone there too. The *Simon Weed* cruised on toward Providence, rising to the crest of each wave and dropping gently into each trough

like two kids going lazily up and down on a teeter-totter.
I spoke her name, but Mary didn't seem to hear me. She
kept staring into that same land of visions, and I wondered
if that faraway place was a certain day she'd never been
able to remember. At first, I figured it could only be a
coincidence, that little red hat, but I couldn't get the
picture of Marian Prince out of my head. Granddad said
Marian and her mother had been washed overboard twelve
years ago. Mary would have been about six, the same age
as Marian Prince.

"Otter," said Mary, "being on the *Simon Weed* has
swept some cobwebs from my mind. That red hat? My
grandfather gave it to me. I remember him! It was my
birthday. We were going home across the lake on a ferry.
The clouds got terribly dark and a storm came up. The rain
poured down in a torrent, and the wind blew harder and
harder. Giant waves piled against the ferry, row after row of
them, and the boat pitched about like a bucking horse."

Mary was excited, and I wanted her to tell me more, to
remember more, but then Granddad opened the door and
yelled so he could be heard above the drumbeat of the rain.

"Otter!" he called, "we're almost to the island, but if we
land, they'll hear us coming in, and they're likely to be
waiting for us. I was thinking, though, if we paddle your
canoe, maybe we could surprise those fellas."

"Sure, Granddad," I said. "I'll get ready."

"All right, young fella. Grab your rifle and a slicker.
It's still raining. We'll go see if we can find your dad. Too

Tall is going to pass between Providence and Phelps Point on South Hero. He'll wait for us at the beach around the corner and just east of the point. We'll leave in a couple minutes."

When Granddad went forward again, I stood up and turned to Mary. I should have been scared silly, but looking at her, I couldn't help grinning like a fool. "I'm glad you're beginning to remember," I said. "I've got to go. I'll be seeing you."

"You'd better," she said, and then she reached across the table, grabbed my hand, and squeezed. "Listen, be careful. Chance is no Roddy Bragg."

"Don't I know it," I said. "He or one of his boys almost took my head off with that rapid-fire rifle. I'll be careful, Mary, and if I'm not, Granddad will be. You can bet he's thought this out. We'd never bother with Chance if it was just booze or a boat, but my dad—well, we're not going to leave him to that devil."

"I know," she said. Still holding my hand, she got up from the table and came to my side. Before I knew what she was about, she kissed me on the cheek.

"Most of the men I've met have been pretty worthless, Otter, even worse than worthless," she said, "but you're not—I know you're not. We've just barely met, and I've learned to be careful, but what if...?"

"What if what, Miss Mary Mack?" I asked.

"What if something happens? What if you get hurt? I just wanted to say thanks."

"That's what that kiss was? Thanks?"

"And something to remember me by," she said, smiling.

"Well, here's something to remember *me* by," I said, and I took her in my arms. The kiss, long and tender, opened our hearts. "You're right, Mary, we only met a few hours ago, but with all that's happened I feel like I've stepped on board a runaway train. I can barely take it all in. I've got a line on this much, though. I feel like I know you better after this one night than I've known most girls after a year. And what I've found out so far only makes me want to know you better, so I'll see you soon." I kissed her once more, jammed on my cap, and smiled broadly as I headed after Granddad.

WITHIN THE HOUR WE WERE IN THE CANOE fifty yards from the island. Granddad was paddling in the stern, Jake was curled up in the middle, and I was in the bow. The Babe's bat was at my feet, and my rifle was wrapped in canvas and slung from the thwarts. A twenty-foot wall of rock rose from the water directly before us. I didn't see how we could possibly deal with this little obstacle, but I had learned long ago not to question Granddad's judgment. Sure enough, as we got closer, I saw the route. Starting somewhere back in the long ago, when the lake monster and his kin were perhaps a common sight on Champlain, this part of the lake bottom had been pushed up and the layers of rock left on a tilt. Eons of freezing and thawing, and eons of pounding waves had gnawed at a vein of softer

rock sandwiched between harder layers and opened a slot
just big enough for our canoe.

"That's Bill's Hole-in-the-Wall," said Granddad.
"Get ready. We've got to ride in on the next wave." On
Granddad's say-so, we paddled hard and caught the crest.
We rushed forward like the King of Hawaii headed for
pineapple and roast pig on the beach. You could barely
see "the hole" behind a screen of cedar branches, but
Granddad pushed through with a last, deft stroke of the
paddle, the wave spent itself on the rocks, and we dropped
into a small pool at the bottom of the cave.

"Grab your rifle and jump out," cried Granddad. Jake
and I leaped after him onto a narrow ledge. It was still
raining as hard as ever and curtains of water streamed
down the walls from some hole above. It was darker than
the Devil's doorstep in that hole, but I heard a scratching
sound, and Granddad's face suddenly appeared, piratical
above the flaring light of a match. He touched the flame
to the wick of his storm lantern and began climbing. I
saw now that we were in a natural chimney, and a cedar
tree leaning against one side led up and out. Some axman
had notched small steps in the trunk long ago, and, old
as he was, Granddad was climbing them nimbly. I tied the
Melodie to a root to make sure she stayed out of reach of
the waves that crashed into the cave, and then I followed.

"Granddad, how did you ever find this place?" I asked.
"Bill Three Rivers."
"How did that happen?"

"We were your age, paddling down the lake in a canoe like yours. Must have been forty years ago. We were camping and fishing, but a few days after we left Swanton, the lake puckered up with an ugly storm that blew in from the Adirondacks. We swooped in off the open lake through that same strait between Providence and South Hero. The wind wasn't so bad, but the waves were still trying to swamp us. I don't know how he did it, but Bill spotted this little hole even at dusk, and we rode in here on the back of a wave like a couple cowboys on bucking broncs. It was providence indeed. We camped for the night, which is where that story separates from this one because we aren't going to be camping out."

"What *are* we going to do, Granddad?"

"We're going to hustle our bones to the lodge on the other side of the island, the one Muff described, and we're going to do it before the sun comes up." With that said, he poked his head up out of the cleft in the rock like a woodchuck checking for danger before going out to eat his clover. He peered into the dark and listened for two or three minutes. Naught was to be heard but the rain spattering against the ground and the waves pounding the bluff, so we crept out of the crack in the ledge and—boy, dog, and old man—we slunk like thieves into the woods.

We found a deer trail along the shore. Granddad put out the light. As my eyes adjusted, I could see that it was still dark, but it wasn't the pitch-black dark Jonah faced in the belly of the whale. The sun was poking around somewhere off to the east. His light was more of an idea than a fiery torch right then, but he was coming. We sensed the path more than we could see it, and we glided invisibly toward the summer folks' lodge on the other side of the island. Half an hour later, Granddad stopped. We stood at the edge of a grove of trees, and looking over Granddad's shoulder, I saw what he saw—the *Thorpedo* tied up at a concrete pier below us, and across the way a steep set of stairs that some clever fella had rigged against the face of another rocky bluff.

The stairs disappeared into darkness, but when Granddad nodded in that direction, I knew what he was thinking. A sentry must be posted nearby. We waited, and sure enough, leaning against a tree not far from the pier, I finally made out the silhouette of a man. I pulled gently on Granddad's sleeve and pointed, but there wasn't any need. He'd seen him too. As best we could tell, the man was looking out toward the lake. Granddad pointed toward a giant oak and whispered the plan.

"When I get behind that tree, you come down the path and make enough noise for him to hear you. Call out and then wait for him a couple yards shy of the oak." I nodded. He gave me his rifle, and I gave him the Babe's bat. Then he crept down the path to disappear in the shadows. When I judged him safely hidden, I followed and before I reached the tree, I sang out.

"Hey there, fella. I'm the caretaker for this island. What's going on here? You got engine trouble?" I surprised the guy, but he recovered quick enough.

"Stop right there and raise your hands," he said. "I've got a shotgun, and I'll use it if I have to."

"Just as you say, mister. I don't want any trouble."

He stepped toward me cautiously, and I could see the glint of the shotgun barrel. It wasn't such a help to him as it might have been though. He passed the oak tree and stood a few feet away with his twelve-gauge at the ready.

"You alone?" he asked.

Jake chose that moment to growl. "Not exactly," I said.

"Hey, what the devil?" The sentry caught sight of Granddad out of the corner of his eye and would have said more, no doubt, but Granddad walloped him with the baseball bat. The fellow dropped to the ground like a poleaxed steer.

"Home run," I whispered.

"Come on," said Granddad. "Let's see if we can find your father." We clambered up the stairs lickety-split and kept our eyeballs peeled as we snuck toward the house, but Chance must have figured the one fella on guard duty was enough on such a nasty night because we didn't meet anyone else. Steps led up to a grand porch that stretched across the front of the lodge. Halfway down the length of the porch, light shone from a picture window and lit the underside of the porch roof. Granddad grabbed my shoulder and came close to my ear.

"Take a look through that window," he whispered. "I'll

circle around the house just to make sure we don't have more company." If I'd been a foot away, I wouldn't have known he'd spoken, and that warned me to be careful. I crept up those stairs like an Indian. I'll bet Bill Three Rivers in his best moccasins couldn't have slipped along any quieter. I tested every floorboard against a squeak, and it took me several minutes to reach the picture window thirty feet away. Prob'ly I was being more careful than I needed to be. The waves rushing into the cove below me boomed against the rocks and made enough racket to cover any small noise I made. In daylight, I could have looked west from that porch across the lake to Valcour Island and maybe even the Adirondacks, and it would have been a fine view, but the only one I wanted to see right then was through that window. *Is my father inside?* I wondered.

After a near eternity, I stood a few feet from the window and beheld Chance's gang of ruffians with some surprise. *Only two of them?* A fire blazed in a stone hearth big enough for trolls, and they were playing cards in the flickering light. I could see them clearly. One had prematurely white hair and blue eyes that seemed kind and merry. *How tricky appearances can be,* I thought. *No doubt he's a hardened killer.*

To my astonishment, the other man was a giant on the scale of Too Tall. His long, curly locks of red hair were capped with a plaid tam. When he laid two cards on the table, I noticed that he was missing the little finger on his left hand. As I watched him, he drew a long knife from a sheath on his belt, scratched his long nose with the tip of it, and then scowled as if thinking hard. Then I saw a rifle leaning against the wall behind him. *Holy Moly,* I thought, *that's a Browning Automatic Rifle. He was the one popping off rounds at me and Louis.* Then my thoughts returned to Dad. *Where is he?* I wondered, *and where is this Chance?*

I felt the hair rising on my neck just then, and at the same moment Jake growled deep and menacing. "Quiet," I said to him softly. "They'll hear you." Jake didn't stop entirely, but instead went to growling deep in his throat. I knew something was wrong, and my mind zipped through possibilities trying to figure out what. I studied the two men carefully, knowing they couldn't see me. I spooked a little when one glanced in my direction. *Did he sense something? No.* He went back to his cards, and I knew he only saw his own reflection in the window. Both these fellas looked rough, but neither looked like the man Mary had described seeing in the Angel's Perch. No eye patch for one thing, and no scar for another. They had glasses and a whiskey bottle between them, but the bottle was nearly full, so they weren't drunk. I looked about the room carefully and finally satisfied myself that my father was nowhere to be seen. *Where was he? Locked in a bedroom maybe?*

Then, somehow, I knew what was wrong and why the hair was still standing up on the back of my neck. I had wasted valuable seconds. Jake was still growling, and that meant danger. I turned slowly, very slowly, to my right and my heart jumped. In the shadows beyond the window, almost invisible in the dark, a man sat in a chair tilted back against the wall. He wore a slouch hat tipped down low.

"That's a large dog," he said in a deep, rich voice. He leaned forward then and brought the chair down quietly on four legs. In his right hand he held a revolver, and it was aimed right at me. My heart sank.

"Why don't you take a seat," he said motioning with the gun.

I set my rifle against the window trim and then sat down at a small table next to the railing.

"Light that lamp," he said. I took a match from a box on the table and struck it. I lifted the glass chimney off the kerosene lamp, lit the wick, and replaced the glass.

"Why, you're just a boy," he said. I didn't say anything. Jake was still growling.

"Does he bite?" the man asked. I smiled, but then he added, "because I'd hate to shoot such a fine animal." Still, I said nothing.

"You're not real talkative are you?" he asked. "What's your name son? Maybe you can tell me that."

"Otter," I replied. I couldn't see too well with the lamp right in front of my face, but I could have sworn that his head turned suddenly, and he looked more directly at me. That was when I saw the eye patch. It was Chance!

"Say that again," he demanded.

"My name is Otter," I said.

"What are you doing here?" he asked. Before I could answer, a voice spoke from behind the man.

"He's looking for somebody, mister." The man across from me turned his head and saw the silhouette of a figure standing on the porch fifteen feet behind him.

"Careful now," the figure said. "I've got a Savage in my hands, and I don't miss from this distance. Take your pistol by the barrel and hand it to the boy real slow."

"Granddad! 'Bout time you showed up," I whispered cheerfully. I took the man's gun, and then I went back to the window and grabbed my rifle.

"I see that. What are they doing inside, Otter?" he asked softly.

"They're still playing cards," I whispered. Then I turned back to the man in the chair. "Now, mister," I asked, "where is Royal St. Onge?"

"That's something I've been wondering about myself," said the man.

"You're Chance, aren't you?" I asked.

"Some call me by that name."

"Mister, we don't have time for games. Royal St. Onge is my father. Are you holding him prisoner? If you know where he is, you'd better tell me. I mean *now*."

"I wish I could, son. I wish I could."

"Just a minute," interrupted Granddad. "Take a seat at that table, mister. Real easy now. I want to see your face." The man sat down across from me, and the lamplight shone on his face.

"Take off your hat," ordered Granddad.

I don't know quite how to tell this part. I looked at Chance, this gangster we had been chasing so hard, this ruthless character who had shot at Louis and me, and then I looked at Granddad. Granddad's expression mirrored what I felt—shock and disbelief. The man had been handsome once. Now his face was disfigured by a jagged scar that ran from the black patch over his left eye to his mouth and down his chin. I found myself staring. Whoever had sewn him up hadn't done a very good job.

But as bad as Chance looked, it wasn't the scar that caused me to stare at him in disbelief. Suddenly, in the flickering light of the lamp, I recognized him. He was the man in uniform whose picture I had memorized, who I had last seen at the age of eight. Chance's real name was Royal St. Onge. Sitting before us, looking like half a grinning devil and half a handsome soldier, was my father.

"Royal!" exclaimed Granddad. "It *is* you!"

My father didn't speak but only sat at the table, staring at me, studying *my* face. "Oui," he said finally, "what's left of me."

CHAPTER 10

The Doozies

YOU COULD HAVE KNOCKED ME OVER with a butterfly wing. *Give me my daily bread and dunk it in gravy!* I thought. *My father!* I forgot about being a tough guy, and I hugged him hard. He hugged me, and I was laughing and firing questions at him like a machine gun, and we just stood there like a couple boxers in a clinch, and then we finally broke apart. He stepped back and looked at me curiously.

"Otter, you're not a pup any more are you? I think you just broke a rib," he said. He smiled, but his smile was twisted by the scar and didn't look much like a smile. "I'm glad to see you."

"What happened, Dad?" I asked. "Why didn't you come home?"

"A guy named Corbin Lenoir was one reason. And your mother."

"Mom?"

"Look at my face, Otter. I know your mother would

have taken me back, but I didn't want to ask her. I could play Frankenstein's monster, and I wouldn't need make-up. I can't ask your mother for something so hard to give, son. I can't walk through her door now, out of the blue, and ruin whatever life she's made, but I've missed her so. How is she? Is she all right?"

Break my heart into more pieces than Humpty Dumpty! He doesn't know Mom is dead. How in the name of hard luck am I going to tell him? I wondered. I couldn't, and I guess Granddad knew it.

"Royal, have a swig of this," he said handing Dad his flask of Moonbeam. Dad stared at him.

"What happened, Amos?"

"Just have a drink first." Dad knew right then it was serious. He took the flask and drank. He handed it back to Granddad who took a swig himself.

"I don't know how to tell you this, Royal. Sweet is gone. She was up in Halifax, Nova Scotia just after the war when the troopships were bringing the boys home. She caught the Spanish flu and passed away."

"Why did she go to Halifax?" asked Dad.

Granddad looked away for a moment and then turned back to Dad. "She was looking for you," he said.

Dad didn't answer. He blew out the kerosene lantern and left us all in the shadows. Granddad sat down with Dad and me. We gazed into the darkness where the waves of the lake rolled toward us. When they met the shore, they said *hush, hush.* The rain drummed on the porch roof, and I felt troubled like I had at the Hotel Champlain. I thought maybe the rain was bad luck, that it was building toward a misfortune, but maybe I was just worried about Dad.

We sat like that for a long time and didn't speak. The coming dawn sorted itself into shades of gray, into shapes that almost looked like things we knew. Trees appeared and disappeared in the mist like ghosts. We glimpsed a dark bird passing the mouth of the cove, flying fast, a cormorant prob'ly. Its wing beats whispered to us in a dark language. Still, no one said a word. Finally, so slowly I wasn't even sure when it happened, a gray light snuck around from the east side of the island. It was weak, no match for the rain and the endless stretch of cloud that hung low over the lake, but it signaled the dawn. The limbo of darkness and silence lifted. A new day was begun. Dad rose from his chair.

"Well, why don't you two come in and meet a couple of my friends," he said.

"Now there's a good notion," said Granddad. "Let's get in out of the cold and damp. After all the chasing around we've done in the last twelve hours, I feel like I've been to China and back. Wet too. I've never seen it rain like this. Can we pull a couple chairs up to the fire and wangle some breakfast?"

"Sure. Come on in and we'll fry up some bacon and eggs." Inside, we stood over the two card players who

were now sleeping by a dying fire. The white-haired man
was sprawled on an overstuffed couch. He was lean and
rangy, tall until you compared him to his companion.
The Scotsman, with his tam o' shanter and unruly red
hair, was snoring contentedly and sleeping as soundly
as the Cyclops after he had feasted on the sailors of
Odysseus. Stretched at length by the hearth like the
entire country of Russia, he was formidable. I didn't
think to ever find another man such as Too Tall on God's
green earth, but I was learning just how narrow was my
acquaintance with the wide world. The Scotsman's head
was turned to the side, and he breathed in and out like
a mighty bellows. Dust motes fluttered about his nose.
A fleck from this small storm was pulled back into his
great lungs, and he stuttered and snorted like an engine
about to stall. Then he smoothed again to a steady roar.
My father bumped him gently with his boot and spoke to
both men.

"Angus, Lucien, this is my son Otter and my father-in-
law, Amos Waters."

Lucien, the man with the white hair, opened his eyes
and rose from the couch, awake almost at once. Angus,
continued to snore but no longer on all cylinders.

"Well, isn't this a surprise!" said Lucien, rubbing his
eyes. "Bienvenue. Welcome. Otter, is it? Lucien Renard.
Pleased to meet you. Royal always claimed he had a
son, but I thought you were just another one of his tall
tales. Amos? The pleasure's mine. Are you hungry, mes

amis? Sit down," he said, pulling out a couple chairs from the table. "We'll brew a pot of coffee and make some breakfast. I'll get Boyce first." He stopped at the door. "Did you talk with him on the way up from the dock?"

"Otter did. About your friend, Boyce," Granddad said a mite sheepishly. "We thought to find some desperadoes here, and I had to knock the poor fellow on the noggin. I hope he doesn't have too bad a headache when he comes to."

"Don't worry. We'll put a shot of Robbie's whiskey in his coffee and give him a good breakfast. That'll revive him." Lucien smiled and left. Angus was awake now too.

"Weel, lad," he said to me. "I ken ye and yer grandda must be stairved. Sit doon! Sit doon. Dreepin ye are, and cauld ye must be too. We'll git ye some hot tatties, and ye'll feel better." He took slabs of bacon from the icebox and laid them in a skillet Dad had already moved to the hot part of the cookstove. They sizzled instantly, and the wonderful smell filled the kitchen. Minutes later he put the bacon on a plate, moved it to the back of the stove to stay warm, and broke two dozen eggs into the bubbling fat. He also started a pot of coffee, warmed up some leftover hash browns, and cut thick slices of bread for toast. Breakfast was ready when Lucien returned with a befuddled Boyce. The poor fellow was none too chipper, and he cast baleful glances at Granddad and me.

Dad helped Angus get all that good food on the table, and the lot of us tucked into the meal with great appetite. We talked with Dad and his friends between mouthfuls. They had met in France, and the four of them had fought together at the Somme and then at Vimy Ridge. I still didn't understand why Dad hadn't come home, but I guessed that he would get to the story in his own time.

Boyce said we had enough eggs to give Jake one, so I dropped one in a bowl, and the great wolf dog lapped it up in one gulp. Then he moseyed down to the beach to see if a dead fish might have washed ashore. Granddad apologized to Boyce for konking him on the head, but Boyce only grunted. Then Lucien tried to coax his pal into conversation and a better humor.

"Amos tells me he's a farmer, Boyce," he said. "Has a small herd of Jerseys. Aren't they the ones that give such rich, creamy milk?"

Boyce was gazing at us with an understandably hurt expression, but now he seemed to thaw a little. "I would have guessed he was a Mic Mac hockey player the way he hit me with that stick," he said. "I've got a bump on my brow big enough to make me two-headed. Every time you say something, Lucien, feels like my head's in a bell, and you're ringin' it."

"Boyce," said Lucien, "that's good! Amos prob'ly jarred a couple ideas loose, and you're hearing them rolling around in there, bumping into each other. That's something you're not used to, mon ami. No wonder your head feels funny. It's nothing a good breakfast won't cure. Drink your coffee and forget about the ringing in your head. Wolf those eggs down and you'll be frisky as a pup in no time." Turning to Granddad and me, he continued. "Boyce grew up on a farm, and all he ever talks about is owning a herd of cows, marrying, and raising a passel of kids. Me, I was a locksmith in Quebec before I joined the Van Doos. I want nothing to do with getting up before dawn to milk and do chores."

"The Van Doos?" I asked.

"The Vingt-deux—if you parlez Français—the Twenty-second Infantry, the only regiment of Frenchies in the Canadian Army. The Anglos called us the Van Doos. Because the four of us gained a certain reputation with the Twenty-second, the brass at Vimy Ridge called us the Doozies. We raided the enemy trenches. There were five of us then," Lucien glanced at my father when he said this.

"Were you one of the Doozies, Mr. MacAskill?" I asked.

Angus smiled good-naturedly. "Aye, that I was, lad," he said. "My mither's name was Parenteau." By this time Angus was mopping up the remains of six runny egg yolks with a slice of toast. He was almost as tall as my Uncle Hercule, and he was bull-necked, broad shouldered and barrel-chested. I had heard that a man like Angus, with his long red hair and bushy red beard, was likely to be hot-tempered. His smile and the funny tam perched on top of his huge head made me doubt that, but if he ever got angry, I didn't want to be in his way. I could as easily stop a rutting elephant as slow him down one whit. I was still marveling at this giant when my father spoke.

"How did you find us, Amos?" he asked.

"To boil it down," replied Granddad, "blind luck led us to the Angel's Perch, and Otter's new girlfriend led us to the Hotel Champlain. At the hotel landing, Otter captured a fellow named Muff, and Muff led us here."

"That was you at the hotel?" asked my father. "The devil it was! Did any of your men get hurt?"

"Well, your nephew Little Roy got a good thump on his brainbox, but otherwise we're fine."

"You mean that big galoot Angus knocked out was Little Roy?" asked Dad.

"The one and only. Louis was shooting at you from the building on the wharf. Hercule was up at the hotel with Otter and me. We thought this fellow Chance we'd been hearing about was a hijacker who'd kidnapped you and the *Thorpedo* back on Goose Bay. We were trying to track him down to rescue you."

"Can you believe we didn't all kill each other, Royal?" exclaimed Lucien. "What a tangle? Muff's all right too then?" he asked, turning back to Granddad.

"Yut. We did a little fishing with Muff—strictly speaking, he was the bait—and he almost ended up like the biblical Jonah, but we saved him before that came to pass. He didn't want to tell us where you were, but Champ scared the bejeekers out of him. He looked a little frayed afterward, but I don't think he's really any worse for the wear. Course, his mind's never been a Swiss watch has it?"

Dad grinned. "I want to hear about your fishing exploits later, but I'm glad he's okay. Life's a muddle for him sometimes, but Muff's a good boy. I'm glad he's alive. We saw him drop and thought he took a bullet."

"He took a baseball bat," I said.

"What do you mean?" asked Dad.

"I'll tell you later, Dad, but first, would you answer a few questions for me? You've been gone for eleven years, and my curiosity is building a head of steam."

"Fair enough, Otter. What do you want to know?"

"Everything," I said. "I want to know what happened to you after you left me and Mom at the farm."

He sat back and pulled a pack of Gauloises from his shirt pocket. He lit one and blew a smoke ring toward the ceiling. The rain had picked up, and now it thrummed steadily again on the roof of cedar shingles. Angus had built up the fire to drive off the damp. If we hadn't wanted so badly to know the story of why Royal St. Onge hadn't come home, Granddad and I would have fallen asleep, I'm sure, but we were wide awake, both of us sipping from a second, steaming cup of coffee. Jake had come back from the lake, scratched at the door and now lay at full length on a rug before the fire. He breathed out contentedly and the rank odor of dead fish wafted to my nose. Dad grinned, but with the scar, his expression was half impish, half ghoulish. He was still looking up into the rafters, following the smoke from his cigarette.

"Well," he said, "If you want to hear that story, it's a good thing we have all day." He said nothing more but continued to stare at the smoke curling upward. I was tempted to drum my fingers on the arm of my chair, but bless my stars and garters, I had enough sense to be quiet. Demons were trying to disorder his mind, no doubt, and he needed time to lock them away. When he had settled himself, he began.

"THE VAN DOOS WERE MUSTERED RIGHT IN my home town of St. Jean, and I joined in 1916. We trained in Quebec for a few weeks, but the French needed us so badly, our training was cut short, and the bigwigs put us on troopships. We arrived in time for the Battle of the Somme. For many of us, new and young and green, the war was a great adventure, *the* great adventure. It didn't take long to find out what a fool's idea that was.

There were no gallant cavalry charges with valiant men fighting hand-to-hand. We wallowed in the mud like pigs. We saw rats feed on corpses and felt them scurry over our faces when we lay down to sleep. The moaning minnies and the whiz-bangs gobbled us up by the hundreds. When those infernal bombs hit the trenches, blood and bits of body flew everywhere, and if the bombs didn't kill us, we died of trench fever or went crazy from shell shock and fear.

At the Somme, that thick-headed Haig thought if he threw enough troops against the German machine guns, they'd finally clog the barrels. That's how bright he was. So many men died on October 25th, the troops called it the Day of Death. I wish Haig had tried to make a run across No Man's Land himself. They called him the Butcher of the Somme, not because of what he did to the Jerrys, but because of what he did to his own men. He should have been hung on razor wire and used for bayonet practice. Canadian boys dropped by the thousands! The bodies piled up like cordwood, and for what? For nothing! The line moved a little this way or that, and then we sat in the trenches for a few more months waiting to get blown apart by a stray bomb or hit by a sniper.

So the great adventure turned into the great nightmare. We reached Vimy Ridge in time for Christmas—such as it was. Vimy was General Julian Byng's show. Bingo Byng, we called him. I'm not much for generals, but he, at least, was blessed with a brain. He cared about his soldiers, and he wasn't one, such as Haig was, to line them up like dominoes in front of machine guns if he could find a better way. Five months later, during the Battle of Vimy Ridge, he did. They called it the "creeping barrage." They set the cannons blasting early one April morning in 1917. The Canadians marched right behind the cannon fire, a hundred yards every three minutes, tickety-tock, and when they reached the trenches, the Germans had either been blasted to smithereens or were caught off guard and shot like woodchucks coming out of their holes.

But that attack didn't come until spring. All through the winter we prepared. By the time we reached Vimy, I was sick of spending all my time in the trenches eyeballing rats and gagging on bully beef. When the Van Doos brass asked for volunteers to raid the German trenches, I signed up. If I was going to die, I wanted to die shooting at Jerry, not hunkered down in a ditch waiting to be blown apart by one of his coal boxes."

"Coal boxes?" I said.

"Yut. They were artillery shells that belched black smoke when they blew up. Moaning minnies were mortar rounds. They wailed something awful on their way down. Whiz-bangs were smaller caliber rounds from field guns. They zipped into the trenches like mad bees and tore up whatever they hit.

Anyway, I took the bull by the horns and told Villy— Captain Roland Villier, my officer commanding—that I would head up a raiding party. Villy was an eccentric, scrawny character who strutted like a banty rooster and managed to look like a spit and polish officer even in the trenches. He screeched and stammered when he addressed the men, and sometimes seemed on the verge of a fit, but they didn't snicker behind his back. They loved him. He had read every book written on military strategy since Caesar's *Gallic Wars,* could explain the mysteries of trigonometry and calculus, was a walking encyclopedia of modern weaponry, a master mapmaker, and not least of all, was as shrewd as a gypsy horse trader in his dealings with superior officers, quartermasters, and anyone else who might affect the safety of his troops. His men respected his brilliance and loved him for using it to keep them alive.

I had earned a sergeant's stripes at the Somme, and Villier was happy to have me scout behind the German lines. 'You can pick four men to go with you,' he said. 'Bring me the locations of the German guns, their dugouts and tunnels, their ammo dumps, anything you find, and I will put them on maps. Next spring, during the Big Push, McNaughton's gunners will fire on the exact coordinates of Jerry's artillery and machine guns, and for once, most of our men will reach the enemy's front line without being put through a sausage grinder.'

"These fellas," said my father, "Lucien Renard, Boyce Goudreau, and Angus MacAskill went with me. So did Chance Tatro." He drew on his cigarette again, and when he didn't continue, Lucien spoke in his stead.

"Chance died on our last raid. It was Easter weekend, and les hasards de la guerre—the fortunes of war—turned against us. Chance died and so did a man named Jacques

Lenoir. That's why Corbin Lenoir is looking for your father today."

"What happened?" I asked. I looked to my dad, but he was staring into the fire, and I think he was seeing horrors in the flames. I waited. Finally, he continued.

"In March and April of 1917 the Doozies raided the German trenches many times. We'd crawl back across No Man's Land before dawn, and Villy would mark his maps with what we'd found. Then he'd give us passes, and we'd doubletime it through the Lichfield or Goodman subways to the rear.

The subways were tunnels we used to travel back and forth between the trenches and the staging areas without being hit by a sniper's bullet or one of Jerry's howitzers. Once out of the subway, we'd hitch a ride with a truck driver to Mont St. Eloi or the Château de la Haie to sleep in a real bed and maybe even get something decent to eat.

As Lucien mentioned, time passed and our reputation grew legendary. Villy was astonished that we kept coming back from raid after raid, and all the more so because we kept bringing him good information. He was so happy with what we told him about the Jerrys, he gave us our nickname. 'Vous êtes les Doozies. You are Doozies,' he said and then cackled at his own joke.

We were on such a raid the night we first met the Crows. They were trench raiders too, attached to the Fifth Brigade, and they too had a reputation—for brutality.

They were called the Crows because they picked over the dead—and the not-so-dead. They took German helmets, insignia, sheath knives—whatever was worth money and easy to carry—and they sold them to collectors. Their O.C. turned a blind eye. I'm not sure why. Maybe it was because—whatever else the Crows did—they still brought back the information they were sent to get. Maybe the O.C. was scared of them.

The sergeant commanding the Crows was Corbin Lenoir. Before the war, he lived on Cadieux Street in Montreal, a part of town running over with whores and hoodlums. He worked for a gangster named Nicodemo Cotroni. The way I heard it, when the cops arrested him for cutting a prostitute, they gave Lenoir a choice of going to prison or enlisting in the army, so that was how he ended up at Vimy Ridge. He wasn't a big man, but he was strong for his size, and quick. He was also as twisted as a pretzel.

Lenoir's Crows were given a mission behind enemy lines on Easter. As it happened, so were the Doozies. At midnight, the Crows were to bomb the Bavarian Reserves' headquarters in the village of Vimy on the other side of the ridge. At the same time, the Doozies were to cut the telegraph line and blow up the railroad tracks a few miles east of the town. Villy didn't tell us *why* we had to do any of this, but he did say it was crucial. I figured it could only be for one reason—so Fritz couldn't bring up reinforcements from Lens once

we started the battle to retake Vimy Ridge. We got our
assignment the day after Good Friday while we were
resting at the Château de la Haie.

As it turned out, that was to be our last raid before
the Push. I'm sure Villy didn't tell us that because if we
were caught, the brass didn't want the Boche to know
the hour of attack. We knew the Push was coming, and
so did the Boche. On April 2nd McNaughton's artillery
crews had doubled their shelling, and four days later the
big guns were still firing at that rate when we met with
Villier. It was as clear as a bug under a microscope. Old
Bingo was getting ready for the attack. We just didn't
know exactly when the attack would happen.

McNaughty, as we called him, was in charge of all the
big guns. College boy, he was, and maybe the smartest
man at Vimy. He had spent the last four months sighting
in our cannon and locating the Jerrys. He put spotters
up in balloons and planes, and on the ground. They
looked through binoculars for the muzzle flashes of the
Boche artillery, they listened for Boche cannon fire with
microphones, and they took pictures from heavy cameras
mounted on planes. They also used information gathered
by trench raiders like us. Then they ciphered with their
pencils and formulas. When the battle began, McNaughty
knew where to aim every Canadian gun. On the day
after Easter, when all four of our divisions attacked Vimy
Ridge, he demolished Jerry's artillery just like Villy said
he would.

But when Captain Villier told us about our little mission, the Big Push hadn't happened yet. Our job, he said, was to find and destroy the railroad track and the telegraph line. If we accomplished that, we were to stay behind enemy lines and wreak as much havoc as possible. We were to leave that night.

'If you can't get the job done and get back Sunday night, go to the Goulot Wood southwest of Vimy and hide. McNaughty is going to soften up the Thelus sector Monday and Tuesday, and the Push will come some time after that. You don't want to be making your way back to the Van Doos when McNaughty's boys shell the Thelus Wood. We'd be lucky to bury your brass buttons.'

By the time we left that evening, we had another mission, one we assigned ourselves. If we could, we would rescue a pilot. Just before sunset we watched a dogfight take place over Vimy Ridge and the Douai Plain. Six of our flyboys were escorting a B.E.2 recon plane back to Filescamp Aerodrome. The two-seater lumbered along like a great blue heron, big and steady but awful slow, and he needed those fighter pilots for protection. The B.E.2 was taking pictures, no doubt, for McNaughty.

We watched the planes from the lawn of the Château de la Haie, and we envied those flyboys soaring amongst the puffy clouds, looking down on us Canucks mired in mud and filth. We shouldn't have envied them too much. Those clouds weren't as innocent as they looked.

Four German Albatros suddenly swooped down from those clouds like hawks after chickens in the barnyard. We could hear the *rat-a-tat-tat* of Jerry's machine guns, and we watched our boys scatter. I quickly focused my field glasses, and I don't mind telling you—I was agog. It was the German ace, Baron von Richthofen, and his flying circus. Those flyboys swooped and dove like barn swallows, and did everything but turn somersaults to catch each other or escape. Always they jockeyed to get on the other guy's tail and drive some slugs up his backside.

Our fighter pilots were holding their own, but the fellow in the B.E.2 was in trouble. One of the Jerrys had stayed in the clouds, but now he dropped a wing, streaked down at dizzying speed, and closed in on the spotter plane. That Canuck was an awful good pilot, but twist and turn as he would, he couldn't escape the Albatros. It was only a matter of time until Jerry got him in his sights. In desperation, the Canadian dropped the nose of his B.E.2 and dove. I held my breath. That boy headed straight down, falling from the sky like a rebel star. The German followed, and soon he was close enough to fire. We heard him let loose with a burst from his twin Spandaus, and I could have sworn I saw the B.E.2's observer slump in his seat behind the pilot.

Then we saw a welcome sight. Just as Jerry fired again, a Nieuport Scout won his duel with another plane and came to the rescue. Within seconds he was

hard on the German's tail, shooting his Vickers gun.
It was Billy Bishop, our best pilot, and he peppered
that Albatros. We knew it was Billy from the trademark
blue paint on the nose of the Scout. The Jerry swerved
and darted, and forgot all about the spotter plane, but
he couldn't shake Bishop. Billy fired again, and when
Fritzie banked hard to the left, Billy led him with the
Vickers. The Albatros caught fire and exploded in
midair. Meanwhile, the B.E.2 had pulled out of the
vertical dive, but the pilot was still in trouble. We could
hear his engine sputtering, and then it died. The last we
saw of him, he was gliding east, skimming the treetops
of Vimy Ridge and prob'ly hoping to reach a farmer's
field on the Douai Plain.

 'Well, if we're going to be in the neighborhood
anyway,' said Chance, 'we might as well look for the
poor fellow.'

 'Oui,' I agreed. And so we added a rescue attempt to our
itinerary.

BY LATE AFTERNOON WE HAD PACKED our kits
and were hurrying up the Lichfield Subway to one of
the jumping-off trenches the boys had just dug into
No Man's Land. We had a shot of rum with some of
our friends in the Van Doos, and then we cleaned our
pistols, rubbed burnt cork on our faces, and waited
for dark. An hour after sunset, we were on our bellies
cutting through barbed wire and wriggling toward the

enemy trenches. I led the way, crawling twenty yards at a time and signaling Chance to move everybody up at intervals.

I had just reached an enormous bomb crater when a cloud drifted away from the full moon rising over Vimy Ridge. In the ghostly light, I saw a figure at the bottom of the crater and recognized Corbin Lenoir. He crouched over a Jerry who was sprawled lifeless on the ground. Corbin was about to chop off the man's ring finger with his bayonet. He wanted the man's wedding ring, but the finger was so swollen, he couldn't pull it off. Then I saw the German turn his head. He was still alive. I drew my service revolver.

'Lenoir,' I whispered. He peered up at me in surprise.

'St. Onge,' he replied. 'What do you want?'

'Wait.' I skittered down the side of the crater and stood six feet away with my revolver in plain view. I looked at the German. He had been hit by shrap in the stomach, and with his free hand, he was trying to keep his insides from spilling out. He looked at me like a dog about to be put down.

'Water,' he begged.

'Put your bayonet away, Lenoir, and give him some water.'

'St. Onge,' he said, 'the great hero, St. Onge. The bold and daring St. Onge who steals through No Man's Land night after night and picks Fritzie's pockets and goes home again with all Fritzie's secrets. What do you

care about *this* Fritzie, St. Onge? You think he is your
business? Why?'

'Just put the bayonet away and give him some water.'

'Or what?' asked Lenoir.

'Or I'll put a bullet in you and leave *you* for the Crows.'

'You do that, and you might get the attention of Fritzie's
friends.'

'I'll take the chance.' Corbin Lenoir looked down at the
wounded soldier and then at me again.

'All right, St. Onge. I didn't know you liked Fritzie so
much. To me he's food for the rats, but I guess you've got a
soft spot for him, eh St. Onge?'

'You've got a soft spot in your head, Lenoir. For the
last time, put your bayonet away and give him your
canteen.'

'Bon, St. Onge. Très bon. You outrank me with that pop
gun. Sure, I'll give him water. I hope he chokes on it.' He
reached for the canteen at his belt but grabbed a sheath
knife instead. In the shadowy crater, I had no warning
until his hand snapped toward me like a striking cobra. I
dodged. The knife sliced my tunic and opened a wound in
my shoulder.

Lenoir whirled, raised his bayonet, and brought it
down on the German's left hand. He severed four fingers,
grabbed the one with the ring, and raced up the side
of crater. The Jerry screamed. I steadied my pistol with
both hands and saw Lenoir in my sights, but I couldn't
bring myself to fire on another Canuck. I've regretted it

ever since. Lenoir called from just beyond the rim of the pit, and I realized with a cold chill running up my spine that if he decided to use his own gun, I was a sitting duck.

'Beware the Crows, St. Onge! They'll peck out your eyes and eat your innards. Look for me, St. Onge,' he cried. 'I'll be looking for you.' Then, *caw-cawing* like a demented bird, he disappeared into the darkness. Meanwhile, the Jerry moaned in agony, and blood gushed from his maimed hand. Once more he begged for water, and I gave him a swallow from my canteen. He drank and then stared at me, pleading, too weak to move. I nodded. Just then Chance called softly from the crater rim.

'What in the name of the Holy Pope is going on, Royal?' he asked.

'Bring up the others as soon as it's safe,' I replied, 'but keep them spread out in case Jerry's machine gunners wake up. Then look for me up ahead.'

'Bien,' said Chance. Then he vanished. I turned away from the German and pulled my own knife from its sheath. It was razor sharp. 'May God have mercy on us both,' I whispered, and I quickly cut his throat. I crawled out of that crater and inched my way forward with a sick feeling in my gut. Clouds covered the moon again. Every twenty yards I signaled Chance and the others to move up. An hour later I heard two Boche soldiers talking softly and saw the barrel of their machine gun poking through the slit of a first line bunker. I was congratulating myself on reaching Fritzie without being seen when a small rocket hissed into the night sky. One of Fritzie's buddies had fired a flare directly overhead. Suddenly, No Man's Land glowed with an eerie, red light, and all was visible. I froze. And then I waited for machine gun bullets to tear me apart.

CHAPTER 11

The Raid

C HANCE, ANGUS, BOYCE, AND LUCIEN lay as quiet as corpses behind me. None of us breathed. None of us moved a hair. Five seconds passed. Ten seconds. Twenty. Then the flare burned out, and the wavering red light faded into darkness. Praise the saints, Otter, they didn't see us. I raised my head slowly and looked at the sky. In a minute, maybe two, the moon would reappear. Chance touched my ankle and crawled forward without a word. Then we wormed our way together. When the two Germans talked, we slithered through the mud, and when they didn't, we stopped. Just as the clouds revealed a crescent of moon, we slid silently into the trench and surprised the two Jerries in the bunker.

We killed them both, I'm sorry to say. I know it was war and we couldn't take the chance of knocking them out and having them raise an alarm later. Still, jamming a knife up under a man's breastbone as he stares you in the eye and chokes on his own blood isn't what I like to dream about at night. Up close like that is a lot worse than shooting into a clot of soldiers storming toward your trench across No Man's Land. When that happens, you don't really know if you killed somebody or not. I'll always regret that boy's death, and I'll always remember his face.

Anyway, that is war, and there was no choice. By then, Angus and the others were on our heels. They made short work of the four Jerrys who heard the scuffle and appeared from around a dogleg in the trench. We yanked off their boots, stole their trousers and tunics, and clapped on their helmets. We knew we'd be shot if the Jerries found us in German uniforms, but we had to take the risk. Soon, we found a tunnel with a signpost pointing to Les Tilleuls and followed it toward Fritzie's second line of trenches.

As the night passed, we climbed toward the crest of Vimy Ridge. After we put Les Tilleuls behind us, we only met with the occasional sentry, and most of those never saw us. Twice we were challenged. Lucien and Chance both spoke German fluently, and in the dark we managed to fool Fritzie into thinking we were fellow soldiers of the Kaiser. Just before dawn we started down the east side of Vimy Ridge and slipped into Goulot Wood.

At the foot of a rock outcrop, we found a small clearing in the trees and hunkered down for the day. Before it was light enough to see the smoke, Boyce lit a fire and heated a pot of water. We broke our fast with oatmeal and tea. Then the others dozed while I stood the first watch. It wasn't long before the sun rose over the Douai Plain in a sky as pink

as the stripes on a rainbow trout. I didn't know if it was a
beautiful sight or a bad omen. I looked to the east and saw
fields sparkling with dew. The grass was sprouting, and in
the islands of forest that dotted the plain, hardwoods were
unfolding new leaves. Where were the blackened spikes of
bombed trees we were used to seeing? Everywhere I looked
was a shimmering plain, green with new life instead of gray
with mud and death. It made me think of home.

I saw farmhouses and barns shining like gold in the
morning sun. I saw the villages of La Chaudière, Vimy,
and Farbus with their church steeples still standing. At
my feet, I saw forget-me-nots and violets in bloom. You
can't imagine what a welcome sight that was, Otter! The
mud and muck of the Front, the corpses and the stench
had vanished. For the first time in months the air felt truly
warm, and I thought that spring might come after all. A
sense of peace hung over the plain like a mirage.

The sun rose higher and higher, and with a pair
of binoculars slung from my neck, I scrambled to the
top of the outcrop and climbed a tall oak while the
Doozies napped below me. I trained the field glasses
on the scene below, and at the foot of the ridge I spied
a railway embankment. Following the rail line north to
the village of Vimy, I saw gray-coated soldiers—Fritzie's
reserves. Three men cleaned a howitzer at the south
end of the village. Two other Jerries stood guard at the
town's railway station. They stood next to a machine
gun surrounded by sand bags. From the station, the

train tracks led off to the east toward the city of Lille. I followed that line out of town until I came to a sight that made me grin. On a siding was a flatbed railcar, and on that car was a piece of artillery. A couple soldiers were stockpiling ammunition for it, and by the look of the shells they were carrying, I guessed it to be a 12-inch siege gun—a Big Bertha. Also on the siding were two cars being used as barracks by the gun crew. I studied Jerry's camp. Maybe fifty men. I knew it wouldn't be easy with so many troops around, but I wanted to blow that gun. If we could detonate the artillery shells, we could knock out the supply trains and the gun. 'Wreak havoc,' Villy said. Yes, that would do. With the glasses, I searched the railway for landmarks I'd recognize later and made a mental note of the woods a quarter mile down the train track between Vimy and the Big Bertha. 'We'll see,' I whispered. 'We'll see.'

As I continued to study the plain east of Vimy, I saw a farmer plowing a field. He had a team of handsome Belgians, and he was leaving good, straight furrows. In a corner of the field far from the road that bounded its western edge, I saw something curious. In a low spot at the edge of the woods, and prob'ly out of sight of the road, was a big pile of brush. I supposed, at first, that the farmer had been trimming the edge of the field. Something about it struck me funny, though, and then I realized what it was. If the farmer was keeping the woods from invading the field, why did he go to the trouble of hauling all the brush to one spot? Why didn't he just drag the limbs into the woods right where he cut them? As I was about to give up on the answer and shift the glasses away from that corner, I saw a spot of blue in that brush pile. I sharpened the focus of the glasses, and Otter, what did I see hidden beneath those new-cut tops but a glimpse of paint on the tail flap of a plane. I was sure of it. *How about that,* I said to myself. *It's the two-seater we watched disappear over the ridge yesterday.*

A couple hours later, when Chance stood watch, he put the glasses on it and agreed. It had to be a plane and prob'ly the one we had seen the day before. The pilot must have landed it, and if he had camouflaged it, he must be alive.

'But,' I asked, 'where is he?'

'In the woods near the plane?' replied Chance.

'Could be. But here's my guess. He needed help when he landed. I'm pretty sure his observer was hit. He might hide in the woods and wait for the Push, but he doesn't know when that's going to come. What if it doesn't happen for a week?'

'It'd be pretty risky to do anything else.'

'Yut. It would. But what if the engine in that crate is fixable? Maybe the pilot went to see the French farmer I saw plowing that field earlier today, and maybe that farmer doesn't like Heinie firing Big Berthas and scaring his cattle day after day. Maybe that farmer has some tools that could repair a plane, or maybe the farmer's wife is good with a needle and thread and could be persuaded to sew up a bullet wound.'

'Lot of maybes,' said Chance.

'You're right about that,' I said.

'Come nightfall, we've got a lot of work to do.'

'Right about that too.'

WE SNUCK INTO VIMY A COUPLE HOURS after dark. With our Jerry uniforms, we passed through the streets without attracting notice. Lucien, Boyce, and Angus nosed about town looking for the Jerry's ammo dump. If they could scrape up more explosives, we'd be supplied for later mischief. When Chance and I arrived at the railroad station, we surprised the two Jerrys on duty by the machine gun nest and knocked them cold. We gagged them, tied their wrists behind their backs, and dragged those boys as far as a shed just beyond the station. Inside, Chance struck a match, and we found what we hoped for—a railroad handcar. We brought it outside and set it on the tracks.

'What do we do with these guys?' he asked.

I pointed to a boxcar on a siding fifty yards down the track. 'We'll load them on the handcar. I'll roll'em down there and tuck'em in. You grab that machine gun and the ammo. We can make good use of that,' I grinned.

I tied the Germans to some rings on the walls of the boxcar, said nighty-night to Fritzie, pumped the handle up and down like a teeter-totter, and rolled the car back to Chance. By the time we set up the machine gun, Angus, Boyce, and Lucien appeared with Angus pushing a wheelbarrow covered with a scrap of canvas.

'We found a machine gun,' said Chance with a smile. 'What did you find?'

Angus looked apologetic. 'Jerry's ammo dump had more sentries than a wee dog has fleas. We couldn't find a way in. But!' he said, suddenly cheerful, 'we did meet a Frenchie who worked in the bloody coal mine nearby. Weel, he hid a cache of amatol when Fritzie rolled in and took over the town.' He swept the tarp off the wheelbarrow and said proudly, 'Look here, lads!'

'That will make a nice bang,' I said. 'Well done.'

'We ain't done yet,' said Boyce.

'Boyce, always your jaw set and your feet on the ground,' said Lucien. 'Live a little, mon ami!'

'Go fry ice, Lucien,' said Boyce.

'No time for squabbling. Climb aboard this chariot,' I said, pointing to the handcar, 'and let's go wreck Big Bertha and the railroad.' We all crowded onto the small platform with our packs, the explosives, and the tripod machine gun, and soon we were riding the rails away from Vimy. After soaking up sunshine all day, we shivered and buttoned up our field jackets. The temperature was dropping, and it felt like a change in weather was on its way. It didn't take us long to get to the woods just west of the Jerry's cannon.

Angus, Chance, and I jumped off the car and trotted

down the railbed on foot. We had twenty minutes, and then Boyce and Lucien would arrive, rolling as slowly and quietly as possible, even pushing the car by hand to muffle the clacking wheels. They would set up the machine gun where they could fire at the barracks if the Boche discovered us and tumbled out of bed with their rifles. But that was a precaution. We had no more intention of waking Jerry than we did of kicking a hornet's nest.

Five minutes after leaving Boyce and Lucien, the three of us crept toward the siding where Fritz kept the Big Bertha. Angus choked the first sentry till the man blacked out. The poor fellow kicked up a couple stones, and that alarmed the other one who turned to look. The sky was overcast, but enough moonlight filtered through the cloud cover for him to spy Angus. He put a whistle to his mouth to sound the alarm, but Chance stepped out of the shadows and clubbed him. Fritzie's eyes rolled up, and he dropped in a heap with the whistle still in his fingers.

Boyce and Lucien showed up on cue. They rolled the handcar along the siding to the pile of shells I had seen the Heinies stacking earlier that afternoon. The five of us loaded as many shells as we could onto the deck of the handcar. We put a charge of amatol in with the shells that remained, and we even put a charge into the breech of the big gun. As quiet as dead men—which we hoped not to be—we rolled the handcar back to the main track and unloaded the hefty, twelve-inch shells. Angus, Boyce, and Chance wired amatol and Big Bertha ammo to several

lengths of track. Lucien and I jammed timbers against
the doors of each of the railcars so the Jerries couldn't get
out. Thanks to the buzz saw snores of some of the soldiers
inside, nobody heard us.

When we finished trapping the Jerries in their
barracks, we found the nearest telegraph pole. Lucien
placed one foot in my clasped hands, climbed onto my
shoulders, and stood. Then he shinnied up the pole and
cut the wire. After that, we rolled the handcar back to
where we could fire on any of the Boche who escaped
through the barracks windows. We set up the stolen
machine gun, and Lucien unlocked the safety and
prepared to fire. I glanced at my watch. It was a quarter to
twelve. At midnight the Crows would blow up the German
headquarters back in Vimy, and we were to set off our
charges at the same time. Angus and Boyce had finished
placing theirs. Fifteen minutes was more than enough
time for Chance to finish with his. Just then, however, we
heard a thunderous explosion in the distance. Glancing
over my shoulder to the west, I saw flashes of light over
Vimy. Bon Sang! The Crows were early.

'Hurry, Chance!' I called. 'That imbecile Lenoir just blew
up the command post in Vimy ahead of schedule! We're
going to have our hands full now! Lucien and Boyce, hustle
your britches!' The Heinies, hearing the explosions, had
already begun yelling inside the railcars and thumping
against the doors. A couple brave and reckless souls dove
out the windows, and Lucien squeezed the trigger of the

machine gun. The gun chattered, the Jerries crumpled, and the others stayed put. Meanwhile, Chance was still placing the last charge of amatol.

'C'mon, Chance!' I hollered. 'Let's get out of here!'

'Don't get your bowels in an uproar!' he answered. 'I've got it.'

As he ran to join the rest of us, we saw a muzzle flash from under the railcar, and Chance dropped. One of the Jerries was still alive. Lucien fired again, sweeping the gun barrel back and forth, raking the area where the Jerry was hiding. I was about to go help Chance, but he was up again and running. He threw himself on the handcar, and Boyce and I began pumping the handles. The Jerry non-com in the rail car must have organized his men at this point because suddenly they were tumbling out of the windows like popcorn jumping out of a pan. Lucien was still firing the machine gun, and Angus added the Browning. Slowly at first, and then faster, we pulled away from the siding and headed back toward Vimy. The Jerries were firing at us now, but they had no time to aim in the hail of our machine gun fire, and their bullets whizzed by without hitting anyone.

As we disappeared into the darkness, Boyce continued to pump away while I rummaged in my pack for a flare. I lit it and threw it as far as I could toward the main track where we had placed the amatol. Then I grabbed the handle again and helped Boyce. 'Blow the charges, Angus!' I yelled. 'Now!' Boyce and I pumped like a couple whirly-

gigs, and the handcar picked up speed as we reached
a downgrade. In the light of the flare, Angus aimed the
Browning gun.

On his second burst, one of the amatol charges exploded
with a tremendous boom. Lucien's machine gun stuttered
as all the Jerries buried their noses in the dirt, and then
the sound of the machine gun was drowned by an erupting
volcano of noise and dirt and twisted steel. The charges
exploded, one after another, and the siding disappeared
in flying debris and billowing smoke. The last glimpse we
had in the light of the dying flare was of two bomb craters
where the main track had been, an overturned Big Bertha
with its barrel split like a pea pod, and a small group of
stupefied Jerries staring after us balefully as we passed
beyond rifle range.

'Are you all right, Chance?' I asked.

'Happy as a cow in clover. That bullet nicked my ear, but
thank God, close only counts in horseshoes.'

'Good. Well boys, I brought a flask of rum just for this
occasion. Have a swig and let's toast the Push. If Bingo
Byng could see those two craters we just blew, I dare say
he might forget himself and find a smile on his face. Let's
see if we can find that pilot now. We'll ride these rails for
a little bit, and then we better get off and saddle shank's
mare. Jerry may have an engine in the roundhouse at
Vimy, and he'll no doubt be coming to see what the big
ruckus was.'

When we reached another downgrade halfway to Vimy,

we braked and slowed. Everybody else jumped off the car, and then I pumped for all I was worth. The trees whizzed by as I reached a curve two hundred yards down the track. I jumped, rolled a couple times, and came to rest in some bushes. The handcar left the rails at the corner and pinwheeled into the puckerbrush where it was hidden from sight. I set off into the woods and rejoined the Doozies under the trees. We hiked toward the side road I had spotted earlier that day. It was less than a mile away, and after walking south on the road for ten minutes, we found the field where I had seen the plane.

We found the pilot too. I was worried that the Boche might ambush us, so we crept up on the plane as quiet as Indians, which I am—at least partly. In spite of that, I suddenly found myself grabbed from behind. An arm locked around my neck, a gun barrel pressed into my back, and a voice whispered in German.

'Allein?'

'No, I'm not alone,' I gasped.

Before the man could ask more questions, Chance spoke from a few feet away.

'We borrowed these Jerry uniforms. Be kind of a shame to kill him, flyboy. We're here to help you.' The man breathed a sigh of relief and let me go.

'Captain John Prince. I'm an American flying with the Sixteenth Squadron, Canadian Expeditionary Force. How in blue blazes did you get here?' he asked.

'Sergeant Royal St. Onge, St. Jean, Quebec, more

recently of the Twenty-second Infantry, CEF. We walked here,' I said with a grin, and I introduced Chance and the rest as they stepped out from behind trees.

'St. Jean!' he said as he shook my hand. 'We're neighbors. I'm from Burlington, Vermont.'

'Well, that's a fluke and a half!'

'It is,' grinned Prince. 'If we ever get back home, we'll have to do some fishing on Champlain.'

'And toast our good luck with a dram of my father-in-law's homemade whiskey,' I said, 'but right now we'd better talk fast. All hell is about to break loose. What's your situation?'

'I had to put this bird down here yesterday. Jim Henderson and I were being escorted back to Filescamp after taking some pictures of Jerry's guns on the east side of the ridge. Richthofen and his pals were waiting for us. One of those Jerrys got behind me, and I couldn't shake him. He shot my gas line clean in two. I was too far away to risk gliding to Filescamp, especially against a headwind, so I had to put down on this side of the ridge.'

'We watched you,' said Chance. 'Bishop got the Heinie that brought you down.'

'Bravo for Billy!' he said. 'At the rate he's going, he might rack up as many kills as Richthofen.'

'How about your spotter?' I interrupted. 'Did he make it?'

The pilot shook his head. 'No,' he said quietly, 'Jim was dead when I landed. I buried him near the plane.' He motioned for me to follow, and we passed beneath the trees

until we reached the dim outline of the brush pile and the
B.E.2.

'Were you good friends?' I asked.

'We flew twenty missions together. You get to know a
man pretty well.'

I nodded, and we let our silence honor his friend. Then I
asked him how we could help.

'I hope to fly out of here at first light,' he said. 'The
farmer who owns this field was plowing it when I landed
yesterday. He's none too fond of Fritzie. His eldest son died
at Verdun last year. When he saw what I needed, he drove
his team home and came back with a shovel, an ax, and a
basket of bread, cheese, and turnips. We cut some brush
and covered the plane, and then he helped me dig a grave
for Jim. He measured my fuel line, and when he went home
later, he was going to roll a piece of copper into a tube,
solder it shut, and bring it back early this morning to mend
the fuel line. I'll wind some wire around the rubber tubing
to make it leak-proof. I've still got fuel in the tank, and if
Fritzie doesn't show up, I should be able to fly that bird
right back across the ridge. Clever old duck, that farmer.
Victor Bachand. What a character, and what good luck for
me that it was his field I landed in.'

'If this Bachand's a decent sort, you've had all the luck
a man could wish for, John. Now, let me tell you how *we*
happen to be here.'

'Does it have anything to do with that explosion I heard
an hour ago?' John was no fool. I quickly told him about

Lenoir blowing up Jerry's headquarters in Vimy and about
the Doozies doing the same to the railroad east of us.

'The Boche will send out patrols to investigate. If you're
going to fly out of here, you'd better do it at first light. The
Push is coming, John. I don't know when, but it'll be soon.
We're going to storm Vimy Ridge. When we do, the Boche
will stampede the road next to this field. We'll take you
with us if you want to come. We're going to cause a little
more mischief on our way back to the Canadian lines, but I
promise we'll do our best to get you to Filescamp.'

'Thanks,' he said. 'I appreciate you coming to find me,
but I'll stay. I want to fly this bucket out of here if I can,
and Victor promised to come before the sun even makes a
shadow.'

'Bonne,' I said. 'We'll go then. Who knows, maybe we'll
see you again.'

'Adieu, Royal. May your aim be true and your enemy's
be wide of the mark.'

'Bonne chance, mon ami,' I answered.

I WASN'T SURE WHAT WE WOULD DO to cause Fritzie
more trouble, but as it turned out, our next adventure was
already in the works. Ten minutes after leaving Captain
Prince, we heard gunfire coming from around a curve in
the road. Angus and I slipped into the trees on the left.
Chance, Lucien, and Boyce vanished into the woods on
the right. Four men in civilian clothes had taken cover
behind a car overturned in the ditch, and eight Jerries,

who had left two motorcycles and a truck a hundred fifty yards beyond them, were converging on the men, moving from tree to tree, encircling them. As we watched, one of the men in the civilian clothes was shot. He slumped down, dead or badly wounded.

We outflanked the Germans and surprised them. I shot two before they even knew we were there, and as soon as I fired, Angus opened up with the Browning Automatic. Bullets whizzed through the trees, leaves fell, and so did two more of the Jerries. One was hurling a grenade at the three civilians still crouched behind the car, but when Angus fired, the soldier was hit, and the grenade fell short. It exploded, and some of the fragments slammed into the car's gas tank. It lifted off the ground with a boom and burst into flame. Shooting continued on the other side of the road, and then the wood was silent. Boyce stepped from beneath the trees and gave the "all clear" signal. I did the same, and then Angus and I hurried forward to pull the men we had rescued away from the burning car.

One of the men had been knocked unconscious by the grenade. Two men were dead. One was the man we had seen shot as we arrived, and the other had been killed by the piece of shrap I saw in his neck. The last man was gutshot. He begged for help with his eyes, and it was clear that he couldn't move. I dragged the unconscious man away from the flames, and then Angus and I picked up the other wounded man as gently as possible and laid him beside his comrade. I noticed, as we moved them, that the two men looked a lot alike. The face of the unconscious man was familiar. I tipped his hat back to see his face better. It was Corbin Lenoir. With disgust I remembered what he had done to the wounded German in the crater, but there was no time to linger. More Jerries might arrive at any minute.

'Boyce,' I yelled over the roaring flames. Get the Jerries' truck and bring it down here. Where are Chance and Lucien?'

Boyce didn't answer, but the look on his face alarmed me.

'Boyce?' I asked.

'Chance was hit in the chest. He's bad, Royal.'

I was already running when I called back. 'Get the truck! Angus, come with me!'

OTTER ST. ONGE AND THE BOOTLEGGERS

CHAPTER 12

Corbin Lenoir

E FOUND CHANCE SEATED ON THE GROUND,
leaning against the trunk of a big oak tree. Lucien
had already opened his shirt and exposed the wound. I
put two fingers to the artery in his neck. The pulse was
fast but still regular. Blood ebbed out of the wound, small
bubbles popping, but it didn't spurt. The bullet had gone
through a lung.

'Let's get him to the road, Angus. Lucien, get one of the
motorcycles.' Angus scooped up Chance in his arms and
carried him gently to where Boyce was waiting with the
truck. He propped him up in the back, bracing him against
the cab with an army blanket for a cushion. Chance said
he could breathe easier sitting up. Lenoir had come to and
was struggling to his feet. He recognized me, I'm sure, but
he didn't let on. He prob'ly didn't want to talk about the
dead Jerry with the severed fingers.

'Angus, help me get this one in the truck. He's hurt
bad.' We picked up Lenoir's man, and at every move he

screamed in agony. We laid him gently beside Chance and put a blanket under his head.

'Be careful with him!' snapped Lenoir.

'Like you were when you chopped off that German's fingers to get his wedding ring?' I glared at him. He glared back, but clenched his teeth to keep his mouth shut.

'There's a farmhouse back that way,' Lenoir said, pointing down the road toward Bachand's. 'Maybe they would help us.' I tried to ignore Lenoir's arrogant tone.

'That's where we're headed,' I said. 'Boyce, you drive. Angus, get the other motorcycle. Ride ahead with Lucien and scout for patrols. If you meet any, take them on a wild goose chase. We'll meet at the farmhouse.'

During the short ride to the farm, I pulled a first aid kit from my pack and bandaged Chance while I talked to Lenoir. 'You blew up the German's headquarters fifteen minutes ahead of schedule,' I said. 'Why?'

'I don't have to answer to you,' Lenoir replied.

'This man almost got shot earlier because of you,' I said coldly. Now, he *has* been shot. That's your doing.'

'How is that *my* doing? Maybe it was just time for his ticket to get punched,' said Lenoir.

'Keep talking that way, Lenoir, and maybe your ticket will get punched. I wouldn't need a lot of arm twisting to dump you and your friend beside the road and leave you for the next German patrol.'

'We didn't have any choice. We *had* to blow the charges early,' said Lenoir. He spat out the words. 'An officer found us wiring the detonator. I killed him, but not before he blew a whistle. A Jerry patrol appeared at the end of the street and started firing. If I hadn't detonated the explosives, they'd have stopped us.'

'Then what happened.'

'We left. Fast. I lost four men in the street fight that followed, but Yves LeDoux hotwired that Dusenberg that's back in the ditch, and four of us got out of there. A Jerry patrol on the Vimy-Farbus road saw us before we reached Vimy Wood. They chased us, shot out the tires on the car, and we ended up in the ditch where you found us.'

I didn't ask any more questions. We drove into a neat barnyard, and I jumped from the truck and talked to an aging farmer. It was Victor Bachand. He had snow-white hair and was stoop shouldered, but his blue eyes were sharp and his grip was strong. I quickly convinced him that we were Canadians in spite of the Boche uniforms. He could tell that the accent in my French wasn't native, but it wasn't German either. I described our meeting with Captain Prince, and when I asked him if he had soldered the tubing to repair the gas line, he was convinced that I was an ally not an enemy.

'Yes,' he said, 'I made it last night. I just finished the milking, and I was hitching up my team to bring the part to Monsieur Prince. If I drive the team, I can tell any nosy Jerries that I'm on my way to finish the plowing I started yesterday.'

'We left a burning car and several dead Jerries on that road. The time for tricks is past. I have a wounded man, and I want to get him on that plane with Prince. Would you be willing to give me that tubing? I can take it to him, and Captain Prince can leave before Fritzie is any the wiser.' The old man looked doubtful.

'Show me the wounded man.' He followed me to the back of the truck where Chance and Lenoir's man were lying pale and sweating in spite of the cold.

'You have two men wounded,' he said. Then he handed me the copper tubing he had made.

'Yes, but only one can go with Captain Prince.'

'What's going on?' demanded Lenoir.

'We have a Canadian pilot nearby,' I said, returning to English. 'His recon plane was shot down Friday afternoon. If we can fix his plane, we can send one of these men out with him,' I said.

'Jacques should go!' Lenoir insisted. 'My brother is badly wounded, but with a surgeon's help he could survive. Your man won't. You know that.' I suspected Lenoir was right, but I didn't say so.

'Your brother?' I asked

'Yes! My brother!' he snarled. 'You're wasting time. Allons-y!'

'I'm sorry about your brother, Lenoir, but I'm putting my man on that plane. He was shot trying to rescue you. If it weren't for my men, you'd both be dead right now.' Lenoir stared at me with burning hatred.

'If my brother dies, you'll rue this day, St. Onge,' he said.
'I will hunt down your wife and children—everyone you
love. Only then, will I kill you.' He turned on his heel and
climbed back onto the truck.

I ignored him and turned back to the farmer. 'Merci,
Victor,' I said.

'De rien, mon ami,' replied the farmer. Then he added in
a whisper, 'Don't turn your back on that one.'

'I won't. You'd better get rid of the tire tracks we've left in
your driveway. The Jerries will be here soon. If they think
you've helped us, who knows what they'll do.'

'I'll exercise my team in the yard,' he grinned. 'Go now.'

I PARKED THE TRUCK A SHORT DISTANCE from the
plane and asked Boyce and Lucien to keep an eye on
Chance and Lenoir. John Prince was both surprised and
glad to see us. 'I thought you were long gone' he said. Then
he saw Chance and Jacques Lenoir lying in the truck bed.
'Good lord, what happened?'

Pointing to the Lenoirs, I explained quickly. 'We found
these men being attacked by Fritzie on the road to the
Bachand farm. We killed the Jerries, stole this truck, and
drove to Victor's to get the tubing you need. Here it is,
John.' I handed him the copper pipe. He quickly inspected
Victor's handiwork and then grabbed a pair of pliers and a
roll of mechanic's wire from his tool box.

'Victor,' he smiled, 'is a genius. I'm coming back after
the war, and I'm going to buy him the best bottle of wine in

the province.' He lifted a cover on the engine housing and worked the tubing onto each end of the severed gas line. Angus and I threw the brush into the edge of the woods.

'John, I need to ask a great favor,' I said.

'Ask away,' he replied without looking up.

'Chance was shot in the chest. The bullet hit a lung,' I said quietly.

'Yes?'

'Will you take him to Filescamp and get him to a doctor?'

'Of course,' he said. He looked at me. He knew as well as I did that Chance wasn't likely to survive the trip. 'I saved Jim's flying jacket to help me stay warm last night,' he continued. 'Give it to him. It gets cold up there. Then strap him into the seat. It's light enough to take off. If Victor's tubing doesn't leak, I'll leave immediately. I should have just enough gas to get back to the landing strip. There's always a doctor on duty.'

We cut away Chance's German tunic and put on the dead spotter's jacket. It was lined with sheepskin which was good because Chance was starting to shiver. Angus and Boyce lifted him into the cockpit. I checked the bullet holes Jerry had put in the plane. The rear half of the fuselage was Swiss cheese, but it looked like the plane might still fly. Then Chance called to me, and I stepped to his side while Prince climbed into the cockpit and checked the flaps and instruments.

'Royal,' he said, 'there's a letter in my pack. Can you give

it to my parents in Quebec and tell them what happened?'
He was terribly weak but still conscious.

'You'll be telling them yourself, Chance,' I said. 'Hang
on. You saw Captain Prince on Friday. He's a crackerjack
pilot. In less than an hour, he'll set down at Filescamp, and
you'll have a doctor taking care of you. A pretty nurse too,
no doubt.'

The corners of Chance's mouth twitched upward. 'Just
in case, bien?'

'Sure, Chance. I'll take care of it.'

Then, with great effort, he lifted his fingers to his cap
in his usual mocking salute, but this time it was also
heartfelt. 'You're a doozy, Royal. So are the others. Raise a
glass for me when this hellish mess is over.'

'I'll pour you one, and you can drink it yourself. Don't
give up. Prince will get you out of this.' I wanted to say
more, but Captain Prince was ready to take off. I returned
Chance's salute and wished him Godspeed.

'Royal, can you help me start this contraption?' asked
John.

'Sure. What do I do?'

'When I give the word, snap that prop down. It's just like
using a crank to start a car. Pull it down hard, but make
sure you let go quickly and stand clear. That propeller
will take your head off if you get in its way.' I stretched up,
grabbed the prop with both hands, and whipped it down.
The engine sputtered and sputtered again, and then, with
a roar, it started.

We had trigged the wheels with chunks of wood. Now we tossed them aside. Captain Prince increased the throttle, and the plane crawled from its hiding place and taxied toward a nearby hedgerow. When he reached it, Prince turned the aircraft and pointed the nose toward the far end of the field. He waved and then gave his full attention to the takeoff. The plane rolled down the field, gathering speed, going faster and faster, the engine roaring louder and louder, and then, suddenly, the wheels bumped once, twice, and the plane was airborne. We watched it climb. It grew smaller and smaller, and then it flew straight over the ridge and disappeared from sight.

Ten minutes later we heard the thundering of guns. We didn't know what to think. Were they our guns? The Germans? Then, as the bombardment continued, we realized what was happening. It was the Push. McNaughton's gunners had just begun an artillery barrage that was heard in London across the English Channel. If Byng's plan worked, the Jerries would be swarming down the east side of Vimy Ridge in a matter of hours. We needed to get to the Goulot Wood. That was the Brown Line on Byng's battle plan. If we could dig in there, our boys in the Second Division would reach us by some time later that day.

'Lenoir,' I said, 'we'll go back to the Bachand farm and see if Victor and his wife will tend to Jacques. Byng has started the Push, and we can't take your brother with us.

He'll never make it. You can't stay with him. You've got to come with us.'

'Who died and made you king,' he said fiercely. 'You don't outrank me.'

'No, I don't,' I said, 'but like it or not, you'll come along. I won't leave you with the Bachands. You'd put them in more danger. Besides, now that Chance is gone, we could use another hand, but the Doozies only have one leader, and that's me. We'll leave Jacques at the farm and head for the woods. Angus, take the motorcycle and scout the road.'

The truth was, I didn't want Lenoir with us at all, but I didn't trust him as far as I could throw an elephant, and it's better to keep your enemy close. I didn't know what mischief he might do on his own. Fifteen minutes later we returned to the farm. Victor was in the yard listening to the bombardment and looking completely amazed and bewildered.

'Is it the end of the world?' he asked.

'With any luck, it will be the end of the Boche in the Vimy countryside,' I replied. 'Victor, can you do us one last favor? The Jerries won't be looking for us or these men anymore,' I added, pointing to the Lenoirs. 'They'll be too busy trying to save their own skins for the next few days. Would you look after this fellow? He's badly hurt, but with any luck Canadian troops will be here in a couple days— maybe sooner—and an army doctor may still be able to save his life.'

'We'll do our best,' he said.

'Good. We'll bring him inside then.' Madame Bachand had come to the door. Grief-scarred by the loss of her son, she still took charge.

'We will put him in Henri's room,' she told her husband firmly.

'Oui, Madeleine,' replied Victor. We followed her to a small bedroom with a low ceiling. Madame Bachand turned back the clean, white sheet, and we laid poor Jacques Lenoir on a comfortable feather bed. Jacques was groaning and barely conscious by this time.

'Stay alive, Jacques. I'll be back for you,' said Lenoir softly. Then he looked at me with all the malice he could muster and returned to the truck. We said goodbye to Victor in the yard and drove up the road toward Vimy. Before we reached the village, we met a staff car full of Fritzie's officers heading east toward Lens and away from the bombardment. Our Jerry uniforms gave us the advantage of surprise. We held the officers at gunpoint and made them get out of the car. Angus fired quick bursts from the Browning into the car's radiator and tires. We took the officers' shoes to slow them down and made a lieutenant give Lucien his hat, jacket and trousers.

When we reached Vimy, the village was in chaos. With Lucien looking like one's of the Kaiser's elite and speaking fluent German, we drove through several checkpoints without being challenged. In a matter of minutes, I was watching Vimy disappear in the rear view mirror as we motored toward Farbus. When we reached the Goulot

Wood, we found a place to drive the car in under the trees.
We hid it just before several trucks of German infantry
zipped by, headed toward Vimy.

When it was safe, we shouldered our packs and walked
a quarter of a mile into the forest. For three hours that
morning we dug into the hillside with trenching tools. We
found the trunk of a grandfather oak that must have come
down in a storm that winter and tunneled beneath it with
two separate holes. By the time McNaughty started shelling
our side of the ridge at midday, we had wormed our way
into burrows six feet deep. Even then we weren't safe.

If you've never been through an artillery bombardment,
it's hard to imagine. I've seen grown men go crazy with fear
and run from a dugout with shells exploding all around
them. That's what Lenoir did, or at least that was what I
first thought. He and Angus and I were in one hole. Boyce
and Lucien were in the other. In the middle of the barrage,
I lifted my head and saw Lenoir's boots disappearing up
the hole to the surface. I don't know why I followed the fool.
I guess I thought I could grab him and pull him back in.
When I popped my head out of the hole, he was waiting for
me with his knife. He slashed me and left my face the way
you see it now. Then he warned me again.

'If my brother dies, St. Onge!' he screamed, 'I'll kill
your family. Don't think you can hide them. I'll kill them
all. Then I'll kill you. After the war, St. Onge! After the
war!' Then he ran off through the exploding, fire-blasted
wood and vanished in the smoke. Right then, I went crazy

myself. Blood streamed down my face, but I didn't care. I scrambled out of the hole and ran after Lenoir. Geysers of dirt leaped into the air, and the noise of the bursting shells was deafening. I glimpsed Lenoir ahead of me, and I could see that he was running for the road. I followed him through the smoke, sprinting, sometimes throwing myself on the ground when I heard a shell screaming close by. When I finally reached the road, Lenoir was gone.

I saw a truck full of Boche infantry coming toward me, headed for Vimy, but then a tremendous roar filled my ears. Everything went black. The war ended for me that day. A shell exploded nearby and slammed my brain so hard inside my skull that it scrambled my wits. When I woke up, I was in a bed with clean, white sheets. The nurse who brought me a cup of water spoke German. I was pretty bewildered, and all the more so because I didn't know who I was. The doctors and nurses were puzzled too because I couldn't speak for months, and when I finally did, I spoke English.

The Jerries in the truck must have seen my German uniform and figured I was one of theirs. They must have picked me up and put me on a train to Germany when we reached Vimy. I was so badly shell-shocked, I didn't know who I was for four years. Four years, Otter. For much of that time, I sat in a wheelchair and twitched. Every day Nurse Klein took me out of that chair and moved my limbs. Slowly, feeling came back, and one day I moved the fingers of my right hand. Months later, I began to walk again, with canes at first, and then on my own. I began to speak, and finally I began retrieving bits and pieces of memory, but that had its drawbacks. Some of what I remembered gave me horrifying nightmares. One day a nurse dropped a metal bedpan on the floor. It landed with a bang. I put my hands over my ears and dove under my bed. I thought it was a bomb.

Eventually, I remembered your mother and you, Otter, and my life here in Vermont and Quebec, but I didn't tell anyone because I also remembered Lenoir's threat, and it haunted me. I still saw his face and heard what he said in the Goulot Wood with explosions shaking the ground and smoke filling the air. 'I'll kill your family,' he said. 'I'll find them.' I knew he might be dead or that he might have made an empty threat, but what if he was alive, and what if he still wanted revenge? What if he still meant to kill you, Otter, and your mother? No—I kept my mouth shut. As far as they knew at the hospital, the memories of my life before the war were permanently lost.

In the spring of 1922, five years after I was admitted, I was discharged. Dr. Schiller said they had done all they could, that some day my memory might return, but nature must take its course. The hospital gave me a suit of clothes and some money for travel. I boarded the first train west, changed trains in Lens that afternoon, and arrived in Vimy that night. I walked past the spot where the Germans had caught up with the Crows, the spot where Chance had been shot in the chest. I finally reached the Bachand's farm at dusk. Victor was in the barn milking. I put hay in the mangers while he finished up, and then we went to the house. Madeleine hugged me, and then we all sat down to a dinner of steak, potatoes, and asparagus.

The way the two of them kept glancing at me uneasily, I knew something must be wrong. Later that night, when I looked in the mirror in Henri's room, I saw what it was. I stared at the image in the glass and barely recognized myself. I don't know why I hadn't noticed before, but suddenly I saw the face Victor and Madeleine must have seen—the face of a sad, hollow man whose life has drained out of him and left only a shadow. I was shocked. It wasn't the scar on my face that bothered me. It was the haunted look in my eyes, the look of a shipwrecked soul.

'What happened to you, my boy?' asked Victor. I told him and Madeleine about how we had dug holes in the Goulot Wood, about Corbin's threat to kill you and your mother if Jacques died, and about how I had chased him down to the Vimy Road with shells dropping all around us.

'He was gone when I reached the road. Then a shell whistled so loud I knew it was going to land almost on top of me. I dove into the road ditch, and that's all I remember. I must have been close to the blast. I woke up in a German hospital in Lille a month later. I was paralyzed, and I couldn't speak. From Lille, they moved me to a special clinic for shell-shock victims in Hanover, Germany. I only learned all this later when I began talking again, and they assigned a doctor to my case who could speak English. It's taken five years for me to get well enough to leave. Now, I have to figure out what to do next. This didn't come from the exploding shell,' I said, pointing to the scar on my face. 'Corbin Lenoir did this right before he told me he would kill my family if his brother died. Victor, what happened to Jacques Lenoir?'

Victor looked at Madeleine before turning to me. 'He died an hour after you left. I built a coffin and dug the boy's grave myself. We buried Jacques Lenoir at sunset right after milking.'

'And his brother, Corbin?'

'He was there. He came just in time to help lower his brother into the ground.' Victor glanced at his wife again, a little worried, and went on. 'He tried to give us money for taking care of his brother, but I refused it. I told him we hoped someone would have helped our son Henri if he had been wounded. Madeleine asked Lenoir if there was anything else we could do. He said no. It was too late. You had made sure of that. When he spoke your name, Royal, it was like a curse. He is a bad one, a man who will never forget. But you are safe, are you not? Who knows that you were in a German hospital? By now, everyone must think you are dead. Is this not true?'

'I hope so, Victor,' I replied. 'I hope so.' I stayed with the Bachands for a week. Then I crossed the Channel, boarded the Cunard Line's *Antonia,* and sailed for Canada. I wanted to come back here, Otter, but the closer the ship got to home the more I began to doubt."

"Doubt what?" I asked.

"Everything. Your mother. You. Most of all, myself. I didn't want to see the look on your mother's face when she saw mine. I wasn't sure I could live with you and your mother, that I was fit to live with you. Back then I still had bad headaches and black moods. And I wasn't sure if you'd want to see me after all this time. I wasn't sure I knew who you were anymore, and I realized you might feel that way about me too. Maybe you wouldn't want me coming home and interrupting your life. I was still sinking then, down, and farther down into a dark well, and I didn't know if I was ever going to touch bottom.

Even so, I meant to come home. I wanted badly to see you and your mother. But then, one day I boarded a tram in Montreal. I had only arrived that morning. I was headed to Robbie MacAskill's distillery looking for Angus. The car stopped several times and began to fill up. I gave my seat to a woman with a baby and stood. I held onto a metal pole as the car lurched along the tracks. In St. Timothee a mob came aboard and packed the car so tight we all had to inhale at the same time. I was standing in the crush, remembering how tight it was sometimes in the tunnels at Vimy, and suddenly I felt the point of a knife in the small of my back. A voice hissed low in my ear like a venomous snake and made the hair stand up on the back of my neck.

'St. Onge. Figured you for dead. Don't make a fuss, my friend, or you'll find out just how long this blade is, and by the time anyone figures out what happened, I'll be getting off at the next stop.'

'Lenoir,' I said. 'What rock did you crawl out from under?'

'The same one that's going to drop on your head, St. Onge,' he said. The knife point broke the skin and slid an inch into my back, and I was sure I was going to die right there on that bus surrounded by a crowd of people.'

CHAPTER 13

Going to the Devil

A S IT TURNED OUT, LENOIR HAD no intention of killing me right then. That would have been too easy—on me, that is. No doubt he pulled the legs off bugs as a boy.

'I'm not going to kill you, St. Onge,' he said. 'Not yet. I want to watch you squirm.' He twisted the knife and pushed it in a little farther. Everything started going black, and I saw flashing lights, but I held on. 'When the tram stops at the next corner, you and I are going to get off.'

'Then what?' I said as blood oozed from the wound and down my back.

'I'd like you to meet some of my friends.'

''Magine that,' I said. 'I'm not much in the mood for visiting today. Do you suppose we could meet tomorrow?' Lenoir's answer was to probe with the knife and give it another twist.'

'On the other hand,' I gasped, 'I've always said it's poor manners to spurn the hand of friendship.' I knew I had to escape—and fast. If Lenoir and his friends got hold of me,

I'd sure enough be a dead duck. When the tram stopped, we crowded out the doors and onto the sidewalk with everyone else. I no longer felt the knife, but he was right with me, speaking in my ear.

'Try to run,' he whispered, 'and I'll sink that blade into your kidney.'

'I feel more like walking anyway,' I whispered back. After saying that, I walked heavily on the heels of the man in front of me. The fellow's reaction was exactly what I hoped for. When he whirled around all indignant and began to rant, I stopped short. Then—in the same second—I swung my elbow hard and fast back into Lenoir's face. I felt his knife pierce my coat and slice my side, but I had ruined his aim. I whirled around now myself, and he lunged at me. He shouldn't have thrown all his chips down on that one play, but he was afraid I'd get away. When he charged me, I stepped back like one of those bullfighters waving his red cloth, and when his knife hand flashed by, I grabbed his wrist and yanked down. He somersaulted forward and landed with a bone-crunching thud on his back. I grabbed the knife and ran. When I looked back, Corbin Lenoir was still down. He was shaking his head, looking dazed, but— much to my disappointment—not looking badly hurt.

I ran to the next trolley stop, climbed aboard the car waiting there, and didn't breathe normally for two hours. By that time, I had ridden so many tramcars and criss-crossed so many alleys and avenues that not even my Abenaki grandsire could have followed my trail. At dusk I raised the brass knocker at 46 LeGrande Avenue and beat a tattoo. Much to my surprise, it was Angus himself who answered the door. It was his brother Robbie's house, of course, and Robbie was living so well from the profits of his whiskey mill, he had a veritable mansion, leastways for a fella that came up the hard way.

I'll shorten up the rest of the story as best I can. I knew I couldn't come home—not with Lenoir looking for you and your mother, Otter—so Angus and I decided to try our luck at bootlegging. Robbie supplied us. We drove out to Ontario, far from Corbin Lenoir, and rented rooms at Elly Day's Guest House in Belleville. We took up with Ben Kerr, the King of the Rumrunners as they called him. Two nights after we arrived, he was playing piano at the Watch Dog Saloon. Angus bought him a beer, Ben returned the favor, and soon they were as thick as thieves. Two nights later the three of us ran whiskey to Oswego, New York in Ben's boat the *Martimas*. I don't think Ben needed to hire us. Most of the time he chummed with a vet named Alf Wheat, but Alf liked to pop a cork a little too often and couldn't always be depended on. Besides that, the three of us got along well. We enjoyed many an evening in the Weather Eye in Oswego, drinking, telling tall tales, and eating Polly Kittings' excellent cooking. Ben refused to serve in the war himself, but he was keen for the stories Angus told about it, especially the ones where we had managed to pull the wool over the eyes of arrogant or stupid officers who seemed bent on getting us killed. After three years of smuggling, Ben had a few stories of his own, but most of all, it was a pleasure to listen to him tickle the ivories on the battered upright piano in Polly's bar. Those times with Ben and Angus did more to heal my soul than any doctor's pill could ever do. One night Angus elbowed me in the ribs, and told me to stop.

'Stop what?' I asked.

'You just smiled, laddie' he said with a grin. 'I thought you'd best stop in case it gave you palpitations of the heart.' Ben laughed at that until I thought he'd have a calf. He was a good friend, Ben was, and he gave us steady work too. In six months Angus and I raked in enough money to buy the *Thorpedo*, and after about a year we went off on our own and started socking away the dough with an eye to a rainy day.

That day came, of course. Running illegal liquor across the lake was pretty easy in the beginning. It was mostly independents like Ben and Gentleman Charlie Mills, and most of us got along fine. Governor Al Smith thought Prohibition was foolishness, and he only put sixteen state police to work on the border. More often than not, the local cops felt the same as the governor and looked the other way when they saw any bootlegging going on—especially if the bootleggers shared the odd bottle and some coin.

All that changed when the mob moved in. Gangsters working for Rocco Perri hijacked loads from the locals. More and more feds appeared in Oswego and other towns on the south shore of Lake Ontario. Last year, the U.S.

Coast Guard fired on the *Andy* with a machine gun and killed poor Leo Yott. Then Perri's man, Joe Sotille, sold a batch of bad liquor, and dozens of people died or went blind. That was when the feds cracked down. They turned over every rock big enough to hide a bootlegger, and Angus and I were under one of them.

We were hauling a load out of Kingston. The night we got caught, we were supposed to meet Liam Carey and his helper, Rub Spiller. As we entered Boomer Cove and got closer and closer to the silhouette of a boat, I realized suddenly that it was too big to be Liam's. I slammed the throttle forward in the *Thorpedo* and Angus threw sacks of whiskey over the side like they were coming off the stove top, but when bullets started ripping into the woodwork around us, I idled down and waited for the feds. They boarded, all eager beaver, but Angus had already dropped most of the booze overboard. I don't know for positive who tipped them off to our rendezvous, but Rub's last name was a hint, size large.

We were jailed in Watertown. Without more evidence, the coasties couldn't nail us for more than a month in jail, but if they'd known the true penalty they levied on me, they'd have been overjoyed. A local reporter wrote us up in the *Watertown Daily Times*. Then, Montreal's biggest daily, the *Gazette*, picked up the story. It was just a short piece, not on the front page, but Lenoir must have seen it. I was going by the name you heard—Chance Tatro—but the *Gazette* ferreted out my real name for the article, and included a photo of Angus and me being escorted in handcuffs through the back door of the Oswego Police Station."

"How did you know Lenoir had found you?" I asked.

"I got a letter while I was in jail." He unfolded a piece of paper from his wallet and read:

Well, well, the worm turns. Imagine my surprise at seeing your picture in the Gazette. *You pop up like a jack-in-the-box. I'm sure you're wondering about the promise I made regarding your family. Don't worry—I'll deliver, and the scales will balance. Go with God for now, St. Onge. You'll soon enough go to the Devil.*

"As soon as Angus and I got out of jail, I sent your grandsire a note asking him to meet me at the fish camp. We wrote to Boyce and Lucien asking them to rejoin the Doozies for one last raid, and they met us in St. Jean. I was at the fish camp the day before last, just after dusk, waiting for you, but for your sake and Granddad's, I didn't dare stay. The four of us were sitting at the table when we heard a motorboat in the distance. It grew louder, and from the window, Boyce saw its running lights a couple miles to the north. It was heading in our direction. I had a bad feeling, so we put out the kerosene lantern, slipped out of the shack, and got back on board the *Thorpedo*. We untied, and let the boat drift away into the dark. The other boat idled down as it neared the camp and turned off its spotlight. I saw four men in the pale glow of the running lights. Suddenly, a man in the bow opened fire with a Thompson submachine gun. Splinters flew from the cabin

like confetti, and gunshots echoed across the bay. After a
second burst, another man signaled him to stop, switched
on a spotlight, and swept the beam over the platform and
the walls of the cabin.

Two of the four men climbed the ladder and stood
outside the door of the shanty. One of them shouted that
if there was anybody inside, he'd better come out pronto.
I'd know that voice anywhere. It was Corbin Lenoir. When
nobody showed, his buddy kicked the door open and fired
another burst from his Tommy gun. Then the two of them
went in. They lit the lantern on the table. I raised my
binoculars, and I could see Lenoir's face lit from beneath
like a ghoul set loose by the Devil himself. We kept watch
for a good five minutes, maybe more, all the while drifting
farther and farther away. I wondered how Lenoir had found
me so quickly. One thing I knew for sure. I had to draw
him away. What if he and his gang had arrived at the
same time as you and Granddad, Otter? No, I wasn't ready
to deal with him right then, especially with that Tommy
gunner at his side. There was too much chance that one of
the Doozies might get shot or that you might show up.

I made up my mind before Lenoir and his sidekick
stepped out of the shack. The *Thorpedo* had drifted a
hundred yards or more east of the camp. I started the
engine and we roared off with considerable speed. By the
time Lenoir and Mr. Tommy Gun clambered down the
ladder and into their boat, we were well away. And that's
the story, Otter. We lost Lenoir out on the open lake—the

Crow was no match for the *Thorpedo*—and we ran down to Plattsburgh to sell a few cases of booze at a couple waterfront taverns and the Hotel Champlain. You know the rest."

When he finished, we were all silent for a stretch of time. Lucien placed a chunk of pine on the fire, and the pitch popped and sizzled. The rain still drummed on the roof. Through the big window facing the lake, we could barely see the few stunted trees on the finger of ledge that protected the cove where the *Thorpedo* was moored. They came and went in the drifting mists. The lake beyond the ledge was hidden in the ceaseless fog and rain.

I sighed inwardly and felt sadness creep into my soul. My father had been twenty-five when he boarded a troopship to France. Not much older than me. He was thirty-six now, and he had seen such horrors as I didn't even want to think about. The scar on his face wasn't the only one he carried. I doubted the one inside would ever heal. As I watched him, I felt the room fill with silence and waiting. A tongue of flame flared up in the fireplace, and then vanished. The wood had burned down to coals. My father gazed at the red glow on the hearth. Finally, he spoke.

"I've got to find Lenoir," he said. "Either he'll go to the Devil or I will, but one thing's certain. There's not room on God's green earth for the two of us, not by a long shot."

"I want to help you," I said.

"I appreciate that, but no, Otter. I can't risk that. I want you to go to the King Street Tavern and stay with your grandmother for now. I'll be back as soon as I can."

I was half tempted to argue, but I knew it wouldn't do any good. Besides, Granddad chimed in before I could say a word.

"I'll go with him, Royal. He's got somebody he's got to look after himself. We'll come to no harm. You find that bird Lenoir and send him to the bottom of the lake. Then you can rest easy."

The Doozies passed the rest of the day playing poker and sleeping. Dad and I buttoned on slickers after lunch, pulled on rubber boots, and walked a shore path around the whole island. Jake trotted at my side. The rain poured down like God Almighty had just tipped over his punch bowl. Darned if I didn't think it was time to gather animals two by two. Wet as it was, I was as happy as I'd been in a coon's age. I couldn't believe I was taking a walk with my dad. A few short weeks ago, I had thought he was moldering away under the sod in France, feeding the worms, nothing left, maybe, but his buttons. Now, he was standing by my side. I could hardly fathom it. We walked and talked and walked some more through the soggy wood, and the whole afternoon flew away like the downy seed of a milkweed pod.

I wanted to help him fight Lenoir and his men. I was a good shot with a rifle, but I knew he didn't feel right about putting me in danger, maybe getting me killed. What he didn't know was that I felt the same way about *him* getting killed. What if he did? When I thought about it, my gut twisted, and I felt sick, but there was nothing I could do. I bit my tongue, hard as it was. At dusk we slogged through the infernal rain back to the lodge. Everybody was packing his kit and getting ready to leave.

"Otter and I will paddle the canoe back to the *Simon Weed*," Granddad said. "With any luck, they'll still be waiting for us off Phelps Point at the southern end of South Hero."

"Amos," said my father, "I want to thank you."

"What for?"

"For looking after Otter. I've been gone a long, long time. A long time. Every step of the way, I wanted to get back here. I guess if I hadn't gone in the first place, Sweet would still be alive."

"You can't blame yourself for that, Royal. Who could have seen that cursed Spanish flu coming down the pike? You couldn't have seen that any more than you could have seen the coming of Corbin Lenoir. We never know where the Grim Reaper will swing his scythe. All we know is that he will reap. Don't bother yourself with what's passed. As to thanking me for keeping Otter out of mischief, save it for his Grandmother Melodie. I have to say he's caused me no end of trouble"—and here, he grinned at me—"but he's quite an Otter, and if he's given me gray hairs, he's also provided Petrice and me with some amusement. If there's any justice in the world, which I often doubt, he may some day earn his keep. I see signs of this, and if that day comes it will be a happy one because he eats almost as much as that giant brother of yours." Dad laughed at this. Then he spoke solemnly again.

"Well, just the same—I can't begin to tell you how grateful I am." His voice caved in right then which surprised me. After what he'd told us about his time in France, I guess I didn't imagine him getting worked up about something like this. I figured he was hardened like a piece of steel that's come out of the forge and been hammered into a new shape.

"Now, Royal, don't give it another thought. Otter and I have had many a good time, and he has worked on the farm like a man every summer since he was twelve," said Granddad. "Come on. Let's head for the boats. The sooner we get going, the sooner we can get back home to where we belong. The Good Lord willin' and the creek don't rise, this will all be behind us soon. No, strike that about 'the creek don't rise.' I imagine every river in Vermont topped its banks a while ago. With this much rain, that Mooney lot I got down by the Mississquoi must be a lake. I hope Petrice has got enough sense to get herself and the cows to higher ground. Welt, nothing to be done about it right now. Let's go ride the flood."

At that, the Doozies came forward and shook hands with both of us.

"Sorry, again, about that bump on the noggin, Boyce," said Granddad.

"No harm done, Amos," said the farmer. "If we weren't practically drowning already, I'd say I'm as right as rain, but I won't press my luck. You and the boy take care."

"That we will. Lucien, Angus, keep your powder dry," he
said with a grin, and then he tucked his rifle in the crook
of his arm and walked out the door. He disappeared down
the stairs that led to the boat and reappeared at the edge
of the woods on the other side of the cove. Dad crushed me
in a bear hug and then held me at arm's length.

"Keep your eyes open," he said, "and if my plans go
haywire, and Lenoir comes after you and Granddad, be
ready and don't hesitate to shoot that son of a bunghole
dead. I guarantee, that's what he's got in mind for you."

"I'll be on the lookout, Dad," I replied. He gripped my
arms tighter.

"You promise?" he asked.

"I promise. Jake's pretty good at knowing when
somebody means to do me mischief. He's helped me out of
a couple jams already. And there's Too Tall and Granddad.
We'll be all right," I said. "You be careful too, okay?"

He nodded, and I smiled. Then Jake and I raced out
the door and down the steps. Granddad was waiting like a
ghostly statue near the tree where we had tricked Boyce.
I looked over my shoulder and waved to Dad who stood at
the top of the steep stairs. He waved back. Then Granddad
and I passed into the wood and vanished into the
darkness. The Doozies still had to load the *Thorpedo*, but
I knew they would be leaving Providence soon in search
of that devil Lenoir. *Holy Mother Mary and her bouncing
baby Jesus*, I thought, *I hope they clip his wings for good.*

WALKING THE ISLAND WITH DAD, I HAD FOUND a
shorter trail to the canoe, and twenty minutes later I was
crawling down that same chimney in the rock we had
climbed out of on the previous night. We gave Jake a little
help, and soon the three of us were safe at the water's edge.
The *Melodie* was still there, bobbing on each new wave that
reached into the cave like a cat reaching its paw into a
mouse hole.

I got in the bow and Jake curled up in the middle.
Granddad and I wrapped our rifles in canvas, and when
the next wave washed in and reached its limit, we pushed
hard and slipped out the entrance. Ahead, the next wave
loomed over us like an angry giant and gathered itself for
its run against the rocky bluff. We paddled for our lives up
to the crest and just managed to drop down the other side
before it could smash us against the wall ten feet away. We
climbed wave after wave like this, gaining only a few feet
every time, but finally we left the island behind and found
ourselves halfway across the strait between Providence and
Phelps Point.

We had to paddle too hard to talk, and as it turned out,
that was just as well. When Dad and I had walked the
shore of Providence earlier, I had taken the hand compass
Granddad had pocketed from Jack Halstead's boat. At the
north end of the island, I had taken a bearing on Phelps
Point. Now, I could see the little dot of radium on the end
of the compass needle just well enough to steer Granddad
a few degrees east of the point toward White's Beach. If a

south wind wasn't driving big rollers against the beach, that was where we would find Too Tall. I wasn't too hopeful. The wind was blowing from the south at a good clip, and I didn't expect the waves to get much smaller when we rounded the point.

We had reached the boiling waters at Phelps Point and were veering off to the east and the beach when I saw a flickering, yellow light to our left. As quickly as it had appeared, it vanished. Was I getting lightheaded? Seeing things? Then it showed again like a will o' the wisp, and I understood. It was a lantern. Jake growled quietly down in his throat, and I stroked his head to quiet him. A boat was anchored in the fog ahead of us, and we were about to pass near it. I turned toward Granddad in the stern and cupped my hands around my mouth. "Did you see it?" I whispered.

"Yes. Keep Jake quiet. Look for the name." Minutes later, the rags of fog around us reformed into the shape of a motor launch, but it was doubly hard to see because the entire boat was painted black. Standing in the stern was the shadowy figure of a man who looked away from us toward the open lake where the *Thorpedo* might soon appear. We passed beyond the ring of the lantern light but still close enough to see gold lettering on the transom. *What does it say?* I asked myself. *A stroke closer Granddad. Good!* I made out the name a letter at a time. *C-R-O-W.* The word sent a shiver down my spine, and instinctively I reached for my gun. *Tighten my suspenders and set me to singing opera,* I thought, *it's Lenoir's boat!* Granddad's next

paddle stroke sent us far from the limit of the lantern light,
and I breathed again. Suddenly, three more men appeared.
One of them spoke, but his voice was lost to the wind and
waves. He raised his hand and pointed west. I was puzzled
at first until I saw, far off, winking dots of green and red,
the running lights of a boat traveling fast. And then the
wind brought the sound of its powerful engine, muted at
first but growing louder and louder. Finally, I dared to
speak.

"Granddad," I whispered. "Is it the *Thorpedo?*"

"Yut," he replied. "I think it is."

When Dad's boat appeared, the lantern behind us was
snuffed out. We heard a low rumble and the clanking of
an anchor chain. The rumble grew louder, and the *Crow*
moved away, gaining speed. Soon, Lenoir would be flying
toward the *Thorpedo*. prob'ly he and his men were already
pulling out guns and switching off the safeties. One of
them, no doubt, was holding a Tommy gun. I tugged my
own rifle out of its canvas wrapping. *The Devil is loose,* I
said to myself, *and Dad doesn't even know he's coming!*

OTTER ST. ONGE AND THE BOOTLEGGERS

CHAPTER 14

The Flood

"GRANDDAD, THEY'RE GOING AFTER THE DOOZIES."

"Hold steady. When they rev the engine, put
a bullet into the *Crow* at the waterline. Do you hear the
waves crashing ahead of us?"

"Yut."

"That's White's Beach. As soon as you put a hole in the
Crow, paddle like the Devil's breathing down your neck.
More than likely, he will be. If Lenoir and his boys come
after us, we'll ride a wave onto the beach and get out of
sight before they can spot us."

The *Crow's* engine roared as Corbin Lenoir sped away.
I flicked off the safety, lined up the bead of the front sight
in the notch of the rear one, and raised my rifle barrel an
inch at a time. I breathed out slowly, let my muscles loosen,
and when I saw a ripple where the water met the black
hull of the boat, I squeezed the trigger. *Crack!* I saw a tiny
spout of water, and then I set my rifle down and grabbed
my paddle. Nothing happened right off. The *Crow* sped
away as before, and then, sure enough, the growling engine

changed pitch. It faded. Then it grew louder as the boat carved a wide arc back toward us.

"Devil take the hindmost, Granddad!" I said. "Somebody in that gang heard the shot, and they're coming after us."

"Dig hard!" shouted Granddad.

We leaned forward, knifed our paddles into the water, and pulled hard. *Stroke, stroke,* I said to myself, and we drove the *Melodie* toward the beach like galley slaves under the whip. Thirty yards behind us, the *Crow* slowed and switched on a spotlight. The beam swept through the darkness like a one-eyed monster searching for its prey, coming closer each second.

The canoe rose to the top of a wave bigger than the others, and I knew we were close to shore. We paddled ahead of its crest and rode it pell mell to the beach like a couple whalers on a Nantucket sleighride. Out of the corner of my eye, I could still see the spotlight combing the lake, and then it swept over us. Granddad jammed his paddle hard and sent us lurching to the right. Then he pushed down on the right gunwale, and water poured into the canoe.

"Jump!" he yelled.

I didn't need a second invitation. "C'mon, Jake!" I cried. I held my rifle in one hand, my paddle in the other, and leaped overboard. "Harry Houdini on ice," I sputtered. "Here I am getting dunked again in November. Two swims in two days is too much! Dang it's cold!" I didn't know how I was going to swim without my hands free, but luckily my feet touched bottom, and I stood up in water to my hips.

"Run!" yelled Granddad. I slogged forward through the crashing waves, and when I got free of the lake, I saw Jake racing up the beach, and I sprinted after him. Granddad's dodge had given us a few extra seconds to escape the spotlight. It had swung back to where the canoe should have been, but missing us, it had moved left instead of right. Now, it was sweeping back and about to find us.

"Get to the trees!" hollered Granddad. I dashed toward a stand of cottonwoods about thirty feet away, but when I glanced over my shoulder, Granddad had run into the circle of the spotlight! *Holy hotcakes! What's he thinking?* I wondered. Suddenly, bullets zinged through the air like Hell's hornets, and he dove behind a log half-buried in the sand. I kept running, and with the few extra seconds he had given us, Jake and I reached the shadows and dove behind a tree trunk. Luckily, Lenoir's men were shooting from the heaving deck of the *Crow*, and we escaped without a scratch. I thought Granddad was okay too, but his log was lit up like midday in the spotlight, and suddenly the night exploded with a burst from the Tommy gun. Splinters of wood flew up from the log, and I saw that Granddad couldn't hide there for long, or he'd be chewed up himself.

My rifle was wet, but I had no time to dry it out. I prayed that it would fire, aimed, and pulled the trigger. Lenoir's spotlight blinked out with a sharp pop, and the beach was dark. Seconds later, Granddad landed beside me. He settled his rifle into a low spot on a tree root and peered around the trunk toward Lenoir's boat.

"Where'd you learn to shoot like that?" he asked with a laugh.

"From you. Will they come ashore?" I asked.

"I doubt it," said Granddad. "We can pick them off too easy. Whatever Lenoir is, I suspect the man's no fool."

"What in the name of the late, great Ethan Allen do we do next?" I whispered.

"Wait."

"I hate waiting."

"I know it. So do I."

"Hang that dog, Lenoir!"

"What's wrong?"

"The Babe's bat was in the canoe."

"That's a shame. Maybe it'll still be floating around out there when he leaves."

We waited. The rain slowed to a drizzle, and I stared into the darkness so long I couldn't tell up from down. After ten minutes, the helmsman revved the engine, and we heard the *Crow* motor slowly away from the beach and out into the strait.

"Shall we rescue the *Melodie* before those big rollers stave in her ribs?" I asked.

"Yut, but let me go first. They may have left somebody standing in the surf. Maybe that fella with the Tommy gun."

Granddad grabbed a big chunk of driftwood and threw it half way to the water's edge where it landed with a thump. A minute later he threw a stick.

"Go get it," he said to Jake. I wasn't too keen on using Jake for bait, but it turned out okay. No one fired at him. It suddenly occurred to me to ask the question I'd wondered about when we landed.

"Granddad, why did you swamp the canoe?"

"Because if Lenoir had seen it, he and his boys would have peppered it with bullet holes and turned it into a sieve, and we'd be stuck here right now." With that, he cradled his rifle in his elbows and crawled after Jake.

"The coast is clear, Otter," he called moments later. "Come give me a hand." I ran down to the lake and splashed into the surf. The canoe was shifting about on the bottom, being pushed around by each new wave. I scrabbled around in the bow, and—praise the god of good luck—my bat was still there, lodged in the canvas tied to the thwart. I threw it on the beach, and then Granddad and I rolled the canoe and emptied it of water.

The food we'd brought was now a picnic for the fishes, but otherwise we were in good shape. In a trice we stowed our rifles and my bat, settled Jake in the middle again, and were paddling east in search of the *Simon Weed*. Since we had seen no sign of Too Tall at White's Beach, Granddad figured he had steamed southeast and anchored off the north side of Colchester Point out of the wind. If we didn't find him there, we would find him at the King Street

Tavern. We settled into a rhythm of long, easy strokes and made good headway until we turned south and into the wind. For three hours, while the wind rose and the waves piled against us, it seemed as if we were shoveling sand against the proverbial tide. Still, we paddled on, and at least the spray in our faces kept us awake. An hour or so after I took the potshot at the *Crow*, the rain picked up, and the night was once again as dark as a murderer's heart.

I hoped that by now, water had pooled in the *Crow*, and the boat was slowly sinking. How long would it take Lenoir to notice? Long enough so that he would have to go ashore to bail it out and plug the hole? I hoped for that too. Thinking about Lenoir caused me to remember a troubling question, and I yelled to Granddad above the noise of the wind.

"How do you think Corbin Lenoir knew about our fish camp on Goose Bay?"

"I don't know, but I've wondered the same thing myself."

"How do you suppose he knew Dad was on Providence Island?"

"Mystery number two."

"Do you think there's a spy," I asked, "somebody who knows Dad and who's been telling Lenoir where he is?"

"Hard telling, Otter, but the thought has crossed my mind."

"But who would—?" I started to ask the question then stopped when something occurred to me. I didn't even want to think it, much less say it, but I had to ask. "Could one of the Doozies be a traitor?"

"Yut."

"But why? They went through the war together. Dad helped them get home alive. Why would one of them do such a thing?"

"Money maybe. Or maybe this traitor is afraid of something."

"Afraid of what?"

"You ask a lot of questions, you know that?"

"I'm sorry, Granddad."

"That's all right. Doesn't hurt to chew it over, but let's talk later and just paddle for now. I'm too tired to do both."

Granddad wasn't the only one. I thought my arms were going to drop off. We'd been paddling for hours, and I was all in, but we couldn't rest. We still had four more hours to paddle before sunrise. By the time we dipped into the cold bottom of night, I had an entirely new idea of the words "dead tired." Old man that he was, I don't know how Granddad kept paddling mile after mile, hour after hour. Pure grit, I guess.

After a while, I slipped into a waking trance. I was settling down into the fresh, clean sheets of my goose down bed back at the farm—in my trance, anyway—when I realized the world was no longer coal-black dark. A weak light shone in the east, and I knew the sun would rise over Mt. Mansfield in the hour. I also knew I wouldn't see the old man's profile in the mountain today. He would be

hidden in a cloud, looking heavenward as always, talking
to God perhaps, but whatever they said today would
stay between the two of them. It was still raining, and I
was beginning to think it would always rain. The feeble
light finally brought the morning, but the world was still
muffled in a gray, low-hanging fog. *Not exactly a cheerful
prospect,* I thought. To make matters worse, my stomach
started to grumble. Then I perked up. From somewhere in
the mist ahead, the honking of Canadian geese rose clear
and loud.

"Do you hear that, Granddad?" I asked.

"I sure do," he replied.

"Are you hungry, Granddad?"

"Mister man, I'm so hungry I could eat a squirrel with
the fur still on it, but I'd a lot rather eat a goose. What
about you?"

"I'd love some goose meat, but where are they?"

"Just ahead. Look!" he whispered.

The murky dawn was spreading, and through the
tatters of fog drifting across the lake in front of us I
glimpsed an enormous flock of geese in the near distance.
Behind them, I could see a strange sight—trees but no
land. With all the rain that had fallen during the two days
since we had left the Mississquoi, the lake had risen, and
here it had flooded low-lying land. If we had wanted to,
we could have paddled out into the woods. This flooding
happened every spring during the snowmelt, but I had
never seen anything like *this*. The lake wasn't just up

around the foot of each tree. It had climbed well up each
trunk. I turned back to ask Granddad if he knew where we
were, but when I did, I saw a dark, squat shape looming in
the fog behind us.

"Is that Law Island back there?" I asked.

"Yut."

"So this must be Colchester Point in front of us. Well,
praise the patron saint of sailors! Granddad, you're like a
migrating bird! How you found your way through the pitch-
black night is a marvel."

Granddad chuckled. "Well, let's see if we can *plug* a
couple migrating birds. I don't know how we're going to find
any dry wood to cook them, but we'll think of something."

"Seriously, Granddad, I know you have the compass
from Jack's boat, but you couldn't see the map in the dark.
How did you get us all the way down here to the Winooski,
right where we wanted to go?"

"I used the compass. And I used this."

I turned around. He was holding a forked stick. "A
divining rod?"

"Yut."

"I thought that was only for finding a vein of water so
you could dig a spring."

"I thought so, too, but Fordyce McCaul taught me
different."

"Fordyce?" I asked. "What kind of name is that?"

"One like yours. A little off the beaten track. He was
a Scot. He taught me how to hold the stick. 'Grip each

branch of the wye lightly,' he said, 'palms up, thumbs oot.
Hold it gently and wait. If ye hae the gift, lad, a buzzing of
sparks will set up in your arms and hands. You'll feel the
stick twitch and pull, and then it will point like a bird dog.
It's a *divining* rod, Amos. If ye ask it the right question, a
seeker's question, it'll steer ye right.'"

"I'll be jiggered!"

"Indeed," laughed Granddad.

"Will you teach me how to hold the stick?"

"I will, but for now, let's look for our breakfast."

We paddled silently and because of the swirling fog,
we snuck in close and shot two geese before the sentries
sounded the alarm. The flock rose and wheeled away to the
south. Granddad paddled to the dead birds, and I dropped
them in the canoe. Jake, who had been napping, raised his
head and stared at them with interest. I warned him in no
uncertain terms not to chew on our breakfast. He looked
at me with an expression that said either "I'll have a little
chew as soon as your back is turned" or "how could you
suspect me of such rude behavior," and then he settled his
muzzle back on his paws and closed his eyes again.

We had rounded Colchester Point to reach the flock
of geese, and I had been so wrapped up with them, it
was only now that I heard a tremendous roaring like a
hurricane wind rushing through the trees. The mouth of
the Winooski River lay before us—or so I thought. Dawn
had broken, and more holes in the mist appeared. Through
the rain, I looked for landmarks, but I was baffled six ways

from Sunday. I knew this part of the river well. Usually, the
current poked along its main channel through a big swamp
full of cottonwoods. At the lake, it slowed down, fanned
out, and dropped silt like it had been doing since ancient
times. But now, the main channel had vanished, and so
had the sandy beach where my friends and I often came
to swim. The roaring that filled my ears was the sound of
a once-tame animal turned into a howling beast, the river
gone mad.

The rain in October had filled every crack and cranny,
every hollow and sag between Montpelier and Burlington.
Now, with the downpour of the last few days, the rain had
no place to go. The cup had run over, and water rushed
down the hills in a fury. Every brook had become a river,
and every river had burst its banks. The swamp and the
beach at the river mouth had been drowned in a great
flood.

Before us, the mouth of the Winooski had widened to
that of a monster. The current raged headlong into the lake
and spewed its victims out upon the bay. A full-grown tree
bobbed along on the torrent a hundred yards before us.
River boulders had ground its branches down to jagged
spikes, and this juggernaut was bearing down on two
frantic Jersey cows. They bawled in terror and swam away
from the rolling, dangerous tree. Three barrels surged past,
along with the wreckage of a hay wagon, a watering tub
with a wide-eyed cat clinging to the rim, and more trees.
Then—and I know this will sound like a whopper—a two-

story farmhouse came tearing along. Most of the bottom story was underwater, and the house was on a wicked tilt. I figured it would sink to the bottom when the river calmed down out in the bay, but for now the madness of the flood kept it afloat.

Then I saw a scary thing. A chair flew through a second story window and smashed out the glass. A girl's face appeared. She looked to be about my age. She climbed through the window opening, swung an ax in a high arc over her head and buried it in the roof just above the eaves. She grabbed the ax with one hand and reached back through the window with the other to pull a woman out onto the wall with her. Then the girl used the ax handle to scramble up onto the roof. The roof was still canted at a steep angle but nothing like the side of the house which was practically a cliff. Once she gained the roof, she grabbed the ax head with one hand and reached back again for the woman. Just then, though, the house ran over something on the lake bottom.

"Holy catfish on a spit! Granddad, look!" I could see it coming. The house rose and then, when its weight shifted, it rolled to one side. The woman reached upward, and her fingers came within an inch of the girl's outstretched hand, but when the house rolled, the woman had to clutch the window frame to keep from being thrown. Then the house turned like a great millstone, and the woman—looking sadly at the girl above her—clung to the window and disappeared underwater. The girl screamed.

"Otter! Put your back into it, boy. We've got to reach them before that house drops to the bottom and sucks them down with it!"

We slashed our paddles through the water as if the whole night of paddling was but a bad dream, and the canoe skimmed the waves like a live thing. Nearer we came, and suddenly, like a wallowing ship that rights itself, the house rolled back up, but the woman was gone. The girl screamed again, but now she had seen us, and she was pointing. Twenty yards from our canoe, and in the wake of the house, the woman flailed, trying to keep her head above water. She couldn't swim a stroke and went under a couple times as we bore down on her. She wouldn't last much longer. Then, out of the corner of my eye, I saw a worse threat. Another one of those trees with the spiked limbs was headed her way.

Leapin' Lamb of God! I said to myself. *That tree trunk is going to drown her sure.* Granddad and I pushed off our paddles so hard the shafts bent, and the canoe rocketed forward. We drove the *Melodie* toward that woman with every ounce of strength we had. Doom rode on my shoulder with his hot breath stinking and his voice croaking in my ear, "You're not going to make it. You're not going to make it." I braced myself for the crash with that damn battering ram. The roar of the flood grew louder. If we could beat the tree we could save the woman, but I saw now that we couldn't do it.

With the Grim Reaper about to harvest our hapless

souls, a blast from a steamboat whistle rent the air so
loudly I almost upset the canoe. In the same instant, the
Simon Weed squeezed by us, hit the tree with a great
crack, and nosed it out of our way. One more tremendous
stroke from Granddad's paddle brought us alongside
the woman. Before she disappeared again beneath the
waves, I grabbed her long, black hair and pulled her
back from the clutches of Davy Jones. Half-drowned as
she was, and with her skirts and petticoats dragging her
down, I couldn't hoist her into the boat, but I kept her
head above water while Granddad brought us alongside
the *Simon Weed*. Too Tall, Mary, and Muff stood on
deck waiting to help us come aboard. My Uncle Hercule
plucked the woman from the lake like she was a child.
Then Granddad and I scrambled aboard with bow and
stern lines in hand. Granddad brought the woman into
the cabin to get her some blankets and a warm spot near
a radiator.

"Otter!" cried Mary. "Oh, I was hoping you'd find us."
Before I could answer, Too Tall shouted to my cousin in the
wheelhouse.

"Louis, get us closer to the girl! If the house sinks, she'll
sink with it."

"Oui, mon père" said Louis. Glancing at the wheelhouse,
I saw the spokes of the wheel flicker in his hands, and the
launch shifted direction.

I turned back to Mary. "Granddad's like a homing
pigeon," I told her with a grin. "Give him a forked stick, and

THE FLOOD

he could find Lost Atlantis." Before I could say more, Jake began howling.

"I guess somebody else needs attention," said Mary.

The *Simon Weed* was jostling my canoe six feet below, and Jake sat between the thwarts with an indignant expression on his face that said "Did you forget something?" Feeling sheepish, I called to Too Tall, and we quickly hauled the *Melodie* right up over the rail. Jake jumped out, wagging his tail, and was so glad to be on the roomy deck of the *Weed* after lying in the canoe all night that he ran in circles around the main cabin. On one of his laps, he was so overcome with excitement, he jumped up on Muff, and with his paws on Muff's shoulders, he licked the poor fellow's face. Muff tumbled over backward and lay on the deck protesting and pushing the huge dog away.

"Help! Help!" screeched Muff. "Get wolf dog off Muff! Him kill poor Muff! Go you dog! Him drown Muff in slobber! Awful dog him is! Let go Muff's arm! Go chase him cat!"

Meanwhile, I felt the deck shiver beneath us as Louis pushed the throttle forward, and the boat's engines drove her through the waves. In no time, we caught up with the house which was settling lower in the water every second. I grabbed the life buoy that hung from a post at the bow. With the ring in my right hand and the coiled rope in my left, I peered through the falling rain at the young woman. We were close enough now for me to see her face, but she was clinging to a lightning rod and looking the other way. I called to her, so I could throw her the rope.

Miss, over here!" She turned, and I almost dropped the buoy. It was Bridget Murphy.

"Mermaid and a muckle fish! Bridget! What are you doing here?"

"Throw me the rope, Otter darlin', and I'll be telling you."

"Darling?" came the voice at my side. I glanced nervously at Mary, and then I threw the ring buoy with all my might. It was easily sixty feet to Bridget. The ring fell short and landed in the water just shy of the house. Bridget had been crouching down on the other side of the roof ridge holding onto the lightning rod at the gable end. Now she let go of the rod and stood up, ready to scramble down the roof and get closer to the buoy. The house was still being carried along by the flood, wobbling and tipping, and just as she stood, it lurched forward hard. Bridget lost her balance, reached for the sky, and pitched sideways off the gable into the roiling waters.

"Otter, the canoe!" yelled Too Tall. I tossed him the buoy rope and picked up the *Melodie*. In a jiff I dropped her over the side and clambered into the stern. Too Tall threw me my paddle, and before I could stop her, Mary seized the other one and dropped into the bow. I didn't know if the girl had ever handled a paddle in her life, but she must have been watching Granddad and me real close because she took to it like an Indian. We paddled hard, but at first the current was strong, and we got nowhere fast.

Then a new disaster reared up. Dragged along by the torrent, the house had been bumping along the bottom, but now Old Man River was fading into the deeps of the lake, and the house was slowing down. The river current coming from the east, and the wind blowing from the west, ran into each other here and worked up waves as big as haystacks. After its last lurch, the house had drifted along smoothly, but now in deeper, slower water it was sinking fast! We spied Bridget trying to swim away, but her dress was heavy, and the haystack waves tugged her to and fro. As the house sank to the roof eaves, a powerful eddy caught Bridget and held her captive. When the roof went under, she would be sucked into the hole the house made and follow it down.

"Otter!" she cried. "Here!"

"We're coming!" I yelled, but I put more hope in my voice than I felt. As the house slowed, we got closer, but now the chaos of waves pushed us about too. The timbers in the house groaned, and suddenly it headed down. The suction of the whirlpool began, and all the water around us hurried toward Bridget and the disappearing wreckage of the house. *That's it,* I thought. *She's a goner,* and I looked on helplessly as terror spread across her face.

CHAPTER 15

Secret Passage

E WERE JUST A STONE'S THROW AWAY, but that was still too far to help. Then, with a great slap, a ring buoy landed in the water close enough for me to reach out and snag it. Too Tall! Louis had maneuvered the *Simon Weed* close enough for his father to throw the buoy maybe eighty feet and land it right beside me. I skimmed it off the water, gathered a few coils of rope, and flung it just beyond Bridget. When I pulled the ring toward her, she snatched it. Then I wrapped the rope once around the thwart in front of me and knelt on the loose end.

"Hang on, Bridget!" I hollered. "Mary, paddle hard, girl, hard as you can, or we're going down!" I paddled with all *my* might to turn the bow away from the yawning hole opening up in front of us. The roof of the house was sinking beneath the waves. I paddled like Corbin Lenoir was in that house trying to pull us down after him. We didn't budge for endless seconds, and then, breathing hard, we inched away from the vortex. A few minutes later, when we had paddled out of the terrible waves and reached the *Simon Weed*, I pulled Bridget to the canoe. She had blacked out, and I grabbed her hair like I had the other woman. It was a minute or two before we could maneuver the canoe close to the hull of the *Weed*. When we did, Too Tall reached down, plucked Bridget from the lake, and laid her on the deck of the launch. Mary and I scrambled aboard to find Granddad kneeling over her with Muff looking on, bewildered as usual.

"She's not breathing!" Granddad said. "Too Tall, fetch that wine cask from the dining cabin." Too Tall rushed off and returned with a sizeable barrel tucked under his arm.

"What old man him do?" cried Muff. "Toast drownded girl? Pour him wine down her gullet, make *sure* poor girl her really dead?"

Granddad ignored Muff. "Otter," he said to me, "make sure she hasn't swallowed her tongue. If her windpipe is clear, we'll drape her over this barrel." I scooped two fingers into Bridget's mouth and peeked in before I pulled them out again. She wasn't choking on anything, so Too Tall laid her over the barrel, face down. Mary and I held her arms out of the way, and Too Tall held her legs like she was a wheelbarrow, and then he rolled her back and forth.

If she'd been awake, I guess she'd have been pretty embarrassed about where her skirts were, but none of us were thinking about that. She still wasn't breathing, just rolling back and forth as limp as waterlogged spaghetti.

Then she gurgled, and on the next roll, she sputtered and spewed water onto the deck. She coughed up more water on the next couple passes, and then, when she could breathe on her own, Too Tall carried her into the main cabin. The older woman, who I discovered to be Bridget's Aunt Molly Murphy, was one minute praising the saints and the next, mewling over her and Bridget's near trip to the lake bottom. I thought she'd be better served if she was busy, so I asked her to follow Muff to the galley where he could show her the makings for some hot tea. Then I asked Mary if she would strip Bridget of wet clothes and wrap her in blankets.

"Maybe you'd like to do it, *darling*," she teased. "Seems like you two are already acquainted."

"She says darlin' because she's Irish. All the Irish say darlin'."

"Ah, do they now? And next you'll be tellin' me ye barely know the lass? Is it that daft, ye think I am, Otter St. Onge. Sure it is that butter wouldn't be meltin' in yer mouth, ye rascal."

"Well, Mary, yer right, lass. Bridget's me own true love, and I'll thank ye to treat her like yer own dear sister, and to be sure she's warm and safe." I said this with a straight face, but Mary looked suddenly so downhearted, I couldn't help but grin. I kissed her on the cheek, and then I hurried off to join the rest of the crew in the wheelhouse. When I shouldered through the door with the rain streaming off my hat brim once again, Too Tall was talking to Granddad.

"You mean to say that Chance, the guy we thought had kidnapped Royal, is Royal himself?"

"Yut."

"Chance ain't him real name?" asked Muff.

"Nope."

"Incroyable! Fantastique!" Too Tall said. "So now we're on the lookout for a man named Corbin Lenoir?"

"Right."

"And he was headed after Royal when Otter put a bullet hole in his boat. How are we going to pick up his trail?"

"Yeah, him got the whole wide lake to vanish himself like thin air. How you find him Lenoor and him black boat?" asked Muff.

"Muff, my friend," said Granddad, "I have never heard anyone murder the English language quite the way you do. How far *did* you go in school?"

Muff turned red. "Muff go fiff. Not like teachers. Teachers not like Muff. In fiff, Little Muff kick him teacher in shins once. School send Muff home. Muff not go back."

"The world lost a scholar," sighed Granddad. "Too Tall, why don't we go to the King Street Tavern. Royal may have already called Melodie's new-fangled telephone and left a message. He planned to spread a rumor that he was headed to St. Jean, and he figured Lenoir would follow him there. Royal is hoping to spot him from the broken-down fort just north of Rouses Point. If he does, he and the Doozies will follow the *Crows* down the Richelieu toward Montreal and settle this business once and for all."

"Très bon! Good plan! To the King Street Tavern," rumbled Too Tall.

"Good plan my elbow," said Granddad feigning disgust. "You just want to eat again."

"Bien sûr, Amos. While you and Otter were eating high off the pig on Ile de Providence, I and mine were turning upside down the *Simon Weed* and finding precious little provender for men of our bulk."

"Yes," said Granddad with his crooked grin, "I can see you've skinnied right down to nothing. Why, you turned sideways a minute ago, and I lost sight of you."

"Granddad?" I said. "Can I interrupt?"

"Sure. What's on your mind, Otter?"

"Do you remember that story you told us about Doc Eastman? How his daughter and granddaughter drowned?"

"I do."

"Welt, I think Mary is Doc Eastman's granddaughter." I had Granddad's full attention now. He stared at me.

"What makes you think that?" he asked.

"After we trolled for Champ with Muff—sorry, Muff—and we were headed to Providence, Mary and I talked."

"Snuggled up in the main cabin, wasn't it?" asked Little Roy.

"We were trying to get warm."

"Mais oui, Otter, a bonne idée! Did you get warm? You looked a little feverish to me," said Too Tall.

"All right, boys. I want to hear this," said Granddad.

"She told me she was raised by a man and woman named Rotmensen down in Whitehall, New York, but they weren't her real mother and father. When I asked her about her parents, all she could remember was a hat."

"A hat?" asked Granddad.

"Yut. A red hat. Later, she remembered that her grandfather gave her the hat at a birthday party, *and* she had a brother named Scott."

"Good Lord! She *is* Marian Prince. She's Evelyn's daughter!"

"The very same, Granddad."

"You know what else, Otter? Her father is alive."

"What!" I said. Now, it was my turn to be surprised. I wasn't the only one. Louis let out a long whistle. "How do you know this?" I asked.

"Doc told me when he was patching up Luc. John Prince came back to the States five years ago just after I visited the last time. Scotty stays on with his grandparents during the winter—has to finish his schooling in Plattsburgh—but during the summer he barnstorms across the country with his father. John bought a war surplus bi-plane. He takes people up for rides and does some stunts. 'Parently, he makes good money at it."

"John the Baptist on a bicycle! Mary's father is alive! Did you tell Dad about John Prince when we were on Providence?"

"Yut. He couldn't imagine how John survived the cannon fire over Vimy Ridge that morning, but he's going to track him down and find out. At least, he will if he can take care of this Lenoir fella."

"Granddad, I want to tell Mary about all this, but it'll be a lot for her to take in all to once. We're headed to the King Street Tavern?"

"Yut."

"Would you mind if she and I follow the *Simon Weed* in my canoe?"

"That's a worrisome prospect, Otter. What if Lenoir should happen by? You'd be a sitting duck in a canoe. Your father would never forgive me."

"What are the chances of Lenoir showing up, Granddad? He was headed north last time we saw him, chasing Dad. He might even be tied up somewhere on Grand Isle looking for a hole in his boat. If he does show up down here, he doesn't even know what I look like."

"He's right, Amos," said Too Tall. "Otter might even be safer in the canoe than on the *Simon Weed*. If Lenoir, he catch sight of me, he will know certain sure I'm Royal's brother, but Otter? He favor his mother more than Royal."

Granddad paused to think. "All right," he said finally. "Muff, be a good lad and go send Mary out here, will you? Then stay in the cabin with Bridget and her aunt. I'll see how they're doing in a few minutes."

"Oh no, Muff him don't mind. Go here, fetch this, do that. Muff happy him be servant to great man use him as fish bait. Muff do any little thing for man who try to drown him. Muff take hat off, bow to Granddad him, walk backward from his highness presence. Muff grovel and wait for him majesty throw poor Muff him bone." Off Muff went, muttering his grievances to entertain himself, the most abused poor soul in the world.

"Thank you, Granddad," I said.

"That's all right. I suppose you've got more than one thing to talk about with Mary," he replied.

"And would yez be wantin' your canoe lowered over the side now, sir?" asked Too Tall grinning.

HALF AN HOUR LATER, THE SIMON WEED had steamed out of sight, and Mary and I were paddling the canoe in the rain. Jake was snoozing in his customary spot amidships. My rifle, as usual, was slung from the thwarts in an oil-soaked square of canvas.

"So," Mary ventured, "Bridget's not really your sweetheart?"

"Not any more."

"She was once?"

"Yut."

"Why isn't she now?"

"Mary, do you really want to hear me talk about Bridget Murphy?"

"I guess not, but—"

"There's only one girl I want to talk about with you."

"Who?" she asked quickly.

"Yourself darlin'. Miss Mary Mack."

"Oh," she said with a laugh.

"For instance, I'm wondering where you learned to paddle a canoe."

"I watched you and Granddad."

"You watched us? That's where—? You mean you never paddled a canoe before today?"

"No. Never."

"How in the name of Mother Mary and her miracles did you catch on so fast? You handled that paddle like you were born to it."

"Things like that come naturally to me. Back in Whitehall? When I was a kid? The boys laughed at me when I wanted to play baseball. Then I bet Lucky Boone I could pitch better than him, and I struck out three batters in a row. They let me play after that. In Kansas City, Mr. Wilbur, the track coach, saw me run one day and asked me to try out for the team. I knew I couldn't join, but I ran the hundred-yard dash.

The coach wouldn't tell me what my time was. He muttered something about his stopwatch and asked me to run again the next day. After I ran the second time, I jogged back to where he was staring at his watch. Finally, he looked up. 'Mary,' he said, 'you just ran the fastest hundred-yard dash of any student I've ever coached, and I've been coaching here for ten years. I looked up the school record last night, and you broke it, and I don't mean the girl's record. I mean, the record. Period. For girls *and* boys. Yesterday, I thought my stopwatch was broken, but I borrowed another one, and today you ran two-tenths of a second faster than you did yesterday. Will you run for the team?' I told him I would, but then DePrae pulled me out of school. Anyway, Otter, I don't mean to go on and on about myself. I was only trying to answer your question."

"Mary, I love to hear you talk." She didn't say anything to this. She just kept paddling, each stroke graceful and strong.

"Look," I said, "I dated Bridget, but that's over."

"I'm sure it's none of my business." I didn't say anything in return. Suddenly, I didn't want to talk. I watched the mist rise slowly from the lake. I opened my mouth and tasted raindrops on my tongue. I scratched Jake behind the ears. I watched Mary, kneeling in front of me in the bow. I saw the wet curls of her thick, beautiful hair falling below her shoulders. She sat as straight and tall as a flower growing toward the sun. I was wet and cold again, but I was as happy as a hired hand on Saturday night.

WE SPIED BURLINGTON HARBOR A FEW HOURS later, and I still hadn't talked to Mary about her family. The time hadn't seemed right, or maybe I couldn't find the right words. It would have to wait, I decided. The waves outside the breakwater were canoe swampers, but Mary swung her paddle through the water as regular as a pendulum, and that helped me handle the steering. I hooked my paddle blade at the end of each stroke just enough to keep the stern from being pushed sideways. I didn't want us to broach. A wave would have dumped in the canoe for

sure, and even if I couldn't get much wetter, I didn't want
to go for another swim. I'd had enough of that cold lake to
last a considerable while. We weren't in any real danger,
but I had to crank my head around and watch for big
waves sneaking up from behind, so it wasn't until the lake
smoothed out inside the breakwater that I could look at the
King Street Ferry Landing.

"Otter!" said Mary, "there's the *Simon Weed*! Look at the
boat tied up beside it."

"Curse the Devil and his demon sons!" I muttered.
"That's hard to stomach."

"It's Lenoir's boat?" asked Mary.

"Yut, it's the *Crow*. He's found us. I'll bet they're all at
the King Street Tavern right now."

"What can we do?"

"I think I'd better pay a visit to Uncle Rinx and Aunt
Josey, pronto," I said.

"Who?" asked Mary.

"My aunt and uncle. They live next door to the tavern."

"I'm coming with you," she said.

"I don't think that's a good—."

"I'm coming with you," she said firmly. I could see she
had made up her mind, and she wasn't going to change it.

"All right," I said. "Let's go." We walked up King Street
side by side, Jake trotting a few yards ahead, sniffing at
hydrants and fence corners marked by other dogs. I talked
to pass the time. "Grandma Melodie runs a tavern in the
house that once belonged to Gideon King. A hundred years

ago folks called Gideon the Admiral of the Lake because
he held the mortgage on just about every boat that sailed
Champlain. That's why they named this street after him.
He made most of his money trading lumber, but crusty
old Gideon wasn't above smuggling now and then. When
the customs agents came to his house, he was never
there. He—." Suddenly, I steered Mary off King Street onto
Ormand Ploof's lawn. We stood behind a hedge just down
the street from the tavern. She started to speak, but I
interrupted.

"The fifth house on the right is my grandmother's,"
I said, "the brick one with the chimneys built into the
gables. I'd bet a buffalo head nickel that's one of the *Crows*
standing near the front door."

"What do we do?"

"I'm going to slip into the house next door without him
noticing. That's where my Aunt Josey and Uncle Rinx live.
My uncle isn't likely to be home, but Aunt Josey will be,
and I know she'll help me." Mary looked puzzled.

"An old lady? How is she going to help you against
Lenoir?"

I hesitated. A tunnel led from Grandma Melodie's
cellar to Aunt Josey's. Gideon King had prob'ly built it for
smuggling. When Prohibition came along, Gram Melodie
socked away her profits and bought the house next door for
her sister Josey. The tunnel had never been used as far as
I knew. Still, it might come in handy. If the cops raided the
place, somebody like Granddad could slip down the cellar

stairs, crawl through the tunnel, and the law would never be the wiser. I was wasting valuable seconds thinking about all this without saying anything to Mary because the tunnel was a family secret. Then she put two and two together.

"You said Gideon King was never at home when the customs agents came? Would that have anything to do with the house next door?"

"Yut," I said. "All right. I guess the cows are already out, so there's no point to closing the gate." I told her about the passage and swore her to secrecy. "I'm going through the tunnel into the cellar at Gram's house," I said.

"You left your rifle in the canoe."

"Yut. Thought it might draw attention on the sidewalk. Uncle Rinx has guns. The question now is, what are you going to do?"

"I'm going to the King Street Tavern to see Mrs. Waters about a job as a waitress."

"What will you do if Lenoir's man won't let you in?"

"Nothing. I'll walk back to the waterfront and wait. But he'll let me in."

"And if he does?"

"Give me a knife. I'll slip it to Granddad. If I can't get it to him, I'll get it to Little Roy. Louis says he's quite a hand with one."

"I don't like it. It's too dangerous."

"And it's not for you?"

"That's different."

"Otter," said Mary softly, "we don't have much time, and I'm going in there whether you give me a knife or not. If I go in, at least Granddad will know you are nearby."

"All right," I sighed. I handed her the hunting knife Granddad had made for me from an old file. It had a sharp, six-inch blade and a slim, bone handle. She stuffed it into her boot top.

"That's good tucked down in like that. There's a chance he'll miss it if he"—Mary raised her eyebrows as I paused— "if he frisks you."

"He won't do that."

"Why not?"

"Because I won't let him."

"You might not have a choice when you get inside," I said. "Are you sure you want to do this?"

"Yes."

"Okay." I placed my fingertips against her chin and gently tilted her face so I could look into her eyes. "Be careful," I said. "I'd like to see you again."

"Would ye now, Otter St. Onge? Oi'd like that fine meself," she said, teasing me again. "But I'm going now, lad. Anything else to tell me about what ye're going to do?"

"No," I said. "I'll figure it out when I come up from the cellar. Granddad will know I'm close by when he sees you, but look down at the floor, if you can do it without Lenoir seeing you. Then Granddad will know I'm coming through the tunnel."

"You be careful, too," she whispered. She stood on tiptoe

and reached up to kiss me. Then she turned away and strolled up the street toward my grandmother's tavern. I peered through the hedge and watched her for half a minute, and then I followed. She hailed Lenoir's man as she drew near the tavern, said she was looking for a Mrs. Waters, and he perked right up. By the time I reached Aunt Josey's house, he was much too busy with her to notice me. I opened the gate in the white picket fence and mounted the porch steps. I knocked, and Aunt Josey opened the door. She was a tall woman, straight-backed and proud. She was also stern, practical and intelligent, prob'ly the most book-read person in the family. One look at me told her trouble had come to town.

"Come in, you scamp," she said quietly.

"Thank you, Aunt," I replied, and inside I quickly explained. She reached into a closet and brought out a twelve-gauge, Winchester shotgun.

"Otter, I hope you know what you're doing," she said. "If you have to shoot a man, you'll carry the weight of it for the rest of your life."

"Aunt, this Lenoir wants to kill our family—me, Granddad, Gram, even you maybe. He already shot at Granddad and me last night off South Hero."

"All right. Then don't hesitate. Here," she said, handing me the gun. "It's loaded. Uncle Rinx left for Barre in the Model T two days ago, and with all the flooding, he must be stranded. 'Parently most of the bridges are out on the Winooski. Anyway, he says this shotgun kicks like a bad-tempered mule, so snug it to your shoulder before you pull the trigger."

"Yes, Ma'am. And thank you. I didn't want to tote my deer rifle up the street. Would have stood out like a sixth finger." Aunt Josey nodded and struck a match to a kerosene lantern. We clattered down the stairs into the gloom of the cellar. I stood the shotgun in the corner, and the two of us wrestled a cupboard full of Mason jars away from the stone wall. She pulled on an iron handle, and a small wooden door swung outward on creaking hinges. I took the shotgun and plunged into the hole on my hands and knees like a terrier after a rat. Aunt Josey held the lantern up to light my way and wished me good luck. Jake stood at the entrance, whining a little, his tail wagging uncertainly. For once, I decided he'd better stay put.

"Aunt," I asked, "will you look after my dog?"

Aunt Josey looked down her long nose at Jake with interest. "Maybe he'll look after me," she said. "Scoot now. Who knows what that gangster is doing to your grandparents."

I wriggled through a passage shored up with half-rotten timbers and got soaked right off. Six inches of water lay in the low spots, and water dripped from the walls and ceiling. *God bless a bull frog,* I thought, *if we ever finish with Corbin Lenoir, I'm going to live in the desert. With all this rain I'll be lucky if the tunnel doesn't cave in on me.* I turned a corner and passed beyond the friendly shine of my aunt's lantern. I kept the gun up out of the water by keeping it in the crook of my elbows. I heard a squeak and something scurried up my arm, brushed my cheek, and fled down my back. *Ugh! A rat! That's it,* I said to myself. *Next time I get to the hardware store, I'm buying one of those Eveready flashlights. I sure could use the darn thing right now.*

A couple minutes later, the worst was over. I bumped against the door at the tavern end of the tunnel. I groped for the latch and breathed a sigh of relief when the door opened into Gram's cellar. A murky light pooled under a couple small windows high up in the cellar walls, and I stood beneath one and inspected Uncle Rinx's shotgun. *Rub my rabbit's foot,* I thought, *dry and ready to fire. I like that.* I pulled my trapper's pistol from the small of my back where I had stuck it down my britches. I opened the cylinder and spun it. Each of the six chambers held a bullet, and the pistol, too, was dry. I could hear voices in the room above now. I flicked off the safeties on both guns, stuck the pistol in my belt, and crept up the stairs.

The door at the top opened into the kitchen. With my ear pressed against the crack where the door met the frame, I listened. I couldn't hear a sound in the kitchen, but I could hear those same voices in the taproom. Ever so slowly and gently, I lifted the latch and cracked the door ajar. I saw no one. I pushed the door slowly, slowly with my foot and held the shotgun ready. No one was in the kitchen. Then, through the window over the sink, I saw a man standing guard on the back porch. Fortunately, he had his back to the door. If he expected trouble, I guess he figured it would be coming from outside. The voices in the next room were clear now, and one in particular I didn't like at all.

"Old man, I'm going to kill the giant—a brother for a brother, you know—but I want the son too. Tell me where he is right now, or I kick the chair out from under the old lady here, and you can watch her hang." I was already headed to the swinging doors that led to the front room and the bar, when I heard my grandmother's voice.

"Amos, don't you say a word. Mister, if you're such a coward you'd kill an old woman, then go ahead and kick that chair. I'll never help you hurt my grandson, and no one else here will either."

"Gag her, Henri. I'm sick of listening to her. What do you say old man?"

"M-m-mister, I'm s-s-so nervous, I can hardly open my mouth," stuttered Granddad. "Y-you've got so many guns pointed at us, I'm getting heart p-p-palpitations. You've got everybody but this girl here b-b-bound hand and foot. Th-that fella behind the bar pointing the T-t-tommy gun at us seems to have an itchy finger. The fella by the door has a shotgun, and you've got a pistol. Wh-wh-what are you afraid of? Don't you think you've got the s-s-situation in hand? Wh-wh-what the heck are we going to d-d-do? I *w-w-will* make a deal with you, but untie my hands and l-l-let me have a drink. Holy M-m-mother of M-m-mercy, I'm shaking all over."

There was dead silence. I couldn't move for fear of

making a noise. I knew what Granddad was doing. He knew I was there, and he was telling me where Lenoir's men were. I had moved close to the swinging doors while everyone was talking. I would shoot the Tommy gunner first and then the man with the shotgun if I could. But I was still a step away, and then Lenoir spoke again and made the hair stand up on my neck.

"What are you up to, old man? You just described everyone's location in the room. He's here, isn't he?" Granddad didn't answer.

CHAPTER 16

The Dead Men

A S CORBIN LENOIR WAS ASKING GRANDAD that question, I took the last step to the edge of the doorway. Aunt Josey's words rang in my head, "Don't hesitate." With the shotgun jammed against my shoulder, I stepped around the corner and shot the man behind the bar holding the Tommy gun. I ducked back into the kitchen just as the guy by the door blasted the spot where I had been standing. Some of the shot slammed into the doorjamb, and some of it flew by me and into the wall above Gram's cast iron cookstove. I levered another shell into the chamber as the man on the porch opened the back door. I pulled the trigger. He teetered like a tree cut through but still on the stump, deciding which way to fall. Staring in wide-eyed surprise, he back-pedaled across the porch and crashed into my grandmother's rose bushes. Then Lenoir's voice came from the taproom.

"Come on in here, boy. I've got a gun to your grandmother's head. If you're not in here by the time I count to three, I'll pull the trigger."

On two, I walked through the swinging doors with the shotgun aimed at Lenoir. He was clinging to Gram like a vine, and reaching up, he did indeed have a pistol barrel against her temple. What he didn't see was Mary. She was bending down, pulling the knife from her boot, and I spoke to keep Lenoir's attention on me.

"What's the point in killing my grandmother? *Her* last name is Waters. My father's is St. Onge. She's my mother's mother, not my father's. If you shoot her, you'll die too, Lenoir. I'll make sure of it."

"Don't think so, boy. You shoot me now, and you're bound to hit your grandmother too. But André, that fellow by the door, he'll drop you in your tracks at a nod from me."

That was all the time Mary needed. She darted forward as quick as a bobcat and stabbed Lenoir in the arm. He dropped the pistol with a howl, and it skittered across the floor toward Granddad. Lenoir tried to grapple with Mary, but she jabbed him with the knife again and held him at bay. I dove behind the bar just as André's shotgun boomed again. He hadn't dared shoot at Mary because of Lenoir, but I was a clear target. I popped up over the bar and fired back, but he was already ducking through the open door, and I missed.

Meanwhile, Granddad had Lenoir's pistol. His hands were tied behind his back, but he had got a grip on the gun, and now, with Mary diving to the floor, he was firing, a little wildly, but steadily, and if Lenoir's reaction was any gauge, Granddad was getting closer with each shot. With Granddad's bullets whistling by, Mary out of reach, and me walking out from behind the bar levering another round into the breech of the Winchester, he ran out the door about as fast as a bullet himself.

I chased down the street after Lenoir, but I couldn't catch him. From the Ice House on the corner of Battery Street and King, I watched him, André, and the third man board the *Crow* and leave in a big old hurry. Little Roy and Too Tall caught up with me in time to see the *Crow* pass the breakwater and head north.

"Don't worry, Otter, mon neveu," said Too Tall. "He won't be so much lucky next time. Go on back now. Your grand-mère wants to see you."

"Yes, Uncle Hercule."

I walked up King Street. The rain poured down, and I felt my insides turn over. I knelt down in some bushes and heaved. When I shot the Tommy gunner behind the bar, I saw what happened to his face. It wasn't pretty. I'd had no choice. I knew that. My grandmother was about to die. Lenoir wanted to kill my family, and he wanted to kill me. I thought it through from every angle, and *thinking* about it, I was sure I'd done the right thing. But I'd never killed a man before, and as much as I told myself I'd done right, my gut churned. I had opened a door better left shut, but it was too late to close it now.

When I was done retching, I tipped my head back and let my mouth fill with rain. I rinsed the sour spit away, and then I stood up again. I felt queasy, but I had to get back to the tavern. When I walked unsteadily through the door, everyone was gathered in the taproom. Louis leaned against the bar, quiet as usual, and I felt like a stranger the way he looked at me. Granddad and Gram, and Mary and Aunt Josey stopped talking. Mrs. Murphy glanced up from her prattle with Bridget. Even Muff was speechless. Their solemn, staring faces scared me, and I wondered if I had been wounded after all and hadn't even realized it. I looked down at my shirt front and my trousers, but I saw no sign of blood. Then Jake bounded toward me, leaped up, put his huge paws on my shoulders, and licked my face. Everyone laughed, and I felt the tension go out of me like air escaping from a bladder.

"Otter," said Gram, "when the Hound of the Baskervilles is done washing your face, I want to give you a hug."

I pushed Jake aside, and my grandmother threw her arms around me and hugged and kissed me and whispered over and over, "Bless you, Otter, bless you." Feeling embarrassed and happy at the same time, I hugged my grandmother with my free hand and grinned at Granddad and Mary. Aunt Josey stepped forward and took Uncle Rinx's shotgun when she realized Gram wasn't going to let go right away.

"All right, Mother," said Granddad, "don't smother the boy."

Gram finally sat down at a table to blow her nose. Mary had been waiting patiently. She held out my hunting knife, and I sheathed it. Her eyes glistened, but she wasn't crying. She threw her arms around my neck, and I clasped her to me.

"Otter," she whispered, "I was scared."

"You didn't look scared, Mary. You looked like a wildcat. I don't think I ever saw anybody move quite so quick as you with that knife."

"I wasn't scared for myself, Otter. I was scared for *you*."

"Well, truth be told, I was scared for the lot of us."

Just then Too Tall and the others walked through the door.

"These two," he said, shaking his head at Granddad. "They're like magnets. Every time they get near each other—zip, click, bang! You can't keep 'em apart!"

Mary flushed scarlet. Looking over her shoulder, I saw Granddad grin.

"Won't be me getting in the way," he said. "Listen," he continued, "the cops could knock on the door any minute. Too Tall, can you and the boys get the bodies into the cellar? Josey, if it's all right with you, we'll drag them through the tunnel to your house. Mother, we'll load them into your wagon tonight and bring them down to the *Simon Weed* after dark."

As always, Granddad was thinking ahead, and as always, he made sense. We set to work. Too Tall, Louis, and Little Roy got rid of the corpses. I mopped up the blood behind the bar, which didn't improve the ill feeling in my gut, but at least it gave me a job. As Gram was fond of saying, 'Satan finds mischief yet for idle hands to do.' I don't know that this made sense when I was younger and making plenty of mischief, busy or not, but it made sense now. I needed a simple task, and strangely enough, this one allowed the knot in me to unwind a little.

Gram brought Bridget and her Aunt Molly to an upstairs bedroom so they could rest and clean up. They were an inch or two shorter than Gram, who was tall like Aunt Josey, so the dresses she laid out for them were a smidge big, but they were dry and warm, and Bridget and her aunt, still shivering in their sodden clothes, were more than grateful. Mary and Aunt Josey set to work in the kitchen plucking the geese we'd shot and putting bread in the oven.

Granddad sat in a Morris chair by the stove in the taproom. The tobacco in his pipe glowed red now and then, and a puff of smoke swirled around his head and drifted to the ceiling. His eyes were closed, and anyone else might have thought he had dozed off, but I knew better. He was thinking. When the others had gone off to their chores, he had taken me aside and explained how Lenoir had caught them unawares.

Little Roy had let Lenoir and a companion into the dining room when Lenoir claimed to be from the Burlington Red Cross. He had come to talk to Mrs. Waters, he claimed, to ask if she could provide temporary room and board to a few poor souls whose homes had been washed away by the flood. Overhearing this, Gram came into the

dining room from the kitchen. Granddad stood up from
his table, suddenly suspicious, but by the time he reached
for his revolver, Lenoir had a knife to Gram's throat, and
his man André had a pistol cocked and ready to shoot
Granddad or Too Tall between the eyes. I pretty much
knew the rest, he said, and if I hadn't shown up when I did,
well—he was just glad I had. Then he clapped me on the
back and looked me straight in the eye.

"I know how you're feeling right now," he said. "If you
kill a man, even with good reason, it leaves a mark on
you. Your father knows, doesn't he? All that he did in the
war? He was your age, Otter. Still, you did have cause.
Remember that. You'll never feel *good* about killing those
men—I'd worry about you, if you did—but you'll carry the
weight easier over time. And you *can* feel good about this—
you saved a lot of people you care about."

I nodded. I'd never known it until then—he had never
told me—but Granddad had killed a man, maybe more
than one. I had no doubt. He settled down with his pipe.
I grabbed the mop and filled the bucket again. *You saved
a lot of people you care about.* I couldn't imagine higher
praise from Granddad.

I SETTLED INTO A RHYTHM WITH THE MOP. I started
behind the bar and swished it back and forth where the
Tommy gunner had bled to death. Again and again, I
dunked the mop, wrung it out, and swabbed the floor.
Slowly, the stains disappeared. I worked my way backward

to the kitchen, where Aunt Josey was getting to know Mary, and then mopped my way out the back door. I dragged the mop back and forth across the porch where Lenoir's guard had spurted blood as he staggered backward and tumbled into the roses. The rain pouring down had washed the blood off the bushes. I cut the broken ones with my hunting knife and threw them on top of some brush that Gram had piled next to the neighbor's fence. Then I went back inside. I had just finished emptying the bucket into the washroom sink when Gram's phone rang.

Neither Granddad nor I were used to telephones—Gram's had just been installed that summer—but we knew how they worked. I took the listening piece off the hook and handed it to him. He murmured yes a couple times, but mostly he listened. When it was his turn, he talked about a flock of pesky crows roosting in the trees around the tavern, and about a local boy having to shoot a couple of them before they would fly away. No, he said, who could tell where they went? He didn't think they'd be back, though. Then he said he wished he could follow those crows because they were a darned nuisance, and he didn't like them roosting next to the house. He'd like to follow them all the way to Canada and shoot every last one if he could. No, of course he didn't think the crows were going to Canada. Who could tell where a flock of crows would land? He had only thought of Canada because they had headed north.

If anyone had been listening on the party line, they might have thought Granddad a bit eccentric, but they wouldn't have known, like I did, that he was telling the other party I had killed two of Lenoir's thugs and that Lenoir and his remaining men might be headed in Dad's direction.

"What did *he* say?" I asked when Granddad put the listening horn back in its cradle.

"Your father said that boy did the right thing to kill two of those crows because that was a sure way to discourage them from pestering the tavern. He also said he didn't know much about crows, but he seemed to remember that they are unpredictable creatures and can turn up anywhere."

"What does he think we should do now?"

"He thinks we should all stay here and protect your grandmother and each other."

"What do you think?"

"I don't know. I'm still thinking."

"Granddad?"

"Yut?"

"I want to go help Dad."

"I know." With that Granddad sat down again and relit his pipe.

A FEW HOURS LATER WE HAD FINALLY CLEANED the tavern to Granddad's satisfaction. By then, Gram, Aunt Josey, and Mary had finished roasting venison, the geese Granddad and I had shot, and a pan of onions and potatoes. They had baked several loaves of bread and three apple pies. They had heated a kettle of corn chowder and a couple gallons of mulled cider. My mouth waters just remembering it. We locked the doors, and we all sat down at the big harvest table in the middle of the dining room.

Granddad and I hadn't eaten a meal since the previous day, and after all the excitement we'd had since leaving Providence Island, we were hungry enough to eat everything but the pig's squeal. Too Tall and the boys had fared a little better. In spite of what he had said, I knew my uncle had found some food on board the *Simon Weed*, but he and my cousins could always be depended on to eat like a swarm of locusts.

We had finished the goose meat and polished off most of the venison by the time the church bell at St. Paul's struck one o'clock. Mary and Bridget had just gone to the kitchen for more bread and home-brewed stout, when we heard boots on the stoop and a sharp rap from the lion's head knocker that decorated the tavern's front door. I heard a click, and I knew Granddad had just cocked his pistol under the table. I slipped into the kitchen, pulled Uncle Rinx's shotgun out of the broom closet, and stood to one side of the swinging doors. Louis grabbed his rifle and left the washroom door ajar. Too Tall opened the tavern door.

Before him stood Henry "Stub" Wilson of the Burlington Police Department. Stub was named for his modest height, so he had to crane his neck and look up at quite an angle to speak to Uncle Hercule.

"Good afternoon, sir. I'm with the city police," he said. He opened his lapel to show his badge and peered around Too Tall's hulking figure in search of my grandmother. "Good day, Melodie, Amos, everyone. We had a report of gunfire in this neighborhood, and I was detailed to make inquiries."

I tucked my shotgun back in the closet and strolled back into the dining room with Mary who carried a cutting board with the fresh bread. She had left the stout in the kitchen. Mary set the bread on the table, and I drew her chair back so she could sit down. Then I sat beside her and returned to my venison and potatoes.

"Oh, Otter," said Stub, "I didn't realize you were back in town."

"Hi Officer Wilson," I said politely. Granddad had always taught me to be as respectful to the authorities as I was to everyone else. He said it was a hard job being a cop or a warden, and until they proved otherwise, a fella should figure them to be ordinary folk just trying to do a job. It wasn't our part to make that job any harder unless our interests ran cross-grained, and when that happened it was nothing personal and didn't need meanness in the mix. I think Stub knew Gram was selling spirits in the tavern, but the sign out front advertised nothing but meals, and since her customers were not the hard-drinking, carousing type that caused an uproar in the streets when they left her premises, Stub had never pressed her with questions. Besides, Stub had courted her for a year during their days at Burlington High School, and maybe he was still a little in love with her even if he had a wife and five kids.

"Yut, I and Granddad came down from the farm to visit."

"Oh. How did you get down here, Amos? I don't see your old T out front."

"We hitched a ride with a drummer passing through Swanton, Stub. You say somebody heard gunfire in the neighborhood? I heard a couple backfires from a car a while ago. At least, I thought it was a car. Can't imagine what else it could have been. Should we be worried?"

"It never hurts to keep your eyes open, does it, Amos? Probably it was just a backfire like you said. How long ago was that?"

"About an hour ago, maybe an hour and a half. I wasn't keeping track of the time."

"Ah. That was about the time someone phoned the station. I had another call, so I couldn't come over right away. Well, everything seems quiet in the neighborhood now."

"Yut. Seems so. Would you like to join us for lunch, Stub?" asked Granddad.

"Thank you kindly, Amos, but I'd best get back to the station. The sooner I make out my reports, the sooner I can go home." He tipped his hat toward Gram and Aunt Josey. "Good day to you all. Enjoy your meal." He paused at the threshold and turned. "By the way," he asked, "does anyone know why that steamboat, the *Simon Weed*, is tied up down at the King Street ferry dock? I didn't see anyone on board, which is strange. If memory serves, that launch is owned and operated by the Hotel Champlain across the lake."

"Nobody on board you say, Stub?" replied Granddad. "That is strange. I wonder if it's got something to do with all this rain. Maybe the hotel sent the launch over here to carry supplies to folks turned out by the flood."

"That's a clever deduction, Amos. Doubtless you have hit on the answer."

With that, Stub passed through the door and closed it behind him. Too Tall had already returned to the table and his overflowing plate. Now, Louis came out of the washroom and did likewise.

"He knew more than he let on, didn't he Granddad?" I asked.

"Yut," nodded Granddad. He had risen from the table and stood now at the window looking down the street.

"Has he gone?" asked Louis.

"Almost. He's coming to Battery Street." Granddad lingered. "Yut. He's turned the corner."

"Bon," said Too Tall. "He seems a smart little man, him."

"He is," said Granddad coming back to the table. "Too smart. If he comes back with a warrant, he might turn into a real pest."

"Should we leave now?" asked Louis.

"No," replied Granddad. "It would be too risky to move those bodies in the daylight. We'll take them as soon as it gets dark and hope Henry is too fond of Mrs. Waters to bother coming back."

Granddad was sitting at the head of the table, facing the door and the big window on the street, and suddenly I noticed that he was staring at Mary.

"What's wrong, girl?" he asked. I turned and saw that her cheeks were wet.

"What is it?" I asked. Bridget, who had taken to her right away, sat in the chair on Mary's left, and now she hugged her.

"There, there, darlin'. It's all right, it is. Worn out is what you are, that's all. What a fright we've had today. No wonder the tears 'ave come. Have a good cry now, and you'll feel better, sure you will."

"Thank you, Bridget, but I'm not tired. It's just that—." She paused, unable to to go on.

"What is it, Mary?" asked Aunt Josey. "What's on your mind, girl?"

"I've never seen this before," she said.

"What's that, dear?" asked Gram.

"Family. I've never sat at a table surrounded by family before. You all look out for each other. It's wonderful."

Granddad was still staring, but now he was staring at me. I nodded my head.

"Mary," I said, "I've been meaning to tell you this all day, but I was waiting for the right time. Maybe that's now." Hearing the earnest tone in my voice, she turned sideways in her chair to face me.

"On our way to Plattsburgh two days ago, Granddad told us a story, me and Too Tall and my cousins. Too Tall's old friend Luc had been shot by Jack Kendrick of the Champlain Boat Patrol. We were bringing him to a Doc Eastman who lives on Cumberland Head."

"Otter," said Mary, "what are you talking about?"

I took her hand in mine and continued. "Uncle Hercule was curious about how Granddad came to know a doctor living all the way across the lake, so Granddad told us the story of how they met. In 1916—you would have been six—Granddad and Doctor Eastman were traveling on the Lake Champlain Ferry from Grand Isle to Plattsburgh. Doctor Eastman was in the company of his daughter Evelyn and his two grandchildren, Marian and Scott.

In a storm that sprang up during the crossing, a terrible accident happened. Evelyn and her children fell overboard. Granddad saved Scott, but it was thought that Evelyn and Marian drowned." Suddenly, Mary was gripping my hand tightly, and her eyes were wide.

"But that's not what happened, was it?" she asked.

"No."

"I was that little girl?" she asked.

"The girl had a red beret, and she had just been to her own birthday party. Yes, I'm sure that girl was you. Your real name is Marian Prince. Your mother must have drowned that day, but she gave you life a second time. She hit her head going overboard, but she just managed to get you into a life preserver before she blacked out. That's the way Granddad told it." Mary turned sharply to Granddad and seeing his slight nod, turned back to me.

"I have a grandfather and a brother?" she asked.

"Your brother's name is Scott Prince. Doctor Harold Eastman and Beverly Eastman are your grandparents on your mother's side. Your father—."

"My father? Yes, what happened to him? Where is he?" The questions came rapid-fire. Mary covered her open mouth with her fingers, and her eyes filled with longing. Before I could answer, the rap of the brass knocker sounded for the second time that afternoon, and we all froze. Then Too Tall scraped his chair back from the table and went to the door. Again, I heard the familiar click of a pistol being cocked. Too Tall looked over his shoulder at Granddad who nodded. Then my uncle opened the door.

CHAPTER 17

The Felix

TOO TALL BLOCKED OUR VIEW, and then, keeping an eye on the stranger, he stood to one side. The man in the doorway was tall and handsome and strangely familiar. He peered past Uncle Hercule into the dim light of the taproom and spoke to the bunch of us seated at the long table.

"Excuse me, folks. I'm sorry to interrupt your dinner. Is Mrs. Amos Waters here?" he asked. I turned from the visitor to Granddad. If ever I knew a man who was quick to size up a situation and act, it was Granddad, but right then he was positively stymied.

Then, looking at the man again, I realized who he was. *Lord light a candle for the righteous,* I thought, *isn't this a happy chance!* Granddad spoke up before I could say it aloud, however, and I waited to see what would happen.

"Well, Johnny-on-the-spot! Pull up a chair. Did Doc send you here?"

"Mr. Waters?" said the man, "why, it *is* you. I didn't

recognize you at first. Thank goodness you're here. It's you I really came to see. My father-in-law said Mrs. Waters would know where to find you."

"Call me Amos, John. We're well beyond the "mister" stage. I'm not surprised you didn't know me right away. There's been considerable water over the dam since we last met. I'm not quite in my dotage, but it has been eleven years since you went off to the Great War."

"Amos, you look as spry as ever. If I didn't recognize you, it was only because I couldn't see around this colossus who opened the door." He smiled at Too Tall who grinned back. "You're right, though, a deal of water has rolled over the dam, especially in the last few days. What a storm! Ah well, we'll survive it. But enough of the weather. Doc said you might need a pilot, Amos. He said you might have news for me, too, but he was awfully close-mouthed about it all."

"Young man," said my grandmother, "before you and Amos settle down to business, sit down by my grandson and chew on this." She handed him a plate piled high with slabs of venison, potatoes and everything else that was on the table. "You're probably famished."

"Like a dog turned out in the cold, Mrs. Waters. Pleased to meet you by the way, and thank you for your kindness. I flew straight here from Buffalo, New York, and I'm so hungry, I think my belly button is touching my backbone. But excuse my bad manners, Ma'am. I haven't even properly introduced myself. My name is...."

"Wait a minute," interrupted Granddad. "You flew here, John?"

"I did. When Doc said you might need help, I left at once. I flew about three hundred miles in four hours."

"Where's your plane? In one of the hayfields south of town?"

"No sir. It's moored to a buoy inside the breakwater right down at the end of King Street." Granddad looked puzzled at this. "It's a flying boat, Amos," continued Mr. Prince. "I can land on water almost anywhere."

When I heard this, I couldn't hold back any longer. "Holy Moses and his rulebook, mister! You flew a seaplane into Burlington Harbor? Is it a Curtiss? How many people can it carry? Are you a wingwalker? Would you take Mary and me up for a ride?"

"This exuberant youth with all the questions is my grandson, John. Meet Otter St. Onge." Mr. Prince stood up and shook hands with me. He had a firm grip. His blue eyes looked right into mine, and I knew, if a first impression can be trusted at all, that he was a good man.

"Otter, I'm glad to meet you," he said excitedly, "especially glad because I met your father once, but I'll tell you about that later. First of all, I'm not a "wing walker," but I did recently crawl out on the wing of my plane— mortally afraid, mind you—to free a jammed aerilon cable while flying over Lake Ontario. That's why I was in Buffalo. I was getting new cables fitted to the *Felix*.

"*Felix?*" I asked.

"The Felixstowe F.2a. After the war, I flew one for Britain's Royal Naval Air Service. When I left the service, the Brits started selling them as war surplus, and I bought one. The *Felix* is modeled after the Curtiss flying boats, so it uses some of the same parts. It's a lot like the American airship Putty Read and his crew flew across the Atlantic in 1919, but it's a British Navy plane that was used for submarine hunting and reconnaissance during the Great War. It carries four passengers, and I would be happy to give you and Mary a ride, but who's Mary?" he asked with a laugh. Once again, Granddad interrupted.

"Mary is the pretty girl sitting beside my grandson, John. We were just talking about her childhood when you knocked on the door. You may find her story interesting. She was raised by a Coby and Helen Rotmensen in Whitehall, New York, but they weren't her parents. She doesn't know who her parents were. The way the Rotmensens told it, they found her abandoned and wandering the streets of Plattsburgh. That was about eleven years ago." Granddad lowered his voice now and spoke softly. "Take a good look at this young lady, John. Does she remind you of anyone?"

John turned to Mary, and I saw a look of curiosity on his face that grew as he gazed at her. "Remind me of anyone?" he asked with puzzlement. "I don't understand, Amos?"

"You will, John. As I said, Mary couldn't remember

her life before the Rotmensens. She couldn't remember
her real parents. Sometimes that happens when a person
experiences something terrible. That's what happened
to Royal, you know. I guess those last days at Vimy were
enough to shake any man's marbles loose. He was almost
hit by a shell the day you lifted off from Victor Bachand's
field, and he spent the next few years in a German hospital
trying to remember who he was. Something like that
happened to Mary, John. It was a terrible accident, but just
lately her memory has started to return. Isn't that right,
Mary?" asked Granddad turning to her. Again, his voice
had become soft and gentle.

"Yes, Mr. Waters." Mary's voice was a mirror of
Granddad's, barely more than a whisper.

"Good God, Amos, will you tell me what's going on?"
asked John.

"This'll make your heart skip a beat, John. Two days
ago, while we were crossing Lake Champlain, Mary
remembered something that had been erased from her
memory for years. She remembered making the trip before.
It was raining then, too, and it was very stormy. She
remembered that she'd been to a birthday party that day,
and she also remembered her grandfather who had given
her a red beret as a birthday gift."

I glanced at Mary. She knew who he was now, but the
stranger named John looked stunned.

"Amos!" he cried mournfully, "I think you may be
slipping after all. My wife and daughter are dead! You saw

them slide off the deck of the Grand Isle Ferry and drown
in November, 1916. You told me so yourself!"

"Calm down, John. I did tell you that, and that's what I
thought, but Marian survived. Evelyn saved her. The ring
buoy kept her alive, and that scoundrel Rotmensen found
her and never told a soul. I couldn't believe it at first either,
but look at her. Look at her hair. It's Evelyn's. And her
features, John. Look in a mirror, if you want to see where
they come from. It's Marian, John. It's your daughter. Mary,
this is your father, John Prince."

The puzzlement and pain in Mr. Prince's expression
passed like a summer squall. I could see that he knew her
now, but he was still stunned. He had been haunted for so
long by the ghosts of wife and daughter it was hard for him
to believe in the young woman before him.

"Marian!" he whispered finally, "I'm sorry. You
must have been terrified. We ran ads in papers, in the
Plattsburgh Sentinel and the *Daily Press.* We heard nothing.
No one came forward. Your grandfather and I searched
and searched. We walked the shores north and south of
Cumberland Head, but we found not a sign. I lost hope. Six
years old and gone overboard in a storm on Champlain? It
would have been a miracle if you had survived. But here
you are! I'm so sorry. I gave up too easily. But here you
are!" he cried. "Here you are. Alive. It *is* a miracle. Can you
forgive me?"

I was thinking that Coby Rotmensen and Todd DePrae
hadn't exactly left Mary prepared to trust a newfound

father, but I guess one thing Mary had learned from being on her own was how to take a person's measure, and she liked what she saw in John Prince. "There's nothing to forgive," she said. She got up from the table then, and so did he. Tears streamed down her face as John Prince hugged her to his chest.

"Why don't you two go sit in the parlor where you can talk," said Gram. "We'll clear the table, and the menfolk can stay here and cipher their plans for later."

The parlor, as Gram called it, was a sitting room where she and Aunt Josey spent afternoons playing rummy with friends or reading. It was also a place to sew, knit, crochet, or mend. The doilies on the overstuffed chairs and couch were Aunt Josey's handiwork. I guess if my aunt or grandmother had a gentlemen caller, the doilies kept his pomade from staining the horsehair upholstery. I always found the horsehair to be itchy, so the parlor wasn't my favorite room, but my grandmother and aunt were fond of it and whiled away many an hour there chatting happily.

That afternoon, they were only too happy to give it over to John Prince and his long-lost daughter. As I shoveled in one forkful after another of apple pie, I listened, a little guiltily, to Mary and her father. Mary's voice rose clear above the clatter of dishes in the kitchen. She asked one question after another about her mother, her brother, her grandparents, and about Mr. Prince himself. When she had soaked up all the answers she could hold, her father asked her about *her* life. Her voice sank to a murmur then, and I knew she was telling him about the Rotters and Todd DePrae and some of the awful things they did to her.

MARY AND HER DAD HOLED UP IN THE PARLOR for an hour before she called me in. They had a lot to talk about, of course, and I smiled to think she had found her real father, but I was glad she finally got around to inviting me in there. I was beginning to think about my own dad again, and I was getting uneasy. I didn't like the idea of Corbin Lenoir loose on the lake again. I had no doubt he'd shoot another man in the back as quickly as he'd step on a bug. Mr. Prince stood up as soon as I entered the room and shook my hand again.

"Otter," he said, "I owe your grandfather a great debt for saving Mary's younger brother that day on the ferry. Now, I'm in your debt as well for helping Mary escape from the Angel's Perch and for looking after her ever since. Let's go talk to your grandfather now and see how I can help. Maybe we can find a way to get you up in the *Felix*, too."

"That would be great!" I said, and I grinned from ear to ear because I had always wanted to fly. Then Granddad called, and the three of us returned to the taproom. *I'm going to like this John Prince,* I thought, and I soon learned I was right.

"John," said Granddad when we joined him by the fire, "we don't have much time. I wanted to give you a chance to visit with Mary, but the clock is ticking, and we'll be leaving soon. Do you still want to help?"

"More than ever, Amos."

"Good. I'll fill you in on what we're doing, but there's one thing I'd like to know first."

"Ask away."

"What happened that day when you lifted off from Bachand's field and flew back toward Filescamp Aerodrome?"

"Chance and I headed straight into Hell. The artillery barrage started when we reached Vimy Ridge. Shells screamed through the air all around us, and the world exploded. Fountains of mud and towers of flame shot upward, and clouds of black smoke blinded and choked us. I clawed upward to escape the cannon fire. We burst free of the smoke minutes later, and I pushed the B.E.2 several hundred feet higher before leveling off. By then we were so far above the battle, it looked like it was being fought by toy armies, but on the ground it was a slaughterhouse.

Lady Luck was with us. We flew out of the firestorm unscathed. Well, not completely unscathed. When I touched down at Filescamp an hour later, Chance Tatro was dead." The smile that had seemed so much a part of John Prince had vanished.

"I'm sorry to bring this up, John, but a man named Corbin Lenoir wanted his brother Jacques to go with you that day. Jacques was also wounded. Royal sent Chance instead."

"Yes. I remember."

"Well, Jacques Lenoir died that day too, and Corbin Lenoir blamed Royal. He vowed revenge and swore he would kill Royal and his family. This afternoon he held a bunch of us hostage in this very room. He put a gun to Mrs. Waters' head and would have killed her if Otter and Mary hadn't rescued us. Otter killed two of his men, and Lenoir fled in his boat with the other two. Now, he's on the loose again, prob'ly headed north to look for Royal, or headed to Montreal for more men. We need to find him. Royal called here by telephone earlier, and he has left Rouses Point for Fort Montgomery at the head of the Richelieu River. He figures Lenoir will show up there on his way to Montreal, but if we can find Lenoir this afternoon with your plane, maybe we can make sure he doesn't slip past Royal in the night and escape."

"If we can get gas, we can fly. It'll be at least three hours before it gets dark, so we'll have a good chance of spotting Lenoir."

"Gas won't be a problem. There's a Texaco pump at the ferry landing."

"Granddad," I said urgently, "I want to go."

"So do I," echoed Mary.

Granddad and Mr. Prince exchanged glances.

"It's all right with me," said Mr. Prince.

"Your father will shoot me if anything happens to you, Otter, but okay—grab your gear. We leave in ten minutes."

"Bring warm clothes," warned Mr. Prince. "It'll be as cold

as a well digger's posterior when we get aloft, and it'll be
wet enough to drink through your pores."

WE SAID OUR GOODBYES TO GRAM AND AUNT JOSEY,
were told in no uncertain terms by Aunt Josey not to take
foolish risks, and then left the tavern. I glanced over my
shoulder when we reached Battery Street. Bridget waved
from an upstairs window, and Gram and Aunt Josey still
stood in the doorway of Gideon King's old house. I waved
to all of them, lowered my head once again in the endless
rain, and wondered what story the next few hours would
tell. I hoped Uncle Hercule and my cousins would escape in
the *Simon Weed* without Stub Wilson being any the wiser.

Before we left, Granddad and Too Tall had devised a
plan for getting rid of Lenoir's men. Too Tall and Little
Roy were to roll the corpses in squares of canvas before
carrying them out of the house. Just after dark, Louis and
Muff would post themselves at the nearest street corners
above and below the tavern. When they whistled "all clear,"
Too Tall and Little Roy would hustle the bodies to Gram's
Ford flatbed truck. Loaded on the flatbed would be four of
the huge barrels called firkins that Gram routinely stored
in her cellar. Too Tall and Little Roy would place the bodies
in two of the firkins and haul them to the *Simon Weed*
along with coils of rope and other salvage equipment. If
Stub Wilson returned to the tavern that evening, Gram
would steer his eye away from the felonious undertaking of
my uncle and cousins by inviting him into her parlor where

she would ply him with tidbits from the tavern kitchen and lull his suspicions through the exercise of her feminine charms.

Once free of Burlington Harbor and safely alone out on the broad lake, Too Tall would weight the corpses and drop them overboard under the cover of night. Muff was encouraged to stay at the tavern, but he would have none of that. He insisted on going with Uncle Hercule and my cousins. They would steam to the Gut and raise *Le Bûcheron* because the *Simon Weed* was too big and slow for the work ahead, and Granddad figured we had hijacked enough boats. They would rig booms on the deck of the hotel launch and raise *Le Bûcheron* using two gigantic pulley blocks that had once belonged to Gideon King. They would float my uncle's boat with the firkins, patch the hole in the hull, and pump out the water. Then they would have to overhaul the engine, and that might take hours. Still, if all went well, and the Coast Guard didn't show up, Too Tall figured they would be done by mid-afternoon of the following day. They would anchor the *Simon Weed*, leave a note thanking the owner for his hospitality, and race northward to find Royal and the Doozies.

That was Too Tall's task. Ours was to track the *Crow* and then rendezvous with Dad. So it was that the four of us and Jake were now plodding down the sloping end of King Street to the pier, heads down, rain sloshing off our hats and slickers. When we reached the landing, Granddad rousted Abraham Lincoln Richards, the pump attendant, from his shack, and the two of them began filling four big gas cans. I didn't know if old Abe had gotten his name because he was born during the Civil War, or if it was a nickname he was given because his beard was a twin to that of the Great Emancipator. In any case, I could see that neither he nor Granddad needed my help, so I stepped under the canopy with Mary and Mr. Prince and looked out across Burlington Harbor at the plane. There it was, moored to a buoy about a hundred yards away.

"Jumpin' John the Baptist! That's the *Felix?!*" I asked.

"Right you are, Otter," said Mr. Prince.

"It's enormous! The wingspan must be a hundred feet!"

"Close. The upper wing is ninety-five feet from tip to tip."

"What a behemoth! It must weigh tons."

"About five if it's fully loaded."

"Five tons!" I said with astonishment. "How does it ever get off the ground?"

"Two 345 horsepower Rolls-Royce engines at high rev. So, what do you think—do you want to go up?" asked Mr. Prince.

"Genie in a jug of Moonbeam, sir! The last time I wanted to do anything this badly was when I went deer hunting with Granddad for the first time." This was a white lie because I'd wanted to kiss Mary more than either of these things, but I thought it best to keep that to myself. And, anyway, I really *did* love airplanes. To be able to fly!—it was the stuff of dreams. "I can't wait, sir," I continued. "Last summer, a pilot barnstormed here in a Curtiss

Jenny. A farmer in Shelburne filled the woodchuck holes in his hayfield, smoothed out a landing strip, and the pilot took people up over Champlain. I didn't go, but I've been in love with airplanes ever since."

"Genie in a jug? Otter, you can coin a phrase, I must say. Well, if we're going to catch up with Lenoir, we'd better fill the tanks, and get the *Felix* in the air."

He was right, I knew, and I hurried after him to help carry the gas cans. We wrestled them over to the tender Abe pointed out. We plunked them down on the bottom, and then Mary stepped into the boat and found her seat. For the first time, the grizzled dockhand noticed Jake standing beside me.

"Holy carp!" he exclaimed, "is that a dog or a moose?"

"He's about as big as a moose, isn't he?" I grinned. Jake didn't see the humor. He wrinkled his nose at Abe, jumped lightly into the boat, and curled up at Mary's feet. The rest of us jammed in too, and Abe rowed us out to the plane. As we drew close, the gray curtain of rain parted, and the airship loomed even larger and more fabulous than it had seemed from the pier. It was like the roc, this ancient bird in a story about Sinbad the Sailor. That was a bird so big it could pick up an elephant and carry it away.

"The two of you plug your ears and wear these," said Mr. Prince. He handed us a few cotton balls, a couple of sheepskin hats with earflaps, two wool scarves and two pairs of goggles. "Then shoehorn yourselves into the gunner's pit in the nose. I took out the Vickers, so there's enough room for you two. Take turns with these binoculars, and if you think you've spotted the *Crow*, make a "C" with your thumb and forefinger. Point down if you want to get a closer look. Amos and Jake can sit in the main cockpit with me."

"Can you find room for your rifle up there?" asked Granddad as Mary and I got settled.

"Yut."

"Well, take it then," he said, handing it forward. "Lenoir prob'ly won't shoot at us because the son of a biscuit prob'ly won't know who we are, but if he does shoot, then shoot back."

"I will, Granddad."

"It's going to be miserably wet, windy, and cold," said Mr. Prince, "and once we take off, we might have to stay in the air for a few hours to find Lenoir. Mary, you can sit back with Granddad and me behind the windscreen if you want. What do you say?"

"I'll be all right," said Mary. "I'd like to be up front with Otter and help look for Lenoir."

Mr. Prince grinned. "Suit yourself, daughter," he said. "Wind those scarves around your necks and cover what you can of your faces. You can hunker down behind that little windshield I bolted on if you start shivering, but if you're going to spot Lenoir, you'll have to sit up in the wind where you can really see. Button the ear flaps of your aviator hats under your chins and put on your goggles. When I say it's going to be cold, I mean colder than sitting down in the outhouse in January. I mean colder than an Eskimo's icebox, so batten down the hatches and get ready for the hurricane. This beast cruises at eighty miles an hour, and it'll do ninety-five if we need it to."

With that, Mr. Prince scrambled into the cockpit with Granddad and started the engines. Without the cotton plugs, the roar would have been deafening. I think those two Rolls-Royce Eagles made as much noise as the looms in the Queen City Mill where Bridget worked. The airplane rattled and shook like a whirligig in a windstorm, and Mary and I traded glances, wondering if the contraption would hold together. We taxied around the breakwater toward the open lake where we could take off.

Mr. Prince revved the engines higher and higher, and we tore across the surface of Champlain faster and faster, thudding on the wave tops. I remembered the turkey I'd shot in October, how it raced across Granddad's cornfield and just couldn't seem to get in the air. Finally, it took wing and flapped to a low branch on a sugar maple. We raced across the lake like that turkey, more earthbound than airborne, but then—almost to my surprise—the flying boat was no longer banging against the waves. We were skimming the crests like a skipping stone, and suddenly—we were up!

I pushed my scarf below my chin for a second. "Hallelujah sings the choir! This crate *does* fly!" I yelled to Mary. She nodded and laughed and looked as happy as

Cinderella putting on the glass slipper. The *Felix* climbed
and we craned our necks and scanned the lake in every
direction. Behind us, Burlington was shrinking fast.
Already, we were coming up on the mouth of the Winooski
River, and I could see that it still boiled with skinned
trees, the wreckage of farms, and the bodies of dead cows
and horses. We flew pretty low, maybe eight hundred to a
thousand feet up, because otherwise the rain made it hard
to see.

Law Island and Sunset whizzed by beneath us as Mr.
Prince followed the Rutland Railroad causeway from
Colchester Point to South Hero. Then he veered off to the
west and we flew over Stave and Providence Islands. I
guess Granddad wondered if Lenoir might have gone back
there to look for Dad. After Providence, we crossed to the
New York side of the lake and flew over Valcour Island,
the Hotel Champlain, and the City of Plattsburgh. Jack
Kendrick's patrol boat was still tied up at the hotel, but
there was no sign of the *Crow* anywhere.

Just north of Plattsburgh, Mr. Prince turned back east
on a course parallel to the one we had just flown. He criss-
crossed Champlain this way for the next couple hours,
and I figured he had prob'ly done this as a recon pilot
during the Great War. Back and forth we flew like a giant,
prehistoric bird seeking its prey. Mary and I peered down
through the rain searching for boats on the gray expanse
of the lake and in the coves and bays of its islands and
endless shoreline. We took turns with the binoculars, and

with them I could see as well as an osprey, but I didn't see that cursed boat, the *Crow*, anywhere.

The wind-driven rain stung our faces and worked its way into our clothes. It put a chill in our bones but not in our spirits. Once, Mary signaled her father to drop down for a closer look at a boat she had spotted. I pulled my rifle out and sighted down the barrel ready to fire at the small figures on the deck as we got closer, but I rolled it in its square of canvas again when Mary said the boat wasn't Lenoir's. I was beginning to think Lenoir had given us the slip as we reached the north end of the lake. My eyes were tired from staring into the rain. For the first hour, I had wiped the moisture from my goggles and binoculars time and again, but my bandana was sodden now, so I stopped. Beside me, Mary was shivering. For her sake, I was glad dusk would force us down soon, but I was pretty agitated, too. *Where is Lenoir?* I wondered for the umpteenth time. *We had to find him before he found Dad!*

We were running out of time, and we were running out of lake. In the distance I could see Rouses Point and Fort Montgomery beyond it. South of Rouses Point was a place called Catfish Bay. I put the binoculars under my coat and wiped them quickly on the driest part of my shirt. Then I pushed the goggles up on my forehead and peered through the field glasses again. I scanned the shoreline and studied each camp, but I saw nothing that looked like the *Crow*. Then, through the drizzle and the curtains of mist, I saw a rambling, two-story lodge and a carriage house. The lodge

sat alone at the end of the point on the north side of the
bay. It was prob'ly a tycoon's get-away before the Great War,
and it was three times as big as any of the other camps
around. One thing about it caught my eye. It had a jetty
hidden away in a small cove, a perfect spot for a smuggler
to unload boats without being seen by the neighbors.

I turned the focus wheel to sharpen the image in my
binoculars, and when I stared through the eyepieces again,
I gasped. In those few seconds, the *Felix* had drawn closer,
and I saw a boat that might have been the *Crow.* I raised
my hand and pumped it in the direction of the ground. Mr.
Prince brought the nose down and we began a sweeping
turn. We circled back over the lodge a few hundred feet
lower. Looking through the glasses, I saw that men were
tying the boat forward and aft. It was a dark boat, but
in the rain-washed gloom, I couldn't tell if it was black.
The *Felix* dropped even lower, and I kept the binoculars
trained on a third man who had just stepped from the
deck onto the pier. *Look up, you rapscallion,* I thought. To
my surprise, he did, and you can bet I recognized him in a
second. It was Lenoir.

OTTER ST. ONGE AND THE BOOTLEGGERS

CHAPTER 18

Rendezvous at Fort Blunder

I CONFESS. RIGHT THEN I WISHED that Mr. Prince hadn't taken the Vickers machine gun out of the nose of the *Felix*. I had a tremendous mish-mash in my head. I didn't want to kill anybody else—not really—but the picture of Lenoir holding a gun to Gram's head was still fresh in my mind. I think if I'd held the Vickers, I'd have squeezed the trigger and blown Lenoir and his Crows to Kingdom Come.

Instead, I pointed to the sky, and Mr. Prince took us up again. I looked back at him and Granddad, made the "C" with my hand, and pointed down toward Catfish Bay. They got the point. Up and up we went, and for a few precious moments I forgot about Lenoir and his vendetta against my family. We climbed and climbed, and to my astonishment we suddenly burst out of the clouds into sunshine.

"Whoa!" I cried, "Look, Mary!" and look we both did. What a sight! Below us, an ocean of cloud stretched as far as the eye could see. To the west, the red disk of the sun glowed above the mighty Adirondacks like a red hot penny. Across the lake to the east and south, Mt. Mansfield and Camels Hump poked up through the clouds, tall and grand. Sunbeams streaked across the sky like flaming arrows, and the two mountains shone crimson in the last light of day. When Mary took my hand, I could tell she too was wonder-struck. We roared through the ether, and I was drunk with the beauty that surrounded us.

"How high do you think we are?" shouted Mary.

"Must be at least a mile up," I replied.

"Splendiferous!" she shouted again, and then she grinned like a kid with an all-day sucker.

Five minutes later, with the light fading, Mr. Prince adjusted the wing flaps to bring the nose down. We circled lower and lower, corkscrewing into the enormous cloud that stretched out of sight in all directions, and soon the rain pelted us again. Round and round, and down and down we flew in a funneling gyre. Mary's hand tightened in mine, and then I saw what she saw—the lake rushing up at us. High above the earth, the *Felix* had seemed to cruise along in no great hurry, but now, as we dove toward the cold, dark waves, our speed was dizzying.

Just as I began to wonder if Mr. Prince knew what he was about, he pulled the nose up, the plane leveled off, and we skimmed the surface of the lake, touching and rising, touching and rising, and all the while slowing down. Finally, the roar of the engines softened, and the rags of mist no longer zipped by. We landed, and like Jesus himself skimming across the top of the water, the *Felix* taxied

north toward the entrance to the Richelieu River. Ahead
of us, blending in with the New York shore at dusk, was
Fort Montgomery where my father and the Doozies were
standing watch. Mary pointed at the towering stone walls
growing larger in the gloom.

"It's enormous!" she yelled above the noise of the
engines.

I nodded. Soon, the great bastions loomed above us,
dark and eerie. Once upon a time, Fort Montgomery
was all that stood between us and the British. Now, it
was abandoned. Granddad told me the story when we
were duck hunting once on Kelly Bay a mile to the east.
The Brits had sailed down Champlain and attacked
Plattsburgh and Burlington during the War of 1812. In
1816 the feds built a fort to stop that from happening
again. It was nicknamed Fort Blunder when a mapmaker
found out the land belonged to Canada. About thirty
years later the Canucks gave us Island Point in a treaty,
and the feds went back to fort building. This time they
named the site after Richard Montgomery who tried to
capture Quebec during the Revolution and got killed for
his trouble.

I'd visited the fort a few times when I was fishing the
upper lake, and I was amazed by the size of it. I was also
amazed that anything so big was empty. Granddad's Great
Uncle Zeke laid stone there in the 1860s, and he said the
only time he'd ever seen soldiers there was during the Civil
War. It was strange to paddle by that great stronghold

and see nary a soul atop its ramparts. A half century
after masons had capped the walls, new, stone-smashing
cannons like the ones used at Vimy Ridge made the fort
useless, and now it sat derelict.

Besides the door set in the west wall at the end of the
drawbridge, the only other entrance to the fort was at the
bottom of the southeast bastion. Barges of black limestone
quarried on Isle La Motte had unloaded at a dock outside
this door when the fort was being built. We headed for
the remains of that dock, a few beat-up pilings that the
winter ice had not yet ground into kindling. Soon we were
close enough to see the gunports and slits through which
soldiers might have trained their cannon and rifles. I gazed
up at the top of the bastion as we neared the old pilings.
The parapet loomed fifty feet above the water. The rain ran
into my eyes, and in the dying light, it was hard to separate
the gray of the wall from the gray of dusk, but suddenly I
saw my father's scarred face peering down from the bastion
like a hobgoblin that haunted the fort. *Praise the Pope and
all his church folk,* I thought. *Dad is safe.* I waved, and he
grinned and gave me a mock salute.

Just then, John Prince cut the engines, and I turned
my attention to the *Felix.* As our momentum carried us
toward the pilings, I took off my aviator's hat and goggles.
When we had drifted to within thirty feet of the fort, Lucien
stepped out from the shadows and threw us a rope. I
caught it, and he made us fast. Then he shoved a battered
rowboat toward us, so we wouldn't have to swim the last

bit. In a trice we were ashore. Given its head, the *Felix* swung around and drifted clear of the stonework and the pilings.

"Bienvenue, Otter!" said Lucien. "I didn't know who was coming, and then off comes your chapeau and your eye goggles, and here you are. I was glad to stop squinting down my rifle barrel when I saw you in my sights instead of Corbin Lenoir. A lot of bootleggers are using planes now, you know? But never mind that. Tell me, who is this pretty girl?"

"Meet Mary, Lucien. Mary, Lucien is one of my father's closest friends."

"Welcome Mary! Vous êtes un très jolie jeune fille. A very pretty girl, yes? Bienvenue, everyone! John, John Prince, is it really you? It is a great happiness to see you again! That day you fly off toward Vimy—how long ago, mon ami?—and the shelling started, we think you was a dead man, but then Royal tell us you live. C'est bon! Très bon. Come with me."

Jake jumped out of the boat after Granddad and John Prince, and we all traipsed after Lucien, following him through a dark archway and up a winding staircase. High above us a roof had been built long ago to keep the weather out, but the boards were rotten now, and holes let in enough light to see the great, wedge-shaped steps of stone that spiraled upward. Rain leaked through those holes as well, and we tried to dodge the drips and the little streams running down the stairs. Lucien chattered like a red squirrel as we climbed higher and higher, and his words echoed so that at times I thought he had a twin.

When we reached the top of the stairwell, we found Dad and Boyce warming their hands over a campfire, the smoke curling up and out through the holes in the roof. Angus was stationed under the eaves outside keeping an eye open for the *Crow* with a pair of binoculars. After crushing me in a bear hug and shaking hands heartily with Mr. Prince, Dad listened while Granddad filled in the details of what happened at the tavern, and that included not only the gunfight with the Crows but also the reunion of Mary and her dad.

"So that's where Lenoir went," said Dad. "Jesus and his disciples, Otter, it was just what I dreaded! That devil after you, and me on a wild goose chase!"

"As the poet said, Royal, 'all's well that ends well.' " Granddad smiled as he spoke, but Dad's mind was not at ease.

"And ended, I wish it was," he said, and a dark look clouded his face. Then he brightened. "Ah well, maybe that's a wish granted soon. Otter, I can't tell you how glad I am that you're alive, and Mary and your grandmother and Granddad and everyone. Sounds like you and Mary arrived at the stroke of genius. And John Prince! I didn't think I'd ever see you again, not after Vimy. What a miracle that you've come home to your daughter!"

"It's all of a miracle and more," said Mr. Prince, "and one helped out considerably by Otter. You should be proud of him, Royal. From what Marian says, he doesn't miss a lick."

Marian flushed at this, but I was glad to hear she'd been talking about me. Granddad—always one for getting down to brass tacks—chimed in at this point.

"Speaking of which, Otter spotted Lenoir tying up at a lodge on Catfish Bay."

At that, my father turned grim. "When?" he asked.

"A half hour ago."

"Bon," said Lucien. "I didn't think he could have snuck by the fort without us seeing him, not during the day."

"No," said Boyce," but what about tonight?"

"Oui," said Lucien. "Tonight, if he runs without lights, he can slip by."

"Not if we take the *Thorpedo* out to the main channel," said Dad. "We can shut off the engine and hear a boat coming from miles away."

"Aye. We'd better step to the piper then, lads," said Angus. "Very soon t'will be darker than the belly of Jonah's whale." He had come in from the rain since nightfall was almost upon us, and he could no longer see boats passing by the fort on the open lake.

"Mr. Prince and I need to talk," said Dad. "I'll meet you at the *Thorpedo* in five minutes. Check the boat and your guns, and eat some jerky. It may be a long night."

WITH THOSE MEN, WORD WAS ACTION. Jake hadn't even followed his tail three times around and curled up for a snooze before Boyce had doused the fire, and all the

Doozies but dad were headed down the stairwell. But then the troubling thought popped up again—could they all be trusted? Was one of the Doozies working for Lenoir? If he was, he was covering his tracks well. To me, they all seemed true men. If I was told one of them was a traitor, I would have said it was Boyce, but I had no real reason to think so, just that he was gruff. With these notions bothering me, I only half listened to what Lucien was saying as he disappeared down the stairwell.

"I hope Mr. Waters and your son can join us, Royal. Sounds like they're bad luck for Lenoir."

"We'll see," said Dad, and then he turned to us. "We hid the *Thorpedo* in the moat behind the fort. They'll need a few minutes to get it ready. John, what now?"

"The *Felix* won't be of much help tonight, Royal," said Mr. Prince. "With the rain, it'll be like Angus said, as dark as the belly of the whale, too dark to fly. I've got some wool blankets in the plane, and you fellas have left enough wood for a few hours, so I think I'll camp right here. I'm hoping Mary will keep me company," he said, turning to her, "but I'm not about to give you orders, daughter. You've been your own boss too long for that."

Mary hesitated. I'd like to think she wanted to go with me, but Dad spoke before I could find out.

"That sounds like sense to me. Otter, would you stay here with Mary and John?"

"Much as I'd enjoy their company," I said, nodding to Mary and her father, "I want to go with you, sir."

"Otter, do you know what a pickle that puts me in? It's taken me as long to get home as it took Odysseus. Now that I'm finally here, and we're getting reacquainted, what am I going to do if you get hurt?"

"Dad," I grinned, "how did your father feel about you joining the Vingt-Deux?" Dad's scar twisted a little tighter as he frowned.

"That's different," he replied. "I was a grown man."

"But did he want you to go?"

"No! And if I'd known then what I know now, I wouldn't have."

"Dad," I said, and I stumbled over the words I wasn't used to saying out loud, "I look up to you. I'll do what you say, but I do want to go after Lenoir. After hearing about Vimy Ridge, I know it's not going to be some storybook adventure. I also know I'm not a man the likes of you or Granddad. I'm as green as a willow stick. Still, I was there when Lenoir put a gun to Gram's head, and that doesn't set well with me. At all. I know now what it is to kill a man, and I'll take no pleasure in it, but Lenoir can't live. I know you don't want me to get hurt, Dad. I know that. But please—don't tell me to stay here. Not while you and Granddad are going after him." At that point, Granddad figured it was time for him to get an oar in.

"Royal, I've grown partial to this boy over the past ten years. He's a bit of a rascal at times"—and he grinned that crooked grin of his as he glanced my way—"but he has some good points all in all. I don't want him to move up a size on his hat band because I'm saying it, but I have to admit he's not as green as he says he is. For one thing, he can shoot the eye out of a turkey at a hundred yards, and that kind of shooting might come in handy when we catch up with Lenoir. He's got nerve too. You should have seen him at the tavern. I don't want him to get hurt either, but Moses on the mountaintop, he's right, Royal. He's old enough to go with us." Dad sighed, and I could see that clinched it.

"All right," he said, "I know when I'm licked, but stick close to me or Granddad, will you?"

"Yes sir," I said and I meant it.

"Thanks to you, we've got the advantage in numbers. Lenoir must have only a couple men now. We'll have six."

"I wouldn't count on that, Royal," said Granddad.

"What do you mean?"

"Have you ever been to the Bucket of Blood?"

"That bar in Rouses Point? Only once. Too rough for my tastes."

"Yut, that's the Bucket. I'll wager that Lenoir will stop there tonight to hire some new men. He won't chance running into you shorthanded. The fellas that bring their custom to the Bucket are his sort. A lot of bootleggers and a lot of riffraff. Some may even work for him already. I'll bet he sends a lot of booze down the lake."

"Men like us," I said with a grin.

"No," said Granddad. "A few like us, but we've got principles even if we are outlaws," he said. "We aren't wanton killers. Most of the fellas at the Bucket wouldn't know a principle if it was wrapped with a bow and handed to them on their birthday, and quite a few would be willing to kill a man for a glass of whiskey. They do believe in one thing, though."

I cocked my head. "What?"

"Money. Especially, fast money. Misdoubt me not. Lenoir will have as many guns as we do—prob'ly more."

"Maybe we should go down to Catfish Bay now and catch Lenoir before he goes to Rouses Point," I said.

"Too much chance for Lenoir and his men to scatter. Too much chance for someone else to get hurt," said Granddad.

"No," agreed Dad. "We'll follow him down the Richelieu and find a lonely spot on the river for this business."

"Royal," said Mr. Prince, "I can't do much tonight, but Mary and I can fly at first light. Would an airplane be of use?"

"I hope not, John, but it might," said Dad. "If anybody gets hurt, could you fly them down to your father-in-law's surgery?"

"Sure," said Mr. Prince. "Glad to do it."

"I've got a couple flares on board the *Thorpedo*. If we need help, I'll fire one off."

"I'll be looking for it."

"Très bon," said Dad, and then he turned to me and Granddad. "We'd better leave now. Are you ready?"

"I'll be right down," I said.

"I'll go down too," said Mr. Prince. "I want to move the

Felix to the moat where it won't get tossed around if the wind picks up overnight."

"We'll give you a hand," said Dad. He and Granddad said goodbye to Mary, and John Prince followed them down the spiral stairs. I guess they knew Mary and I wanted a minute alone. When they left, we stepped out under the eaves of the guard tower. The light was dying fast. The rain washed off the eaves and made a curtain in front of us.

"This will all be over soon," I said.

"I don't know whether to be mad at you for leaving me behind or proud of you for risking your neck."

"Don't be proud of me. I'm not going to stick my neck out if I can help it. I'm sure Lenoir would be more than happy to take my head off. To tell the truth, I'm scared of getting shot."

"That just proves you've got some sense."

I hadn't been accused of that very often, and since I didn't know how to reply, I changed the subject. "If I'm still in one piece when we sort out this mess, I'd like to spend time with you, Mary. You'll prob'ly want to live with your dad, but I'd still like to see you." From below came the rumble of the *Thorpedo's* engine. Mary turned toward the sound as if suddenly interested in what the Doozies might be doing down below. When I moved close, she turned back to me. I don't know if it was a raindrop on her cheek or a tear, but she brushed it away quickly.

"Yes," she said, and she was in my arms, her hair like an angel's touch against my cheek. We held each other close, breathing as one, and three minutes passed like three seconds. I couldn't let her go. Then Dad's deep voice called from the stairwell.

"Otter," he boomed above the drumming of the rain, "we're leaving!" Mary loosened her grip and stepped back.

"Be careful," she whispered. I nodded—I didn't trust myself to speak—and then I kissed her eagerly enough to remember the softness of her lips long afterward. I grabbed my rifle and hunting bag and headed for the stairs.

"You'd better come back," she said.

"I will," I called over my shoulder, "just like a bad penny or a boomerang." Then I grinned that crooked, Waters' grin and bounded down the stairs with Jake right behind me.

FIFTEEN MINUTES LATER, DAD SHUT off the engine of the *Thorpedo*. He stopped south of the Richelieu, and we drifted. The hours slipped by. We followed three boats coming to us from down the lake, but the first two had running lights, and we didn't have to get very close to see that neither was the *Crow*. The third must have been a bootlegger, but when we pulled alongside and turned on the spotlight, the boat was clearly not Lenoir's. The hours after midnight dragged by like a convict pulling his ball and chain. Dad sat at the wheel and played solitaire on a bench, the rest of the Doozies snoozed in the cabin, Jake snoozed at my feet, and Granddad and I stood watch. The rain still poured down like the good Lord was bent on drowning all us poor humans and making the fish his chosen people. We stared into the black gloom to the south looking for the small, red and green lights of boats running at night, but in the lonely hours before dawn, when every creature of darkness is at last slinking back to its lair, we saw nothing. Then, as my eyelids drooped, and I drifted toward the Land of Nod, I heard a boat in the distance. In the shake of a lamb's tail, I was wide awake.

"It's coming from the south," I said, "and I don't see any lights."

"Roust Lucien and the others. It may be him," said Granddad.

It was no trouble to wake the Doozies. Only Angus was sleeping soundly, but when Lucien whispered "Jerries" in his ear, he bounded out of bed with his rifle in his hand. In seconds the bunch of us were posted fore and aft, waiting for the boat as the noise of its engine grew louder and louder. A shudder passed through the *Thorpedo* as Dad started our own engine and left it idling. Granddad and I were hunkered down in the bow, and Lucien and Boyce were amidships on opposite sides of the cabin. Angus stood by the spotlight ready to train it on the other boat when we got close enough to see a name on the transom.

I peered through field glasses and searched the inky blackness for the other craft. As I realized that seeing anything in that murk was about as likely as seeing a leprechaun in my soup, the engine of the other boat roared its loudest and then began to fade. To my great surprise I saw a red dot wink on and off. It was sixty or seventy yards to the east. My eyes were tired now, so I blinked and looked for it again. Sure enough, the tiny, red glow reappeared.

"Somebody is smoking a cigarette," I whispered to Granddad. "They're passing by about sixty yards to the east."

Granddad passed the word back to the stern, and Dad turned the *Thorpedo* toward the other boat. Slowly, he added speed. I heard Granddad's safety click, and I took mine off too. The bow waves made a light, slapping sound against the boat now, and we cut the water faster. Slowly, slowly Dad let out the throttle, and we gained on the other boat. No doubt they would hear us soon, but for now we drew closer and closer and fastened ourselves to their wake like a burr in a dog's tail.

We were prob'ly a hundred feet away when Angus snapped on the spotlight. He flashed the beam along the hull to the stern. The hull was black. On the transom, in the fancy, gold lettering, was Lenoir's trademark—*Crow*—and just as I read the word, I saw the man himself, standing above it, aiming a rifle in our direction. His face was well-lit in the spotlight. It was him—the man who had sworn revenge against my father. I drew a bead on Lenoir, breathed out calmly, and squeezed the trigger.

CHAPTER 19

Chase Down the Richelieu

ITH ALL THE FLASHES AND BANGS, I thought I'd just lit a string of firecrackers instead of pulling the trigger on my deer rifle. Somebody on that boat—I'd bet a buffalo nickel it was Lenoir—smacked a bullet into the *Thorpedo's* spotlight just as I pulled the trigger, so I couldn't tell if I'd hit him or not. Rifles spouted flame on the *Crow,* and we fired back. Luckily, Lenoir didn't have another Tommy gun, but his men knew how to put another round in the chamber even if they didn't know exactly where they were aiming. In the dark, they were counting on luck and full cartridge belts to do some damage, and it wasn't a bad plan. A storm of bullets spattered against Dad's boat, and splinters flew in all directions. One ricocheted off a steel handrail next to me and zinged off into the dark. I had just fired again and was levering another round into the chamber myself when a bullet cut through the middle finger on my left hand and blew out a chunk of my rifle stock.

"Lenoir, you boil on the Devil's bum!" I muttered. "You

just poked a hornet's nest!" A smile and a kind word to a stranger is my way generally, but right then I was bent on destruction. I worked the lever action and fired one shell after another at the spot where I'd last seen my father's nemesis. I didn't stop until I'd shot every cartridge in the rifle. It was a foolish waste of bullets because I was shooting blind, but I'd had that rifle since I'd shot my first buck at the age of ten, and I wasn't any too happy about the damage to the stock which was a prime piece of black walnut. Of course, I wasn't happy about my finger either, but it was dark, and I couldn't exactly tell how bad it was. It did seem pretty useless when I tried to bend it, and it did smart some.

When I dropped to the deck to reload, the *Crow's* engine roared, and Lenoir streaked away down the Richelieu like a rabbit with a beagle on its track. Dad opened the throttle of the *Thorpedo*, and we gave chase. Enough blood was flowing from my mangled finger now to know it wasn't just rain streaming off my fingertips, so I figured I'd better get tended to. That was when Granddad squatted beside me and shielded a match flame from the rain.

"How bad is it?" he asked.

"Could be worse," I said. "Middle finger on my left hand is about cut in two."

"Yut. I see it. We need to stop the bleeding. Let's duck in the cabin where we can use a lantern."

Moments later, Granddad had my hand stretched out on a rough, wooden table and was swabbing it with a scrap of cloth soaked in Moonbeam. Jake sat next to me and licked the fingers on my good hand. Dad stepped inside. He'd seen the lantern and given the wheel to Lucien.

"What happened?" he asked.

"Take a look," said Granddad.

Dad bent low and studied the wound. I dared a glance too. A storm lamp swung to the rocking of the boat and scribed circles over the table. Shadows leaped up and down on the walls of the cabin. In the wavering light of the lamp, I watched the blood pumping from my nearly severed finger, and all of a sudden I felt woozy.

"Bon sang! I'm sorry, son, but we'll have to take it off between the knuckles," said Dad.

"He's right, Otter," said Granddad.

I'd seen that myself. The bullet had smashed the bone and left a pulpy mess. I was going to lose half the finger.

"Go ahead," I said.

"Empty this," Granddad replied and handed me his flask of Moonbeam. I gulped down the rest of the whiskey, and it burned a trail of fire down my throat. In seconds, the heat spread to my limbs. Then my mind came untied and drifted from its mooring. Pain still seared my hand, but it wasn't screaming now. Just growling.

"Bite down on this when I tell you," ordered Granddad. He rummaged in a pouch at his belt and gave me a round of basswood to put between my teeth. "And don't look at your hand. Look at the lantern. Watch it swing back and forth. That's right. Kind of soothing isn't it. You just watch that light swing back and forth, back and forth, like a baby rocking in its cradle," he droned, and then he pulled his hunting knife from its sheath. From behind, Dad leaned over and pressed what was left of my finger onto the table edge. He clamped my hand to the scarred wood with his. Then he wrapped his other arm around me and held me still. I followed the sweep of the lantern like Granddad said. Back and forth it swung like the pendulum in the old hall clock on the farm. The creak of the chain from which it hung reminded me of the ticking and tocking of that clock. Back and forth, back and forth it swung, and a dreamy, liquor heaviness settled over me so that Granddad's voice seemed to speak from another room.

"Bite down," he ordered.

Kathunk! went the knife against the tabletop. I almost cracked the stick in two when the blade took off the rest of my finger, but thankfully the edge was sharp enough to shave with, and the operation—such as it was—only lasted a second.

"I think I'll lie down," I said.

"You hold on a pinch longer," said Granddad. Even though the world was spinning, I watched him daub a sticky gob of something I didn't recognize on the stump of my finger and wrap it with a strip of cloth. Then Dad helped me totter over to a bunk. The last thing I remember was Jake licking my face. Then I wobbled off to a dark attic of dreams where I could rest.

I WANDERED THROUGH THE LAND OF MORPHEUS
where Father Time has no bite, and when I returned to the
world of men later, I heard a steady, far-off rumble like the
Winooski River rushing over the dam at the Champlain
Mill. It flummoxed me for a time. *Is it a waterfall?* I
wondered. I wanted to know, but my mind wouldn't come
to heel. It was like a dog that's broken its chain and
refuses to heed its master's call, on the track of a squirrel
one minute and a woodchuck the next, forgetful of all but
the smell in its nose and the here-and-now. Was I in a
boxcar listening to the hum and clatter of heavy wheels
eating up railroad track? Was I in the *Felix* hypnotized
by the thunder of the Rolls-Royce engines? Louder and
louder grew the noise. I raised my hands above my head,
and I swam toward it, escaping from a black cave at
the bottom of a lake. I rose with every stroke, bubbles
streaming from my nose. I needed to breathe, to find my
way out of the abyss. Up and up I struggled, and then I
broke the surface.

I was panting when I realized where I was. My finger
stump was a howling Shakespeare with many clever ways
to say pain and more pain. That steady rumble I'd heard
was an aircraft engine, but it didn't belong to the *Felix*.
It was the engine of the *Thorpedo* cranking along at just
above an idle, and I remembered finally that we'd been
headed north on the trail of Lenoir when I had passed out.
I'd slept for two or three hours because now, when I opened
my eyes, the light of dawn was a pale thing creeping on all

fours. Wouldn't you know it—rain still beat on the roof, and the world was still awash in the great storm.

I threw off a wool blanket to jump out of bed, but Jake clamped his mouth around my wrist and squeezed just hard enough to make me reconsider. Then I realized my left arm was hanging in a sling above my chest, and Shakespeare was going to howl even louder if I did any kind of jumping, out of bed or otherwise. I lifted my arm gingerly out of its canvas cradle and shuddered to think of how I'd almost yanked it.

"What a smart dog you are!" I said. I scratched Jake fondly behind the ears and shuffled out of the cabin to find Dad and Granddad and the Doozies chewing venison jerky, drinking coffee, and scanning the shore.

"What did I miss?" I asked.

"Rien," said Lucien. "You miss nothing, Otter. We follow the *Crow* as far as Île aux Têtes. Then she give the slip to us in the dark, and if she ahead or behind, we don't know."

"Île aux Têtes?" I asked. "En Anglais, Lucien!"

"It mean Island of the Heads."

"What?"

"Oui," said Dad. "The Abenaki met a band of Mohawk there during King William's War. They killed them all and stuck their heads on stakes down on the beach to warn away other Iroquois."

"Bloodthirsty Beezlebub!" I said, "that was a grisly deed! Picture those Mohawk faces staring at you through the mist as you paddled in close to shore. What a ghastly sight that would have been! Just knowing about it would give me the jitters if I went there now."

"Certainment," said Lucien. "Even today, so many year after, I would not sleep easy in such a place. The ghosts of those warriors, I think, would haunt still that island."

"Well, maybe one of those ghosts helped Lenoir last night. He vanished in the dark, that's sure, but I think he's ahead of us, Lucien," said Dad. "If he waited on the other side of the island as we motored past, he could have doubled back, but I don't think he did. It's just a hunch, but I think he kept going. He'll try to stay ahead of us and reach Montreal. He knows he's the one being hunted now, and it's too risky for him to fight us on the river. He won't do that unless he's cornered." He turned to me then.

"How's the hand?" he asked.

It felt like somebody was squeezing it with pliers, but I didn't say so. "Not as handy as it once was," I replied, "but I can still pull a trigger."

"If that's so," said Granddad, "what do you say, Royal? Do you want to light a fire under this torpedo boat of yours? I think the sun just rose in that blessed murk to the east, so we'll soon see our way. If we're going to catch Lenoir, today may be our only chance."

"C'est une bon idée, Amos," said Dad. "I was thinking just so." He opened the throttle, and the rumble of the engine became a deafening blast. I saw why Dad had named the boat after the great Indian athlete, Jim Thorpe. The *Thorpedo* leaped forward, and soon we were racing

down the river like the boat's namesake. We sped down
the main channel searching the banks and the river ahead
for the *Crow*. It wasn't long before we reached Île aux Noix
where we saw Fort Lennox, another broken-down outpost
left over from the French and Indian Wars. We circled the
island but finding no sign of Lenoir, we sped north again,
down the Richelieu.

Angus trained a pair of binoculars downriver in search
of our enemy, and the rest of the Doozies scanned either
shoreline. Granddad beckoned me into the cabin to change
the dressing on my wound. He pulled off the bandage and
laid bare the mysterious wrapping he had put on after
the gun battle. The sticky stuff he had gobbed on was
now blood soaked, but it had done its job and had finally
stopped the bleeding.

"What in the name of the healer Hippocrates did you put
on the stump of my finger, Granddad?"

"Cobweb," he said in his laconic fashion.

"What?" I asked again. He grinned lopsidedly.

"Cobweb. Helps the blood clot. But now we'll get rid of
the sticky mess and put some of this salve on the wound.
Supposed to be good for man or beast. That stump will be
tender for a while. Try not to bump it. You don't want it to
start bleeding again."

ONCE GRANDDAD REWOUND MY BANDAGE, he and I
went to the bow again. He lit his pipe and puffed on it now
and then as we scanned the shoreline for the *Crow*. We

kept our rifles within easy reach. Jake nuzzled my good
hand, and I stroked his fur. I rested my wounded hand up
on the rail where it didn't throb so much, and I thought
about what we were doing. A voice in my head bothered me
like a mosquito whining next to my ear. I couldn't seem
to get rid of it, but I couldn't really make out what it was
saying either.

"Granddad?" I queried.

"Hmm?"

"I got a bad feeling about all this."

"Why?"

"I don't know. But something's not right."

"Any idea what that 'something' is?"

"No."

"Well, cipher on it. Let me know if you get an answer."

With nothing more to say, I settled down to the business
of watching. We flashed by farms and farmers' fields,
diving deeper and deeper into Canada. An hour passed,
and houses crowded out the farms.

"St. John," said Granddad, "or St. Jean if you want the
French."

"This is where Dad grew up?" I asked.

"Yut. This is as far as I've been in Canada. Your mother
and father got married in a church here. Now we get off the
river for a bit. Your dad said there's a twelve mile stretch
of rapids between here and Chambly, so we'll use the
Chambly Canal."

I had pulled out my own binoculars and was only

paying half a mind to Granddad as I scanned the docks and boathouses of St. Jean. Sweeping the shoreline, I glimpsed a stripe of black and then lost sight of it. I moved the glasses back upstream, searching carefully. "Granddad," I said excitedly, "there they are!" About three hundred yards away, a dark boat was tied up at the public pier. I couldn't see the name on the stern yet, but I was pretty sure it was the *Crow*. A small, black figure was hurrying down the dock toward the boat. Even at that distance, I recognized Lenoir's furtive movements.

"Yut, I think he's right. It looks like the *Crow*, Royal," called Granddad over his shoulder, "up ahead at eleven o'clock."

Dad kept the engine revved, and seconds later Angus backed me up.

"It's Lenoir, all right. I'd know that hound anywhere."

Lenoir and his men must have spotted us, too, because they pulled away from the dock in such a hurry that the waves set the other boats to bumping. The *Crow* was picking up speed every second, racing to the middle of the river and the deepest water. The bow lifted, and we saw seven men in the boat. Then the *Crow* turned into the main current and flew like an arrow downstream. Dad opened the throttle too, and once again we gave chase. Soon, I saw the entrance to the first lock on the Chambly Canal, but Lenoir was not slowing down.

"What in the name of Sam Champlain? Is he going to run the rapids!" shouted Boyce.

"He's as crazy as a coon-bit dog! This stretch of river will chew up his boat and spit out nothing but toothpicks," cried Lucien.

"Maybe. Maybe not," said Dad. "The river's up in the weeds with all this rain. I think it can be done. One thing's sure. If he does make it, we'll never catch him by piddly-putting down the canal. He'll skip right up to Montreal ahead of us and dive down a rat hole."

"Might as well try to marry off the Pope as to smoke out Lenoir if he reaches St. Timothee," said Boyce. Everybody looked at Dad.

"You fellas willing to swim if this rig comes apart?" He turned to the Doozies, and they all nodded. Then he turned to me. "Otter?" he asked.

"I'll follow that devil down to the Kingdom of Fire if that's what it takes to get rid of him," I said.

"All right," he said grimly. "Let's see if we can jam a stick in that fella's spokes." He opened the throttle wider yet, and the *Thorpedo* bounded forward. The *Crow* had lengthened its lead, and suddenly it dropped from sight. Moments later, I realized why. I saw a tongue of the river in the distance, but beyond that the Richelieu disappeared. Granddad and I had returned to the bow. Now, he reminded me to look to my rifle. I double-checked to see that it was fully loaded, and I tied it with a slipknot to a railing stanchion so that if we got to bouncing around, it wouldn't fly out of the boat. Then I stood in the prow and waited eagerly to see the rapids as we rushed toward the river horizon. I felt a furry presence next to me. Jake pushed his head gently against my thigh and licked my fingers.

"Good boy," I said softly. "Good boy." I don't know how he knew mayhem was ahead, but he knew. We slid forward and farther forward toward that tipping point beyond which we could not see. Closer and closer we came, and then, even above the noise of the engine, we could hear the crashing of waves and the booming roar of tons and tons of water sluicing downward and disappearing in shrouds of mist.

"Steady, Jake," I said. "Steady." Then we were over the edge, and there was no turning back. I quickly realized as I studied the river below that I was the one who needed to stay steady. Since Jake could do nothing but swim if bad went to worse, he curled up again in the bottom of the boat and pretended to nap. Looking downriver, I wished I could do the same. Below us, the water boiled and foamed around scattered boulders. Hitting just one would crack our boat like an egg and spill us into the drink. Other rocks hid just beneath the black water and waited to gut the boat from stem to stern. Huge waves geysered up from drowned ledges, and in other spots the current swirled around and around in deep pools like someone had just pulled a drain plug off the bottom. In the middle of it all, a couple hundred yards downstream, was our quarry, Lenoir and the *Crow*.

They had their hands full, but so did we. For the time being, none of us could worry about anything but dodging

the rocks and staying right side up. Dad had to keep
us moving a little faster than the current, so he could
steer. He gunned the engine in fits and starts to skirt
the boulders and the worst of the whirlpools. Angus and
Lucien lashed two oars together to make one long one, and
then lashed the whole thing to the transom. Angus swept
it back and forth like a fish's tail to help Dad with the
steering. Boyce and Lucien called out "Left!" and "Right!" to
help Dad avoid rocks he couldn't see from the helm. For the
next hour the four of them worked together like they were
all one body, and the one job that body had to do was keep
the *Thorpedo* from breaking apart on a rock or a ledge.

Slowly, we gained on the *Crow*. I knew this for sure
when a bullet hissed by a few feet off the starboard bow,
but we were still too far away for anything but a lucky
shot, especially when both boats were jumping around
like kangaroos. Still, Granddad was never one to discount
luck. He had his Savage 99 rifle, and although he usually
snuck up close to his deer and shot them at forty feet or so,
I'd seen him shoot a bottle off a fencepost at two hundred
yards.

"Get down," he said, and then he emptied his rifle of two
rounds. He placed these bullets back in the ammunition
belt around his waist. Then he took two different bullets
from the pouch attached to the belt and reloaded. They
were cartridges he had loaded himself, and he used them
only for a long shot. They had a bigger charge of powder,
and they'd send a bullet farther with less drop. As he

was reloading, I heard a new thundering downriver, and I wondered what new monster Mother Nature had spawned to swallow us whole. Were we about to pitch over Niagara Falls? I knew we weren't in the right geography for that, but good God in his galaxy, what a racket! It didn't bode well, if I could hear it over the hubbub all around us.

When the call of Doom sounded from downriver, something else happened. The rain stopped. Hallelujah sings the choir! I had begun to think I would always hear squelching in my boots and the drumming of the rain. I'd been wet so long, I thought I'd have to iron myself to get the wrinkles out. The downpour had started when Granddad and I left the mouth of Mississquoi on Tuesday night and hadn't stopped. Now it was past noon on Friday.

"What do you know about that, Otter. Only rained four days instead of forty. Judgment Day has come early. At least for one of us." With that, he stood up and asked me to steady him. I grabbed his belt with my good hand and looked downriver again. Granddad wasn't grinning, and I knew from his tone that he wasn't expecting me to laugh. If his aim was true, Granddad was about to send Lenoir or one of his men to meet his maker. We had gained on Lenoir, but we were still a hundred fifty yards away. For the next twenty yards, we would have a smooth ride with no boulders in the way and no big waves. I raised my binoculars with my left hand and studied the river as Granddad aimed. Below the *Crow*, I saw that the river dropped from sight again. That was the explanation for the sinister rumble I'd heard. There was a falls! As I realized the danger waiting for us, Granddad pulled the trigger.

The rifle cracked and through the field glasses I saw the man at the helm of the *Crow* fall. Without his hand on the wheel, the stern of the *Crow* swung sharply to the right. The helmsman pitched out of the boat into the river. Another man jumped for the wheel to bring the boat back under control, but he was too late. The *Crow* surged over the brink going sideways and was lost from sight. I was about to tell Granddad what a legendary shot he had made—few men could have done it—but I held my tongue. I knew he took no pleasure in his skill right then. We had no time for such talk anyway. We were about to follow the *Crow* over the rim of the falls, and I guessed it would be like an elevator in free fall. Maybe we'd soon be knocking at the Pearly Gates ourselves.

"Hang on!" hollered Dad from the stern. "We can ride her down!" I hoped with all my heart that he was right. I stroked Jake one last time.

"How'd you like to go for a swim?" I asked. Then we plunged over the falls, and I gripped the rail with my good hand, ready to jump clear.

Otter St. Onge and the Bootleggers

CHAPTER 20

Chambly Falls

O VER THE FALLS WE FLEW. Angus saved the *Thorpedo* and us too. He worked the steering oar and brought the boat in line just as we slid over the edge. The river tumbled over a giant ledge and dropped twenty feet in about the same distance. Huge spines of rock ran like an old man's gnarly fingers down to the base of the falls, but luckily we barreled down a narrow chute between the worst of these. The boat bumped and thudded, but it held together. At the bottom we dove like an osprey after a fish right into the water and out again. I held my breath and clung to the rail. The *Thorpedo's* charge carried us beyond the base of the falls, which was good because otherwise we'd have been trapped by the undertow.

Captain Nemo and the good ship Nautilus! We burst out of the spray and foam and floated out onto the Chambly Basin. I couldn't believe we were still right side up and still afloat! I shook my head like a dog. My flat cap was gone, but I counted myself lucky not to be blowing out water like a whale. It wasn't raining anymore, so maybe I wouldn't need a hat. We must have cracked a strake in the hull what with all the rock and ledge we'd run over in the last couple hours. A little water sloshed in the bilge, but it wasn't flooding in. I glanced at Granddad who was unruffled by our wild scamper over the falls. He was already drying his rifle with a rag taken from his oilskin wallet. Still, I felt something was wrong. With relief, I heard Dad's voice behind me, but then I realized what troubled me—Jake was missing! I scanned the whitecaps around us, but I saw no sign of his wolfish head. Where was he?

"Granddad!" I cried, "Jake went overboard!"

"Otter!" shouted Boyce, "behind you!"

I looked back, and sure enough, Jake's head was bobbing up and down as he struggled mightily to keep it above water and escape the current pulling him back into the boil of water at the base of the falls.

"Dad!" I shouted. "Do you have a rope?" He was trying to restart the engine, which had stalled when we played submarine, but he ducked into the cabin and threw me a fifty-foot coil of manila as I scrambled to the stern. Watching Jake, I took the free end of the rope in my left hand and began swinging the coil in my right. He was still pretty far from the boat, and he was swimming madly but not making much headway.

"C'mon boy!" I hollered. "C'mon, Jake! You can do it! Just a little closer!" A minute passed. Suddenly, caught by one of the worst waves, Jake dropped from sight. He popped up again, but I wasn't sure how many times he could do that. I gauged the distance, swung my right hand far back, and threw for all I was worth. The rope end landed ten yards short. Snatching at the rope and coiling it fast, I stood ready for another throw. Jake paddled a few yards closer, and again I swung the loops back and forth in my right hand. Finally, I threw, and the coils unwound into an arcing snake. This time the rope landed three feet from Jake's nose. He drove himself forward, lunged, and once more dropped from sight. When he surfaced, he had the rope in his teeth.

"Hold on, Jake!" I yelled. "Hold on, boy!"

I pulled Jake steadily to the side of the boat where Angus was waiting.

"Here, wee dog," said the Scotsman, and then he scooped up Jake. "Let's get you back on board. Aye, laddie, ye're as big as a horse."

Jake stood on deck with his four legs splayed, drenched and bedraggled but really none the worse for wear. He shook himself furiously and showered Dad and me which seemed to brighten his outlook considerably. With Jake now safe, Dad returned to the engine, and I to the hunt for Lenoir. Looking to the west, I saw a church steeple in the village of Chambly and closer to us, Fort Chambly on a point of land jutting into the river. Below the fort, the Chambly Basin spread out ahead of us. It was more or less round and about three miles across before it narrowed again at the north end on its way to the St. Lawrence River.

Still a couple hundred yards ahead of us was the *Crow*—or what was left of it.

It had taken a wicked beating from the falls. It must have rolled at least once because the cabin was all stove in. The hull got crunched too. Bow to stern it had been twisted out of line, and the whole shebang listed to one side. I pulled my field glasses out from under my coat and studied the wreck. It was on the verge of sinking. An eddy was pulling it toward a big patch of cattails on the west side of the river, but it looked like it might easily go to the bottom before it drifted to shore. I didn't see anybody left aboard, but maybe they were only shy of Granddad's rifle now. I turned and searched the basin between the *Crow* and the falls, and that's when I spied a body.

"Granddad," I said, "look!" I pointed, and he gazed in that direction.

"Is that him?" he asked.

"Yut," I said. It was the man Granddad had shot. He had the same green-and-black checked shirt, the same red suspenders. Just then the current rolled him. His bearded face rose from the water, and he stared accusingly in our direction. He slid beneath the roiling waves, and I knew he wouldn't come up again until his bowels filled with gas. Then he would rise like a balloon, caught maybe, on the hook of a surprised fisherman.

While Granddad and I searched the basin for other men who might have been thrown overboard when the *Crow* tumbled willy nilly over the falls, Dad cranked the

engine a few times, but he soon quit. I looked back to
see him and Angus drying the spark plug wires and the
distributor cap, and I knew we might as well be poling
Huck Finn's raft on the Mississippi. We weren't going
anywhere fast—not for a good while. Then from the south
came an insistent, buzzing sound. With the Chambly Falls
roaring behind us, I hadn't noticed it at first. I looked up
and saw an airplane flying a thousand feet or so above
the river, coming from the direction of St. Jean. Over the
basin it dropped into a wide, banking turn and touched
down north of the fort. It zipped across the water toward
us, and I felt a thrill when I recognized the gigantic flying
boat. It was the *Felix*, of course, and Louis and Little
Roy were in the cockpit with Mr. Prince and Mary. The
biplane finally slowed and taxied toward us. When Mr.
Prince switched off the engines and stepped out on the
wing, Lucien threw him a line. Everyone came aboard,
and when I saw Mary, and she smiled, my heartbeat
quickened. *That little fella with the bow and arrow,* I
thought, *he's a deadly shot!*

"Bienvenue, nephews!" said Dad. "You are here quicker
than I expected and a good thing too! We need your help."

"And you are welcome to it, mon oncle," said Little Roy.

While Mr. Prince told Dad about Too Tall, who was on
his way down the canal with *Le Bûcheron,* Mary and I
stepped around the corner of the cabin for a little privacy.

"Well, Wild Otter, I'm glad to see you're still in one
piece," she said teasing.

"Yut, I'm in great shape," I said. I was lying a little, but the finger wasn't worth mentioning.

"I was worried," she said.

"About what?" I asked.

"You, mister!" she said, pretending to be annoyed.

"I'm glad," I said, laughing. "I can hear the affection in your voice."

She squinched up her face in a mock frown, but then she reached out for my hands and smiled. I pulled my left hand away, and the smile vanished. She glanced down and saw the bandaged finger.

"Otter! Oh God, you're hurt! I'm so stupid. I didn't mean to tease you. You said you were still in one piece!" she cried.

"I am," I said. "Well—mostly."

"Tell me! What happened?" she asked with a worried look.

"Lenoir or one of his henchmen shot a piece of my finger off, but Granddad stopped the bleeding, and now it's fine—just a little short," I said with a grin.

"How can you joke about it?" She looked stern but then her face softened. "Doesn't it hurt?" she asked.

"It does," I said.

"Is there anything I can do?" she asked.

"There is," I smiled, "Come closer. It's a secret, and I'll have to whisper it."

We were in the middle of telling secrets—not ones told with words—when I heard Dad's voice rise above the others in the stern.

"There they go," he said.

Mary and I drew apart and looked to the western shore. The *Crow* had grounded in the cattails, and Lenoir's men were slogging through the mud toward the riverbank.

"Well, the scales are out of whack today," I said.

"What do you mean?" asked Mary.

"I mean that if there was any justice in the world, some of Lenoir's hooligans would have drowned, but there they are, every blasted one crawling ashore, but for the man Granddad killed, and they're all carrying guns. Come on. Let's find out what we're going to do."

Granddad was talking as we rounded the corner of the cabin.

"If we keep drifting, we'll fetch up in the cattails too, and we don't want that. They'll sit up there on the riverbank behind the trees and pick us off like turkeys in the corn."

"If we tie the *Thorpedo* to the *Felix*, I can tow you downriver and land you around the point just below the fort," said Mr. Prince.

"That'll pull our fat out of the fire nicely," said Dad. "Let's get busy."

Mr. Prince climbed back into the cockpit of the *Felix*, and Boyce and Lucien rigged a tow line to the *Thorpedo*. When the rope was tied, Mr. Prince started the *Felix*. The engines sputtered, as usual, and then caught. In less than five minutes, we were motoring out toward the middle of the Chambly Basin. When we got out of rifle range, Mr. Prince pointed the *Felix* downriver.

The *Crows* scurried through the trees along the riverbank, trying to reach the crumbling walls of Fort Chambly ahead of us. If they could reach the abandoned fort, they knew they could hold us off until dark and then escape. Mr. Prince revved the engines, and we scooted right along, but the race was lost before it was begun. Lenoir and his cronies got the jump on us, and they were within a stone's throw of the fort when we were still rounding the point. Mr. Prince stopped beyond the nearest walls, and we dropped anchor in quiet water. I grabbed my rifle and jumped into the shallows next to shore. Jake leaped over the rail and landed with a great splash beside me. He paddled furiously until his feet touched bottom. I waved to Mary who stood now with her father.

"Remember," she called, "we have a date when this is over, so don't make yourself a target." She was smiling and joking, but I heard the worry in her voice. I smiled too, like I didn't have a care in the world, but when I slipped into the trees, the smile disappeared like a drop of water on a hot stove. A worm of dread wriggled in my gut, and I still sensed some ill luck in the wind. It wasn't just having my finger shot off that caused the clenching in my bowels. It was something else, and it didn't bode well.

NOT MUCH LATER, DAD POSTED BOYCE AND ANGUS as sentries in a grove of trees near the west wall of the fort. Lucien borrowed my field glasses and went off to scout the fort itself. The rest of us made a temporary camp under the

trees and out of sight of the Crows. The land butting up
to the fort was clear of cover, and in daylight we couldn't
get close without getting shot. Since we had to wait, we
cleaned and dried our guns, ate some bread and cheese
and sausage Little Roy had brought, and talked about
what would happen at nightfall. Lucien returned with
discouraging news.

"We get in this fort not too easy," said Lucien. "The
walls, they be fifty feet high if they be an inch. The one
door, she have oak planks twice as thick as a man's fist
and heavy, iron hinges. No, not too easy."

"Impossible, maybe," said Little Roy.

"The Green Mountain Boys took Fort Ticonderoga," said
Granddad.

"Oui," said Lucien, "but the redcoats weren't waiting for
no one."

"You're right, Lucien," replied Granddad. "Lenoir
knows we're coming, and he's not going to open the door
and invite us in for tea. You can bet your bottom dollar
on that." He was puffing on his pipe looking at the fort
through a screen of tree trunks. "We need to figure out a
way over that wall or under it. And," he emphasized, "we
need to do it without tipping our hand."

"Over? Under?" said Lucien. "It is a tall order, oui?
We could build a ladder maybe, but a ladder of fifty feet?
Beside this, they would hear us chopping. They would
know and be ready. And going under? Mon Dieu! How to do
such a thing?"

Granddad didn't answer. Neither did Dad. We all sat in the woods thinking and being quiet. Maybe a quarter hour passed. Then I got an idea.

"Dad, did I see a grappling hook in one of the lockers on board the *Thorpedo?*"

"Yes, but Otter, look at that wall. Lucien's right. It's up there mighty high. I don't know if one of us could even throw a hook to the top."

"I bet Angus could," I said. Granddad's pipe glowed, and he blew out a smoke ring. Dad rubbed his chin. Angus raised his eyes to me and looked interested.

"He might. He just might," said Dad, "but then what? You mean to say you can scale that wall?"

"I can, Dad." He looked at me doubtfully.

"Even with the end of your finger gone?"

"I can do it."

"Are you sure?"

"Yut." I saw Granddad nod slightly when Dad looked his way.

"And what if Lenoir hears the clang of the grappling hook when it hits the wall?" asked Lucien. "He'll stick a gun in your face as soon as you reach the top."

"I ciphered on that. If a couple of you fire your guns under the wall next to the river, he'll never hear me, and his men will be drawn away. Once I'm in, I'll drop to the other side and open the gate."

"Somebody may be guarding that gate," said Dad.

"I know," I said, "but they won't hear me coming."

Granddad blew another smoke ring. "It's a good plan," he said, "or if it's not, it's as good a one as we're likely to get."

"I don't like it, but I guess your grandsire is right. Just be careful," warned Dad.

AFTER DARK LUCIEN SET THE LONG HAND of his pocket watch to match Granddad's. I snuck out from the trees at five till nine with Granddad and Angus. While we waited beneath the wall, I took off my boots, tied the laces together, and slung them around my neck. As the hour came nigh, Angus started swinging the hook, and when the Doozies started shooting at nine, he let it fly. It caught on the first throw—the clang muffled by the rifle fire—and I tugged on the rope to test it. It held. Angus boosted me up. I stood on his open palms, his arms stretched above his head, and then I stepped off and started scaling the wall. I gripped the rope, felt for jutting stones with my toes, and walked upward. I knew I was dead if they caught me on the wall, so I climbed like a cat, quick and quiet. The rifle shots tailed off, and Granddad and Angus melted back into the woods. I was on my own.

A few minutes later, as I neared the top, the angle of the rope no longer allowed me to walk up the wall, and I had to pull myself up hand over hand. My finger throbbed. The wound opened, and I could feel blood soaking the bandage again. I was getting wicked tired. Sometimes I could perch and catch my breath when I found a stone big enough for a toehold, but I didn't dare rest for long. Finally, I reached up with my good hand and curled my fingers around the edge of a stone set in the top of the wall. I tensed, ready to throw my leg up and over. Then I stopped and hugged the rock. Twenty feet away, I saw the glowing red end of a cigarette. So close I could almost touch him, another man hissed a question.

"Où êtes vous? Where are you?"

"Ici! Here! Je suis fumeur," said the man with the cigarette.

"Allons-y, Peris. Let's go. Lenoir wants us to keep walking to make sure no one is coming over the wall."

"Over the wall, Hector? Zut alors. What will they do? Fly?"

"Allons-y! Allons-y! Or you want to tell Corbin maybe, he is a fool?"

"Très bien," grumbled Peris. "Je viens."

Their whispers faded as they padded off toward the next lookout tower. Now or never, I thought, and I heaved myself up. I clung to the top of the wall, gasping. *Rope a rubber ducky and ride it straight to Hell,* I thought as I breathed a sigh of relief. *Couldn't have had a closer shave with a straight razor.* I lay on my stomach and peered down to the old parade ground looking for Lenoir's men. When I satisfied myself that all was quiet, I put my boots back on.

I pulled the rope up from the outside wall and listened for the Crows' possible return, but I only heard the evening breeze whispering through the gun slits. I reset the grappling hook and lowered the rope inside the fort without a sound. I stripped off my shirt and used it to protect my hands. Then I slid down that rope as fast as a fireman sliding down the stationhouse pole. At the bottom, I slowed down and landed softly. I shrugged my shirt back on and crept toward the gate. The guard didn't hear me coming. I hit him in the back of the head with Mary's sock full of birdshot. He crumpled, and I laid him down easy. The stout timber sitting in two huge brackets and holding the double door didn't want to budge, so I lay on my back and kicked like a mule with both feet. It jumped from its place and landed with a hollow thump right where I'd been lying before I rolled clear.

Then, everything happened at once. Rusted hinges screeched as one of the heavy oak doors swung inward, and the Doozies ran inside. Rifles cracked from the parapet, bullets spat in the dirt, and suddenly a flare lit the parade ground bright as noon. For a split second, we froze. It was barely long enough to blink, but that was all it took for one of those dogs to drop Boyce. Boyce struggled to one knee, and Angus scooped him up and followed the rest of us. We ran like rabbits, twisting and turning, trying to dodge the gunfire popping all around us. My shoulder burned suddenly like somebody had just whacked me with a hot poker, and I knew a bullet had gouged my flesh. I raced on and reached the doorway right behind Dad. Inside, I aimed at a gun slit in the northwest tower. I'd seen a muzzle flash, and I fired at that spot. Then I slipped into the shadows of the old barracks and joined the rest of the Doozies. Angus laid Boyce gently on the ground, and the Doozies crowded around him, worried that he might have been badly hurt.

"Strike a match," said Dad.

"Take this," said Louis, and he handed Dad a pocket torch.

"Louis, you and Little Roy spread out," he said. "Some of those jackanapes may be down here already or headed our way. Otter and Angus, stay and help."

Dad handed me the torch, and I shone it on Boyce.

"It's my right leg," he said. He was gritting his teeth, and his face was the color of skim milk. Dad sliced open the trouser leg and asked Angus to press his palm hard against the wound in Boyce's thigh.

"Sweet Jimmy Christmas and his lovely Mother!" muttered Boyce between clenched teeth. "You don't have to add a broken bone to my misery, Angus!"

"Hush now, ye squawling bairn. I've got to stopper this hole or you'll bleed yourself as dry as teetotaling Carry Nation." He took a thick bandage from his pocket and clapped it on the wound. Then Dad wound a long strip of cloth around and around the leg to hold the bandage in place.

"Boyce," said Dad, "we've got to find Lenoir. Angus will stay with you."

"No need," said Boyce. "I'll fire on those toads if they show their faces. You'll hear me. I can hold them off until somebody gets back here." Dad looked doubtful, but then he agreed.

"Bon," he said. "We may need the Scot. You hold on. We're going to the guard tower where they've holed up, but we'll be back."

"Where's Granddad?" I asked as we moved off to find Louis and Little Roy.

"I don't know exactly. He said he wanted to scout the tower, and he'd catch up with us when the shooting started." As I followed Dad through the old barracks, I wondered if Granddad had more in mind than scouting, and I wondered, too, how we were going to roust Lenoir and his men from the tower. The only way to reach them was to climb the stairs to the guardroom, but with those scoundrels firing down from above, it was a dicey proposition. I didn't like the odds, and suddenly I had a notion.

"Dad," I said, "somebody should be waiting outside the fort at the foot of the tower to stop Lenoir's men from going out a window and sliding down a rope when you bust into the guardroom."

"You're right," he said. "Go on out and find yourself a spot to shoot from. You've got plenty of time. We're going to build a smudge fire and look for something a couple of us can hold up over our heads as a bullet-stopper. Maybe with a smokescreen and a shield to catch lead, we can knock those buzzards out of their roost."

Dad was happy about me standing guard outside the

fort. I guess he figured I'd be safer there. Of course, I didn't
tell him everything I had in mind. With a nod, I slipped
into the dark and snuck back to the open gate. Dad's
plan improved the odds for the Doozies, but it was still
going to be wicked dangerous—especially if Lenoir had
brought back any grenades from the Great War. Outside
the fort, I sprinted into the trees and made a beeline for the
Thorpedo. Mary's father was holding a rifle in the crook
of his elbow and looking watchful when I arrived at Dad's
boat. Mary was nowhere in sight.

"Mr. Prince," I called breathlessly, "I need to fill a bottle
with gasoline from the fuel tank! Can you find a hose?"
Mary stepped out of the cabin, her eyebrows arched in
surprise.

"Otter," she asked, "what are you doing here?"

"No time to explain," I said. Then I handed her the sock
with the birdshot. "Thanks for the loan. It worked slick, but
you might need it."

"Keep watch will you, daughter?" asked her father. He
rummaged through the tool chest, and I corralled a quart
bottle of Moonbeam in the cabin. Much as I hated to do it,
I dumped the contents and brought it back to Mr. Prince
who began siphoning gas with a length of rubber hose. By
the time he finished, I had torn a strip of cloth off an old
towel. I pushed it down in the bottle like a lantern wick
and jammed some extra material into the neck so the
bottle was well plugged. I put it in my hunting bag, jumped
over the side of the boat, and splashed toward shore again.

Looking over my shoulder, I saw that Mr. Prince had the same questioning look that Mary had.

"Going to make it hot for the Crows," I grinned, and then I vanished into the woods.

BACK INSIDE THE FORT, I SLITHERED ALONG the wall to the rope I had left hanging from the grappling hook. I didn't hear a peep from the northwest bastion, but I knew that wouldn't last. Once again, I shucked my boots, grabbed the rope, and climbed. It was a mean piece of work to hoist myself up onto that wall a second time, but huffing and puffing, I finally threw a leg over the top. I stepped into my boots and tied them fast. Once I freed the hook and wound up the rope, I poked my head through the coils and let them hang from my shoulder. Creeping toward the tower, I worried that one of Lenoir's men might see me from the window facing the parapet, but when wisps of smoke began appearing from the tower, I practically ran.

In the twilight, I stopped and looked for the chimney I had spotted on top of the bastion. I could barely see it now, a darker stripe against the sky. More smoke billowed out the windows, and now gunfire chattered from the Doozies somewhere down in the lower stories of the tower. I twirled the hook a few times in a widening circle, and then I launched it toward the chimney. It caught! The Crows were shooting back now. *In for a nickel, in for a dime,* I thought. I pulled the bottle from my pouch, struck a match, and lit the gas-soaked strip of rag poking out of the top.

Earlier that afternoon, when I lay beneath a big maple studying the fort, I had noticed that the windows facing the woods had no bars. Why put bars in a window no one could get to? It was one of those windows I had to reach. The wick was burning fast. I reached up, grabbed the rope, swung out from the wall, and swooped toward the window. As I passed by, I threw the bottle as hard as I could through the opening. I heard the sound of breaking glass, and as I reached the limit of my swing, I heard a giant *whoosh* behind me. I kicked against the wall to turn myself, and when I swung back in the direction I had come from, I faced an enormous tongue of flame reaching out from the tower room where Lenoir and his men were shooting at my father.

CHAPTER 21

The Burning Man

RATHER THAN GET BURNED, I loosened my grip on the rope and slid down a few feet. That saved me from the fire, but when I swung back to the wall I was too low to grab it and hoist myself back up. Instead, I scribed shorter and shorter arcs back and forth beneath the window. The flames died back—which was good because the rope was getting singed—and then screams came from the tower room. Even before the pendulum swing ended, I began climbing the rope again. I didn't want to be left hanging under the window like a fish waiting to be reeled in.

More gunfire cracked in the stairwell. Up the rope I shinnied, gripping with my bare feet, and gritting my teeth against the pain in my hand. Finally, I reached the window ledge and peered in. A few flames still licked the walls and danced on the floor of the guardroom. One man, whose face I couldn't see, was writhing on the floor, and his were the screams I heard. He must have been pretty scorched by the homemade fire bomb. Both the other men had been burned but not so badly that they couldn't fight. I kept climbing, hoping that neither of them would look my way.

One man was shooting down the stairwell. The other was on the floor, reloading his pistol. His head was turned away, but I knew him. It was Lenoir. Why those two didn't see me, I'll never know. When I stepped onto the windowsill, the man at the stairwell must have been shot because suddenly he jerked and tumbled through the open trapdoor. I heard shouting and a commotion below, and then, as Lenoir flicked the loaded cylinder back into his revolver, my father's head appeared. Lenoir thrust the barrel of his gun in Dad's face just as Dad's pistol came up, but Lenoir was too late. I landed on him with both boots before he could pull the trigger. The gun flew from his hand and skittered across the floor. He rolled out from under me and sprang to his feet with a knife in his hand. Dad burst into the room and leveled his gun at Lenoir.

"Drop the knife," he ordered. At that distance, Dad couldn't miss, but Lenoir hesitated. Footsteps clattered on the stairs, and then Lucien appeared.

"Drop it," repeated Dad. Lenoir straightened from his crouch, and strangely, he smiled. It wasn't the smile of a man who knows he is beaten and takes his bad luck in stride. It was the smile of the carnie who knows he has gaffed another sucker. That dread I had felt earlier stirred in my gut again, and I tasted bile in my mouth. I still didn't understand. *What's wrong?* I wondered.

"I don't think you'll kill me," said Lenoir.

"I warned you," said Dad grimly. He was about to squeeze the trigger, but a small noise caught his attention, and he froze. The noise was a pistol being cocked. All my attention had been on Lenoir, but now I shifted my gaze to Lucien. He was standing three feet behind Dad, and his gun was aimed at my father's head.

"Slowly, Royal, s'il vous plaît," said Lucien, "very slowly, put your gun on the floor." Dad bent down and did as he was asked.

"I couldn't figure out how this scalawag always knew where we were, Lucien, but now je comprends. I understand. I just didn't think it could be you."

"If it comfort you, I did not do these thing for money," said Lucien.

"That's enough," said Lenoir curtly. "Where are the others?" As he asked this question, Lenoir stooped to pick up his gun.

"Boyce get a shot in the leg. He go nowhere. I knock out Royal's nephews in the dark. They be no trouble."

"Bon. Now you must do a thing, Lucien, to see are you with me. I want that you shoot the boy." Lucien's eyes narrowed.

"In front of his father?"

"Mais oui. That is the point. In front of his father," he said.

"Non, I can't."

"You can, or what happens you know."

"I know." And I knew right then from the fear in his voice that he would shoot me. Dad must have sensed Lucien's gun swinging in my direction. He turned, but Lenoir stepped forward and pressed his pistol against my father's temple. *Tie a tin can to the Devil's coattails,* I thought. *I'll be jiggered if I'm going to stand still and wait to get shot.* I tensed my leg muscles and was about to fling myself on Lenoir when the man on the floor moaned loudly and thrashed more violently. He rolled onto his back, and I saw a revolver in his hand. Lucien shifted his aim, but it was too late. The man shot him in the chest, and Lucien dropped to the floor. Lenoir had brought his gun to bear too, but then Dad chopped down on his forearm, and Lenoir dropped his pistol. I dove for the gun. Lenoir hurled himself through the window, caught the rope and slid down. I ran to the sill, and his cry rose up from the shadows.

"I'll be back for you and the boy, St. Onge!" Then a raggety, croaking sound echoed through the darkness, the sound Dad remembered from a battlefield at Vimy. It was the *caw-cawing* of a crow. I couldn't see the fiend, but I fired off a round like a prayer for his destruction and thought I saw a shape blacker than the darkness darting into the trees. When I turned, I glanced first at Dad who was kneeling by Lucien. He was pressing both hands against Lucien's chest, trying to stop the bleeding, but I could still see a lot of blood soaking Lucien's shirt. The man who had shot Lucien was standing now, bent over his pistol, reloading, and with his hat brim tipped down, I couldn't see his face.

"Mister," I said, "My name is Otter St. Onge. Yours must be Johnny-on-the-spot. If it hadn't been for you, my dad and I would both be dead men. 'Thank you' doesn't hardly cover the tab, but I don't know what else to say. We're in your debt."

"Call it even, young fella," said the man. "It doesn't seem right to call in a chit on family." He looked up then, but of course I'd already recognized the voice.

"Granddad!" I said. "How in the double dickens did you get up here in the tower with Lenoir?"

"I knocked out one of his men who was lagging behind, and then I stole his coat and put it on over mine. In the dark, Lenoir was too busy to notice," he said. With that, he knelt beside Dad who was whispering to Lucien.

"Why?" he asked his old friend. Lucien tried to answer, but he was choking on his own blood. Granddad skooched around so he could lift Lucien's head and cradle it in his lap. That eased the man enough to say a few words.

"My wife," he rasped.

"He has her?" asked Dad. Lucien nodded.

"In Lachine. Said he would kill..." He gagged again on the blood.

"We'll find her," said Dad. "I promise."

Lucien nodded. Then he startled us.

"Save Sweet's boy," he whispered.

"What?" asked my father.

"Sweet's boy," whispered Lucien. "Save him."

"*Sssh,*" said my father. Dad understood now. Lucien was in shock. "Otter's right here. Don't fret, Lucien. The boy is safe." With the last of his strength, Lucien grabbed my father's shirt.

"Lenoir has him," he said. "Sweet's boy!" He clung to my father's shirt, pleading. Then he sank back and closed his eyes.

"He's gone," said Dad a moment later. "I don't know what he meant. Must have been out of his head." He stood up, and his hands were red with blood. Just then we heard the clatter of footsteps on the stairs, and Angus appeared.

"What happened?" asked the Scot.

"Amos had to shoot Lucien. He's been helping Lenoir because that sorry piece of slime took Lucien's wife hostage."

"Is he dead?" Dad nodded, his mouth grim, his scar horrible. It wasn't anger I saw though. It was deep, deep sadness.

"Where did Lenoir go?" asked Angus.

"He dropped down that rope hanging outside the window," replied Granddad.

Yes, I thought bitterly, *the rope I left there.* Then I felt the bite of panic. *Mary and her father are in danger!*

"He's headed for the *Thorpedo!*" I cried. I didn't wait. I vaulted through the window and slid down the rope so fast I turned a somersault when I hit the ground. I rolled onto my feet, grabbed my rifle, and vanished into the woods like a cannonball from a big-mouthed gun. My arms were pumping, and my legs were a blur, but I was still on the lookout for Lenoir. A figure hurtled toward me from the trees on my right, and I swerved, but at the last second it fell in beside me.

"Jake!" I whispered, "you scared the bejeekers out of me! Come on, boy. Let's catch Lenoir before he gets to Mary." When I heard Mary scream, I ran faster than Mercury himself. I cleared a four-foot rail fence like a hurdler, and I didn't slow down until Jake and I got close to the river again. When the woods thinned out, I crawled through the puckerbrush until I reached an opening in the branches where I could see Dad's boat.

My heart sank. Five people stood in the bow of the *Thorpedo*, and I knew Lenoir had captured Mary and Mr. Prince. I had to think fast. Once they started the motor, it would be too late to stop them. I couldn't shoot. They were in the shadows, and it was too dark to see who was who. I would have to get closer. Leaving my rifle in the bushes, I crawled backward to the trees. I told Jake to stay, and then I ran in a crouch to the river far enough from Lenoir so he and his man wouldn't see me. Holding my pistol up to keep it dry, I waded into the water and headed for the *Thorpedo*.

As I got close to the boat, I settled into the water like my namesake and swam with just my head and the gun above water. I swam to the river side of Dad's boat, hoping that Lenoir would only be watching the shore. That was how I almost got spotted. Lenoir was talking to Mr. Prince about the *Felix*, asking questions about how to start the engines, how much gas he had, and so on, and I realized with a start that he was going to take the plane!

Then—thank the patron saint of wayward lads like myself—the rumble of a boat engine came from around the point. I cocked my head in the direction of the sound. It was headed our way. One of the men on the *Thorpedo* stepped to the stern and peered into the night in my direction. I stayed perfectly still and hoped he was looking over my head. He was. He whispered an oath, and they all disappeared inside the cabin.

The boat rounded the point, a dark shape lumbering toward us, its engine thumping louder and louder as it came closer. *Well, boots and saddles,* I thought, *here comes the cavalry!* It was Too Tall with Le Buchêron. Quickly, I swam to the *Thorpedo* so I wouldn't get run over. Under cover of all the noise my Uncle Hercule made coming alongside, I boosted myself up over the gunwale at the bow and hid behind a corner of the cabin.

"Slow down, Mister Too Big, or we boat crash and hurt ourself. Little left you go mister. Okay, good job you do. Now you in a right spot." *God help my uncle if he has Muff for a pilot,* I thought. Too Tall cut the engine and shuffled forward like a great, hulking bear as *Le Bûcheron* came to a stop next to the *Thorpedo*.

"Royal?" cried my uncle, "Où êtes vous? You leave no one to gardez votre boat?" I could tell from his voice that Too Tall was becoming suspicious but too late. When he stepped into the stern of the *Thorpedo,* Mary and her father and a third person stepped out of the cabin. The third person was short enough to be a kid or a midget, but in the shadows I couldn't tell which. It struck me odd, this stranger in the mix, but I didn't have time to cogitate on the mystery because directly behind them came two men with guns.

"Très bon," said one of them to my uncle, "another hostage. Put your hands in the air and keep them there. Get back on your boat, Monsieur Too Big, and we will join you eh?"

"We've had radish now, Too Big. Bad men got Muff and Mister Big in nasty bad fix," said Muff, his eyes rolling wildly.

Now? I asked myself. *Yes, now.* I couldn't see well in the shadows, but I gambled that the other man must be Lenoir. After all, I had only seen five people aboard, and I had heard Lenoir's voice. I wished for a little more light so I could be sure, but I couldn't wait. Right then, I had a good chance at both those hoodlums, but if they went aboard *Le Bucherôn,* I might not. I reached under the bench that was fixed to the front wall of the cabin. Yes! The Babe's bat was right where I'd left it. I grabbed it and crept along the side of the cabin. I was almost on the two men when a floorboard squeaked. I didn't hesitate. I whacked one fella with that Louisville slugger, and before the other one could whirl around, I changed his mind.

"Don't," I said. "I've got a shotgun, and it makes a big

hole. Hand your popgun to my uncle. He's the giant." I was feeling pretty good about saying popgun because *I* only had the trapper's pistol, which wasn't exactly a cannon, but I figured he didn't know that. My moment of glory was short-lived. It's just when a fella starts feeling his oats that he's headed for a fall.

I was close enough now to see Mary and her father and the short stranger, and my first glimpse of the stranger sent a sharp buzz of electricity right through me. It *was* a kid, a boy about eight years old. I wasn't surprised by *that*. What jolted me—when the moon showed pale through a hole in the clouds—what made me feel like I'd grabbed hold of a magneto wire, what made my heart thump like a drum, was that this boy I was staring at in the milky moonlight looked like a younger version of me. I shifted my gaze to Mary, hoping to find a clue to this boy, to why he was there. She looked scared—real scared—and so did Mr. Prince. That's why it wasn't a complete surprise when I felt cold steel press against the base of my skull. Lenoir whispered to me, and all my moxie vanished like smoke in the wind.

"Take your gun by the barrel, boy, and hand it to Hector," he ordered. "Do it slow and easy, or I'll shoot you right now." I did what he asked. "Won't your papa be sad when he sees you next, washed up on shore with black holes where your eyes used to be and the sea gulls pulling the meat off your bones?" he asked.

"Yut. He will be," I said. Then, since I didn't have

anything to lose, I showed some bravado. "Did you know he's part Indian, Lenoir? He'll track you down, and believe me, there's no place on earth you can hide where he won't find you. Some day you'll open your eyes from a troubled sleep, and he'll be inches away from your face with a knife at your throat. I know you're good with a knife, Lenoir. You'll appreciate what he can do with his."

"Shut your trap, maggot!" he snarled. He shoved the gun into the small of my back, and I grunted with pain and stumbled. I could have caught myself, but I fell onto my hands and knees to buy some time.

"Hector, get the girl and her father on board the other boat. We're leaving. You, big oaf," he said to my uncle, "pick up Peris. And you," he growled at me, "get up! If your father is anything like you, he won't be too hard to handle." With that, he hauled back and drove his boot into my side. A rib cracked and pain exploded so sharply in my chest I almost blacked out. I should have cringed like a whipped dog—it would have been smarter—but I couldn't give that devil the satisfaction. *Stay with it,* I thought, *stay awake.* When I opened my eyes and saw Mary stepping down into *Le Buchêron,* the pain turned to fury. I knew Lenoir was going to put a bullet in me, but I wasn't inclined to make it easy for him. I got to my feet, staggered forward, and fell in a heap.

I knew he'd kick me again. This time, though, I was ready. I curled up with my back toward him to make him think I was scared. His boots scraped on the deck as he

came after me. Then, the scraping stopped, and I knew he
was rearing back to lambaste me. Suddenly, I rolled back
toward him, and there was his boot coming toward my face
just like I figured. I grabbed it with both hands before he
could split my head open. I twisted so hard, I flipped him
onto his back. I must have wrenched his knee because he
cursed like a trooper. When he landed with a hard thump,
I jumped to my feet. He brought his gun up, but now it my
turn to kick, and I nailed his hand with my size eleven.
He howled, and his gun spun off into the dark. Right then,
Too Tall or Mr. Prince must have rushed Hector, but he told
them to freeze or he'd shoot, so I knew I was on my own
against Lenoir.

He sprang up, and I saw the flash of a knife in his hand.
I scooped up my bat, but before I could use it, he slipped
in and stabbed at me. I leaped back, but he put a couple
inches of blade into my stomach. I swung the bat, aiming
for his head, but he dodged too. Still, I slammed it down
hard on his shoulder and felt the crunch of bone. He howled
again and jumped back out of reach. Then Too Tall shouted
a warning, but it was too late. Hector shot me in the back. I
dropped to the deck like I'd been cut by the reaper's blade,
and Hector whirled, ready to fire at Too Tall or Mr. Prince.
He should have paid closer attention to Mary. I had reached
the *Thorpedo* right after Lenoir, and he hadn't had time to
search her well. Suddenly, she had that sock full of birdshot
in her hand. Hector swiveled toward her, ready to shoot,
but he wasn't as quick as Mary. She darted toward him,

and when that sock thunked him in the temple, his knees buckled, and he slithered to the deck.

Then shots ripped over my head on the *Thorpedo,* and Lenoir hit the deck and scuttled into the shadows after his own gun. *Great Uncle Gamble and the Green Mountain Boys!* I thought. *Amos Waters and Dad to the rescue! It's about time they showed up.* I was beside myself with joy, but I was counting my chickens too soon. Lenoir wasn't going to give up easily. He called from where he was hiding behind the corner of the cabin.

"St. Onge!" he said, "I'm glad you're here. I've got Sweet's boy. You and the old man throw down your guns and come aboard with your hands up, and I'll let him live."

"Not a chance, Lenoir. I saw my son get shot. He's prob'ly dead. Now you just want to kill the rest of us."

"I don't mean that miserable whelp you named after a river rat. I've got him, sure, and he's still alive, but Sweet had another boy, St. Onge." There was a pause after Lenoir said that. A light wind had sprung up, and all I could hear was the creaking of the boats as they rocked on the small waves it pushed into shore, that and the thudding of my heart.

"I don't believe you, Lenoir? You're a lying gutter thief who steals from the dead."

"You'll believe me when you see him. He looks like his mother. Just like her."

"Who's the father?" I heard the edge in Dad's voice. Lenoir heard it too and his own voice sounded gleeful.

"It wasn't you was it, St. Onge? Where were you? She was looking for you. After the Armistice was signed in November, the Crows boarded the *S.S. Olympic*. We steamed into Halifax Harbor in January. Sweet was a nurse at the demobe center. She asked every soldier she met about you, and nobody could tell her a thing. Until me, that is. I told her you had died at Vimy Ridge even though I saw those Jerries cart you off. I told her I lugged you out of No Man's Land on my shoulder when you were shot by a sniper. I told her I held you while you died. She was so torn up over you, I had to comfort her, and you can guess what came of that.

Our son was born in September. We named him René. That was my brother's middle name. You remember my brother don't you, St. Onge? Jacques Lenoir? Your wife gave me the address, and I had a woman write a letter to your father-in-law saying Sweet had died of the Spanish flu. I didn't want him to come up there looking for her. I figured when I was ready, I'd make the trip to Swanton and kill some more of your kin, but I had a feeling you'd show up some day, so I waited. And now, here you are, St. Onge. Oh, and Sweet? She died giving birth. Such a shame! Ah well, c'est le guerre.

So what do you say, St. Onge? You'd better make up your mind, or your other boy's going to bleed to death here. I'll let your brother take him and René aboard his boat, and they can leave, but you and your sharpshooter father-in-law have to give yourselves up. That's the deal."

Oh, he's a sly one, I thought. *He's going to take us all if*

I don't stop him. But how? I was lying on the deck with one
eye open, wondering how much longer I could keep myself
from slipping off into darkness. Then I saw it. The rubber
hose John Prince had used to siphon gas was still in the
gas tank, the end of it trailing on the deck within reach.
I pulled it to me and sucked on it to start the siphon. Gas
poured into my mouth. I spat quietly and laid the hose on
the deck. Gas fanned out toward the cabin where Lenoir
was hiding. I had no time to lose. I pulled a wooden match
from my pocket and got myself ready.

"You show me my son's still alive, and I'll come on
board, Lenoir."

"The old man too!" hollered Lenoir.

"All right, you devil," said Granddad, "show us the boy
first."

"Don't shoot or I'll kill him."

"Losing patience, Lenoir," called my father. I heard
Lenoir scrambling toward me, and I gripped the rubber
hose in one hand and the match in my teeth. I lay face
down with the gas still pouring out of the hose and
running past me in his direction. Then I sensed him
standing above me. Grabbing my shoulder, he flipped me
over and came down close to my face to see if I was alive.

"Speak up, boy, if you want to live. Quick now!" I
grabbed him tight by the collar. With my thumb part way
over the end of the hose to jet the stream, I squirted him in
the face with gasoline. He fell back, digging at his eyes and
howling with rage.

"I'll kill you for that," he screamed. I struck the match and dropped it in the pool of gas at his feet. With all the strength I had left, I rolled to the port side of the boat and pulled myself up. I had time to look behind me and see the deck of the *Thorpedo* alight with fire and Lenoir engulfed in flames. I saw the trail of fire heading for the gas tank as I tumbled over the rail into the river. The *ka-boom* rang in my ears as I hit the water, and chunks of Dad's boat zinged through the air like shrapnel. One whanged into my skull, and I couldn't see the outside world anymore but only the inside one. Then I dropped into the cold water of the Richelieu River where Death was waiting for me with a cruel smile on his thin lips and a look in his eye as cold as a corpse.

Lenoir was dead! Praise the saints and dance with hobnailed boots upon his head! That spawn of the Devil lit up like a human torch, so my father said later. I know it was an ugly, awful way to die, so I'll make my confession here and now, and you can sit at the Lord's right hand and judge me as you wish. I was as dry-eyed as a lizard about that fella's demise. Prob'ly that doesn't show me at my Sunday school best, but then again, Lenoir had just tried to bury his blade in me. He met a nasty end, but a nastier fellow I never met, and that's the God's honest truth.

No, I didn't sorrow over Lenoir, for as I sank to the bottom of the Richelieu, I figured I'd catch up to him before he met the old boy with the pitchfork. I only hoped the

Devil wouldn't put me to work alongside that miserable
son of a snake shoveling coal to keep the hellfires burning,
but being the Devil, I guessed he might. This I thought as
I plumbed the river because, even with a name like Otter,
I couldn't hold my breath much longer, and what with that
chunk of wood hitting me in the head and the dose of 0.22
lead in my back, I wasn't feeling too perky. The truth be
told, I couldn't muster enough gumption to move an arm
or a leg. With all the rain, the river was ten or twelve deep
feet where I toppled over the side of the *Thorpedo*, and it
seemed as if my lungs would burst by the time I settled on
the muddy bottom. I held on as long as I could, waiting for
a miracle and watching the moving picture show inside my
head.

It grew darker and darker, and I tagged along after my
mind, which wandered off to wherever it goes when it's
trying to get away from the boogeyman. Now, somehow,
I could look up through the two fathoms of water and
see black clouds gathering in the sky. They boiled and
swirled, and soon thunder cracked and lightning flashed.
A whipping blue bolt of electricity streaked toward me like
a rope let down from heaven, and down that rope slid a
dark, bearded giant. As fast as he came, he took forever
to get any closer. *I'm losing my mind,* I thought. *Lack of
air prob'ly.* I had a hunch this giant wished me well and
wanted to snatch me from my grave with the fishes, but I
was sure he'd be too late.

Along with this vision sprung from my delirium came

another one. My lungs had become bicycle tires, and someone was pumping them full of air. They swelled fatter and fatter, and I knew they were going to burst. And then— before they did—I blew out. The air *whooshed* from me, and I wanted to laugh at all the bubbles hurrying up and away, but then I had to breathe, and when I did, the river flooded into my chest. A curtain dropped, the lightning vanished in inky blackness, and I traveled beyond the beyond.

I FLOATED IN THAT BLACKNESS FOR SOME TIME, but time was lost, and I don't know if minutes passed or weeks or days. For all I knew, it might have been years. Maybe I was like that Rip Van Winkle I read about in school and was going to wake up as an old man. Or maybe I wasn't going to wake up at all. Finally, I found a door in the bottom of the river, and that door opened into a room and a set of winding stairs. I climbed those stairs, and the stairs turned to ladders leaning dangerous and rickety against steep rock faces. The ladders led to trails barely wide enough for a goat, and the trails corkscrewed around a mountain pinnacle that rose up and up, and finally disappeared in the clouds. I climbed and climbed, and I knew days had passed because a stubble of whiskers appeared on my chin, and I grew ravenous for meat or even a cold potato.

Up out of the dark I climbed, into sunlight so dazzling I was blinded and had to send my hands across the rock like spiders in search of a hold, a horn of rock to haul myself up or a crack in which to wedge a boot. Then I passed into clouds and could see the rock again in front of my face if not the world spreading out far below in a patchwork of forests and fields. By now I had reached a point on the mountain so high that the air was thin and the height dizzying, and only a red-tailed hawk kept me company.

I had thought when I first stumbled upon the room at the bottom of the river to have found Lady Luck's bedroom, and she—in her kindness—had shown me Jacob's ladder, a way back to Mary and the world of the living, but I should have known better. This was no escape. Death was taunting me with a last trick before shuttling me down to the pit of fire. My mind had come unhinged, but I couldn't stop my mad crawl to the top. I ran my fingers over the smooth rock, searching for a new handhold, and I cried out in fury and despair because there was none. I rested and caught my breath. I would not go down. I could not. I had one chance. Jump and grab for a hold. I gathered myself to leap, and then I hesitated. From above, I heard a musical and unearthly voice.

"Otter," whispered the voice. "Can you hear me?"

What a sweet, pure voice! An angel? I wondered. *St. Peter, keeper of the Pearly Gates! I'm on heaven's doorstep. Too bad. The old man will never open up for me. Ah well, in for an inning, in for a game.* With that, I sprang from the ledge and reached with my good hand as high as I could. It was a desperate gamble. I scrabbled at the rock searching

frantically for a cranny or a wart to grab onto, but I found
nothing. For a moment that lasted forever, I was unhooked
in space and about to plunge to my death. Then—pluck
a miracle from the prayerbook!—a hand grasped mine!
I clung to it with all my strength, and even though that
hand held mine ever so gently, even though the skin was as
soft as rose petals, it saved me from falling to my death.

CHAPTER 22

Shooting Stars

HEN I OPENED MY EYES, I saw a miracle even greater than I had expected. An angel held my hand all right, and that dark-haired angel's name was Mary. I was lying in a bed with clean, white sheets, and she was sitting on a chair beside me, looking into my eyes with surprise and joy and hope. I closed my eyes, not sure I could believe what I was seeing. I felt something wet slithering again and again across my other hand. I opened one eye. It was Jake.

"Otter St. Onge," Mary whispered, "it's about time you decided to wake up and stop my heart from breaking."

"Mary, lass" I croaked, "I've got another secret I need to tell you. Come close so I can whisper." She bent down and kissed me tenderly on the lips, and then I knew for sure she was an angel.

"Where am I, Mary?" I asked.

"You're at my grandfather's house on Cumberland Head. My father flew you and Boyce down here in the *Felix*."

"And you barely made it, I might add," said a low voice.

"Granddad, you're here too?" I asked. I turned my head, shocked at how weak I was. He was sitting in a patch of sunlight, a book in his lap and the smoke from his pipe wafting out the window.

"Yut. Four days, off and on. Mary's been here every minute. Took her meals in here and slept in that chair."

"Four days?" I asked. "I've been out for four days?"

"Yut. Out or out of your head. You almost drowned, and when your father got you breathing again, your heart started up, but it wasn't any too strong. John flew you down here as fast as that bird would fly. Then Doc dug the bullet out of your back and cleaned that stab wound in your stomach. Course, you were unconscious. 'Parently you got knocked in the head pretty hard when you touched off that gas tank. I told Doc that wouldn't cause any permanent harm." He grinned as he said this. "Anyway, you didn't wake up, and then you ran a high fever, and—well, we were starting to wonder weren't we, Mary?"

"Yes," she said softly. Now, Jake sidled closer to the bed and reached up to lick my face. I pushed him away and stroked his shaggy head. Finally comforted, he turned two circles and lay down by my bed.

"Did Dad fish me out of the river?"

"No, that was Too Tall." This time the reply came from the doorway.

"So there was a giant," I muttered.

"That would be your uncle," said Dad.

"And I be wondering past few days if I were too much late, but you wake up at last! Mon Dieu, I am glad, you!" boomed Uncle Hercule. That was the signal for a few more people to come into the bedroom. Little Roy, grinning happily, squeezed in past Too Tall.

"Il est bon, cousin!" he said. "It is good to see you alive," he laughed.

Behind him, to my surprise, came Luc the Weasel, who I hadn't seen since he'd been shot during our set-to with the Lake Champlain Boat Patrol.

"Bonjour, Otter," said Luc shyly. "Comment allez-vous? Better?"

"Luc," I said, "I'm glad you beat that bullet. I feel like I boxed a few rounds with Jack Johnson last night."

"No worry for you, Otter," said Luc. "Doc Eastman, he dig bullet out of me, and he do same for you. He tend you whole time you sleep. You be all right, now you is awake." Luc stepped back from my bedside, and behind him stood a tall, distinguished-looking, older man. He had a full head of snow-white hair and a big, drooping mustache, and I thought of the pictures I'd seen of Mark Twain. He looked at me with kindly, blue eyes. I knew it must be Mary's grandfather.

"Young man, I'm delighted to meet you," said Doc Eastman, "not only because I admire and respect your grandfather, but also because I hear you have taken good care of my granddaughter. What a relief it is to see you awake. Let me take your pulse." He put a couple fingers on my wrist and peered at a pocket watch he held in his other hand.

"Good," he said. "Steady and strong." He let go of my wrist and gave my hand to Mary. "Here granddaughter," he said, "you hold onto him. Don't let him jump out of bed, but I dare say he'll be up and about soon. Otter, your wounds are healing nicely. We're having a Thanksgiving dinner of sorts in a couple hours. It's early by the calendar, but we've all got plenty to be thankful for. If you feel like it, you can come to the table and get some nourishment. Now everyone, let's clear out of here and let Otter rest a little longer." And everybody did leave, which was good because my eyes were closing in spite of me.

I slept, even though that's all I'd been doing for days, and woke up sometime later to the sound of a creaking floorboard. I lay with my eyes closed for a bit, watching a parade of pictures in my mind, Angus lugging the wounded Boyce over his shoulder back at the fort, Dad trying to stop the flow of blood pumping out of Lucien's chest, Lenoir's leering face bent over mine just before I set him on fire. I was troubled by these sights, and I banished them with the only one I wanted to see—Mary, smiling and pretty, as when I first saw her at the Angel's Perch.

That floorboard creaked again, and I opened my eyes a little. The light in the room was dim and beset with evening shadows. I opened my eyes wide. Dad had just risen from his chair and now stood looking down at me. Mary still sat right beside my bed. Granddad looked comfortable, tipped back in his chair by the window, reading a book, now and again blowing his pipe smoke out beneath the raised sash.

"Are Angus and Boyce and Louis okay?" I asked. "They weren't here when I woke up earlier were they?"

"No, they weren't, but they're fine. Boyce is back at his farm, hobbling around on a pair of crutches, itching to get back to work before his hired hand Muff runs the farm into the ground. Thanks to Doc Eastman, Boyce is healing nicely. Angus and Louis took *Le Buchêron* up to Montreal. Before he died from a gunshot wound, we persuaded one of the Crows to tell us where Lenoir was keeping Heloise, Lucien's wife. Angus called last night on the telephone. He and Louis broke into a house in Lachine and rescued her. She and her daughter will stay with Boyce in St. Jean for the time being. Angus and Louis are headed down here right now." He paused and stared at me long enough that I knew he had something important to say.

"Otter, I'm glad you are alive."

"Me too," I grinned. He paused again, and I knew that wasn't all he wanted to tell me. He had a stone in his shoe, so to speak. Mary saw it too.

"What's wrong, Mr. St. Onge?"

"The boy," he said, "Otter's half brother." I didn't understand. Half brother? Then, with a shock, I remembered the boy on the *Thorpedo*.

"How do you know he *is* my half brother, Dad?" I asked. "I wouldn't believe anything I heard from Corbin Lenoir."

"No. But do you remember what Lucien said before he died?"

"You think what Lenoir said was true?" I asked.

"Oui. The boy is your half brother. Your mother was in Halifax, looking for me. C'est vrai? How Lenoir must have laughed at his good luck when he found her. What a chance for revenge! To worm his way into her life, always believing that I would come back some day! He set his hooks in Lucien too, recognized him when he got off the troopship in Halifax and set some of his boys after him that same night in a tavern near the docks. Lenoir called Montreal and had Lucien's wife kidnapped. Then he told Lucien to do as he was told or Heloise would be killed.

When Lucien met your mother, she was already in a family way. She didn't say whether Lenoir had forced himself on her, and Lucien didn't want to know. Neither do I. Your mother died giving birth to a boy nine months later. He's the one was on the boat, the one named René after Lenoir's brother."

"What are we going to do with him?" I asked.

"I don't know. He's just a boy, but when I look at him, I think of your mother dead and him the cause of it. I think of Lenoir. This boy is part of his revenge. He has Lenoir's blood. I look at him, and my stomach turns." I didn't know what to say to this. I understood how Dad felt. I thought I might even feel the same. Still, it seemed harsh to judge the kid for his father's sins. Then I looked at Mary, and I saw she was troubled.

"Mary, what is it?" I asked.

"I don't want to meddle," she said.

"Go right ahead," said my father. "Maybe you can help."
She didn't speak at once. Then she looked directly at my
father.

"I know what it's like to be brought up by somebody like
Corbin Lenoir," she said. "Todd DePrae was like him, and
so was Coby Rotmensen. I lived with one or the other of
them from the time I was six until I escaped six months
ago. Anybody might think that their nastiness was bound
to rub off on me."

"But it didn't, Mary," I said. She smiled.

"No," she said, "and I don't think Corbin Lenoir's
nastiness has tainted René either. If he takes after anyone,
he must take after his mother."

"What makes you think so, Mary," asked my father.

"It's just a hunch. He's so quiet, and his face is so
frozen, it's hard to tell what he's thinking, but I know that
look. He's trying to hide, and I bet that has to do with
his father. Yesterday, though, I looked out the window
and saw him playing with Jake. He didn't know I was
watching. Jake would run pell-mell right at him, swerve
at the last second, then circle away at top speed and do
it again. René tried to grab him over and over, but Jake
was too fast and flashed by every time just out of reach.
Suddenly, I blinked. René was smiling, and I felt a tear
wet the corner of my eye. Then, on the next run, Jake
bowled him over and began licking his face. René lay

on the grass and laughed and laughed like a boy being tickled by his best friend.

I don't know what your wife was like, Mr. St. Onge, but I wonder if I wasn't seeing a little of her in René's face right then. He was so happy. He loves that dog. Mrs. Eastman found René curled up with Jake last night sleeping outside this room in the hallway. Maybe it's wishful thinking, but I can't imagine him being like Corbin Lenoir." Mary lowered her eyes and gave my father a chance to answer. For my part, I thought she might be right. Jake had a nose for good guys and bad guys, and if he thought René was okay, who was I to argue? Dad wasn't so sure.

"Mary," he said, "I understand why you feel for the boy, but René wasn't just raised by Corbin Lenoir. He's Lenoir's son, and Corbin Lenoir would tip his hat to you with one hand and stick a knife between your ribs with the other. Maybe René *does* have some of Sweet in him, but what if he's got his father's mean streak?"

"I don't!" The words startled us. René stood scowling in the doorway. How long he had been listening, I didn't know, but I guessed he'd heard plenty. No one spoke for several seconds. Then Mary broke the silence.

"René," she asked, "how long were you in the hall?" René studied his shoes before answering.

"A while," he mumbled.

"You shouldn't eavesdrop," she said.

"I came to see Jake. Then I heard you talking about my

father and me. You think I'm bad." He looked accusingly at
Dad.

"Sorry you heard all that, boy," said Dad. René didn't
reply at first. When he did, he got Dad's full attention.

"Were you really married to my mother?" he asked.

"Yes," Dad answered finally.

"My dad said she died because of me. When I was born."
Nobody knew what to say to this, and the silence in the
room was loud. Then, in a small voice, René spoke again.
"I wish I could have known my mom," he said. Granddad
had been sitting quietly by the window all this time. Now
he spoke.

"I'm your granddad, René. Amos Waters. Your
grandmother and I named your mother Sweet when she
was born, and never did a child do a better job of living
up to her name. She was the soul of kindness. Otter there
is her son, too. I know this isn't the first time you've seen
him, but I guess it's the first time you've had a chance to
talk." René stared at Granddad but didn't answer. Then
he turned toward me, and looking at his shoes again, he
stepped to my bedside. When he finally spoke, he was still
looking down.

"I did see you. I saw you kill my father," he said.

"I know," I said. "I'm sorry."

"Did my dad hurt you?" he asked. "Was that why you
made the fire?"

"Yut," I replied. My voice was husky. René was rocking
back and forth, pushing against the bed and then away

again. Tears trickled down his cheeks. I hoisted myself up so I was sitting. Then I reached out and pulled him in close. I thought he might fight me, maybe even hit me, but he didn't. His breath came in shuddering gasps, and he cried and cried. Mary hugged him and stroked his hair.

"It'll be all right," she whispered. "It'll be all right." He buried his face in my shoulder and let go of all the hurt. He'd been holding back a lot, and when it came out, it came out in a flood. It took him a while to settle down. I didn't blame him. I was only a couple years older than he was when the letters came saying Dad was missing in action and Mom was dead of the Spanish flu. After a while, he calmed down. That was Granddad's cue.

"René," he said, "we've got to get you situated. Do you have family back in Montreal who would take you in?"

"No," he said, wiping his eyes. "Uncle Leonel, but I don't want to live with him." Granddad traded a glance with my father. Then he continued.

"Well, I may need some help. I had a regular farmhand before the flood," he said, smiling at me and Mary, "but he met a young woman in the shining city of Plattsburgh, and I don't know if milking cows will hold his interest any more. What do you think? Would you like to come live with me and help me run the farm?" René's eyes widened again. He wasn't sure whether he could trust Granddad, but I could see he wanted to. He nodded his head slowly and seriously.

"All right then. Why don't you go outside now and play

with Otter's wolf dog. I'm sure the two of you need to run around and breathe some fresh air. Mary will call you when it's time for dinner, and later I'll tell you about the farm." René, without a word, scooted out the door, and I sent Jake after him. Seconds later, we heard the front door close and Dad continued the conversation about my half brother.

"You sure you want to take him on, Amos?" asked Dad.

"He's my grandson, Royal. Sweet's son."

"Yes," said Dad. "You're right. It's just—it's hard to know what kind of man he'll be, whether some day—."

"No, way to know, Royal," said Granddad.

"Some people get stabbed or shot," said Mary, "and a doctor like my grandfather can dig out the bullet or sew up the cut, but some people, like René, get hurt on the inside where nobody can see. If that little boy has even a slim chance of being different than his father, maybe that chance is you and Petrice and the farm, Mr. Waters."

"I hope you're right, Mary. Time will tell the tale."

"Well, now that you've settled that, what's next?" I asked. "I plan to get out of this bed tomorrow. It's chafing me to be lying around doing nothing. Is Lenoir really dead?"

"Most definitely dead, and we are all in your debt for it. You don't have to worry about him anymore."

"And his men?" I asked.

"They're *all* dead," said Granddad grimly. "It was a bad business, but we couldn't have any of them carrying

the tale of what happened at Fort Chambly. It's all best
forgotten now."

I sighed. "Yes. It's over then. I'm glad." And I *was* glad.
I'd had enough of dead men to last me a lifetime. "Now,
what do we do?" I asked.

"Your grandsire and I have been discussing that, and we
thought we'd ask you."

"I want to go home," I said without giving it a second
thought.

"Yes," said Dad, "but where is home? With your
grandmother in Burlington? With Granddad in Swanton?
Do you want to come up to St. Jean and live with me? Are
you going to strike off on your own?" The answer to Dad's
question was not as simple as I had thought. I wondered
about Mary. What would she do next? No sooner did I think
it than my father read my mind.

"Maybe you want to talk to a certain girl before you
decide," he said.

"Yut," I said," but Dad, I want to spend some time with
you one way or another." He smiled at this.

"Well, here's a thought. Maybe you can stay at Doc's
for a few more days until you get your strength back, and
then you can make your way to Granddad's farm. Your
grandsire and I have been talking, and I'm going to stay
with him and Petrice for a while and help work the farm.
Whatever you and Mary decide, I imagine you'll show up
there every so often for a visit. I'm sure Granddad and
Petrice would welcome Mary if you came together."

"With wide open arms," said Granddad, "and your father would be just as welcome, Mary."

"That sounds good," I said, "but how are you going to get back to Swanton?"

"Uncle Hercule will give us a ride anywhere we want to go. He's got your canoe, by the way."

A WHILE AFTER DAD AND GRANDDAD left the bedroom, Mary and I heard the whistle blow for the noon arrival of the Grand Isle Ferry. I was getting out of bed, and every inch of me felt like it had been punched or kicked. My head was fat and fuzzy, and when I stood up, I was so dizzy I had to lean on Mary until I got my balance. I took my sweet time putting my clothes on. She gave me a glass of water and a piece of her grandmother's bread, and I perked up some, and when we went out to the parlor, we heard a car drive into the yard. Moments later, Petrice, Gram, and Aunt Josey bustled through the door, and right behind them came a young fella who looked a lot like John Prince.

"Otter St. Onge!" cried Petrice, "come here you prodigal boy and give Petrice a hug. And you, girl, you must be Mary? You are beautiful, child. Oh, I'm so happy to see you both!" Petrice, who has a heart as big as the wide world, took both of us in her arms and hugged us hard. When Petrice let go, Gram hugged me until my ribs almost cracked again, and then she cried a small river of happy tears while Aunt Josey had her turn. I might have suffocated, but a small woman with snapping black eyes and a big wooden spoon in her hand appeared in the doorway to the dining room. When she spoke, I realized it was Mary's grandmother, Beverly Eastman.

"Scott," she said, "this is Mary," and when he stood gaping, she continued, "so close your mouth before you catch a fly and give your sister a hug." Then she summoned us to the table because Doc had just carved the turkey, and I needed to eat to build up my strength, and especially because a giant everyone called Too Tall said he was starving and would eat the tablecloth if food didn't appear soon.

I sat on one side of Mary, and Scott sat on the other, and he pressed her eagerly to tell him everything that had happened after she had been swept off the Grand Isle Ferry and was thought to be drowned. René sat between Granddad and Petrice, and when she wasn't hugging him and marveling at how handsome he was and how much he reminded her of his mother, Granddad was telling him about the farm. René looked bewildered by all the attention, but he smiled shyly at Petrice and listened to Granddad like he was receiving the gospel.

The men were drinking home-brewed beer, and the women were sampling Petrice's apple wine, and we were all eating more turkey and stuffing and cranberry sauce and mashed potatoes than we could possibly hold, and we were laughing and telling stories, and slowly the platters of food grew lighter, and we reached that lull in the eating that means everyone needs a breather before dessert. I knew that many of us were also remembering loved ones who could not be at the table, which was why my father and John Prince suddenly stood up to speak.

"John and I want to propose a toast," he said, "and for that we need spirits suitable to the celebration." That was Granddad's cue to appear with a bottle of Moonbeam and pass it around the table so everyone could pour a tot in a whiskey glass. Dad spoke cheerfully, but he didn't smile. I think he knew by now that the zigzag scar on his once handsome face mocked that expression. "Otter," he said, "I left the North Country when you were a boy. Now I come back and find you a man, a man not only brave but kind. Your mother would be proud. I know I am."

"And Mary," said John, "only the good Lord knows how you did it on your own, but you became a woman—."

"An angel really," interrupted Dad mischievously.

"An angel," laughed John, "not only as brave and kind as your mother was, but as beautiful as she was, and if there is a heaven or some place where the spirit lives on in its own mysterious way and takes notice from time to time of us mere mortals, she is overjoyed that you are alive and happy and in the full bloom of youth. Now, before we get maudlin, and you all think we're already in our cups, we just want to say how thankful we are that our children are here with us today, safe and restored to their families."

"Mais oui," said Dad. "So raise your glasses everyone. Otter, welcome back to the land of the living!"

"And Mary," said Mr. Prince, "may your life be long and

happy!" Well, you should have heard the wicked racket everyone made then. They clapped and cheered. Some of the men banged on the table with the butts of their knives. The dishes rattled and the silverware jingled, and that crowd of family and friends hoorayed us again and again, and the din was tremendous. When the thunderstorm of noise finally dropped to a summer shower, and when everyone had drunk off a second tot, Granddad, of all people, began singing "Auld Lang Syne." Everyone joined in, and then dessert came, and I went back to bed because suddenly I was tired and wanted to sleep.

EVERYBODY BUT THE EASTMANS AND THE PRINCES and me left on *Le Bûcheron* in the morning. Mary and I stayed for a couple more weeks while I got stronger and Mary got reacquainted with her family. She and I and Mr. Prince and Scott drove into Plattsburgh one day and visited the Angel's Perch. We saw no sign of Roddy Bragg, but we heard some surprising news from Deacon Gates. A Pinkerton detective had come to the Angel's Perch, but he hadn't wanted to bring Mary back to Kansas City to stand trial for murder. Mrs. DePrae had sent him with a letter. *She* had confessed to the murder of her husband, claiming that he had assaulted her and threatened to kill her. When two other women testified at her trial that they too had been assaulted and raped by DePrae, the jury convicted her of voluntary manslaughter with no jail time. She wanted Mary to know that she could come home, that she would be welcomed home with love. I guess Mrs. DePrae found some courage. It came pretty late, but I was glad that she had finally roused herself to protect her adopted daughter. I hoped she was getting better, and I could see that Mary hoped so too. Her eyes were glistening when we said goodbye to Deacon and Angel, and at the Western Union office down the street, she sent the following telegram:

> 1927 NOV 23 PM 1 55
> LEAH DEPRAE
> KANSAS CITY MO
> THANK YOU STOP AM SAFE AND WELL
> STOP FOUND MY FATHER STOP WILL VISIT
> AFTER THANKSGIVING STOP LETTER TO
> FOLLOW STOP
> MARY =

The next day we loaded my canoe with camping gear. Mary and I had decided to spend a week or so camping on the lake, just the two of us—and Jake, of course—and then visit Granddad's farm in Swanton. After that, we would take a train to Kansas City and visit Mrs. DePrae.

Mary was restless. Finding her family was like a fairy tale, and she was as happy as a princess, but we'd both discovered that life isn't a fairy tale. She'd spent a lot of years on her own, and a lot of that time was spent just trying to stay alive. After twelve years with no family, she needed some time to get used to the idea of having one. Suddenly, she had a father and grandparents and a brother, and it was too much all at once.

Luckily, her father and grandfather understood. Mrs. Eastman wasn't so sure.

"Otter St. Onge," she said, "you've barely left your sickbed. You've been stabbed, shot, kicked, and knocked in the head. Now you're going to take my only granddaughter across Lake Champlain which, as you very well know, is the place where she almost drowned. And you're going to do this in a canoe? Are you crazy, young man, or just insane?"

"No, ma'am," I said with a smile. "We'll be careful. We'll paddle close to shore, and we'll only cross the lake when the sky is clear and the wind is calm."

"Do you promise me that you'll take no foolish chances, and that you'll bring Marian safely to your grandfather's farm?"

"I promise, Mrs. Eastman. And I want to thank you for taking care of me." I put my arms around her, hugged her hard, and picked her right up off the ground.

"Put me down! Put me down!" she scolded. "You are a rascal," she said when I set her back on her feet, but she was laughing, and I think she liked it all right. I shook hands with Mr. Prince and Doc Eastman, and I thanked Doc for saving my life.

"From the stories I heard of your adventures during the last couple weeks, I need to thank *you*, Otter. Mrs. Eastman and I are more than grateful. I can't tell you what it means for us to see Mary again." Then Mrs. Eastman cried and cried and smothered Mary with hugs and kisses. When his wife was done, Doc stooped and planted a gentle kiss on Mary's forehead. Then her father hugged and kissed her, and said goodbye to both of us.

"You two have a good trip. After all the rain we've had, maybe you'll have some sunshine. As Too Tall would say, bon voyage, mes enfants." Jake was already curled up with our gear in the middle of the canoe. Mr. Prince steadied the bow, Mary stepped in, and I pushed off from the stern. In no time, the three of them were tiny children waving in the distance. We waved back. Then we rounded Martin Point, and they disappeared from sight.

THAT AFTERNOON, AS THE SUN WAS SINKING into the Adirondacks, we reached Cloak Island off the southeast corner of Isle La Motte. The next morning, we stayed in our blankets for a while. We had slept under a square of canvas that was staked low to the ground in the back and stretched over a level pole lean-to style in the front. A breeze blew toward us from the south, and when the sun rose over North Hero it warmed our campsite. I had a few sticks of driftwood handy, and I threw them on the coals of last night's fire without even getting out of bed. In a few minutes, a curl of smoke rose from the ring of stones. I gazed down the lake toward Point Au Roche and Bixby Island. The water sparkled with diamonds. *I love this world,* I thought. *I do.* I put some strips of smoked bacon in a spider, and set it on a flat stone next to the baby flames dancing around the driftwood.

I slipped from the lean-to and walked through the cedars to a thirty foot bluff on the other side of the cove. Jake trotted along at my side. On the prow of the rock I closed my eyes and felt the heat of the sun on my skin. For a November day, it was going to be warm. I opened my eyes again, ran three steps, and leaped. I hit the water like a cannon shot and water geysered above me. The cold took my breath away. I dropped down and down, just like when I sank to the bottom of the Richelieu, but I wasn't going to lie waterlogged on the bottom this time. I felt strong again. I put my arms out to slow down, and then I swam toward the spears of sunlight slanting into the water above me.

I just had time to shake the water out of my eyes when something rocketed into the lake next to me and sent up another great splash. Seconds later, Mary popped up beside me, laughing and squirting water at me from her mouth. I splashed her and she swam away. Jake lay down on the beach with his head between his paws and watched us. We chased each other and flailed the water, but it was too cold to stay in long, and soon we stumbled onto the beach and lay down on a bare rock. The rock was already warm in the sun, and we dried off quickly. Then, our little piece of paradise was invaded. From around the corner of the island, coming down the east side, we heard the chugging of a boat engine.

"I guess we'd better put some clothes on," said Mary.

"Yut," I replied, "I guess we'd better."

"Last one to the lean-to is a three-legged turtle," she cried. She was already up and running like a deer. I stared after her, and so much joy and love for her welled up in my heart that I called out to her.

"Mary, wait!" She didn't say anything. She just looked over her shoulder and laughed. I sprang to my feet and raced after her, but truth is, I was hard-pressed to catch her.

By the time a motor launch showed up in the cove, we were sitting on the beach eating bacon, eggs, and crusts of Mrs. Eastman's bread for breakfast. I munched on the bread and studied the boat as it putted toward us. The fella in the bow looked familiar. He was directing the man in the stern to go left or right so as to stay in deep water. When they got to where they could talk to us without shouting, the helmsman shut off the motor and threw an anchor overboard. As the boat swung broadside toward us, I saw the lettering on the bow—*Lake Champlain Boat Patrol.* On the canoe ride to Cloak Island, I had told Mary about everything that had happened during the hunt for my father and Corbin Lenoir, so she knew about the sinking of *Le Bûcheron* and our capture of the patrol boat. I nudged her, and then I whispered.

"Holy Mic Mac Indian, if it isn't Jack Kendrick and Eddie Halstead back from their Canadian vacation." Then I called to the men in the boat. "Hello officers! Top of the morning to you!"

"Good morning to you young fella," said Jack Kendrick from the stern. "We saw the smoke from your campfire and came to check on possible bootlegging activity. What are you and this girl doing out here in such a lonely place?"

"We've been fishing, sir. Caught a whopping big walleye last night and cooked it for dinner. Actually," and here I paused and grinned, "we're on our honeymoon. Ellen and I have been sweethearts through high school, and, well, we finally decided to tie the knot. My folks had a farm on the Lamoille River right near Georgia Mountain." Here again, I paused. I looked down sadly and then up again as if taking new heart. "The truth is, sir, my mother died when I was twelve, and when the Lamoille flooded earlier this month, it took the house and barn and all our Jerseys. My dad drowned trying to save some of the herd." I wiped my sleeve across my brow as if wiping away a tear. "So you see, we were going to wait to get married until I saved up more money, but when Dad passed on, we decided that life is short and uncertain, and we couldn't wait any longer." I could see that if Eddie wasn't hooked with this story, he was nibbling at it.

"Why, that's awful about your Dad," he said. "I'm sorry to hear it. My wife and I weren't much older than you two when we got hitched. You'll do just fine."

"Thank you, sir. We appreciate the sentiment, don't we, Ellen?"

"We do," said Mary blithely. If we had Eddie's sympathy, Jack was another breed of cat and not so easily fooled. He piped up again from the stern.

"What's your name young man? Maybe I know your family. The Patrol is based in St. Albans you know."

"Danny Lussier, sir? What's yours?"

"I'm Jack Kendrick, and this is Eddie Halstead." Before he could ask another question, I jumped in with one of my own.

"You say you're looking for bootleggers? That must be exciting work!" I said, and I made it sound as if I were in a state of awe and admiration. "Have you caught any lately?" Eddie turned red at this, but Jack had a ready answer.

"We can't talk about ongoing law enforcement operations," he said, "but I do need to ask if you've seen any suspicious activity in this area." At this point, I saw Jack staring at Jake, and I knew I'd better come up with a good story and do it quickly.

"Well sir, to tell the truth, we have. Last night we were visited by a gang of pretty tough customers. We shared some of that walleye with them, in fact, and they stayed and talked until near midnight. I have to say, tough as they looked, they were a friendly bunch. One of them was an oldtimer, and he pulled a flask out of his pocket and offered us a sip of something he called Moonbeam. Of course, we refused, it being against the law and all, but he helped himself. When I took a shine to this dog"—and I nodded at Jake who lifted his head—"the old man gave him to me. Said he'd picked him up in a trade, but he was afraid the dog was going to eat him out of house and home. Anyway, after he oiled his tongue with whatever was in that flask, he told an interesting story. It seems that he and his gang were overtaken by some lawmen just before the flood.

The bootleggers ran their boat over a rock, and it sank, but then they somehow managed to capture the boat that belonged to the lawmen, and they took those sheriffs prisoner. So there they were, quite a merry crew, I guess, the lawmen and the bootleggers. The bootleggers offered the lawmen some of that Moonbeam, and since the night was cold and miserable, the lawmen were only too happy to oblige."

"Why, that, that ain't..." stuttered Eddie.

"Quiet, Eddie," interrupted Jack. "Let's hear the rest of this story."

"There isn't much left to tell," I said, "only that, after they passed the flask all around, the bootleggers wondered what to do with the lawmen. They didn't want to do them any harm. That's when the old man got an inspiration. They took the boat over to Plattsburgh where the bootleggers were hoping to do a stroke of business anyway, and after they all shared a last drink of Moonbeam, they put the two lawmen on a freight train headed for Montreal. Ellen and I chuckled when they told this—to be polite and because we were a little nervous, them being bootleggers and all—but we didn't think it was a bit funny. Think of how far those two men were put out of their way, up there in Canada with not a buffalo nickel to their names prob'ly.

I'd have been hopping mad, especially if word ever got back to the folks at home."

"Yes, well that's an interesting story," said Jack, and he cleared his throat. "These fellows are notorious liars, however, so you'd best not repeat that story lest you find yourself in trouble for spreading slander. You say the old man gave you that dog?"

"Yes sir, he did, and he was right about this dog's appetite. I had another walleye, and he ate the whole fish himself. I don't know how I'm going to—."

"Yes, yes. Eddie, jump out and take a closer look at that dog. Doesn't he look familiar?" Eddie swung a leg over the side and lowered himself into water up to his knees. He took one step toward shore, and Jake stood up and started growling. He took another step, and Jake started snarling.

"I don't know if I can control him officers. He's brand spanking new to me. He sure seems aggravated, doesn't he?" Eddie looked doubtful about taking another step and stood very still.

"All right, Eddie," sighed Jack, "get back in the boat. It's not worth getting the animal all riled up. Danny, what else can you tell me about these men? Did they drop any hints about where they came from or where they were headed when they left here last night?"

"They were a wicked close-mouthed bunch, mister. They were cagey, those bootleggers. They sat in the shadows, and we never even got a good look at their faces. As to where they lived, they never said a word, but I can tell you this. One of them mentioned Montreal, and for sure, they headed north once they left."

"All right. I strongly suggest that you two find more conventional surroundings for the rest of your honeymoon. As you have already discovered, the islands of Lake Champlain are rife with bootleggers and who knows what other criminals."

"Yes, sir! We had no idea such riffraff were loose. I'll take Ellen back to St. Albans today or my name isn't Danny Lussier. Thank you for your advice!" Eddie Halstead tipped his hat to us. Jack only looked stern, pulled his anchor back on board, and started the engine. They backed away slowly from the beach. At the mouth of the cove, Jack pulled on the throttle, and they disappeared around the point.

"Otter," laughed Mary, "my grandmother was right. You *are* a rascal! Come on. Let's get out of here before they decide to come back and question you some more. You've got a gift for spinning tall tales, but there's nothing to trip you up like a lie."

THAT NIGHT AND THE NEXT DAY, WE CAMPED on Ransom Bay in Alburg. Most often, November comes down cold and gray and wet in Vermont, but Mr. Prince must have cast a spell of good luck on us because we had four days of sunshine and puffy, fair-weather clouds. At Ransom Bay we built a lean-to in a grove of cedars, but we built our campfire where we had a full view of the stars.

After eating another meal of fish and some potatoes I stuck in the coals, we lay back on a blanket and looked at the stars as the fire died down to embers. Along about ten or eleven o'clock, some of those stars began shooting across the great sparkly dome of the night. We held hands, and each time one of those stars streaked through space, I felt it in Mary's touch.

"They are like us," she said, "like our souls. They burn and burn—no one knows how long—and then they streak beyond the horizon of the universe and travel on forever."

"I like that," I said. "My soul burns, Mary. Whenever I'm with you." Mary sat up and looked down at me.

"Otter, wild animal or not," she said, "I think I like you."

"How much?" I asked.

"A lot." She laid her head on my shoulder again.

"Enough to travel on with me forever?" I felt her lips brush my ear.

"Yes," she whispered. There in the dark I smiled. A couple hours later, when we were ready to sleep, we saw two stars shoot across the heavens at the same time. They winked out, and Mary squeezed my hand. She kissed me very tenderly. I kissed her back, and we burned like stars. Then I closed my eyes and passed on to the land of dreams with a smile still on my face.

OTTER ST. ONGE AND THE BOOTLEGGERS

Acknowledgements

MANY THANKS GO TO MY WIFE, DENISE. From the first chapter to the last, she encouraged me, but she also asked questions that caused me to rewrite and revise and settle for nothing less than the best I could do. I could not have asked for a better reader.

Other early readers include my children Jake, Katie, Josey, and Calley; my brother Duncan; my mother-in-law, Sandra Collins; fellow writer Amy Noyes and her son Ian; friend and genuine fan, Janni Jacobs; neighbor Steve Reid; and longtime friends Bill and Sheila Birmingham, and David and Diane Doubleday. A special thank you goes to friends Paulette Staats, Paul Shriver, Linda Clark, Karen Williams, Craig Williams, and again, my wife. They performed a skit inspired by the chapter titled "Muff's Wild Ride" for my sixtieth birthday—what a hoot!

I'm grateful to the members of the Writers' Hotel: Tom Absher, Erika Butler, Bill Gazzola, Steve Swanson, David Rees, Jane Bryant, Sarah Hooker, Michael Macklin, Jan Melampy, Nadell Fishman, Ernie Dodge, and Sue Gleason.

For the past twenty years, I have joined them in a writers' workshop, and they have helped me explore and refine my craft.

If you were able to read this story without being distracted by the too-frequent errors sometimes found in self-published work, much of the credit must go to friend and former colleague, Mindy Branstetter. She kindly lent her editing skills and "vacuumed" the final manuscript.

Thank you Abbey Meaker (photographer), Larry Steeneck (supplier of the vintage canoe), Bill Fabian, Tim Aldrighetti, and Brittany Flint for the photo shoot at the Sandbar State Park on a cold day in December, 2012. A photograph of Bill, Tim, and Brittany became the model for Carrie Cook's excellent illustration of Granddad, Otter, and Mary on the front cover. Thanks to Carrie for the design of the book and her amazing artwork. Our shared nostalgia for our fathers' books and the Golden Age of Illustration translated into a shared understanding and excitement about what would work aesthetically for *Otter St. Onge.* From the front cover to the back, her work beautifully reflects and enhances the spirit of this story.

A hearty thank you goes to my publisher, Stephen Morris. Just when I was getting discouraged with traditional publishing venues, his Public Press gave me a new option for getting *Otter St. Onge* into the hands of interested readers, an option—I'm happy to say—that didn't involve swallowing large quantities of ibuprofen.

Last, but by no means least, I want to express

Acknowledgements

appreciation to my 2010 through 2012 Drop-Everything-and-Read (DEAR) students at Whitcomb High School in Bethel, Vermont, and especially to loyal Otter fans Scott Nickerson and Cody Snelling. The enthusiasm of all these DEAR students for Otter and his friends inspired me to work my way to the final stage of this project—a real book! I hope they, and you, have enjoyed it.

About the Author

ALEC HASTINGS GREW UP IN HAPPY VALLEY—yes, it's true—in the Vermont foothills just west of the Connecticut River. Perhaps his happiest neighbor was the locally famous Warren Bumps or "Bumpy," a logger and jack-of-all-trades who stood as large in the author's imagination as Too Tall in *Otter St. Onge and the Bootleggers.* Warren's father, Elmer, milked twenty-five Jerseys on a small farm near the top of Sugar Hill, and on that farm the author earned his first George Washington from the kindly old man with the twinkling blue eyes.

The author's grandfather, Scott Hastings, Sr., and his father, Scott Jr., were also self-reliant hill folk. His grandfather was driving logs out of the woods with horses at age fourteen. He taught his grandson the names of trees, how to sharpen an ax, and how to drive a war-surplus Jeep. His father taught him how to shoot a rifle, use carpentry tools, and believe in himself. His grandmother Josephine filled him up with sour cream cookies and fresh baked bread! All these elders filled him with stories.

If, as the saying goes, the child is the author of the man, this gives you a glimpse into the author's life. He has six children and step-children, and he is happily married to Denise Martin. At the time of publication, he is still teaching high school English (and storytelling) in those same foothills of eastern Vermont.